THE WALLS OF LEMURIA

(A PURGE OF BABYLON NOVEL)

SAM SISAVATH

The Walls of Lemuria
Copyright © 2014 by Sam Sisavath

All rights reserved.

Disclaimer: This is a work of fiction. Names, characters, businesses, places, events and incidents are either the products of the author's imagination or used in a fictitious manner. Any resemblance to actual persons, living or dead, or actual events is purely coincidental.

Published by Road to Babylon Media
www.roadtobabylon.com

Edited by Jennifer Jensen & Wendy Chan

ISBN-13: 978-0692271841
ISBN-10: 0692271848

Books in the *Purge of Babylon* Series (Reading Order)

My heartfelt thanks to everyone who made this book possible by volunteering their valuable time, including George, Cathy, Dru, Brock, Lisa, Ryan, Sally, Steven, Susan, Elizabeth, Mark, and Zachary. I asked, and you all said Yes. I can't thank you guys enough.

Every survivor has a story.

The Purge decimated the planet almost a year ago, leaving small bands of humanity scrambling to find sanctuary from the hordes of unkillable monsters that reside in the darkness.

Keo is one of the few who made it through that harrowing first night. Trapped in a small town in Louisiana, he finds himself joining forces with a group of strangers to make sense of what's happening.

Like thousands of others around the globe at that exact moment, Keo and his new allies will discover that braving the creature-infested first night is only the beginning. Every day from that moment on will be a struggle, and every night will be a nightmare.

This is their story.

PART ONE

THE SURVIVORS

CHAPTER 1

"SEE THE WORLD. Kill some people. Make some money."

It wasn't an entirely bad plan, and a lot of people had taught Keo to do a lot of things in his twenty-eight years of existence to achieve those very modest goals. He knew how to kill a man in the water, from the air, and on land, but his instructors never bothered to cover what to do when faced with something that didn't die even after you shoved a lamp into its skull.

Keo was out of ideas when the thing rose back up from the motel room floor. The carpeting under its bare feet was already covered with too many stains from past occupants and was now getting a nice new coat of paint in the form of oozing black...*something.*

This is not real. I'm dreaming.

It wasn't blood, exactly. Keo had seen blood before. Human blood, pig blood, horse blood, even camel blood. But he had never witnessed anything this thick and clumpy. So it couldn't possibly be blood. Could it?

Of course not. This is just a really bad dream.

The problem was that it wouldn't die. Not after it smashed its way through the window and took a big chunk out of the pretty blonde waitress *(Danielle? Delia? Something with a D.)* who had come back to the motel with him. The creature had cut itself to ribbons on the glass shards as it crawled inside, leaving an impressive, bloody trail in its wake. It had bled enough for two dead men.

So why isn't it dead?

It should be dead. Keo had bludgeoned it with a cheap lamp with a cheap lightbulb that had been sitting on a cheap nightstand before shoving the top of the lamp, broken lightbulb included, straight down into its skull. It was easy because the thing was crouched like some kind of animal in front of him. He saw the lamp go in—and *through*—the skull, which was surprisingly weak. Skulls were not supposed to be that easy to puncture.

That should have done it. It should have gone down and stopped moving.

Only it didn't.

First day on vacation and you're already stuck in a bad dream. What a gyp.

Twin obsidian globes where eyes should be looked back at him in the semidarkness. It was almost hairless except for strings of what must have been, once upon a time, blond hair. Its teeth were black and yellow and brown, as if someone had grabbed random pieces of bone and superglued them onto its gums. The only lights in the room flooded in through the broken window, the motel's gaudy street sign spelling out "Rearview Motel" in green and red colors, blinking all the way across the parking lot.

Then Danielle/Delia screamed from the open bathroom door across the room. Keo had lost track of her in the last few seconds. She was still just wearing her bra and panties with a towel wrapped around her left arm where the creature had bitten her a few minutes ago. The towel had been white when Keo had first seen it, but it was almost completely red now.

Red blood. Because blood is supposed to be red, not black.

The scream distracted the creature and it turned toward her with an almost curious expression, the lamp jutting out of its head bobbing like some grotesque party hat, the heavy base making it move left and right, then forward and back.

Keo took advantage of the distraction and grabbed the next

closest weapon and smashed it into the side of the thing's temple. The cheap alarm clock shattered on impact, pieces of it sailing in every direction through the air. The lamp, balanced unsteadily on the creature's head, was jarred loose and fell to the floor, taking chunks of flesh and bone and more of the clumpy black liquid *(blood?)* with it.

The creature forgot about Danielle/Delia and lunged at him instead. He dived to his right and out of its path. He expected it to take a second—maybe two seconds, if he were lucky—to right itself, but instead the thing gracefully swiveled to follow his path, seeking him out again like some kind of bony flesh-and-blood living missile.

Then it was in the air and coming at him again. And damn, was it *fast*.

He flung himself to the floor and it sailed over his head. Keo twisted around just in time to see the not-quite-human thing hit the wall, where it somehow ricocheted off, landed on the floor, and was *(How?)* already in the air again. Keo didn't think—he didn't have time to think—and kicked out with both bare feet, catching the creature in the chest as it pounced on him. It was like kicking a bag of flour, and the soles of his bare feet sunk into flesh as he guided it over—then past—him.

Keo scrambled up and ran for the bathroom, realizing how absurd he must look in just his boxers. Danielle/Delia stood frozen in the middle of the open door, holding the bloodied towel to her arm and staring at him with all the alertness of a deer in the headlights.

"Get inside!" he shouted.

She snapped out of it and turned and ran inside, and Keo was almost at the door when he decided to look back and—

It was already on its feet. Not just up, but on the queen-size bed and about to use the mattress as some kind of springboard. The surreal sight of the moving creature with the top half of its head gone made Keo wonder for just a split-second if he hadn't, in fact, died in some shitty backwater country and was now stuck in some kind of purgatory hell. That was entirely possible. He had certainly accumulated enough bad karma to justify this kind of endless and cruel suffering.

Then again, maybe he was awake and all of this was real. Which, he supposed, wasn't really so far from purgatory hell, too.

Move move move!

He grabbed the doorknob and lunged inside, slamming the door almost at the exact instant the creature crashed into the wooden panel on the other side. Its forward momentum generated enough force to make the door and flanking walls quake against the impact.

Keo turned the lock and stepped back.

Thoom thoom thoom!

It was hitting the door. He couldn't imagine with what. Its fists? It had ridiculously small hands with long, old lady fingers. *Boney* would be the right word. Flesh draped over a skeletal form, like some emaciated hunchback the way it seemed permanently bent over, minus a noticeable hump. It had almost no volume to its body, no muscle, but that also made it incredibly swift. He had never seen anything that malnourished move that fast.

Thoom thoom thoom!

The door moved each time, but it was holding. Whatever had happened to the thing outside hadn't given it any special strength. But then maybe brawn didn't matter when you couldn't die. He had literally smashed the thing's brains in. *It didn't even have a brain anymore.*

And yet, there it was, railing against the door.

Thoom thoom thoom!

Pounding, smashing, relentless...

Thoom thoom thoom!

He looked back at Danielle/Delia, sitting on the toilet seat, staring at the door. He hadn't seen it back in the motel room, but under the harsh bathroom light, she had blood on her chest and tummy and legs as well as the side of her neck and parts of her cheek. Her face was white, long blonde hair spread out around her oval-shaped face, giving her the appearance of a wild she-devil. She trembled each time the creature banged against the door behind him.

Thoom thoom thoom!

He walked over and crouched in front of her. "You okay?"

Tears fell silently down her cheeks, and her lips quivered. She shook her head and tried to speak, but when she opened her mouth, the only thing that came out was the sound of her teeth chattering.

"It's okay," Keo said. "It's okay."

She didn't look convinced at all.

Thoom thoom thoom!

"I promise," Keo said. "We'll be—"

The creature stopped.

There was just silence from the other side of the door now.

They both stared at the door, neither one saying a word, as if afraid to jinx the sudden peace and quiet. Keo expected the creature to pick up where it had left off, but it didn't.

They waited, unsure of what to do next besides watch and anticipate.

"Keo?" Danielle/Delia said softly, her voice uneven, on the verge of breaking down.

"I don't know," Keo said. "It could be a trick."

"A trick?"

"To lure us outside. Why would it stop?"

"Maybe it…left."

Maybe it did. Or it was a trap. Was it smart enough to do something like that?

He wouldn't know. Keo didn't know a damn thing about the creature. And that was what it was. A *creature*. It wasn't human. He knew that much. Maybe it used to be human, once upon a time, but not anymore.

"What now?" she asked.

He shook his head. Keo was more than happy to wait inside the bathroom until the authorities showed up. Someone would have heard the commotion by now. If not the breaking window, then Danielle/Delia's screams. A call to the local cops would have already gone out. So how long did he have to wait it out? Morning? It wasn't as if he were in New Orleans or Shreveport. He was in the boondocks of Louisiana. There were probably a dozen cops for the next 200 or so miles. Maybe.

Keo looked back at Danielle/Delia. "Danielle…"

"Delia," she said.

"Right, Delia," he said, and gave her his best smile.

She smiled back. Or tried to. It came out more as half-smile/half-terror.

"I need to look at that," he said, reaching for the towel.

She grimaced when he took her hand away and slowly unwound the cotton material from around her arm. Keo had seen plenty of wounds—knife wounds, bullet wounds, even a good old-fashioned animal mauling—but Delia's arm still made him flinch a bit, though he did his very best to hide it.

Whatever the creature was that had been banging on the bathroom door a minute ago, it had really chomped down with those things it was passing off as teeth. The result was a bite mark almost a quarter-inch deep that was still oozing blood when Keo took away the towel. The flesh around the point of contact was purple and black, and it looked infected even to his layman's eyes. That was the most dangerous part of all. He had seen what infections could do in even the toughest and biggest men. Delia was five foot six and 120 pounds soaking wet.

He covered her arm back up without a word. Delia was watching him closely and when she saw his reaction, she began crying.

"It's okay, it's okay," Keo said. "I've seen worse. Hey, Delia, look at me. I've seen worse."

She either believed the lie, or she wanted to. Either way, her crying lessened, but her face remained terror-stricken, her cheeks covered in tears. "I'm scared, Keo…"

"I know," he nodded. "So am I."

"You too?" she asked, as if she couldn't believe it. Lovely brown eyes watched him closely again.

"Yes." He smiled, hoping it was convincing. "This…isn't normal. It's perfectly okay to be scared, right?"

She nodded hesitantly.

"But we'll get through this, I promise," he continued. "We'll wait in here for the cops. I bet someone already called the local PD. How many cops are in Bentley?"

She thought about it. "Six, I think?"

"So at least one or two of them should be on their way by now. Until then, we're just going to sit tight and wait for them. Okay?"

She nodded with more confidence this time.

"You're doing good," he said. "You're doing really good."

Keo sneaked a quick look at the towel around her arm. He swore it had gotten even redder since a few seconds ago. How was that possible? It wasn't, of course. No one could bleed that much from a simple bite wound.

Right. Because all of this makes perfect sense.

"Keo," Delia said.

"Yes?"

"Can you hear it?"

"Hear what?"

She didn't answer, because she didn't have to. Keo did hear it.

It was unmistakable and it seemed to be coming from all around them, from the other motel rooms to their left and right.

Rearview Motel had one floor and it was spread out, with twenty rooms in a long line from one end of the lot to the other. Their room was somewhere in the middle, #11, which gave him a perfect spot to hear the growing noise, like rolling thunder, getting closer and closer, and louder and louder at the same time.

"Keo," Delia said, her voice dropping to barely a whisper. "Is that...?"

He nodded.

"What's happening, Keo? What's happening out there?"

"I don't know, but we'll get through this. I promise. We'll get through this."

He remained crouched next to her and listened, because it was impossible to ignore. If he pressed his palms against his ears and pushed for all he was worth, he would still hear it.

The screaming.

The people in the other motel rooms were screaming...

CHAPTER 2

THEY SPENT THE next two hours inside the bathroom listening to the screaming. Every now and then Keo heard gunshots, but there weren't enough of them to convince him there was some kind of organized resistance going on. The shots never came from the same location and they sometimes overlapped, which meant the attacks were happening simultaneously across the motel.

There's more than one of those creatures out there.

How many? Depends. How many rooms?

Too many...

Keo didn't have his watch with him, but it had to be well after midnight. Two, maybe three in the morning. They had arrived at the Rearview Motel around ten after Delia got off work early at the bar. He had actually waited for her, which had been a first. Four long, agonizing hours of listening to country music and avoiding fights with locals who thought Delia was spending too much time with a stranger. A six-foot-one Asian guy, no less. In this part of Louisiana, that probably made him something of a freak. He wasn't even supposed to have stopped here, and now he wished he had kept going.

Too late for that. Way too late for that now.

Keo didn't spend a lot of time regretting things in his life. The fact was, if he had to weigh the night with Delia against everything happening now, it wasn't even all that hard of a choice—

"Keo," Delia whispered.

"I hear it," Keo said.

Or rather, what he *didn't* hear.

Silence.

The screaming had stopped.

He didn't think quiet could feel so heavy, but then he had never listened to strangers screaming for the last two hours.

He glanced back at Delia just to make sure it wasn't all in his head.

She nodded, large brown eyes wide with questions. "Is it over?"

"I don't know." He turned back to the door. "I should find out."

"No, don't go out there. *It's* out there."

"Trust me, I don't want to go out there, but we need to know what's happening."

And you need proper dressings and a doctor, he thought about adding, but decided she didn't really need to know that. He had wrapped a fresh towel around her arm only to watch it turn red like the last one. There was no way to actually stop the bleeding, and there was no first-aid kit in the medicine cabinet. And Delia looked painfully pale and seemed to be moving her head with difficulty. More than once, he'd had to check that she was even still breathing as she dozed off.

"I'll be right back," he said.

She nodded, but even that seemed to take a lot out of her. "Just be careful, okay?"

Keo got up from the floor and looked for a weapon.

What weapon? He was inside the bathroom of a cheap motel room, in a part of the country where the only people who came here were either lost or looking to play hooky from marriage. Or, in his case, had just met an attractive blonde at an impromptu stop.

There weren't any weapons. Or at least, nothing he would take with him into battle and feel good about.

He finally settled on the stainless steel tension rod holding up the shower curtain. It popped loose with little effort, and Keo swiped off the curtain rings. The rod was adjustable, so all he had to do was twist it and push inward, turning a seventy-two inch stick into a three-foot long weapon.

He gave it a couple of practice swings, pleased with the *whip-whip* sound it made as it sliced through the air. He would have liked something more lethal—a gun, maybe—but beggars couldn't be choosers, especially ones hiding inside a bathroom in their boxers.

Delia was watching him. Keo couldn't tell if it was with admiration, fear, or pity. Maybe a little of all three. "Are you really going out there?"

"I have to." He crouched in front of her. "I have to find out what's happening out there. I want you to stay in here, and whatever you do, do not open the door for anyone but me. At least for tonight. If I don't come back—"

"Keo…"

"No, Delia. This is important. If it's not me, only open the door for the cops. Understand?"

She nodded uncertainly. "Just…be careful."

"Absolutely. You're not getting rid of me that easily."

He smiled at her, and she tried to return it but came up painfully short. Keo couldn't help but feel guilty about bringing her here. Where would she be now if he hadn't picked her up in town? At home, probably. Maybe somewhere else with one of the locals. God knew there had been plenty of them hitting on her, but for whatever reason she had decided he was the guy she would go home with. If it weren't for him, she would be anywhere but here right now. She would likely be safe and he would be on his way with his week-long vacation.

Live and learn, pal. Live and learn.

He stood up and kissed her on the forehead. "Sit tight."

She grabbed onto his hand with surprising strength. "Be careful, Keo. God, please be careful. I don't want to be in here by myself."

"I'll be back before you know it."

She let go of his hand and leaned back against the toilet seat, closing her eyes. He watched her for a moment and saw the barely noticeable rise and fall of her chest. If it weren't for the fact she was only wearing her bra, he might not have been able to detect that she was still breathing at all.

She'll never survive the night.

Gotta get her to a hospital...

He moved with urgency to the door and put one hand on the doorknob. He leaned forward and listened, slowing down his breathing so he could focus completely on the other side of the door. There was nothing to listen to. No movement that he could detect, no sounds that he could hear.

Did it leave? Am I that lucky?

He waited another minute.

Then another...

There was nothing. Just a big fat nothing.

Daebak. Maybe I am that lucky. Maybe it really did leave...and took all of its friends with it, too.

You willing to bet your life on it?

One minute became two...

...then two became five...

Keo looked back at Delia. Her eyes were still closed and the bright lights reflected off her wet face, as if she were asleep under water. Her skin looked paler than before. If he didn't know any better he would assume she was dead, but her chest still rose and fell. Barely.

Keo turned back to the door.

He took a breath, then pinched the lock and twisted it silently in case someone *(something)* was listening in on the other side. He gripped the doorknob tighter and readied the three-foot steel rod in his other hand. It would have been nice if he had a gun instead of a lousy metal rod. Then again, since he was already daydreaming, why settle for any gun? Why not go all out and daydream about an MP5K?

Another breath. Deeper this time.

This is the stupidest thing you've ever done.

He twisted the doorknob and jerked the door open, stepping outside all in one smooth motion. He was raising his makeshift weapon to swing before he had even completely cleared the doorframe.

Darkness and silence, except for his own heartbeat hammering in his chest.

There was nothing in the room. The creature was gone, leaving behind broken glass and splatters of black blood along the wall, mattress, and carpeting. Even in the semidarkness, the blood looked unnaturally lumpy.

He twisted the lock on the other side of the doorknob, then giving Delia's (impossibly) still form a final look, closed the door back up and didn't take his hand away until he heard the soft but solid *click* as the latch slid into place inside the strike plate.

Keo moved through the room, careful to walk around the bloodied glass shards on the floor. Besides wearing only boxers, he was also barefoot. The possibility of bleeding to death out here from a glass cut made him slightly queasy.

There was just enough moonlight spilling through the broken window to light his path around the debris. He walked past the bed and remnants of the lamp. The front door was still closed, the chain lock in place, which meant the undead thing had left the same way it had come in.

Keo stopped at the window, flattening his body against the wall. The motel wallpaper was cold against his bare back, and he longed for clothes. That would have to wait, though. He peered out into the world outside, saw the concrete sidewalk, then the parking lot beyond that. There had only been a dozen or so vehicles when he first arrived last night. They were still out there, including his Ford sedan rental, sitting under large bright pools of light from the lampposts.

There was light, and silence, and no movement.

Where is everyone?

He remembered the screams and gunshots from earlier. There were others at the motel. Hell, they were probably looking out their windows right now wondering where everyone was, just like him. Right?

Maybe…

Keo tiptoed to the other side of the bed where his clothes were still in a pile. He put the rod down within easy reach, then pulled on his pants and T-shirt. He had to look for the socks, finding them under the bed. He then grabbed his sneakers and shoved them on, all the while keeping his eyes on the window, expecting the creature to return at any moment.

"Psych!" it would say. *"Fooled ya!"*

But it didn't return. Like the last few minutes, the only sound Keo could hear was his own breathing. Was he breathing a little harder than usual? Impossible. This wasn't even close to being the first life and death situation he had been in.

Keep telling yourself that, pal.

He opened the nightstand drawer, pocketed his wallet and car keys, and grabbed his watch. He thought about picking up the Bible and seeing if it said anything about unkillable black-eyed creatures from the pits of hell, but decided he probably didn't have that much time to waste. Besides, the last time he actually read the Bible was…well, it had been a while.

He was putting on his watch when he heard it.

Car engines!

Keo snatched up the rod and jumped on the bed to get to the other side quicker. He was almost at the window when he saw not one, but two trucks blasting up the highway, their headlights slicing through the darkness. He glimpsed figures in the front and more clinging to the backs of both trucks.

Seconds after the trucks appeared, the darkness around the motel parking lot came alive. They had been there this entire time, he realized, hiding *(waiting)* in the shadows, avoiding the lamppost lights.

He was prepared to see one or two of the same hairless black-skinned things that had attacked Delia and him, but not five—no, ten—*maybe two dozen* of the creatures emerging out of the blackness along the corners of the lot and from the motel rooms around him. Three dark figures flashed by the window inches from his face in a blur of black skin and *clacking* bones. He hadn't heard doors opening, so he assumed they had used the windows to exit those rooms.

They moved with preternatural speed, with an almost effortless motion that seemed incongruent with their malformed shapes. They bounded across the asphalt parking lot, slipping in and out of the pools of light in pursuit of the vehicles, like rabid dogs chasing something they didn't have a chance in hell of catching—

The *pop-pop-pop* of gunfire exploded across the night sky, coming from the direction where the trucks had gone. More than one weapon firing simultaneously, judging by the constant rate of fire.

Had they actually caught up to the trucks? They were fast, but he had a hard time believing they were that fast. Likely, there were other creatures already out there that had intercepted the trucks farther up the road. Of course, that introduced a whole new breed of problems, like there being more of the creatures than just the ones at the motel.

Keo shivered slightly at the thought and wished he knew for certain. But that was beyond his control at the moment, and all he could do was stand in the darkness and listen to the chaos. It went on for a while, but inevitably the gunfire began to slowly fade as the action continued on without him.

Eventually he couldn't hear the gunshots anymore. He wondered if the people in the trucks had successfully eluded the pursuit. Or maybe they were all in a ditch somewhere along the highway at the moment, possibly dead. Or worse. Maybe like...

Delia.

Keo stepped away from the window and hurried across the motel room one more time. He picked up Delia's clothes—a too-small miniskirt and red top—and headed back to the bathroom.

He knocked on the door as softly as he could, just loud enough for her to (hopefully) hear, and whispered, "Delia, it's me."

He waited for a response.

After about five seconds, he tried again, knocking and whispering a bit louder this time. "Delia, it's Keo."

He waited five more seconds, then ten…

"Delia?" Slightly louder again. "Delia, it's Keo. Open the door."

Ten seconds became fifteen, then twenty…

Keo looked back at the window, at the parking lot outside, trying to guess how much noise he could make without attracting attention from whatever was still lingering around out there or in the surrounding rooms. It was so quiet (*so goddamn quiet*) that any little sound would travel. He could even hear the *buzzing* from the lampposts, something he had never noticed before in all the years he'd spent in motel rooms like this one.

He knocked on the bathroom door again.

Too loud. Way too loud. Anyone with ears would have heard that.

"Delia, open the door."

Sixty seconds…

He tried the doorknob, but it wouldn't move. He put his shoulder against the door and gave it a push, but he had no leverage without a running start. Keo was just a shade over 180 pounds of lean muscle, so breaking down the door wasn't the problem. The racket that would result, though, would be.

He tried again, even louder than the previous times. "Delia, it's Keo. Delia? Can you hear me?"

She was either dead or dying in there. That was the only explanation. She had looked terrible when he last saw her. If she had succumbed to her wounds, there was nothing he could do. But if she was still alive and needed help…

Dammit.

He stepped back and dropped her clothes to the floor. He gripped the steel rod in one hand and zeroed in on the doorknob and the area around it. Keo took a breath, then delivered a solid kick with his tennis shoe that caved the doorknob in with one blow.

The door swung open and Keo lunged inside.

She wasn't at the toilet anymore. Delia had somehow crawled into the bathtub, where she now lay curled in a fetal position. Bloody handprints covered the smooth porcelain sides, and the towel that was supposed to be wrapped tightly around her arm was instead in her lap. She looked unconscious and her face, covered in the familiar thick film of sweat, seemed drained entirely of color.

Keo did his best to close the bathroom door back up, but the strike plate was damaged and the doorknob hung off one end. He managed to close it anyway but didn't delude himself into thinking it would hold if the creature—or God help him, *creatures*—came. If he was lucky, they had already fled after the trucks and there were none left to hear him break down the door.

If he was lucky.

He waited against the door, listening for the sound of running feet. If they were coming, they were taking their damn time.

After a few minutes, he abandoned the door and rushed over to the tub and leaned over Delia. He already knew what he was going to find even as he reached for her neck. Her face told him everything, and the lack of a pulse confirmed it.

He sat on the tub and stared at her for a moment. Even in death, she was striking. Her eyes were closed and she looked peaceful, as if she had simply gone to sleep. He picked up the shower curtain and placed it over her face and body, then sat for a moment and contemplated his next move.

He looked back at the door.

What was that saying about the world coming to an end with a whimper? There wasn't even that much at the moment. He would have settled for a little whimpering, anything but the oppressing stillness and silence from the dark motel room beyond the open door.

What the hell is happening out there?

CHAPTER 3

THE BATHROOM LIGHT flickered off around four in the morning and didn't come back on again. When Keo poked his head out the bathroom door, he wasn't surprised to see the same darkness in the parking lot beyond the broken window. It was the first clear indication that this was a much wider problem than just something to do with a skeevy motel at the edge of nowhere.

Great. So I guess I'm not the only one SOL.

Of course, knowing that didn't really improve his lot any. He was still stuck in a motel bathroom with no communication with the outside world.

And now the lights were gone.

He spent the next few minutes turning over the few available options he had in his head. The motel room didn't have a corded phone, and he didn't have a cell phone on him. The only people who ever needed to get in touch with him was the organization, and he had a beeper for that. When you worked for the kind of people who employed him, you were summoned—you didn't converse about the job. The problem with that was a beeper received messages, it didn't send one out.

So what was left?

Delia.

Her cell phone was likely still in her purse outside. He had seen her using it before they left Garrity's, where she worked, and again during the short ride to the motel. Even if the power grid was down, cell towers had backup batteries, so there was a chance the phone could still be useful.

Keo picked up the steel shower rod from the counter and, keeping low, moved out of the bathroom and toward the dresser nearby. Her purse was exactly where he had last seen it, on top of the dresser next to the TV. It was a small white thing that somehow, like most women's purses, managed to hold an astounding amount of everything. He picked it up, shuffled in the darkness over to one of the nightstands, and collected his beeper before heading back into the bathroom.

Back inside, he remained near the partially ajar door. He couldn't lock it anymore (or fully close it, really), but if something was coming at him, he preferred to see it as soon as possible. Without the bathroom lights, the entire motel was one big dark room anyway, whether the bathroom door was closed or not.

Keo turned on his beeper first. It powered on, the LED display blindingly bright. No messages. Disappointing, but not unexpected. The organization only contacted you when they wanted you back at work, and it had been a long shot to think this had something to do with them.

He pocketed the beeper, then dumped the contents of De-lia's purse on the sink counter and rifled through them. He found her iPhone among the lipsticks, tissue paper, gum, a box of mints, and a dozen other things for which he couldn't figure out their uses.

He powered on the iPhone. Her lock screen background was a duckface selfie of Delia in her waitress uniform. When he slid the icon to unlock the phone, it asked for a password. But Keo didn't need to know that because the emergency function was still available, as it was on every phone. The problem was the zero bars at the top left corner of the screen. Would the emergency number work without bars? He had no idea, but there was only one way to find out.

Keo pressed the emergency button.

He didn't have to wait very long for his answer. The phone wouldn't connect. For some reason, that didn't surprise him. No bars meant the local cell tower was down. Either his was the only one affected, or all the towers were down everywhere. Not that the answer mattered. Either explanation resulted in the same thing: a big fat nothing when it came to contacting the outside world.

He shoved the phone into his pocket with the beeper. If nothing else, the screen was bright enough that he could use it as a flashlight if he needed one.

Keo glanced down at his watch: 5:16 A.M.

WHILE WAITING FOR morning, Keo closed his eyes briefly and didn't open them again until he felt the warmth of the sun through the (mostly) closed bathroom door. The room had brightened up noticeably, and waking up to the natural glow put him at ease, and for a moment—just a moment—he entertained the idea that last night was just one big bad dream.

He glanced down at his watch: 6:02 A.M.

The heat was building outside, which meant sunrise was very close. Thirty minutes, he guessed, maybe sooner. He hadn't been in the state long enough to know for certain, but it was November, and down South that usually meant sunrise between six and seven, complemented by a very early nightfall. Yesterday, the sun had set well before six in the evening.

He spent the next few minutes trying to recall the map of the surrounding area in his head. If he knew where everything was, he could better formulate a plan of action. Right now, his priority was figuring out what the hell had happened last night, and that meant gathering information. He needed cell reception for that. The Internet, a news channel, even a working radio station would be a boon at the moment.

Bentley was the closest town that he knew of, and that was

only because he had stumbled across it while looking for a place to eat a late lunch yesterday. That was where he had found Garrity's bar and inside, Delia. Seeing her across the room, with her spectacular figure, long blonde hair, and large brown eyes, he was almost tempted to believe in love at first sight. Or at least lust at first sight. Either/or.

Crunch-crunch.

Keo slowly turned his head toward the back of the bathroom.

Crunch-crunch.

His eyes settled on the bathtub and the crumpled shower curtain spread over it. Underneath the shiny vinyl fabric was Delia.

Dead Delia.

So why was the fabric moving?

Crunch-crunch.

Keo stood up as the shower curtain was pushed aside by a long and frail *(and darkened)* hand. She slowly peered out at him with a pair of black eyes, like tar. Her nose had changed and it was sharper, upturned—and her lips were gone. Soft lips, he recalled. Perfect for kissing.

Delia...

He didn't believe in love at first sight, but if he did, she would have been the one.

Delia...

She stood up slowly, bones *clacking* against the tub. Her bra had become too big for her shrunken and slightly hunched over figure, and it hung off breasts that no longer existed. Her hips were narrower and the white panties could no longer be held in place, and they slid down impossibly thin legs. It reminded him of a perverse striptease, except here the purpose wasn't to tantalize, but to disgust.

"Delia?"

She cocked her head to one side and stared at him, strands of blonde hair falling wistfully off a smooth skull, the skin painfully taut and pink. She looked like a newborn, climbing out of some dark womb and now trying to adjust to a new existence.

"Delia, are you in there?"

Her eyes shifted to the rod in his hand before returning to his face. There was an alertness there in the dark pits. Some kind of awareness of him. But as what?

Food, maybe.

"Delia?"

It looked so much like the creature he had fought last night, the one that kept coming even after he had smashed its skull in with a lamp. But this wasn't the same one. No, this was the waitress from Garrity's. Was that thing last night also like Delia once upon a time? Had something bitten it, too?

They bite you, you die…and you become this.

Whatever the hell this *is.*

He remembered the screams last night. The gunshots. The men in the trucks being pursued by a horde of the creatures. Were they all like Delia now? Skeletal and blackened, all traces of humanity stripped away?

"Delia, can you hear me?"

Of course she could hear him. There was nothing wrong with her ears that he could see. There was a lot wrong with her mouth and eyes and body, but those ears looked fine. Was she listening, though? Could she even understand him anymore? Those were the real questions.

She stepped out of the tub, one foot at a time. There was a surprising gracefulness to the way she moved despite her painfully brittle appearance or the grinding noises that her joints made with the slightest movements. In the pooling morning light she looked surreal, like something out of a dream.

Or a nightmare.

Keo took a step back toward the door behind him.

"Delia, stop."

She took another step forward.

"Can you hear me in there? Is that still you? If it is, stop now. Don't take another—"

She took another step.

Aw hell.

She jumped at him. So fast. He wasn't prepared for the speed, even though memories of fighting the other creature were still fresh in his mind. One second she was moving toward him as if she had all the time in the world, one foot at a time, and the next she was in the air and coming *fast*—

He swung the rod on instinct and caught her full in the side of the face. Her entire body jerked sideways and she flew the short distance over the sink counter and slammed into the medicine cabinet, smashing the mirror. She fell into the sink in a pile of bones and flesh, glass raining down on top of her.

Keo's arms were still vibrating from the blow when she snapped back up to her feet on the sink counter. A large piece of glass jutted out of one side of her face, black blood oozing along the jagged edges. She didn't seem to notice it or the collapsed side of her face where the steel rod had impacted. He couldn't even tell if it was a face anymore that looked back at him, though he had no trouble seeing those dead eyes.

"Delia," he said, when she leaped at him again.

He backed up, but it was too late to cock his arms for another swing, so Keo struck upward instead, spearing her through the chest as she was almost on top of him. Her torso had become weak and there was nothing to stop the steel instrument from easily punching completely through the front of her body and out the back.

Keo dropped at the last second and let go of his only weapon. She flew over and past him as his entire body was still sinking to the floor. The sight of it flashing by over him would have been comical if not for the fact that he had just shoved a bathroom implement through a woman whom he had just spent last night with.

By the time he was back on his feet and turning around,

Delia was already rising from the floor, having landed somewhere at the foot of the bed inside the room. Nearly the entire length of the rod had gone through her body, with one foot jutting out of her back and another foot in front of her, the remaining third foot buried within her torso. Heavy clumps of blood oozed from both sides of her face.

Then she grabbed the part of the metal sticking out of her chest and began to pull.

She was directly between him and the door, which left Keo with only one path. He fled back into the bathroom. He could already hear her coming even before he darted back inside and scrambled to find a weapon.

Any weapon.

Instead, all he saw were bloody pieces of glass in the sink and what looked like torn flesh splattered across the countertop. A useless shower curtain in the bathtub. The lowered toilet seat and the tank lid behind it—

Why the hell not?

Keo grabbed the lid—the damn thing was made of porcelain ceramic and it was like lifting a boulder—and pried it free. He spun around just as Delia, or the thing that used to be a bar waitress named Delia, came into the bathroom. She was dripping thick clumps of blood out of the hole in her chest with every step.

He had just enough time to set his feet when she came straight at him, her mouth opening, revealing grotesque teeth and caverns of bleeding gums. Keo swung for the fences and the heavy porcelain lid shattered instantly against her head.

She crumpled to the floor in a hail of white ceramic.

The tank lid had disintegrated completely in Keo's hands on impact, so it didn't take much time for him to realize he wasn't holding onto anything anymore. He leaped over her already moving body, turned, and backpedaled through the open door, watching as Delia picked herself up from the floor—though this time she wasn't nearly as quick.

She's hurt. I've hurt her.

Hurt it.

Or had he? Caving in one side of her face hadn't worked, and spearing her with a rod through the chest had only temporarily slowed her down, so there was very little chance that breaking a toilet tank lid over her head was going to be the magic bullet. At least, he didn't wait around to find out.

Instead, Keo turned and ran.

He ignored the chaotic, bloodied state of the room in the morning light and ran straight for the door. He grabbed the doorknob with one hand, pulled at the chain with the other, and jerked the door open, lunging outside into the hot sun.

Then Keo prepared himself for the inevitable attack. He spun around once, twice, waiting for more of the creatures to come out of the rooms around him the way they had last night. This was where they would surround him and finish the job. He knew without an ounce of doubt that they would be out here, waiting for a victim, an idiot like him to come out of a perfectly good hiding spot—

But there was nothing in the parking lot except for the same cars from last night.

The Ford rental was twenty meters from where he was standing, because he hadn't bothered to move the car once the manager had given him the key. There had been plenty of parking spaces, but Keo had been lazy and didn't want to waste those precious minutes when Delia was already inside the motel room waiting for him.

He was digging out the car keys to the Ford now when he felt her presence.

He whirled around and looked through the open door of room #11. Delia stood inside, peering after him. Bloodied, bleeding, a shriveled husk of the vivacious woman who had demanded his and every man's attention at Garrity's last night.

Keo gripped the keys tighter, his legs already in motion. Twenty meters to the Ford. He could make it, even though she was fast. They all were. But twenty meters was a cakewalk, and he could make it—

But he hadn't moved. He didn't know why he was still standing at the exact same spot outside room #11 where he had come out seconds ago.

The Ford. Run to the Ford!

Except he didn't have to, because Delia hadn't taken a single step toward the door. She seemed content to watch him from the shadows inside the motel room, standing just beyond a splash of sunlight that flooded through the window.

He stared back at her. It was a trick. This was some kind of trick.

Wasn't it?

Then, finally, she did move: She took a step back, leaking *(black)* blood from her head and chest and God knew where else. Then she was gone, having somehow merged into the part of the room that was all quivering darkness.

Keo thought he could still feel her presence somewhere in the blackness, lifeless eyes ogling him. He imagined her in there, waiting for something to happen.

Patient. Eternally patient.

And waiting...

CHAPTER 4

THE REARVIEW MOTEL had twenty rooms, not including the manager's office on the east end. It was every bit a roadside establishment, resting along a mostly deserted state highway with the much more well-traveled Interstate 20 somewhere in the background. The closest town was Bentley, five kilometers down the road.

Keo went through the motel rooms one by one looking for survivors, but after the fourth room it became apparent he was really scavenging for supplies. Most of the rooms yielded very little, and the first three cell phones he found couldn't get reception. The power grid, as he had expected, was down and so were the towers.

He kept Delia's iPhone and an Android smartphone from room #8 and tossed the rest.

He encountered another one of the creatures in the manager's office. It was hiding in the back, away from the sunlight. When it heard him entering, it appeared in the back doorway and watched him curiously from the shadows. He waited for it to attack, but like Delia in room #11, it never strayed into the light.

The sunlight. It's staying out of the sunlight.
Why?

He spent ten minutes trying to lure it out of the back room in order to test his theory. But the damn thing wouldn't budge. It stood silently, unmoving, watching with lifeless black eyes.

He found a broom on the floor and began prodding it with the handle. It was like poking a jellyfish, the wood sinking into yielding flesh. He could tell that it wanted to react. Its eyes followed his every step and he could almost see its limbs twitching with need. Like the one that had attacked and turned Delia (and then Delia herself), this one looked infirm, its chest sunken, arms like twigs unmoving at its sides. Pruned black skin glistened in the shadows, hairless scalp reflecting the sun.

Direct sunlight. It's afraid of direct contact with sunlight.

Why?

When it wouldn't bite despite everything he tried, Keo gave up and left the manager's office. He had hoped to find a gun or some kind of weapon under the counter, but there had been nothing.

He found more of the creatures in four other rooms, hiding in the darkness in the back, sometimes watching him, other times ignoring him completely. Keo took what he could find, including the keys inside room #16 to a blue Lancer truck. There was blood on the bed of #16 and splashed across the carpeting and walls. It was a hell of a mess, signs that the Lancer's owner had fought to the bitter end. The bathroom door was closed and Keo weighed the pros and cons of finding out if anyone *(anything)* was inside, but decided against it.

The Lancer had almost a full tank of gas and was a major upgrade over the smaller Ford sedan. He climbed in, then took a moment to unclip his beeper and checked it again. No messages. Keo tossed it out the window, then started the truck and drove out of the parking lot. It was 7:34 A.M. by the time he turned left at the highway and pointed the Lancer back toward Bentley. If there were other survivors, he would find them there.

He switched on the radio, expecting to hear the Emergency Broadcast System with its long uninterrupted beeping signal, followed by a soothing male voice reading a pre-recorded set of instructions on what to do and not to do.

Instead, there was just static.

Keo turned the dial slowly, searching for a local channel, with one hand on the steering wheel. He had dropped the truck's speed to less than twenty. Not that he really had to. There wasn't another car on the road in either direction, and the only sound was the static from the radio and the Lancer's smooth engine.

When he couldn't get anything on the radio after a few minutes, he switched over to AM and searched again. There was no way the Federal Emergency Management Agency wouldn't have co-opted the airwaves by now.

If FEMA was even still around…

HE WAS HALFWAY back to Bentley when he saw a white Lexus parked along the shoulder of the road at an odd angle. Keo drove the Lancer up alongside it before realizing the car looked awkward because it had crashed into the guardrail. That was definitely not how a Japanese luxury car was supposed to look like.

He parked the truck and climbed out, but not before reaching into the backseat and grabbing the tire iron he had put back there. It wasn't a knife or a gun, and it was shorter than the shower rod, but it was hard finding an effective bludgeoning object these days. His other best option was the broom from the manager's office, but Keo preferred the strength and durability of a tire iron.

The Lexus's side windows were rolled up and tinted, so seeing through them was nearly impossible. He got a better look from the front windshield, which was spiderwebbed, likely from impact with the guardrail. There was blood on the dashboard and more across the front upholstery and steering wheel. When he touched the hood, the engine was cool. The vehicle had been sitting there for a while, probably since last night.

Keo walked around the car and tried the driver side door. It was locked. He stared at his own reflection for a moment before breaking the window with the tire iron. It took two tries—the first time only cracked the glass, but the second blow scattered it into a few hundred pieces along the highway. He reached inside, popped the lock, and pulled the door open.

He heard it almost right away—a scratching noise from the back.

Keo took an involuntary step away from the door, expecting to see something lunging out of the vehicle at him. He was surprised when it didn't happen, though instead of relief, it only made him more anxious.

When had he gotten so skittish? Oh, right; there was that thing with Delia in the bathroom...

He moved to the rear driver side door and broke that window with two more swings. As the glass pelted the backseat, he saw it right away—another one of the creatures huddled on the floor behind the front passenger seat. It was curled up like a ball, bony legs and arms folded impossibly tight around its body. Glassy black eyes peered out at him from within the tangled limbs.

It was hiding. Not from him, but from the sun's rays splashing across the upholstery through the suddenly open windows. Keo couldn't tell what it used to be—a man or a woman, or maybe even a child. It had the small frame of a kid, but it was difficult to tell without hair or distinguishable features. If he didn't know better, this thing could have been the one that bit Delia last night, or even Delia herself.

How the hell had it ended up locked inside the Lexus? It couldn't have locked itself in. No. That didn't make any sense. It was more likely that someone had managed to imprison it somehow and fled. Maybe the vehicle's missing owner. Someone with a key fob. Did that mean the creature couldn't figure out how to unlock the doors from the inside? Maybe. The ones he had seen last night seemed to be acting on almost basic instincts.

Eat, attack, and avoid the sunlight.

It didn't take a smart animal to grasp those simple concepts. What about a brain? He remembered smashing the lamp into the skull of one of the things last night...

He had so many questions, but the answers all belonged to a creature that shouldn't possibly exist, but did, and was staring back at him from the floor of a car.

"What do you have to say for yourself?"

It glared at him. Maybe it knew he was mocking it. Or maybe it just saw him as food.

"Nothing? Can you even talk?"

It looked suddenly agitated. Or was that fear? Annoyance? He couldn't be sure. It was hard to read its face. Maybe he was subscribing emotions to those lifeless black eyes when there were none to be had. But he knew for a fact it wasn't scared of him. And why should it be? Could he even kill it if he tried?

Keo held up the tire iron for it to see. Hollowed black eyes remained focused on his face.

I'm just food to you, aren't I?

"But the sun. You don't like the sun, do you?"

He cocked his head, and the creature mirrored his movement.

"Smart ass. Let's find out what you have against the sun."

He walked around the car and slammed the tire iron into the back windshield. It cracked, but didn't break. The creature on the other side of the glass quickly unfurled its long limbs, but it didn't dare move too far away from its hiding spot.

The sunlight...

He could almost sense its growing frenzy. It definitely knew what he was trying to do.

Keo swung again, and the windshield caved in under the tire iron this time.

He wasn't prepared for what he saw next.

The creature's skin seemed to boil for a split-instant before it turned white, taking the form of some kind of brittle second skin that actually looked like gray cigarette ash. But even that didn't last for very long. The ashy substance began flaking against the air, as if coming unglued at the molecular level. It happened almost instantaneously, like watching acid swallow human flesh, stripping it clean off the bones. The sheer speed of it surprised and shocked him, even more so than the reveal of bleach-white bone underneath.

A very strong acidic odor attacked the air, choking him. Keo instinctively started breathing through his mouth, but he was just a second too late and doubled over and thought he was going to vomit what little he had managed to eat last night. It was a dry heave, though, and he managed to back away from the vehicle with his stomach's contents intact.

This is impossible.

The black-skinned thing wasn't dying; it was *evaporating* before his eyes. Its flesh and muscle, anyway. The bones were still there, along with the skull—though it looked grossly deformed—that was rolling around in the floor of the luxury car.

Keo took another couple of steps back before he felt safe enough to start breathing through his nose again. But the damage was done, and the tainted smell clung to his clothes and hair and skin. He thought about the cheap carry-on he had left behind in the Ford rental back at the motel, and the pair of shirts and pants inside, along with the disposable toothbrush. It would have been nice to have the option of changing clothes right about now...

He regained his composure and moved back toward the car, then stared into the shattered back windshield at what remained of the creature inside. There wasn't very much; just a small pile of bones and the skull gleaming in the sunlight, along with remnants of the ash that used to be the thing's skin and flesh lingering in the air.

*So that's why they're scared of the sun. Because it does...*that *to them.*

That was why the creatures in the motel never left the rooms, or why the one in the manager's office refused to be goaded into the sunlight. But it wasn't just the presence of the sun—it was direct exposure *to* the sun. Direct contact.

What am I saying? This is crazy.

Isn't it?

Keo tried his best to shake it off. He wouldn't have believed a single word of it if he hadn't lived through it last night and this morning. In so many ways, it was similar to his work with the organization. They sent him to places and paid him to do things he could never explain to another human being in any coherent way, unless they had also lived through it with him.

But this...this was insanity.

Wasn't it?

He had to keep moving. That was the only way to convince himself he wasn't dreaming, that this wasn't some bad nightmare he couldn't wake up from.

Keo walked back over to the Lancer and climbed inside and drove off, pointing the truck east, back toward the town of Bentley. All he had to do was keep driving, keep moving. Sooner or later, he would run into something that actually made sense again.

There were answers out there. He just had to find them.

At least he knew more now than he had last night, or even an hour ago.

The creatures weren't stupid, he knew that much. They weren't geniuses by any stretch, but they were definitely operating on some kind of low-level intelligence. Almost primal instincts. And they couldn't be killed. He was almost sure of that now. Well, that last part wasn't entirely true.

The sun.

They're afraid of the sun, and with good reason...

CHAPTER 5

THE TOWN OF Bentley, Louisiana, had a population of just over 3,000. Its only real feature was the flat state highway that ran through it. The road was parallel to the more well-traveled Interstate 20, but if you ended up in Bentley, you were either lost, looking for gas, or a combination of the two. There was nothing else about Bentley that was of note, though last night it had introduced him to Delia at Garrity's bar.

Keo was trying to convince himself that he wasn't completely screwed as he drove the long stretch of road through Bentley. Garrity's would be a few blocks ahead, but he remembered seeing a police station on the other side of town. Not that Keo expected to find help there, but a law-enforcement building meant weapons, and right now he needed more than just the tire iron lying in the front passenger seat.

There were a few cars in the streets, parked haphazardly as if their owners had simply stepped on the brakes and abandoned them. There was a blue pickup buried in the side of a Wallbys Pharmacy, and another vehicle had run down a stretch of hurricane fencing and broadsided a red brick building that looked like a bakery, or possibly a diner. The sign that would have told him either way had been knocked free during the crash.

There were no signs of people on the streets. Bentley was a ghost town.

He continued through town at ten, sometimes fifteen miles

per hour, hoping to spot someone—some *thing*—that would signal he wasn't alone before he arrived at the police station.

Moving slowly was how he noticed there was something wrong with the windows. Something *off*. It took him a moment to realize they were all being covered from the inside. The ones that didn't have curtains now had other things hanging over them. A bed sheet, a blanket, even towels. There were a few with walls of furniture, and one actually made use of a stack of boxes.

Someone—some *things*—had been busy last night.

The sun. They're keeping out the sun.

Keo stopped the truck in front of a convenience store with sheets over its windows and stared at it for a moment. It would be dark in there. Shadows everywhere. No direct contact with sunlight.

Because they evaporate on contact with sunlight.

How is that even possible?

It only took him five seconds to decide that driving on was the better option. He stuck Delia's cell phone out of the open window as he drove, but he might as well be holding a bar of soap. He switched to the Android smartphone just to be sure.

Nada. Nothing. Zilch. Jack shit.

Maybe he'd have better luck when he hit the interstate—

The flickering of chrome snapped him back to the present. Keo jerked on the steering wheel just as a truck flew by. Scarring red paint and white stripes flashed in front of his eyes as the vehicle blasted up the road in the other direction.

Keo climbed out of the Lancer as the other truck kept going. There was a lone figure in the cab, but he couldn't tell if the man was looking back at him or not.

"Nice to see you, too, pal."

The red truck made a right turn and disappeared into a side street. Gradually, the sound of its engine faded.

Keo took a moment to look at the town spread out around him. The place felt different from outside the Lancer. It wasn't just the eerie quiet against the truck's churning engine, either. There was something else. An almost noticeable shift from life to death, from civilization to…what?

Good question.

Keo had never been particularly good at abstract thinking. He was a "see target, shoot target" type of guy. He left the thinking and planning to other people, folks who got paid more than he did.

"See the world. Kill some people. Make some money."

It was a simple mantra (he was a simple guy), and it had been working for him for the last ten years. Of course, that was before last night. Whether he liked it or not, last night had changed everything.

HE SPENT THE next thirty minutes driving through Bentley's streets, moving back and forth off the main highway with his windows rolled down and the speedometer at no more than twenty miles per hour. He dropped down to ten miles per hour whenever he thought he saw something that, inevitably, proved to be a false alarm.

There was nothing and no one out there. Whenever he saw covered windows he kept going, even if he thought he caught glimpses of movement on the other side. He wasn't sure if they were trying to lure him in, or if they were just restless and reacting to his vehicle. God knew the Lancer was probably the only moving thing in the entire town at the moment.

He knew one thing for certain, though: The night wasn't his friend anymore.

Delia could have told him that. So could the guy *(or girl?)* in the manager's office. Or the poor saps who were driving the Lexus.

The night is theirs. Stay out of the night.

He kept the radio on as he drove, occasionally spinning the

dial through the AM bands, hoping for some snippet of conversation. He had always hated listening to talk radio. Too many people with myopic agendas talking about things they didn't really understand from the comforts of their couch. Keo had been out there. The world was a vastly complicated—and bloody—place.

Right now, though, he'd take just about anyone. A sound that wasn't his own breathing. A voice that wasn't his own echoing inside his head.

The fact that the Emergency Broadcast System was still nowhere to be found was the most disturbing part. The EBS *was* the United States government. Keo couldn't imagine what kind of force you'd need to take down the U.S. government. And in *one night*, too. You would need a full-scale and highly coordinated East-to-West coast invasion using millions of soldiers attacking all at once. It was unthinkable and ridiculous.

Wasn't it?

And yet, and yet...

Where the hell is everyone?

What the hell happened last night?

THE POLICE STATION was a single story building with its own parking lot out front and open, undeveloped land in the back. Red-and-black brick walls greeted Keo as he pulled into a handicap parking space and climbed out. There were white-painted burglar bars fastened over the windows and two security gates over the front doors. They all looked intact, and he was relieved to not see anything covering them up on the other side, though one window did have its curtains pulled.

He was disappointed by the lack of activity around the station, but not terribly surprised.

There were two squad cars parked near the front, along with a black Ford sedan, a white pickup, and a red Dodge Durango that stood out. The mid-size SUV looked as if it had simply stopped as close to the front doors as it could before being abandoned. Armed with the tire iron, Keo checked the empty SUV through its open driver side window before moving on to the police vehicles. There were no weapons in the front seats and none in the trunk, either.

Of course not. Why should my luck improve now?

He kicked something small on the ground when he turned. It *clinked* away.

Keo crouched and picked up a spent shell casing. He glanced around and saw more shiny brass spread across the parking lot, glinting under the morning sun. How'd he miss those before?

He headed into the building, retracing a trail of dried blood that stretched from the parking lot to the front doors. Some-one—or *someones*, judging by the large amount of blood—had been dragged in last night. Glass shards covered the concrete walkway closer to the doors. The security gates up ahead had kept the doors in place, but that hadn't prevented someone *(something)* from breaking the glass anyway.

Keo tried the doorknob on the security gate, but it was locked.

"Anyone home?"

He waited for a response.

Five seconds…ten…

"Anyone?"

Five more seconds…ten…

"I swear I'm not selling anything. Honest."

He tried pulling the security gate. It moved a bit, showing obvious wear and tear *(from last night?)*, but it was going to take a lot of effort and sweat—not to mention the right tools—to pry it free from the walls. There were a couple of windows to his right, so Keo moved over to them, stepping on flower beds and skirting bushes along his path.

The only noise for miles belonged to his footsteps *crunching* the damp soil and the *clang! clang!* of a metal latch banging against one of the flagpoles behind him.

The burglar bars were still in place over the windows, and pulling at them for a couple of minutes only tired out his arms. Keo peered in through the curtainless window. Despite the sun, there were too many patches of shadows on the other side, and he could barely make out a group of desks and chairs. If there were people in there, they would have spotted him easily enough.

So where were they? The doors were still locked, which meant someone had made it here last night. So why were they hiding—

The loud *boom!* of a shotgun blast rocked the town behind him.

Keo looked back and across the street at a row of storefronts just as a flock of birds perched on a nearby roof took flight in terror.

A second *boom!* tore through the air.

Keo ran across the parking lot as a third and fourth shot rang out less than a second apart. He was on the road when a figure emerged out of a gas station in front of him. There were clothes draped over the building's windows, along with newspapers and plastic bags. It looked like a makeshift mural of leftovers from an old, dying world.

The man who was backpedaling out of the store lost his footing when he stepped off the walkway and didn't account for the slight drop. He fell down to the hard concrete on his butt, but somehow still managed to hold onto the shotgun.

Keo slowed down as he crossed the gas station parking lot. "That last step's a doozy."

The man scrambled up and spun around at the sound of Keo's voice, taking aim with the weapon. Keo slid to a stop and instinctively raised his hands as high as they would go, praying he didn't get shotgunned to death in the next few seconds.

Right. Crack a dumb joke at a guy with a shotgun. You're a real dumbass.

Something behind the man drew Keo's attention. The store door was slowly closing, and Keo saw two pairs of dark black eyes looking out at him from the shadows. One of the creatures, its black skin almost invisible in the semidarkness, had a hole in its chest and was missing almost its entire left arm, cracked bone sticking out at an impossible angle. The rest of the arm was on the floor in a pool of *(moving?)* black blood. Then the door closed, blocking Keo's view.

The sound of the shotgun racking snapped Keo's attention back to the man. A pair of intense brown eyes looked out at him from underneath an LSU Tigers cap. The face was hardened—mid-fifties, eyes that had seen their share of bad things even before last night. He wore civilian clothes, jeans and a sweat-stained T-shirt, and there was a padded pouch on his left hip, bulging with what Keo guessed were extra shells for the shotgun currently pointed at his head.

"Put it down, string bean," the man said. "Put the tire iron down *now.*"

Keo slowly bent at the knees *(Slowly, don't get shot)* and laid down the tire iron.

"Step back," the man said.

Keo did, raising his hands back up without having to be told. He eyed the man from top to bottom, getting a good feel for who he was dealing with. The man's voice was hoarse, which matched his grizzled face. He was barrel-chested, maybe five-eight, and African-American. He looked in reasonably decent shape for a man his age. Sunlight reflected off a bald head and the grays were liberally spread out across a five-clock shadow.

What Keo really noticed, though, were the man's hands. Despite his recent encounter with the creatures inside the gas station, those hands were rock steady.

That's a man who knows how to use a weapon.

"I was just coming to help," Keo said. "You a cop?"

The man cocked his head, then grinned slightly. "How'd you know?"

"You look like a cop."

"Not anymore. Orlando PD."

"You're a long way from home."

"Yeah, well, I was on vacation."

Keo grinned. "Small world. I was on vacation, too."

That's right. Find something in common with the guy pointing a shotgun at you. Maybe then he won't shoot you dead.

Keo nodded at the door behind him. "What happened in there?"

"I was looking for survivors. I found more of those *things* instead."

"There are more of them, you know. In the other buildings with the covered windows. That's how you know."

The man didn't reply right away. He seemed to be considering what Keo had said. Then, finally, "How'd you know that?"

"They're afraid of sunlight."

"Why?"

"Because it seems to be the only thing that can kill them. I saw it for myself on the way over here."

"How do you know it's the only thing that can kill them?"

"How many shots did you fire at those things inside the gas station?"

The man grunted. Keo wasn't sure if he had gotten through, but the guy hadn't shot him yet, so that was a good sign.

"I'm not the enemy," Keo said. "I'm just trying to figure out what's happening, same as you. I came to the police station looking for help and maybe some answers."

And some guns would have been nice, too, he thought, but didn't say out loud.

Keo heard footsteps behind him. He looked over his shoulder at a man and a short woman with blonde hair running across the street. He had no idea where they had come from, but he guessed from inside the police station. The man was armed with a shotgun and the woman was clutching a police baton. They slowed down as they reached the gas station parking lot, both out of breath.

"Norris!" the woman said. "Are you all right?"

"I'm okay, Rachel," the man named Norris said. "This guy had some interesting things to say about the creatures."

"Does he know what's happening out there? About last night?"

"I know as much as anyone," Keo said. "But if we can all lower our weapons, maybe we can figure this whole thing out. After all, I'm the only guy who's going to get killed here if people start shooting."

Norris made a quick circle around Keo before joining his friends on the other side. Keo turned around to face all three of them.

Norris lowered his shotgun. "He's not armed, unless you count the tire iron. Lower your weapon, Aaron."

The man named Aaron hesitated. "Are you sure?"

"He heard my shots and ran over to help." He eyed Keo for a second, then added, "We gotta trust somebody; might as well be him."

"Do you have a name?" Rachel asked.

"Keo."

"What kind of name is that?"

"John was taken," Keo said.

CHAPTER 6

"THE SUV. THAT'S yours?" Keo asked.

Rachel nodded. "We were on the I-20 when everything started happening. We heard about it on the radio and decided we should probably look for a place to stop for the night, just in case...you know."

"Where were you headed?"

"Texas. Well, Santa Marie Island in Galveston. We were going to visit some family, maybe even stay there for a while."

"Where were you guys coming from?"

"Atlanta. I had a job there until a few months ago." She shrugged. "We were looking for a change of scenery, anyway."

"We" was Rachel and her eight-year-old daughter, Christine. The girl sat on one of the big desks inside the police station, small legs swinging back and forth over the side. She ate enthusiastically from a bag of Doritos and hummed some random pop song he had heard on the radio a few days ago to herself.

Aaron, the other guy with the shotgun, stood at the window peering out through the bars, absently clutching and unclutching the Mossberg 500 in his hands. He wore slacks and a jacket, the pockets stuffed with shells. Every now and then he swiped at beads of sweat along his forehead, though he didn't seem affected by the sun shining in his eyes. He had all the telltale signs of a man who hadn't slept in the last twenty-four hours. Despite the stress spread liberally across his face, Aaron looked young. Early twenties, Keo guessed. Aaron lived a few blocks away and had arrived at the police station about the same time that Norris and Rachel did last night.

Norris looked in direct contrast to Aaron; he was calm despite the incident at the gas station earlier. The fifty-six-year-old ex-cop from Orlando, Florida, was at home with the shotgun, and if last night's events had turned his world upside down, he didn't show it.

"I saw shell casings in the parking lot," Keo said to Norris.

"Wasn't me," Norris said. "We got here after all of that happened. It couldn't have been too long, though; the blood was still wet then. Whoever was in here before us must have gone outside and didn't come back before we arrived. They left the doors unlocked and we found the keys on the floor."

"We came here because it was a police station, like you did," Rachel said.

She sat next to her daughter, occasionally reaching over to flick at a piece of cheese or chip clinging to the girl's pink shirt and dress. Mother and daughter both had blonde hair and blue eyes, and they clearly adored each other. There was no doubt Christine was going to grow into an attractive woman, just like her mom.

If she lives long enough to grow up, anyway.

"You have no idea what happened to the cops?" Keo asked.

"Dead," Aaron said. His voice sounded hollow and drained. "Probably dead. I heard a lot of shooting. Must be dead."

"You said there were reports on the radio," Keo said to Rachel. "What were they saying?"

"Something about attacks in the cities," Rachel said. "It was kind of confusing. I don't think the news really knew what was happening. And no one was telling them, so there was just so much guessing, rumors…" She adjusted Christine's hair, and the girl smiled back at her mother. "I didn't want to risk it out there alone with just the two of us, so I decided to get off the main road and find a place to spend the night. Bentley was the first town we ran across."

"She picked me up along the highway," Norris said. "I'd lost my ride."

"We weren't the only ones who decided to take the first exit off the interstate," Rachel said. "There was a big pileup and Norris was just walking along the shoulder. He looked friendly enough."

"No, I didn't," Norris said, "but she was nice enough to give me a ride, anyway."

Rachel gave Keo a pursed smile. "I took a chance. What about you, Keo? Where were you when all of this happened? Do you have any idea what 'this' is?"

"I was at a motel down the road," Keo said.

"But you saw them, right?"

Keo nodded. "I saw them."

"They're not human. They can't possibly be human."

"They used to be." He told them about Delia. "She was bitten by one of those things. It took a while, but she finally succumbed. That's how it works, I think. They bite you, you die, and then you become one of them. For them to have done what they did last night—in *one* night—there had to be thousands of them spread out across the state when it started. They had to be coordinated, too. This isn't some random thing that just happens. Last night was an orchestrated invasion."

"An invasion," Rachel repeated quietly.

"It must have been hell in places with big population centers. It would spread like wildfire and their numbers would explode exponentially every hour. One becomes two, two becomes four, four becomes eight…"

"Like a disease," Norris said.

"A goddamn effective one, yeah. At least, that's what I saw with my own eyes. I'll leave it to the historians to come up with the fancy words. All I know is, don't let them bite you and stay out of the dark."

Rachel and Norris didn't say anything for a while.

Finally, Norris said, "You armed?"

Keo held up the tire iron. "I got this."

"We can do better than that," Norris said.

NORRIS HANDED KEO a shotgun from a room at the back of the station. He would have called it an armory, except it wasn't really one. It had lockers along the walls and a long wooden bench toward the front. There was a refrigerator in the back corner and an oak table in another. In the middle of the back wall was a weapons rack next to an ammo shelf.

Armory/employee lounge/changing area. Welcome to Boondocks PD 'R' Us.

"We were lucky the doors and windows had bars on them," Norris said. "They couldn't get in no matter how hard they tried, and damn, did they try. They were at it throughout the entire night and morning."

"How many were there?" Keo asked.

"I don't know. More than a dozen. Maybe two or three. Why?"

"Bentley is a town of 3,000."

"Right. Where were the others."

"Exactly."

"Maybe they were busy with...the other townspeople."

"Easier prey," Keo said.

"Yeah," Norris nodded. "They eventually stopped about an hour before sunrise. I couldn't figure out why, but I guess we now know. Sunlight."

"Sunlight," Keo nodded.

"You have any ideas why?"

"Do I look like someone who would know things like that, Norris?"

Norris grunted. "I guess not. We're both out of our element here, aren't we?"

"I think that's a safe assumption, yeah."

The shotgun that Norris handed him was a Remington 870, and there was one more like it still in the rack. Norris tossed him a box of shells, and Keo fed them into the tactical police weapon. It took seven rounds, and Keo put the rest of the shells in a pouch similar to the one Norris was wearing. Except for three shotguns left behind, the rack were empty, which was unfortunate because judging by the boxes of 9mm bullets and 5.56x45mm ammo still stacked on the shelves, the Bentley Police Department had assault rifles stored back here at one point.

Besides ammo, the shelf also had plenty of LED flashlights and two-way portable radios. Keo and Norris grabbed one of each before heading back into the hallway.

The back room had a steel door, which made sense given the weapons inside. There was a deadbolt, but the door was left open when Norris had found it last night. The building was split into two sections connected by a hallway, with the offices, lobby, and jail cells up front, and the armory/employee lounge and a unisex bathroom in the back. They didn't have any other windows except the ones in the lobby to worry about.

"How many cops were using this place?" Keo asked.

"A town this small?" Norris thought about it. "A dozen would be too many."

"It looked like they had some pretty big firepower in there for a dozen cops."

"Small towns and guns. I wouldn't be surprised if most of those were their personal hardware." They walked for a moment before Norris asked, "So, you're what, Korean?"

"Just the *kimchi* half of me. How'd you know?"

Norris smirked. "You mean how did I know you weren't Japanese or Chinese? I've been around, kid. Although I have to admit, I didn't know they grew you Korean boys so tall these days."

"My dad was a full-blooded six-five American serviceman,"

Keo said. "As you can imagine, I'm a bit of a disappointment to him."

RACHEL WAS SITTING on the desk next to Christine, turning the dial on a portable radio. She was only getting static and from the annoyed expression on her face, he guessed that was all she'd been getting for a while now. Christine, meanwhile, had started in on a new bag of chips, all of them from one of the vending machines in the lobby. Keo had seen the girl go through three bags already.

Keo sat down on a desk with a framed photo of a deputy crouched next to a little girl as she was eating ice cream. They seemed to be having a good time at a park or someplace with very green and well-cut grass.

"Anything?" Norris asked Rachel.

She shook her head. "It's like there's nothing out there. That can't be true, could it? Shouldn't there be something? The state? The government? *Someone?*"

"There should be," Keo said. "Unless if what happened to us also happened to the rest of the country. In which case, there's no help coming. At least, not for a while."

"What about the phones?" Norris said. "Still not working?"

"Butkus," Rachel said.

"What about out there?" Norris asked Keo.

"I saw a truck at the other end of town, but he didn't bother stopping to swap war stories. Other than that, Bentley's my first stop. I'm not comfortable telling you there's nothing else out there, because I don't know that for sure."

"You said the sun kills them," Rachel said to Keo. She had turned off the radio. "That they just...turn to ash?"

Keo shrugged. "I'm just a layman, Rachel. That's the best way I can describe what happened to it."

"And everything's gone when this happens?"

"Everything except the bones."

"What about the organs?"

"Those, too."

"That's weird."

"Which part?"

"All of it, I guess."

"We should—" Norris began, but he stopped and craned his head. "You hear that?"

Car engines.

"Yes," Keo said, hopping off the desk.

"Aaron, what do you see?" Norris asked.

"I can't see anything," Aaron said, peering out the window.

"Come on," Norris said, running off.

Keo followed him to the back of the hallway, where Norris climbed up some ladders he had pulled down from the ceiling. When he reached the top, the ex-cop unlatched a metal square hatch above him and pushed it open to reveal a cloudless sky on the other side. Keo climbed up after him and onto the rooftop of the police station.

Norris crunched loose gravel under his sneakers as he jogged over to the edge. He looked out, his eyes shielded from the harsh glare of the sun by the brim of his cap. "Two trucks. Coming fast. Looks like we're going to get company."

"You think they're headed here?"

"It's a police station, kid. It's the first place civilians go in times of emergencies. Just like we did."

Norris was right. The two vehicles began to slow down as they neared the station before turning into the parking lot. Keo glimpsed a lone figure in the red truck leading the way, and two more in the trailing black vehicle. They stopped behind Rachel's Durango SUV, but the passengers didn't climb out right away. Smart move. It wasn't hard to spot Norris and him on the rooftop, along with the shotguns slung over their backs. He remembered how close he had come to getting shotgunned in the face less than an hour ago.

The man in the red truck climbed out first, throwing both his hands in the air. Early twenties, wearing dirty work jeans, steel-toe boots, and a blood-stained white T-shirt. He had short brown hair. "Don't shoot!" the man shouted up at them.

"No one's shooting you," Norris shouted back down. "You folks okay?"

Norris had directed his question at the couple in the black truck, who were climbing out of their vehicle now. A girl and a man at least twice her age. The man had pulled a 12-gauge double barrel shotgun out of the truck with him, though he smartly kept the barrels pointed at the ground.

"We're okay," the girl shouted back.

"Where's the sheriff?" the man asked, peering up at them. "Stan around?"

"No idea," Norris said. "We found the station empty last night."

The young man walked over to the other two and they talked quietly amongst themselves.

"Locals," Keo said quietly.

Norris nodded. "Looks like it."

The private conversation done, the young man walked toward them and shouted up, "Can we come in? I don't think it's safe out here." He glanced around him as if to drive the point home.

"What do you think?" Norris asked Keo, keeping his voice just low enough so it didn't carry.

"The more the merrier," Keo said.

Norris grunted. "That's probably what they said at the Alamo, just before the Mexican army showed up."

CHAPTER 7

THE YOUNG MAN'S name was Jake, and the girl was his girlfriend, Tori. The older man was Henry, Tori's father, and they had come straight from Henry's farmhouse on the outskirts of town after climbing out of the storm cellar where they had survived last night. Their attempts to get in touch with someone on the phone or find out any information from the radio and TV had proven fruitless. It was an all-too-familiar story, and Keo wondered how many other people were saying the exact same thing to each other across the country this morning.

"It's like the world just stopped," Jake said.

"You guys stayed in the cellar all night?" Rachel asked.

Jake nodded. "Henry built it to withstand tornados. I guess it did its job against those things just fine, too."

Norris told them about the creatures' aversion to sunlight and about the covered windows around town.

"That explains it," Henry said. "We knocked on a lot of houses on the way over here, but no one answered. The only house I tried going into was our neighbor's. The door was unlocked, and when I went inside I swore I saw them moving around in the darkness. I ran out and never looked back."

"What are they?" Tori asked. "Does anyone know?"

"Your friends and neighbors and a lot of strangers," Keo said. He told them his story about Delia, and about his invasion theory. "You noticed there aren't any bodies out there? But there's blood everywhere. Why? Because all the dead aren't dead anymore, and they're hiding inside the dark buildings, waiting for nightfall. What happened last night will happen all over again tonight. We all know that, right?"

The others nodded, and no one said a word for a while.

With three extra bodies inside the lobby, the place felt less empty. Aaron remained at the window and hadn't said a word. Keo had to look back at him every now and then just to make sure the kid hadn't taken off yet. Rachel sat on the same desk with her daughter, who looked from face to face, depending on who was talking. She listened and ate her chips, and when she ran out, Rachel produced another one. Keo wondered how many bags the vending machine held and how long it would take Christine to go through all of them.

"What now?" Jake said finally, looking at Keo, then Norris.

"What do you mean?" Norris said.

"I mean, what do we do now? Stay here?" He looked over at Keo. "You said it yourself. It'll start all over again tonight. So, what now? Do we just sit and wait for help that's probably never going to come? If it's this bad here in Bentley, how much worse is it in places like Shreveport, New Orleans, or Baton Rouge?"

"Rachel and I talked about going to Fort Damper," Norris said.

Rachel nodded. "The Army's there. It would be the safest place to be right now in the entire state, wouldn't it?"

"Fort Polk's bigger," Henry said.

"But Damper's closer," Jake said.

Henry nodded. "That's true. But even 'closer' doesn't mean within walking distance."

"That's why man invented cars," Norris said. "We can reach it within a day."

"What about Shreveport instead?" Jake said. "Or one of the other big cities? There has to be some emergency organization in one of them. Maybe even the National Guard." He looked hopeful as he said it, though maybe not necessarily optimistic.

"Cell towers are down," Keo said. "There isn't even anything on the radio. If the cities were still intact, or at least even semi-intact, they would be broadcasting as we speak."

"Even FEMA's gone down," Norris said. "That's not a good sign."

"FEMA is the United States government," Keo added. "If they're down, then this thing is nationwide—not just isolated to Louisiana."

"This just keeps getting worse, doesn't it?" Tori said. Her hands were trembling as they held a can of Coke in her lap.

"I wouldn't say that," Keo said.

"Why not?"

"We're still alive. Most of the town isn't."

She nodded. Jake put his arm around her and pulled her against him. She leaned her head against his shoulder and stared off at nothing in particular.

"Fort Damper is our best shot to find out what's happening out there," Norris said. "If the United States government has gone dark, the base will know what happened, and more importantly, what to do next."

"You think Damper's a good idea, too?" Jake asked Keo.

He shrugged. "I can't say. But I'm not sure staying here is a good idea, either. If we have to go somewhere, I guess a military base is as good a place as any."

"Well, we're going wherever you guys are," Rachel said. "I'm definitely not staying here with Christine."

Christine gave Keo and Norris a hearty salute.

"What about you guys?" Norris asked the three newcomers.

They exchanged a brief look before Jake said, "Sounds like a plan, I guess." He nodded at Norris's shotgun. "You got any more of those weapons? We only managed to grab Henry's shotgun before we left the farm."

"There's one more in the back," Norris said. "Though I don't know how useful it'll be, to be honest with you. I shot two of those things with this shotgun at point-blank range this morning and they just kept coming. And Rachel ran one over last night with her car when we were entering town."

"It didn't stay down," Rachel said. "It got back up and chased us." She shivered a bit. "I ran it over twice. Once with the front tire, then again with the back. But it just got up like nothing happened."

"It looks like sunlight's our only weapon against these things," Norris said. "We need to take advantage of that." He glanced at his watch. "Sunset is at five, so that gives us seven hours of sunlight to get to Fort Damper. That's plenty of time."

"How far is it from here?" Rachel asked.

"About 150 miles. It's three hours on the road if we haul ass, slightly longer if we take it slow and easy. The worst thing you can do during times of crisis is rush on the highways. The resulting accidents usually kill more people than the thing they're running from."

"Didn't you get into a car accident last night?" Keo asked.

"Don't rub it in."

Keo chuckled, then nodded at Aaron. "What about him?"

"Aaron," Norris said. "You have a say in this, too. You coming with us?"

"I guess," Aaron said. He didn't take his eyes from the streets outside. "Can't stay here. Everyone's dead. Everyone's dead…"

They were all looking at Aaron, perhaps thinking the same thing that Keo was *(The kid's not going to last)*, when something *squawked* in the background and they all heard a voice.

"Can anyone hear me out there? If you can hear me, please respond."

The voice was female, and it was coming from the Motorola radio Keo had brought out from the armory with Norris.

"Is anyone monitoring this channel? Hello?"

Keo snatched up the radio and pressed the transmit lever. "We can hear you. Over."

"Oh, thank God," the woman said. "I thought we were alone out here. Who am I speaking to?"

"My name's Keo. What's yours?"

"Gillian. My name's Gillian. Where are you, Keo?"

"Since we're talking on a two-way, I'm guessing I'm close by," Keo said. "I'm in Bentley, Louisiana."

"Bentley! I'm in Bentley, too."

"Where are you, exactly?"

"We're at the hospital," Gillian said. "We could really use some help over here, Keo. I have a dozen people with me, including one in a wheelchair."

Keo looked over at the others. They were watching him anxiously. Even Aaron seemed attentive, though Keo could just be misreading his hollowed, tired eyes.

He turned back to the radio. "Gillian?"

"I'm still here," Gillian said anxiously.

"Sit tight. We're coming to get you."

"Thank you, thank you."

Keo looked over at Norris. "Seven hours?"

"Are you kidding me?" Norris said.

"We can't just leave her," Rachel said. "Norris, you heard what she said. She's not alone at the hospital."

"Rachel's right," Jake said. "We probably know some of those people. We can't just abandon them."

Norris sighed, then fixed Keo with a hard look. "Two hours. If you're not back in two, we're leaving without you. You'll have to follow in your truck."

Keo nodded. "Fair enough."

IT WAS JUST past ten in the morning when Keo stepped outside the police station with Jake. The younger man had armed himself with the last Remington, which looked comically too big for his small hands. Jake was tall and lanky, but he hadn't filled out in his twenty-two years.

"You sure you don't want to stay with Tori and your father-in-law?" Keo asked.

"We're not married yet," Jake said.

"Close enough."

"Anyway, Tori and me talked, and we agreed I should go with you."

Keo smiled. "You both 'agreed'?"

He grinned. "Okay, I agreed and she used some choice words describing what an idiot I am. Either way, I can't ignore a bunch of people trapped in a hospital in town, can I? Doesn't seem right."

"It's the end of the world, kid. Right and wrong don't mean much anymore."

"Look who's talking. You're running off to help people you don't even know. You don't even live in this town. And I'm supposed to sit back and stay safe when you're willing to do that?"

"Don't start worshipping at the altar of Keo yet, kid," Norris said behind them. Keo glanced up at the ex-cop, standing on the rooftop looking down at them. "He's just going for the medical supplies, isn't that right?"

"You can never have too many bandages," Keo said. "Trust me on this. I learned that the hard way last night. If we're making a road trip, we're going to need to stock up."

"For emergencies?" Jake said.

"That, too," Keo said.

"Good luck," Norris said. "You got two hours to get there and back."

Keo nodded. "We'll either see you back here or on the road."

He climbed into the Lancer while Jake slid into the front passenger seat and spent some time adjusting the shotgun. Keo hoped the kid didn't accidentally blow a hole through himself. Hell, he hoped the kid didn't accidentally blow a hole through *him.*

"Last chance to change your mind," Keo said, firing up the engine.

For a moment, Jake looked as if he was thinking about it. But then he shook his head. "Nah, let's go."

"Keep that shotgun on the floor with the barrel pointed up at the ceiling, okay?"

"Oh, okay," Jake said, and arranged the shotgun to do just that.

"I thought all you country boys know guns."

"I was never comfortable around them. You seem pretty used to them, though."

"I've just been around, that's all."

"What are you, thirty?"

"Twenty-eight."

"Sorry, no offense meant."

Keo chuckled. "I don't have a vagina, Jake. I'm not going to tear your guts out over two extra years."

Jake gave him a slightly embarrassed look. "Good to know, I guess."

Keo pointed the Lancer out of the parking lot. "You ever left Bentley before?"

"I was gonna go to the state school, but things didn't work out. Never got the chance."

"It's a big world out there, worth exploring." He unclipped the radio from his hip and keyed it. "Gillian, can you hear me?"

"I can hear you, Keo," Gillian answered through the radio.

"I didn't ask before, but how are you for weapons?"

"What weapons? I only managed to grab this radio from a deputy who was in the lobby when those creatures attacked."

"No gun?"

"I think he lost it after he, you know, died. I'm just glad he had the radio already set to the same frequency as yours, or else I'd be talking to air at the moment."

"Okay. We're on our way now. Stay put."

"Well, I had a hot date, but whatever," Gillian said.

Keo smiled to himself. He decided that he liked the sound of her voice.

"HOW BIG IS the hospital?" Keo asked.

"Not too big," Jake said. "One floor, and a couple of wings and the lobby."

"You've been there before?"

"Once or twice. They expanded it a year ago. I don't know how big it's gotten since the last time I was there, though."

Jake wasn't entirely wrong. Bentley Hospital was a one-story building much like the police station they had left twenty minutes ago, except about three times as wide. There were about two dozen vehicles in the parking lot, including an ambulance parked near the entrance with its doors, including the double doors at the back, left open. Unlike the buildings he had driven past in the last few hours, the hospital's front glass curtain walls were uncovered and sunlight spilled inside, lighting up large portions of the lobby. Portions, but not *all* of it.

Keo parked next to the ambulance and climbed out. He keyed the radio. "Gillian, I'm at the front entrance now."

"You actually came," Gillian said through the radio. "You must be crazier than I thought."

"I've been called worse."

"Like what?"

"I'll let you know when I see you."

"An optimist, too, I see." Then, with surprising seriousness, "Be careful, Keo. We can hear them outside. I think...I think they know you're here. They sound more active than they've been all morning."

"Where are you, exactly?"

"The last room in the back of Hallway C."

"What's back there?"

"The morgue," Gillian said. "It's the only room in the place with a steel door. I think that's what spared us. The only thing."

Keo glanced over at Jake, the younger man's face plastered with uncertainty. "You good?" Keo asked.

Jake gave him a less than convincing nod. "Yeah. You?"

"Stay behind me, keep your weapon down, and only shoot when you see the black of their eyes."

"The black of their eyes," Jake repeated. "Got it."

Keo wasn't entirely sure if Jake really had "gotten it," but he didn't have much of a choice at the moment.

He swiveled the Remington into position. The hospital was going to have a lot of tight spots, and a shotgun with its spreading power would be ideal for that kind of situation. Of course, shooting and expecting them to go down was another story.

Jake must have come to the same conclusion. "What's the point of the shotguns?" he asked. "It's not going to kill them anyway, right?"

"No, but it might slow them down."

"Slow them down for what?"

"To run the hell out of there," Keo said.

"Oh," Jake said.

Keo looked through the glass wall into the lobby as they neared the entrance. Bright sunlight filtered inside, illuminating large swaths of the room. A good sixty, maybe sixty-five percent of the building was visible to him. Keo glimpsed fallen chairs and dried blood splatters on the walls and floor and over toppled furniture. It was like looking into a butcher shop.

Behind him, Jake swallowed audibly.

"Stick behind me," Keo said. "And don't shoot at anything in front of me, understand? Only behind me."

"Only behind you," Jake repeated.

Daebak. The kid is definitely going to end up shooting me in the back.

Keo grabbed the first glass door and pulled it open without resistance. He gave himself a few seconds to breathe in the strong, lingering stench of day-old blood—behind him, Jake might have fought back a choking noise—before slipping inside and stepping over a bloodied white shoe.

If he thought the lobby smelled bad when he first got a whiff of it from outside, it was worse once he settled into the room. The air was suffocating and he started sweating, the combination gag-inducing. The entire building had been baking in the heat since sunrise this morning. That, combined with the bloodied evidence from last night, had badly tainted the air with a thick odor that was tangible against his skin.

Keo started alternating between breathing through his nostrils and mouth.

"You still good back there?" he asked.

"Yeah," Jake said, with all the conviction of a condemned man being led to the gas chamber.

Keeping the shotgun in front of him, Keo moved across the lobby and toward the hallways on the other side. There were three, clearly marked as Hallways A, B, and C, spaced out from left to right, with a nurses' station behind a sliding glass window in the center.

As he and Jake moved toward Hallway C, Keo saw them out of the corner of his eyes. At first there were just the occasional flickering movements, but as he neared, they came fully alive.

Silhouetted figures, dozens *(hundreds?)* of them jammed into the hallways, were impossible to miss even if he couldn't actually see them. He could feel and smell them just fine, though. If he thought confronting one of them at a time last night was daunting, so many of them squeezed into one place— one narrow, oh so narrow passageway—was paralyzing.

I should have kept driving yesterday...

CHAPTER 8

JAKE STARTED BREATHING hard as soon as they entered the lobby, but he really picked it up when they noticed movements from the hallways in front of them. He was practically hyperventilating by the time they saw the amassed horde inside Hallway C.

Keo took out the flashlight and ran the beam across the mouth of the hallway. Creatures, black eyes like seas of tar, glared back at him. They looked rabid and annoyed by the sudden brightness but remained where they were, just beyond the reach of the sunlight that splashed across the lobby floor.

He raised the flashlight over his head in order to see past the massive blob of hunched over forms. He couldn't. They were everywhere. Simply everywhere. There wasn't a single window in the entire hallway, and without the lights along the ceiling, the whole length of the passageway was blacked out. The figures inside grew more agitated the longer Keo shined the flashlight at them.

Impossible. It's impossible.

"*Daebak,*" Keo said under his breath.

"What?" Jake said behind him.

"Hmm?"

"You said day-bat?"

"It's nothing," Keo said. "Just something my mom used to say to me."

"Oh."

"Remember what I told you, Jake. Keep your shotgun pointed at the floor and only shoot away from me."

"Okay…"

He turned off the flashlight and put it away, then unclipped the radio. He didn't press the transmit lever right away because he didn't know what to tell her.

"Sorry, babe, but you're on your own. See ya!"

Not quite.

He keyed the radio. "Gillian."

He hadn't bothered to keep his voice down. There was no point because they knew he was here. They could see him, and it looked as if some of them were sniffing him, getting as close to the mouth of the hallway as possible without entering the stream of sunlight.

"Keo," Gillian said through the radio.

She sounded relieved. Maybe she had expected him to turn and run as soon as he saw what awaited him inside the lobby. She wasn't far from the truth. Keo desperately wanted the medical supplies in the rooms along the hallways, but he didn't intend to die here in this place, at this moment.

But he didn't say any of that. Instead, Keo said, "You were expecting someone else?"

"You're still here. I'm surprised, that's all."

"How many rooms are in Hallway C?"

She didn't answer right away. "One of the nurses said ten," she said finally. "We're in the last room at the back, after a slight right turn."

"What about a side door into the morgue? They don't bring bodies in through the lobby, do they?"

"No. There's a back door at the end of the hallway that they use, and the morgue is right next to it. But I don't think you're going to be able to use that one, either. Sorry."

Of course not. Why should it be that easy?

"Keo, be careful," Gillian said. "I don't think they can be killed. I stabbed one of them in the head with a scalpel last night. Where the brain should be. It just...kept coming, like nothing happened."

Tell me something I don't know, he thought, but said, "Understood. Stay put."

Keo clipped the radio back on his hip.

What now?

"How are we going to get to them?" Jake asked. "Through...that."

Keo shook his head. He had no answers for Jake. A part of him wanted to leave. Head back to the police station. Get on the road with Norris and the others and head to Fort Damper. Yes, he wanted those medical supplies, but he wasn't going to get them. Not with all three hallways teeming with those undead things. And he wanted to help Gillian and the others trapped in the morgue. He liked the sound of her voice, her sense of humor. But that was another pipe dream filled with black-eyed creatures that refused to die.

"See the world. Kill some people. Make some money."

Remember?

Keo sighed.

"Keo? Should we just go back?" Jake said, watching him closely.

"Not yet."

"What are you going to do?"

"I want to make sure."

"Make sure of what?"

Keo didn't answer. Instead, he took three quick steps toward the mouth of Hallway C, lifted the shotgun, and fired from a meter away. Fire stabbed forth from the barrel of the Remington, lighting up the interior of the passageway for a brief second.

Two of the creatures closest to the blast were ripped apart by buckshot. Flesh tore and blood splattered, but neither of the inhuman things went down. Keo didn't know what he was feeling—maybe acceptance, or possibly fascination—as he watched the smelly, pruned-skin forms glower at him. One of them had lost half of its head; black globs of something that probably used to be blood but couldn't possibly be anymore *slurped* out of its shattered skull. The other one had lost its left arm in the blast—not that it seemed to notice.

"Oh, Jesus," Jake whispered behind him.

Keo racked the shotgun and fired again, then again and again.

Fingers flew off, a chest exploded, and the sound of bones crunched under buckshot. A leg buckled and the body collapsed before the creature picked itself back up and stood on one bent leg.

When he stopped shooting, they looked back out at him.

Waiting...

Keo was already reloading the Remington with fresh shells from the pouch when the radio clipped to his hip squawked and he heard Gillian's voice, slightly frightened. "Keo, what's happening out there? Are you okay? We heard shooting."

"Everything's fine," he said into the radio.

"Are you still coming to get us?"

He didn't answer her right away, and instead shoved another shell into the shotgun.

"Keo? Are you still out there? Please answer me..."

"I don't think I'm going to be able to make it back there, Gillian."

There was a long silence from her end. Then: "I was afraid you were going to say that. We can still hear them through the door. I can't be sure how many, but it sounds like a lot."

You have no idea.

"And they can't get through?" he asked.

"No. The door's solid steel, like I said. They stopped trying to break it down last night. I guess they just gave up."

They do that. If they can't get through, they give up. And then they wait, because eventually you'll have to come out. And they have all the time in the world. What does time mean to something that doesn't care if you smash their skull in or obliterate their brains?

"Hey, you still out there?" Gillian said.

"I'm still here."

"I thought you might have left us."

"Not yet." Then, "What kind of supplies do you have in there?"

"What do you mean?"

"Food. Water. How long can you last?"

"We don't have anything in here, Keo. We didn't exactly plan this. When it happened, it was so fast. I was just looking for a place where they couldn't get in. It's my fault we're in here."

It wasn't quite self-pity he heard in her voice; it was more like resignation. She was giving up, likely because she had heard the same thing from him. That, more than anything, made Keo feel all of two feet and stuffed with a big bag of crap.

"Gillian," Keo said.

"What?"

"The town's dead except for a handful of people that I've met so far."

"Oh, God. I was afraid of that."

"What I'm trying to say is, those people in there with you wouldn't be alive now if you hadn't taken them there."

She didn't say anything.

"Gillian?"

"I'm here," she said softly.

"You did good."

"Thanks, Pa."

He smiled. She had a wicked sense of humor. He wondered what she looked like...

"Now, sit tight some more and I'll figure out a way to get to you," Keo said. "I promise."

"Thanks, Keo. Whoever you are."

"I'll talk to you soon."

"Don't be a stranger."

He put the radio away and looked back at Jake. The young man's eyes were focused on the hallway, on the creatures watching him back.

"Jake," Keo said.

Jake didn't respond. His attention remained glued to the hallway.

"Jake," Keo said, louder.

The young man flinched a bit and finally looked over at him. "We can't get to them. They're all the way back there. We'd never make it all the way back there."

Keo nodded. "I know. Let's go outside. See if there might be a back way into the morgue."

"And if there isn't?"

"I don't know," Keo said. "We'll figure something out."

JAKE LEANED AGAINST the hood of the Lancer, probably wondering why he had ever decided to come along in the first place. Keo didn't blame him. Even though he knew it wasn't going to be a quick rescue mission, he hadn't really expected this.

How the hell was he going to get Gillian and the others out of the morgue when he couldn't even access the room in the first place? There were no windows anywhere that he could see, and Gillian herself said there was no other entry or exit out of the place except through the one steel door. The back door that the staff used to transport bodies to the morgue was closed, and when he leaned against it, he could hear the creatures moving restlessly on the other side.

He walked around the building once, then a second time, just to be sure he hadn't missed anything the first time. He hadn't. He could walk around the hospital a third and a fourth time, and a door still wouldn't magically appear for him.

Gillian radioed him back during his second lap around the

place. "Any second now, Keo."

"I'm still looking."

"Where are you now?"

"Outside."

"Must be nice."

He imagined it had to be pretty bleak for her and the others at the moment. Morgues were, after all, where you stored dead bodies, and without electricity the freezing units wouldn't do what they were designed to. In another day the smell would be unbearable, if it wasn't already by now.

Keo circled back around to the parking lot and glanced at his watch. Thirty minutes until noon.

"Norris," Keo said into the radio.

It took a few seconds before he heard the ex-cop's voice. "Yeah, kid."

"You been listening in?"

"Couldn't turn the channel. Real exciting stuff you guys have going on there. So what's your next move?"

"I don't know yet. Are you packed and ready to hit the road?"

"We're all ready to go, but you still have until noon to get back here."

"Roger that."

"Are we going somewhere?" Gillian asked through the radio.

"Fort Damper," Keo said.

"What's there?"

"A fort."

"Smart-ass." Then, "Figured something out yet? It's getting pretty hot in here."

"I'm still thinking."

He heard her sigh heavily. It was overly dramatic and for his benefit, no doubt.

"Sit tight," he said.

"Sure," she said. "I'll call and cancel my day at the spa."

"That's my girl."

"Keo, did I tell you?"

"What's that?"

"I'm very attractive."

He smiled. "Is that right?"

"Yes. I also have green eyes. It's one of my best features and I'd love for you to get lost in them. So please, get me the hell out of here."

"I'll do my best."

He stared at the building in front of him for a moment. Specifically, at the red-and-black brick and mortar that made up the wall. Behind that was the morgue, and Gillian. All he really needed was another entrance that wasn't teeming with blood-suckers on the other side. A new door of some kind.

A door…

"Gillian," he said into the radio.

"Really, really attractive," she answered almost right away.

He smiled again. "Where are you and the others right now inside the room?"

"We're kind of scattered everywhere. Why?"

"I need you to move everyone away from the back wall. As far as you can. Get everyone to the front of the room."

She didn't answer right away. Then, with more than just a touch of concern in her voice, "What are you going to do?"

"I'm going to make a door."

"Oh God, I don't like the sound of that."

"Trust me."

"I don't even know you."

"Trust me anyway."

"I guess I don't have much of a choice, do I?"

"None that I can see. It's a morgue, so it has those steel tables, right?"

"Yes…"

"You'll want to use them as cover, just in case. Understand?"

"Just in case of what?"

"I thought you were going to trust me."

She sighed again. "Okay. And then what?"

He walked back to the Lancer and Jake. "When you have everyone moved as far away from the back wall as possible, let me know."

"Okay," she said. Then, "Keo..."

"Yeah."

"Is this going to work?"

"Definitely."

"You sound very sure of it."

"I am."

"Are you insane?"

"I've been called worse."

Jake looked ready to leave when Keo reached him. "Are we going?"

"Not yet," Keo said.

"How are we going to get them out?"

"Do me a favor and start looking for a vehicle with keys in them."

Jake gave him a perplexed look.

"Like the ambulance," Keo said. "See if the keys are still inside."

"And if it's not?"

"You know how to hot-wire an ambulance?"

"I..." He stopped and shook his head.

"We'll figure it out," Keo said. "For now, you might want to get your stuff out of the Lancer."

THE LANCER WAS a full-size truck and weighed over 5,000 pounds. It had a maximum payload of over 1,500 pounds and was powered by a 5.7L V8. It also had a huge front grill and when Keo backed it up and slammed on the gas, it had no trouble whatsoever punching a hole into the side of the hospital.

Keo hadn't backed the truck all the way across the parking lot because he didn't need that much of a head start. He wanted just enough speed to penetrate the wall, but too much and the collision would send huge blocks of brick flying across the room at Gillian and the others like missiles.

The wall caved in as expected, chunks of it raining down and spiderwebbing the windshield of the Lancer from one side to the other and nearly collapsing the roof of the cab above him. He ducked his head, just in case. Keo knew he had lost the truck even before he saw smoke billowing out of the crumpled front hood. Trucks were not meant to be used as battering rams, but they sure made for a good one in a pinch.

He couldn't see much of anything through the smoke and debris outside the cracked windshield. He tried reversing the Lancer, but the rear wheels spun uselessly on him. After about ten seconds of futility, he turned off the engine and kicked the bent door open just enough to angle his way out.

Jake was there to lend a hand, pulling him free from the destroyed vehicle. "Jesus. I can't believe you just did that."

"Worked, didn't it?"

"Yeah, but... Jesus, you're crazy."

Keo grinned at him.

"He's not wrong," a familiar female voice said.

Figures were climbing out of the rubble in front of the truck through the makeshift hole in the wall. One of them was a tall woman with black hair wearing jeans and a white T-shirt, coughing as she pushed a girl in a wheelchair outside. The girl had her shirt pulled over her mouth and nostrils to keep out the smoke.

"You're insane, Keo," Gillian said with a big smile on her face. "I think I'm in lust."

CHAPTER 9

GILLIAN HAD BEEN hiding in the hospital morgue with ten others—three nurses and six people who had either been waiting to see a doctor or were visiting patients, and a young girl named Lotte, who was in a wheelchair. Lotte, whose broken right leg was covered in a cast from a car accident, was fourteen, and Jake was wheeling her up the ramp into the back of the ambulance.

"How many are coming with us?" Keo asked Gillian.

They watched the cars driving away, all of them in a hurry to get somewhere. There had been a lot of questions about what had happened last night, and Keo had told them everything he knew, which wasn't much. He didn't blame them for not coming to the police station with him and Jake, or going to Fort Damper. They had families, friends, and loved ones they needed to find, despite the odds being against them.

By the time the last vehicle pulled out of the parking lot and disappeared up the street, it was just Keo and Gillian standing next to the ambulance, with Jake in the back getting Lotte's wheelchair strapped in for the drive. Jake had found the keys to the ambulance still dangling from the ignition.

"It's just Lotte, me, and Taylor," Gillian said. "Lotte's family was killed in the accident that put her in the wheelchair about a month ago. Some cousins were supposed to come get her next week."

Taylor was one of the nurses, a pretty girl still wearing her blue nursing scrubs. She stood next to the ambulance, absently scraping at the dried blood on the front of her shirt and along her pant legs with her nails.

"She told me she's only been in town for about a year," Gillian said, looking over at Taylor. "She had a boyfriend, but he left a few months ago for a job in Monroe, so she doesn't have any friends or family, either."

"What about you?" Keo asked. "You're taking the end of the world pretty well."

"Am I?"

"Better than her," Keo said, looking at Taylor.

"I have an ex-husband running around out there some-where. He can stay out there for all I care. Other than that, the only thing the end of the world means is I don't have to pay the rent anymore."

"What were you doing at the hospital last night?"

"I wasn't feeling well all week, and the over-the-counter stuff I was taking was just making it worse."

She caressed her throat. Gillian was tall at five-eight and had a long neck to match. She was a strikingly beautiful woman, and as promised, she had lovely green eyes that he wouldn't mind getting lost in at the first opportunity.

"It was a last-minute thing," she continued, "and the hospi-tal was on the way home from work. It wasn't like I had a social life, anyway."

"So, what did you have?"

"I don't know. All of this happened before I got the chance to see someone. Wouldn't it be ironic if coming here saved my life, all because I thought I was coming down with something? That morgue might have been the best thing to happen to me last night."

"Where were you coming home from?"

"What's with all the questions?"

He shrugged. "We're not going anywhere until Jake's done strapping Lotte in. I don't like awkward silences."

"Bentley Savings and Trust," she said. "I'm a bank teller. Well, I was a bank teller, I guess. Not much use for banks anymore, right?"

"I guess not."

"So, what's your story?"

"I don't have a story."

"Bull. What's a guy like you doing in a two-horse town like Bentley?"

"I was on vacation."

"In Bentley?"

"Why do you sound so surprised?"

"Did you not hear when I called this place a two-horse town?"

"It has its charms."

She smirked. "Where were you on vacation from?"

"Work."

"I got that part. What's work?"

"I did things for people who needed things done."

"That's it?"

"Yup, that's it."

Jake exited the back of the ambulance. "I got her strapped in, and we're good to go."

Keo glanced at his watch. It was almost noon. "I talked to Norris, told him we were on our way. He said he'd wait for us for another half hour."

Jake nodded, the relief obvious on his face. The idea of having to chase after Norris and the others—including Tori and Henry—on the road had made him more than a little anxious.

"Can you drive this thing?" Keo asked him.

"Sure. It's like driving a really big tractor."

"Really."

"I have no idea," Jake said. "Can't be that hard."

"I'll sit in the back with Lotte and Taylor," Gillian said.

"Okay," Keo said. "You can take inventory of what they have so we can clean it out when we reach the station. I was hoping to grab some medical supplies from the hospital, but I guess this'll have to do."

He climbed into the front passenger seat of the ambulance. Jake was already settled in behind the steering wheel and adjusting his seat belt.

"You sure you can drive this thing?" Keo asked.

"Pretty sure," Jake said.

"Good enough." He unclipped the radio and keyed it. "Norris."

"You took your sweet time," Norris said through the radio.

"We're on our way back now."

"Tell me you're not coming back empty-handed. I mean, besides the others."

"We're coming in an ambulance. There might be things in the back we can use."

"Well, that's something, I guess."

"Any troubles on your end?"

"No. Just get your ass back here, kid. No more delays."

"Roger that."

Keo put the radio on the dashboard as Jake started up the ambulance and maneuvered them out of the parking lot. He seemed to be handling the large vehicle well enough, so Keo looked back through the opening between the two front seats. Gillian was sitting next to Lotte, whose wheelchair was strapped against the wall. The teenager was playing with a pebble turquoise bracelet around her left arm. Taylor sat further back, staring out the security glass of the twin doors at the hospital in the background.

"Fort Damper, huh?" Gillian said.

"In absence of any other viable options, it's the best option at the moment," Keo said.

"And that makes sense to you?"

"Sure."

"I don't believe you."

"Are you always this negative?"

"It helps to keep me from being constantly disappointed. What kind of name is Keo, anyway?"

"Fred was taken," he said.

THE RAIN STARTED just as they turned into the parking lot of the police station, thick heavy drops pelting the roof of the ambulance like machine-gun fire. Aaron was on the roof when they pulled in, and he hurried off to get away from the rain while Norris ran outside as Jake parked as close to the front doors as he could.

Keo opened the back and helped Taylor out, then lowered the ramp while Gillian pushed Lotte's wheelchair down.

"Looks like we're in for a heavy storm!" Keo shouted over the rain at Norris.

"This is what I get for waiting for you!" Norris shouted back.

"Do we still go in this?"

Norris shook his head. "The only thing worse than rushing in a crisis is rushing in a crisis during a rainstorm! We still have time. Maybe we'll get lucky and it'll stop soon."

Keo nodded back, though he didn't believe a single word of it.

He saw that Rachel's SUV was parked in the handicap spot nearby, and its back was already full of supplies. Jake and his would-be father-in-law's trucks had also been moved closer to the front doors.

The rain pummeled them, and the parking lot had already been covered in puddles in the couple of minutes since the shower began. Keo felt as if he were drowning; it was difficult to breathe, and his clothes clung to his bones. It didn't help that the wind had picked up and was howling around them like some banshee.

"Let's get out of this monsoon!" Keo shouted.

Norris led them up the walkway to the front doors.

"What about the medical supplies?" Gillian shouted at Keo.

"We'll get them later, when it stops raining!"

She wiped water off her face with one hand and looked up at the skies. They had gotten impossibly dark in such a short time. "Looks like it might rain for a while!"

Aaron, soaking wet, stood holding the doors with Henry for them. They rushed inside, trudging through an obscene amount of water as lightning flashed across the horizon and thunder boomed somewhere nearby.

If this isn't the end of the world, it sure as hell sounds like it.

When they finally made it into the lobby of the police station, Rachel and Tori hurried over with rolls of paper towels and they wiped the water off them as much as they could, but it was obvious it wasn't enough. Keo's teeth were still chattering and so were the others' around him. Christine, Rachel's daughter, looked on with fascination from a swivel chair behind a large desk.

"What about Damper?" Keo asked Norris.

The ex-cop shook his head. "We're not going anywhere in this weather, kid."

"What about when it stops?" Rachel asked.

"Depends on how long it lasts. Same difference if there's still a lot of water on the roads. We'll just have to wait and see. Play it by ear."

"We were safe here last night. They couldn't get in. If we have to, we should be fine staying here again tonight. Right, Norris?"

"If we have to stay, we should be," Norris nodded, though Keo wasn't quite sure if he was trying to convince her or himself.

"So, no road trip?" Gillian said behind them.

"Doesn't look like it," Keo said.

✷

GILLIAN WAS GOING through the personal lockers in the back room. There were two dozen of them, twelve on each side, but only six had anything in them. They had names on the doors and combination locks that Norris and Keo had pried open for their contents, which turned out to be mostly clothes. Keo had been hoping for one of the weapons that would load those boxes of 5.56 rounds.

There were no windows in the room, but there was enough natural light from the hallway spilling in through the open door to see with. They could hear the rain pounding on the rooftop above them. There were no hints that it would stop anytime soon, and, in fact, seemed to be stretching itself out.

Gillian had taken off her wet clothes and put on a pair of men's jeans about a size too big for her. She should have looked ridiculous in them, but she didn't. He watched her flip her hair out of the shirt and tie it back with a cheap rubber band.

"You look good in hand-me-downs," he said.

She smiled back at him. "You don't look so bad yourself."

He looked down at the slacks and T-shirt he had raided from one of the lockers. He had also found socks and sneakers, and his wet clothes were in a pile at the back along with the others'.

"Six deputies and not a single woman among them," Gillian said. "The Bentley PD needs an equal opportunity lecture."

"You can bring it up at the next town meeting."

"What town meeting? I think this is it for Bentley. Maybe for the entire state."

"I'm almost one hundred percent certain it goes beyond the state."

"You think so?"

He nodded.

She frowned and sat down on the bench, pulling on a pair of dry socks. She had found sneakers that looked as if they could fit her, though like the jeans and T-shirt, might be a size or two too big.

"I didn't realize how bad it was until we were driving through town," she said. "I mean, I knew it was bad after last night. All that screaming and people dying, and the blood was everywhere. But I didn't really know for sure until I saw the rest of the town. It was like driving through a cemetery out there, Keo."

"But you're handling it well."

"It's all an act. Underneath this calm exterior, I'm like Taylor—shell-shocked and scared shitless." She looked over at him. "But you're not. It's not an act with you, is it? You're actually...fine with all this."

He thought about Delia...

"About all this?" he said. "No. But I guess I'm good at compartmentalizing."

"How do you compartmentalize the end of the world? Let me in on your secret. I'd like to do a little of it myself."

"On the one hand, everything we know and accept has been irrevocably changed. For better or worse, things will never be the same again after last night. On the other hand, life goes on. And so do we."

"I wish it were that simple."

"It is."

She shook her head. "Maybe for you. Not for us. We're just regular ol' human beings."

He chuckled. "I think I should be offended by that."

"That was a compliment."

"Yeah?"

"Yeah."

He nodded. "You hungry?"

"Famished." She stood up and tucked the shirt into her waistline. "What's for lunch?"

"Vending machine food and warm soda."

"Yum," she said. "The tsunami raging outside notwithstanding, this day's already looking up."

THE OTHERS WERE back in the lobby. Taylor had joined Aaron at his familiar spot by the window, the two of them staring outside at the curtain of rain as if trying to see who could remain catatonic-like the longest. The only time either one of them moved at all was to drink from soda cans and eat granola bars rescued from the vending machines.

Jake and Tori sat together on the floor, Tori with her head against his shoulder, while Henry stood in front of the twin doors looking out. Rainwater had made its way inside through the broken glass frames, and puddles were growing larger near the toes of his boots. Henry stood guard with his shotgun, his face mostly unreadable.

Rachel was rifling through a large duffel bag they had stuffed full of vending machine food for the trip, while Christine sat nearby on a desk, legs swinging back and forth, waiting to find out what Rachel would produce next. Open cans of soft drinks were scattered along the floor and desks around them.

The men had changed out of their wet clothes and into dry ones from the lockers in the back. Luckily for Tori, Taylor, and Lotte, they were all about the same size as Rachel, who had run back outside to grab her luggage from the Durango and spread its contents around. Gillian had tried on a couple of Rachel's clothes before realizing they were too small for her and had settled for the men's wardrobe from the lockers instead.

The room had gotten noticeably darker since Keo went to find Gillian. He didn't have to look very far to see why. Gray clouds covered the skies outside, and the lack of working lightbulbs only added to the gloom.

"Did anyone show up yet?" Gillian asked. "From the hospital?"

"Not a soul," Norris said. He was peering out of a window closer to the doors, keeping an eye on the soaking wet highway beyond.

"They know to come here?" Rachel asked.

Gillian nodded. "I told them where we were going after the hospital, and where we'd be going after that."

"Fort Damper," Keo added.

"Where did they go?" Tori asked.

"Home, work, other places," Gillian said. "They had to make sure, that's all. I can't blame them."

"Saw a few vehicles going down the street before you guys showed up," Norris said. "It was probably them. None of them pulled in though, even with Aaron up there on the rooftop trying to wave them down."

"Were any of them armed?" Rachel asked.

"Not when we left the hospital," Keo said. "Why?"

"I thought I might have heard gunshots when I was up on the roof earlier."

"We're lucky we weren't out there on the roads when this monsoon began," Norris said. He glanced over at Keo. "You probably did us a favor by lollygagging and making us wait for you, kid."

"I guess you owe me then, old timer," Keo smiled back.

"I'm not that old," Norris grunted.

The conversation petered out after that. For a while, they were content to listen to the consistent sound of the rain against the rooftop and outside in the parking lot. It was almost melodic and soothing, despite the howling wind that caused the rain to slash sideways at times.

Gillian wandered over to where Keo was sitting on one of the desks near the offices. She sat down beside him. "Do you mind?"

"Not at all," he said, and handed her a bag of chips and a bottle of warm water. "Don't say I never took you anywhere fancy."

She made a face. "You're such a charmer, Keo." She opened the bag and snacked on cheese-covered chips. "So now what?"

"Wait until the rain stops."

"What if it doesn't stop anytime soon?"

"Tomorrow's another day."

"Yeah, but tonight comes before tomorrow," she said.

He nodded. "There's that."

She looked around at the darkening lobby. "Well, at least this place is better than the morgue."

"Better company too, right?"

She seemed to think about it for a moment before shrugging. "We'll see."

CHAPTER 10

IT WOULDN'T STOP raining.

By 1:30 P.M., they began making preparations to spend the night at the police station. It would be the second time for Norris, Rachel, Christine, and Aaron, but the first for Keo and the others. There was enough food and water on hand to last for one more night, so they decided not to risk searching the surrounding buildings for more.

Keo and Norris ended up looking at the security gate over the front doors. The spaces between the bars were about four inches, too small for most things to slide through. But Keo remembered how thin the creatures were. Some of them were practically skin and bones, and skin and bones could slide through a lot of places…

"We should barricade the doors," Keo said. "Just to be safe."

"What are you thinking?" Norris said.

"Town's empty; it's just us now. If they want to get in badly enough…"

"Yeah," Norris said, "good point. A couple of the desks should do it. We have plenty to go around."

"The windows, too."

Henry and Jake helped drag one of the larger desks over. They turned it onto its side, then slid it forward, pressing the desktop flat against the doors before pinning it in place with a second desk. They did the same to the two windows, but this time using the vending machines, and reinforced those with metal shelves from the offices.

Rachel had found a box of portable LED lamps in a supply closet when she was searching the building earlier in the day. Norris turned two of them on now, putting them in two corners of the lobby to provide just enough light to see with.

"Everyone should get settled in for the night," Norris announced. "We're not going anywhere until tomorrow."

Keo looked around and saw a light glowing from one of the offices. He walked over and found Gillian taking inventory of the drawers on a big desk. The room had once belonged to the sheriff (a man named Stan, according to Henry), with framed photos featuring a large man in a Bentley Police Department uniform and two blondes, one a teenage girl, lining the walls like some kind of museum.

"You look at home," Keo said.

She gave him a pursed smile. "I never had my own office at the bank, and I always wanted a big desk like this one, too. One day, I told myself, I'd be running the place. I guess that's not going to happen."

"The bank's still there."

"Yeah, well, not exactly the same anymore, is it?"

Keo looked back into the lobby at Lotte, sitting with Christine. They were eating chips that the younger girl was pulling out of a pink Hello Kitty backpack.

"How is she?" Keo asked.

"Lotte?"

"Yeah."

"She's handling it well. Or as well as can be expected."

"What about you?"

"I'll be fine. Mostly." She stopped going through the drawers and closed them back up, then leaned her elbows on the desk and put her chin in her palms. "What time is it?"

He glanced down at his watch. "Almost four."

"It'll be dark soon."

"Uh huh."

"No more sunlight."

"That's usually what happens when it gets dark, yeah."

"They'll be out again."

He nodded.

"I'm scared," she said, and looked past him out into the lobby. "At least last night I didn't know what was coming. This time, I know exactly what's going to happen. They're going to come out and we'll be the only ones here." She shifted her green eyes over to him. "Does that scare you, Keo?"

"It's natural to be scared. You wouldn't be human if you weren't."

"But are *you* scared?" she pressed.

He nodded. "I am."

"You don't look scared."

"I hide it well."

She watched him for a moment. Then, "Okay."

"Okay?"

"I believe you. You're scared, too, which makes me feel a little better. If a big, tough guy like you gets scared..."

He chuckled. "Who says I'm a tough guy?"

"You look like a tough guy. Where are you from, anyway?"

"San Diego."

She rolled her eyes. "You know what I mean."

"My mom was Korean."

"South Korea?"

"God, I hope so," Keo said.

THE RAIN STOPPED ten minutes after four, when Keo climbed up to the roof. He walked through puddles and a lingering drizzle. The still-dark clouds gave the impression the day's rain hadn't completely given up on flooding the town just yet, and that it could return at any moment.

The highway beyond the police station parking lot was covered in water, as were large swaths of the town that he could see from up here. Leftover rainwater dripped from the rooftops of businesses and signs along the street, the *tap-tap-tap* filling the quiet air.

Keo kept waiting for something to happen—an explosion of activity, of violence—and when nothing did, it just made him more anxious. He wasn't used to seeing and hearing the world like this.

"On second thought, we might end up wishing we had braved the rain," Norris said. He was already at the edge of the rooftop. "I'm definitely not looking forward to nightfall. We got real lucky last time. I always hate pushing my luck."

"Doors and windows are covered. There's no way in."

"Doesn't look like it."

"So what's got you worried?"

His thick eyebrows furrowed in thought. "I told you we found the station empty, right?"

"You did."

"So where'd they go? The deputies?" He shook his head and ground his teeth together. "Something about this place doesn't sit right with me. Who leaves a solid location like this? And that back room with the steel door; there's no way these things can get through it. So why did the sheriff and his deputies abandon the place?"

"You think we might have missed something? A weakness in the construction somewhere?"

"Don't you?"

"I've gone over the building twice already. Top to bottom. Side to side. Front to back. We didn't miss anything."

"Yeah, but it doesn't make any sense." He shook his head again. "Maybe I'm overthinking it."

"That happen a lot?"

He grunted. "Not since I wore a uniform in Orlando."

"When was that?"

"Last time was about ten years ago. I hung it up after twenty-three years. Could have been stubborn and stayed for another four, hit the max and get pushed out, but what the hell—I'd always wanted to travel."

"How long have you been traveling?"

"On and off for ten years now."

"That's a hell of a lot of traveling, Norris."

"Retirement, kid. You keep waiting for it, thinking about all the things you're going to do when you hit that magic number. Then it creeps up on you, and suddenly you realize you don't wanna do half of the things on your list. So what *do* you do? You look for other adventures."

"Where's your next stop?"

"No idea. Wherever the wind takes me. A few weeks ago I got an itch to see the Deep South. And here I am. What about you? Got plans after retirement?"

"Making plans would mean I expect to live to retirement age, old timer. To be honest with you, I've already overachieved after last night."

"That's a hell of a thing to say, kid."

"It's been a hell of a life," Keo said. "So, about tonight."

"What about it?"

"What you said about the back room. You think it can withstand a prolonged attack?"

"I think so," Norris nodded. "I saw them attacking the windows and doors last night. They kept at it for hours and hours, but they didn't make a dent in the bars. I don't think they're that strong. Hell, I think they're weaker than they used to be—"

He stopped in mid-sentence when they heard the faint *pop-pop-pop* of automatic gunfire coming from well across town. The source was so far away that they would have missed it entirely if they hadn't been standing on the rooftop at that moment.

"You heard that?" Norris said.

"Yeah," Keo nodded, looking in the direction of the gunfire.

"How many shots did you hear?"

"About a half dozen. Maybe seven."

"It's stopped." Norris scratched his chin and thought about it. "Could be anything. Anyone. Maybe one of those people from the hospital."

"If any of them are still out there, they should be making their way to us by now."

"What were they shooting at, you think?"

"Too bad we can't ask them," Keo said.

GILLIAN WAS WAITING for them in the hallway at the bottom of the stairs when they climbed down from the roof.

"I thought I might have heard gunshots," she said.

"You did," Keo said. "But no one showed up and we didn't hear it again."

"It might have been Brent and the others. I don't understand why they're not here yet. It's going to be dark pretty soon."

"I'm sure they're fine."

"You don't know that."

"I'm just trying to think positively."

"Maybe they left town," Norris said, hopping down behind Keo. "That'd be the smart thing to do, rain-slicked roads or not. We probably should have done the same thing. The more I think about it, the more I think we're pushing our luck staying here two nights in a row like this."

"We didn't miss anything," Keo said.

"That's what I keep telling myself too, kid."

"You're just being paranoid."

"I've been called worse," Norris grunted, then walked past them and up the hallway.

Gillian looked after him, while Keo down at his watch.

"We'll get through this. We didn't know what we were dealing with last night, but this time we do."

"You really think that's going to matter when they come out of their hiding places and swarm the building?" she asked.

Keo smiled at her. "Absolutely," he lied.

CHAPTER 11

THE ONE HOUR until nightfall felt like an eternity.

They gathered in the lobby and waited in silence. Keo spent the time checking the Remington while Gillian sat quietly next to him. One of the portable LED lamps glowed a few meters away, throwing a halo around them and half of Norris's face, the ex-cop leaning nearby against a desk. The only noises were the wrinkling of bags, the crunch of chips, and the occasional sloshing of bottled water.

Keo busied himself with duct-taping the flashlight to one side of his Remington's barrel. When he was done, he tossed the roll over to Norris, who did the same to his weapon.

"I used to love the fact that it got dark so fast this time of year," Gillian said after a while.

"Night owl?" Keo said.

"No, it wasn't that. I just liked the quiet. Of course, I didn't know what real quiet was until now." She surprised him by leaning her head against his shoulder. "Do you mind?"

"No. But let me know when my breathing becomes too annoying."

She smiled. "Deal."

"Remember," Norris said, his voice practically booming in the quiet of the lobby. "We turn off the lamps in thirty minutes. We might be the only people left in this town, so let's not draw attention to ourselves."

Keo felt Gillian shivering involuntarily against him.

"We shouldn't be here," Aaron said.

It had been such a long time since he had said anything that the sound of his voice prompted Keo to look around for the source. Aaron sat on the floor next to one of the vending machines that covered up a window. He hadn't moved from the spot even though he couldn't look outside anymore. Keo wondered who (or what) he was looking for all those other times.

"Where else would we be?" Henry said from the front doors, where he sat on the floor with his shotgun resting between his legs.

"We shouldn't be here," Aaron repeated. His eyes seemed to be focused on a patch of wall across the room. There was nothing there that Keo could see. "In this place. This building. This town. We should have left when we had the chance."

"We couldn't," Norris said. "Not with that monsoon earlier."

"We should have tried. Don't you see? They left for a reason. We should have left, too."

"Who's he talking about?" Rachel asked.

"The deputies," Norris said. "The ones who were here before us last night."

"Did we ever find out why they left?"

Norris shook his head.

"They had a reason," Aaron said. His voice cracked a bit and his eyes drifted down to the floor. "We should have left when we had the chance. We shouldn't be here..."

All eyes had turned to Aaron, not that the young man seemed to notice. He looked lost in his own world, staring at a wet spot on the floor.

"We looked everywhere," Norris said. "Every room. Every nook and cranny. There aren't any other ways in here."

"He's right," Keo said. He wasn't sure if Norris actually believed what he was saying, but he had said it with just enough conviction that Keo could see the others almost buying into it.

He thought he'd help out. "There aren't any other ways in except through the windows and doors, and we covered those up. We're good in here, guys. They're not getting in."

Daebak. I almost convinced myself that time.

"Just remember," Norris said, "lights out in—" he glanced at his watch "—twenty minutes. We don't make a peep and they won't know we're here."

THE UNMISTAKABLE SOUNDS of doors opening and closing could be heard up and down the street outside the police station. It was followed by the growing cacophony of bare feet against hard concrete and splashing puddles from this afternoon's rain. All of it flooded across the silent town of Bentley without any resistance.

They're coming.

If the noise outside was impossible to ignore, the quiet inside was deafening. Keo wasn't sure if Gillian was even breathing next to him. Or Norris nearby. Or anyone else. Even little Christine was clutching her mother's waist, the two of them sitting next to Lotte's wheelchair. Rachel was holding the teenager's hand, though Keo couldn't make out who had the tighter grip in the pitch-black darkness.

It didn't take very long for all of them to accept that the creatures knew exactly where they were. Keo realized it right away when the stampede of footsteps grew louder and louder as they got closer and closer.

"They know we're here," Gillian whispered next to him.

"I know," he whispered back.

"What now?"

"I don't know. The doors and windows should hold."

"Are you sure?"

"Yes," he said.

He put his hand over hers and felt her tense at first, surprised by the contact, before relaxing a bit when she realized it was just him. He couldn't see all of her face in the darkness, just the soft green of her eyes.

Norris was to Gillian's left, sitting with his back against one of the desks. Taylor and Aaron had moved away from the windows and were now somewhere inside the sheriff's office to their left in the back. He didn't know what they were doing in there. The idea was always to retreat to the back room with its steel door if they lost the lobby. He hoped the two of them remembered that.

They waited for something to happen because the noise outside was growing, getting louder and somehow more intimate at the same time. Thoughts *(doubts)* swirled around in his head, making Keo question everything.

Did we miss something?

We must have missed something.

Why did the deputies abandon the station last night?

Did we miss something?

Maybe crazy Aaron was right.

Fort Damper's looking pretty good right about now.

Did we miss something?

There was a *click!* to his left. Norris, thumbing the safety off his shotgun. It was a tiny sound, unnoticed by everyone else in the room except him. Keo took his hand away from Gillian's and did the same thing to his Remington.

"Remember, the back room," he whispered to her.

"What?" she whispered back, leaning closer to hear him better.

"If anything happens, go to the back room. Where the lockers are."

"Like we planned."

"Like we planned," he nodded, though of course she probably couldn't see him in the darkness.

Did we miss something?

No. We didn't.

Right?

"Can you hear that?" Gillian whispered.

"Outside?"

"No. Something else…"

"Where?"

"I don't know, exactly."

He stopped moving and breathing entirely and listened, but he still couldn't hear anything. "Where?" he asked again.

"It sounds like it's coming from inside the building," Gillian said, her breath catching a bit as the words came out.

Keo glanced up at the ceiling, expecting to see something, but only saw the dirty tiles visible against a small sliver of moonlight that had somehow managed to invade the room through one of the vending machines stacked in front of the windows.

He was going to ask her again when he heard it.

Clack-clack-clack…

"What is that?" Norris whispered, just loud enough to get their attention. "What's that sound? Where's it coming from?"

Clack-clack-clack…

The noise was getting louder, but Keo couldn't quite pinpoint its exact location. It seemed to be moving. At first it sounded as if it were coming from outside, but the more he listened, the more certain he was it was originating from *inside* the police station.

But that couldn't have been possible.

Did we miss something?

Keo stood up to better track the sound.

Clack-clack-clack…

Norris was moving somewhere else in the room. "Where is it?" he said, just the hint of panic in his voice.

The others were standing up too, the sudden explosion of movement overwhelming Keo's focus and forced him to abandon it. He put his hand against the wall instead and could feel the vibrations. Slight, but they were there.

Clack-clack-clack...

"It can't be from the roof," Norris said. He sounded out of breath for some reason. "There's no way up there from outside."

Clack-clack-clack...

Keo took a step away from the wall. Gillian, standing next to him, mirrored his movement. "Keo?" she said breathlessly.

"The wall," Keo said. "It's coming from the wall."

"Where?" Norris said, almost shouting out the question.

Clack-clack-clack...

"I don't know," Keo said.

Did we miss something?

Shit, we must have missed something.

He clicked on the flashlight duct-taped to the side of the Remington. Norris and Jake did the same with their own flashlights, though Jake hadn't taped his to his weapon. They took another step back and ran their beams along the wall, spreading the three halos from the top to bottom, then side to side.

Clack-clack-clack...

"I don't see anything," Jake said. Tori was clutching his waist from behind.

"Where the *hell* is that sound coming from?" Norris said, on the verge of shouting.

Keo pointed the shotgun at the spot where the wall joined the ceiling. He moved his flashlight beam from left to right until something metallic and soft-white gleamed in the pool of light.

It was a ventilation grill, held in place by two hinges along the left side.

Clack-clack-clack...

Keo took a step toward it, angling the light to look through the elongated, curvy slits that made up anywhere from ninety to ninety-five percent of the grill. He expected to see a box-shaped air filter on the other side through the louvers, but instead there was *a pair of lifeless black eyes* glinting in the flashlight beam.

"They're in the vent!" Keo shouted. "They're in the fucking vent!"

CHAPTER 12

THE VENTILATION GRILL was 24x24 inches, big enough to pour as much cold air (or heat, in the winter) into the police station from a large air conditioner unit somewhere outside. The grill itself was made of sturdy solid steel construction. That was the good news. The bad news was that it was fastened to the wall by two simple hinges and could be easily loosened by twisting two latches in the right direction.

Or, failing that, slamming really hard into it.

And that was what the creature did. The first time it smashed its entire body into the 2x2 feet grill, the result was minimal. If it had given up then, things would have been fine.

But it didn't give up.

It crashed into the vent again and again and again, and each time the latches moved a little bit more. Ventilation grills were meant to be opened easily so that replacing air filters wasn't a chore. Not that Keo thought the creature slamming its entire body into the grill knew that. Just as it didn't know—or seem to care—that it was skewering itself against the louvers, cutting its flesh with every impact. Pools of black wetness had begun to spread and drip down the wall.

Norris's flashlight beam lit up the creature as he stumbled back in shock. "Fuck!" he shouted, and aimed his shotgun.

"Wait!" Keo shouted.

Norris glared at him. "What the hell for?"

"It can't get through yet! If you shoot it—"

Loud rattling sounds from behind them cut him off. He spun around along with everyone else and saw the walls around the windows and doors shaking as the creatures outside began attacking the security gates and burglar bars. The desks in front of the doors shook and the vending machines vibrated against the two-pronged assault.

Keo wasn't too worried about the doors and windows giving way, though. Even if the creatures could pull off the metal bars, there were the barricades to keep them back. No, he wasn't worried about the things attacking the entrances. Despite the tumultuous rattling, it was all sound and fury, signifying nothing. He was worried about the ventilation system and the creature behind it. Because if there was one of those undead things back there, there were probably more.

"The back room!" Keo shouted. "Everyone into the back room now!"

"Lotte!" Gillian shouted and ran off somewhere into the darkness.

Keo tracked her with his flashlight until he heard the screeching of metal and knew the ventilation grill had finally surrendered. Before he could turn, a shotgun blast ripped through the lobby and something sticky and wet smacked him in the legs.

Norris was walking toward him, firing into the creature that had fallen out of the hole in the wall and was now flopping on the floor between them. Keo stumbled backward to keep from catching stray buckshot from Norris's weapon as another blast tore just as many holes in the floor as it did the creature's body.

And the damn thing didn't stop moving.

Keo aimed at its head, the beam of his flashlight lighting it up in all its blackened and malformed glory. The undead thing scowled at him, one side of its face already gone, the jagged outline of its shattered skull torn apart by Norris's buckshot. Keo fired and the rest of the thing's head exploded like a ripe melon, leaving behind just the bottom half where the nose and mouth were.

And it still didn't go down.

Norris had kept moving forward and he was almost on top of the thing when it whirled to confront him, "looking" at him with eyes that it no longer had. The sight of it, with the top part of its head shorn off, what's left of its brain scattered over the floor like clumps of goop, was something Keo didn't think he would ever forget.

Then Norris shot it almost point-blank in the chest, and the concussive force of the blow at such a short distance sent it sliding across the lobby and into the wall in a tangled mess of bony arms and legs. It lay against the wall for a second or two before it began unfurling itself and rising up again.

"Back room!" Keo shouted. "Get into the back room now!"

He turned in time to see Gillian racing across the lobby, pushing Lotte's wheelchair in front of her. Rachel and Christine also ran past him, Rachel holding onto her daughter's arm as the girl struggled with the suddenly slippery floor covered in pools of blood *(and flesh and brains)* the creature had left in its wake.

"Henry, Jake!" Norris shouted. "Get the fuck over here!"

Henry and Jake had Tori between them and they were rushing over from the other side of the room. They hadn't gone more than a few feet when the creature turned its torso in their direction and launched its headless body at them. It slammed into Henry's legs, bowling the older man off his feet, and took Tori right along with them.

"Tori!" Jake shouted.

Screams filled the lobby in tune to the relentless rattling of metal bars from outside the windows and doors to Keo's right. He did everything possible to block them out. They were distractions, unimportant. What was happening inside the building was what mattered, was *all* that mattered. But telling himself that and following up on it wasn't quite the same thing.

Jake's flashlight scoured the room until its bright beam fell across Henry on the floor, the creature's jaw clamped down on the back of his neck. Tori was nearby, screaming. Keo didn't know whose screams were louder—Henry's or Tori's, or father and daughter combined.

Jake was running toward the bloody scene, the flashlight bouncing up and down as he switched his grip to his shotgun. More screaming, though now Keo couldn't tell who it was coming from, and he didn't have time to see what had happened because—

BOOM!

Norris was shooting behind him again, his Remington and flashlight pointed up at the square ventilation opening. His shotgun blast had widened the box, buckshot having torn chunks off the surrounding wall, and a creature was leaning out when a second blast from Norris's weapon blew a hole in its chest. The creature looked annoyed just before it staggered out of the wall and plummeted, hitting the floor with a loud *clattering* of bones.

Norris racked his shotgun and was backing up just as another one of the monstrosities groped its way out of the opening. There was already another one—*no, two more*—behind it, waiting for their turn to come through.

Keo darted across the room, swerving around the creatures as they landed in front of him, the *clack-clack* of bones hitting the floor tiles somehow louder than even the shotgun blasts behind him.

Jake. Jake's shooting. Sorry, kid.

Keo couldn't worry about Jake anymore because one of the creatures spun on him, obsidian eyes glinting in the darkness. Keo shot it from less than a foot away, and large sections of its head came unglued and flew across the floor in a sea of brain and skull and blood (or what used to be blood).

One of ghoulish creatures swiped at him, but Keo side-stepped just in time, actually spinning on his heels like some ballet dancer.

Eat your heart out, Mikhail Baryshnikov!

He might have even cackled. Though, of course, it was impossible to hear anything over the roar of shotgun blasts from in front and behind him. Norris and Jake shooting, one after another, as if they had timed their fire. And there were Tori's bloodcurdling screams, which seemed to go on and on and on...

Keo thought the creature would chase him, but instead it bounded into the darkness in the opposite direction—toward where Keo last saw Jake trying desperately to save his would-be father-in-law.

Run, Jake, run! Save yourself, kid!

He looked back, just as a flash of fire lit up the room, and in that same split-second, Keo made out Henry in a pool of blood and Jake trying to shake off one of the creatures clinging to his own back. Then Jake's shotgun fired again and blew a hole in the wall—*and the top half of Tori's head right along with it.*

Keo stopped and stared for a good second, until the darkness overtook his vision again.

Oh, damn.

"Kid, come on!" Norris shouted behind him.

"Right behind you!" Keo shouted back, before turning and running.

He didn't see where Gillian had gone and prayed she had run straight to the back room at the end of the hallway like they had agreed. His fingers were already busy instinctively reloading the shotgun as he ran past the sheriff's office. He glimpsed Taylor and Aaron inside hiding behind the massive desk, so big that they couldn't bring it outside to use on the doors.

"Run!" he shouted at them.

They stared back at him, clutching at the sides of the big oak furniture, faces barely visible in the semidarkness. He couldn't tell if they were paralyzed with fear or if they couldn't hear him over the screaming and shotguns blasts. Maybe both.

"See the world. Kill some people. Make some money."

Yeah, right.

Then the two of them were gone, vanished from his peripheral vision, as Keo entered the hallway and kept going.

Sorry, kids, can't help you now!

He concentrated on what was in front of him. The back hallway, and almost at the very end, the room with the now-empty gun rack and shelves fully stocked with bullets that had no weapons to load.

And the steel door.

His sneakers had a hard time gripping the floor as he ran. He didn't know why until he remembered all the blood and brains and flesh he had stepped on and collected as he fled from the lobby. He was vaguely aware that he was reloading as he moved through the rectangular shaped darkness that was the hallway, the flashlight beam jolting left and right, then up and down, illuminating just enough to keep him from running straight into a wall.

Someone was moving behind him, shotgun blasting all the way. It was likely Norris. Keo had given up on Jake, and the chances of Aaron and Taylor making it out of the sheriff's office was not even worth thinking about. To find out for sure, he would have to slow down and look back.

Keo ran full-speed down the hallway instead.

He saw the door up ahead, Gillian's face temporarily lit up by his bouncing flashlight beam. She was at the door and holding it open with both hands, shouting something at him that he couldn't hear over the roar of gunfire from less than a meter behind him.

Then, out of nowhere, a voice shouted, "I'm out, I'm out!"

Keo slid to a stop and spun around. "Run, old man, run!"

Norris's face was contorted into a pained expression and there was sticky goo *(blood?)* clinging to his chest and face when Keo's flashlight flashed across him. When the beam of light left him, Norris was swallowed up by the darkness, though Keo could still make out the large whites of his eyes as the ex-cop ran past him.

Then there was just the hallway and the quivering, moving mass of silhouetted creatures flooding into the narrow passageway in front of him, their deformed shapes partially lit by large pools of moonlight splashing across the lobby.

He fired, then backed up and fired again, racked, and fired again.

One shot...two shots...three...

Keo wasn't aiming at their chests, which was the biggest part of them. Instead, he was gunning for their legs, because knocking them off their feet was the only thing that seemed to even slow them down.

Buckshot tore into their long spindly limbs, the strangely satisfying *crunch* of bones snapping at will. Sometimes he shot too high and shattered femurs, which was just as good.

"Keo!" from behind him. *Gillian.* "Come on!"

...four shots...five shots...

...six...

They fell over each other trying to get up the hallway at him. They slipped and slid on splattered and spraying blood, but all that did was delay them for a second, sometimes even less than that.

Daebak. I'm going to fucking die in this two-horse town.

Or worse.

He didn't know where the hell they had come from, how so many had gotten into the station so fast. How many had been in the air ducts? A dozen? A hundred? It looked like *thousands* were now rushing toward him. So many that he couldn't see the lobby behind them anymore, just little slivers of moonlight here and there, trying to pierce through a wall of death that was surging, stumbling, and crawling over the ones he had felled by taking out their legs.

And still they kept coming, and coming...

"Keo, goddammit!"

He fired his last shot and turned and ran. He didn't have far to go because he had backed almost right up to the open back room door. He practically stumbled his way inside as Gillian and Norris slammed the heavy piece of steel shut behind him. They drove the door into its frame with their entire bodies, fueled no doubt by a healthy dose of adrenaline.

Keo's momentum almost sent him right into the bench but he somehow managed to right himself in time. He looked back at Norris and Gillian as they took two quick, involuntary steps away from the door, which trembled slightly each time the creatures smashed into it, producing a soft, almost perversely gentle *thoom-thoom-thoom*, the noise impossibly muted by the metal door's construction.

The door held the way it was supposed to, even against the frantic assault from the other side. It housed guns, after all, and the valuables of the station's occupants.

Thoom-thoom-thoom.

Keo ran his flashlight around the room. Rachel and Christine were embracing each other near the back, their faces hidden from his beam. Lotte sat trembling next to them in her wheelchair, a look of half-shock, half-terror on the orphaned fourteen-year-old's face.

Norris continued backpedaling from the door and reloading his shotgun at the same time. "Did you see Jake and Henry?"

Keo shook his head. "Back in the lobby." He remembered Tori's head exploding under buckshot from Jake's shotgun... "I don't think they made it."

"Yeah..."

"What about Taylor?" Gillian asked.

Keo shook his head again. "I don't know. I saw them in the office when I was running past."

Gillian looked as if she wanted to ask something else, but maybe she already knew the answer, so she didn't.

Behind her, the steel door vibrated slightly against the *thoom-thoom-thoom...*

Keo reloaded his Remington with shells from his pouch.

Jesus, was he hyperventilating? He calmed himself—or at least, did the best he could to stop the pounding in his chest.

In and out, in and out...

Gillian sat quietly down on the bench next to him while Norris leaned against one of the lockers and caught his breath. The three of them didn't say a word and barely moved as they fixed their eyes on the piece of steel that was holding back the night. The *only* thing between them and a fate worse than death at the moment.

The creatures continued their attack, though by now the *thoom-thoom-thoom* had mostly faded into the background.

Not that they stopped. Not for a second.

Thoom-thoom-thoom.

He wondered how long they were going to keep it up.

Thoom-thoom-thoom.

Maybe all night. Maybe through tomorrow. Maybe well into the next night...

Thoom-thoom-thoom...

CHAPTER 13

THOOM-THOOM-THOOM.

Thoom-thoom-thoom...

"Why won't they stop?" Gillian asked around eight, three hours after nightfall.

He could barely see her in the darkness. Every now and then, either he or Norris turned on their flashlights and looked around to make sure everyone was fine. Or as fine as could be, locked inside a room where there were, possibly, hundreds of unkillable things squirming in wait on the other side of the only way out. Jake, Henry, and Tori were dead. He wondered if they were out there now, having joined the mass of undead.

Right. Because three more or less is going to make much of a difference either way.

"They can't get through," Gillian said. "They know that. So why don't they just stop?"

"I don't know," Keo said. "Maybe they don't know how."

"That doesn't make any sense."

"Doesn't it?"

"No."

He shrugged. "I'm out of ideas."

"You're useless."

"Sorry."

Thoom-thoom-thoom.

"Did you see what happened to Taylor?" she whispered.

"No."

"What about Jake and his girlfriend?"

"I didn't see what happened to them, either," he lied.

Thoom-thoom-thoom...

THE GIRLS FINALLY went to sleep around midnight after trying in vain to stay awake. Lotte simply closed her eyes and leaned back against her wheelchair, while Christine laid her head on her mother's lap and drifted off. Gillian moved from the bench to the floor next to the lockers and slid a pile of clothes under her head, then curled up into a ball and went to sleep.

Keo remained sitting on the bench facing the door, while Norris sat with his shotgun over his knees behind him.

Thoom-thoom-thoom.

"Jake and the others?" Norris said, his voice so quiet that Keo barely heard him.

Keo shook his head. He remembered flames stabbing out of Jake's shotgun, Henry on the floor, then Tori's head exploding against the wall...

"Dammit," Norris said.

"Yeah."

Thoom-thoom-thoom.

"They're a persistent bunch of fuckers," Norris said.

"It's not like they got anywhere else to be."

"What about the surrounding towns? The cities? You said it yourself. This thing isn't just statewide, it's probably nationwide, too. It's a full-scale invasion. So why are they wasting time on a half dozen people in Bentley?"

"Did you see how many were out there?"

"Looked like the whole town, and then some."

"Yeah. Looked like the whole damn town. If it's this bad here, think about the cities. There must be thousands—maybe tens of thousands—of those things running around in places like New Orleans and Shreveport. Maybe they're running out of...food."

"Already?" Then, "You think it's gone, don't you?"

"What?"

"The country. Good-bye, America."

"It's the lack of anything from FEMA that worries me."

"No FEMA, no United States government."

"Yeah."

Norris didn't say anything for a while. Finally, he said, "You're good at this."

"What's that?"

"Surviving."

"I've had practice."

"Who exactly did you use to work for, kid?"

"You wouldn't know them. They pride themselves on staying in the shadows. But if you're ever in Downtown Raleigh, North Carolina, they have a building there. Nothing special, but they're always looking to hire people like you."

"People like me?"

"Ex-law enforcement types. People not shy around guns. Bonus points if you're not queasy around blood."

"Sounds like swell guys."

"Oh yeah," Keo smiled. "Not that it matters now. They're probably gone, too. If Uncle Sam can't survive this..."

"Was it good money?"

"Good enough."

"But not great."

"It depends on the gig. Every call out's different."

"So why do it if the money isn't always great? I'm guessing your life's at stake each time you go out there."

"It's what I'm good at," Keo said. "I've never been good at very much else. Some people know they're destined to become a singer, an actor, or go into outer space. Me? I realized I could do this pretty well."

"What is 'this'?"

"Fight. Survive. Make a little money while I'm at it. You

know, the American Dream."

"You're crazy," Norris said.

"Don't tell anyone," Keo said.

THE CREATURES STOPPED trying to break down the door around two in the morning. There were no hints that they were getting tired or signs of anything else happening outside. One second they heard the constant *thoom-thoom-thoom*, and the next there was just silence.

Keo and Norris remained where they had been for the last six hours. Keo wasn't sure what Norris was thinking, but he was wary of the quiet and tried focusing on Gillian snoring lightly on the floor next to him instead. Rachel, Christine, and Lotte were still in the back somewhere, though it was harder to hear them.

It's a trick. Some kind of sick, twisted trick.

He waited a minute. Then two…

…then ten…

And there was just the stillness inside and outside the back room.

"They've stopped," Norris finally said. "You think it's a trick, too?"

"Has to be," Keo said.

"Go find out."

"Why me?"

"You're younger. You probably have better hearing."

Keo stood up and moved through the darkness, walking as lightly and silently as he could manage, and leaned against the cold steel door.

He could hear them outside. Moving, but not frantically. Not like creatures with purpose. Almost…bored?

"Well?" Norris whispered behind him.

Keo took a couple of steps backward. "They're still out

there."

"What are they doing?"

"Do I look like I have x-ray vision?"

"What did you hear, then?"

"They're moving around. Like they're…"

"What?" Norris pressed.

"Like they're settling in for the night." Keo tiptoed back to the bench and sat down. "They're going to wait us out. You know that, right?"

"How long, do you think?"

"You don't understand, old timer. They don't have to go anywhere. You remember this afternoon?"

"What about it?"

"Sunlight doesn't reach this far back into the hallway."

"Shit."

"Yeah," Keo said.

He wondered how many were out there right now on the other side of the steel door, waiting in the darkness.

A dozen? A hundred?

How many could possibly fit into the narrow space of the passageway?

Too many. Too damn many…

HE FELT MORNING rather than saw it. There was the sweat pooling under his armpits and dripping from his temple, and the suddenly noticeable stench of the blood on the front of his shirt and pants. Or, at least, he thought it was blood. It was too dark, too clumpy, and hadn't really dried the way blood should overnight.

Keo glanced down at his watch: 6:44 A.M.

It had actually sneaked up on him. Norris, too, from the way he opened his eyes and stood up, sighing as his joints popped from sitting all night. Or just old age. He stretched and looked around. Visibility had increased enough that everything wasn't just black lumps around them anymore.

Keo used the precious little light available to look for new clothes in one of the lockers. He found an Under Armour T-shirt and pulled it on, then shoved the stained one inside. There were no spare pants, so he made do with the ones he had on. Norris did the same thing, finding only a white T-shirt that was just one size too small. He didn't look happy with the fit as he pulled it on.

A T-shirt wasn't the worse article of clothing they could have on at the moment. It was going to get hotter in a few more hours. There were no windows in the back room, and although there were two vents along the walls, they were both half the size of the one in the lobby. Thank God, or the creatures would have just followed them into the back room.

I guess we missed something after all...

Gillian stirred on the floor before sitting up. She squinted at him from behind a curtain of black hair.

"Hey," he said.

She rubbed her eyes. "We're still alive."

"You sound surprised."

"After last night? Hell yes." She stretched her arms. "I don't think I can take another night like the last two." She stood up and looked back at the girls, then at the door. "Are they...?"

Keo shook his head. "I haven't checked in a while."

He did that now. Norris and Gillian watched his every step. He put his hand against the warm steel door before pressing his ear against it.

He listened.

"Well?" Norris said after Keo didn't move or say anything for almost a minute. "Are they out there or not?"

Keo pulled his head back before giving them an uncertain look. "I can't hear them anymore."

"That's good, right?"

"Yeah, but I should be able to hear *something*, even if they're just standing around. There were a lot of them out there last night, remember?"

"Maybe they're sleeping," Gillian said. She glanced back at the sleeping forms of Rachel, Christine, and Lotte again. "They sleep, don't they?"

"I think so," Keo said.

"They definitely sleep," Norris said. "Inside the buildings where they were hiding, the ones with the covered windows. Yesterday morning I woke up a whole nest of them at the gas station, remember?"

Keo leaned back against the door and held his breath. He listened again...

...and still heard nothing.

"Keo?" Gillian said.

He shook his head.

"Why would they just leave?" Norris said. "They have us trapped in here. The only way out is through that door."

Keo didn't have any good answers for him. He saw the frustration on Norris's face. Gillian's, too. He shook his head. "I don't know, but I can't hear a single thing. Even if they were asleep, I should be able to hear...something."

"So what do we do now?" Gillian said. "We can't stay in here forever. It's already getting hot. And we don't have food or water."

"We should risk it," Keo said.

"Go out there?" Norris said.

"Yeah."

"That sounds like a bad idea."

"Gillian's right. We can't stay in here forever. No food, no water. Sooner or later, we'll have to make a run for it. What if they had left this morning and we didn't take advantage of it? What if it's our only chance?"

Norris shook his head. "What if you're wrong about everything? Maybe they're out there, just waiting for us to make a mistake."

"I don't see how we have any choice, old timer."

"It's suicide."

"Only if they're still out there."

"You really can't hear anything?"

"No. Nothing."

"Why would they leave? It doesn't make sense."

"Norris," Keo said, "we're dealing with creatures that die in sunlight but can't be killed even after you've destroyed their brains. If they even have brains anymore. What about any of this makes any sense to you?"

"Shit," Norris said.

"Yeah."

"Look, just make a decision," Gillian said. She sounded resigned but defiant at the same time. "We can't stay in here forever. We have to try something eventually, and it might as well be now, while we still have the strength. Us here, right now, is better than us after twenty-four hours of no water or food. Or am I wrong?"

"What's going on?" a voice said behind them. They looked back at Rachel, rubbing her eyes, Christine still sound asleep in her lap. "Are they still out there?"

"That's the question of the century," Keo said. He glanced at Norris. "Now or later, old timer."

Norris sighed. "I'm too old for this shit."

GILLIAN GRIPPED THE lever and waited as Keo established himself to her right and Norris did the same to her left. They readied their Remingtons and each took a long, hard breath.

"This is such a bad idea," Gillian said. "I've changed my mind. Is it too late to change my mind?"

"Yes," Keo said.

"Dammit."

Behind them, Rachel, Christine, and Lotte sat on the floor

with their backs against the wall, all three using the overturned bench and Lotte's wheelchair as their first line of cover. They looked terrified—all except Christine, who held up her hand and gave Keo a thumbs up. He grinned back at her.

"Ready, kid?" Norris said.

"No," Keo said. "But do it anyway."

"God, this is so stupid," Gillian said between them.

"It's your idea," Keo smiled at her. "You're the one who convinced us to do this."

"I know; that's why I think this is such a stupid idea. I'm just a bank teller, for God's sake. No one ever does what I say."

"See, you're already more important than you used to be." He changed up his grip on the shotgun for the fifth time in the last minute. "Whenever you're ready, Gillian."

"Okay." She took a deep breath. "Just to be sure, we're really doing this—"

"Yes," Keo and Norris said at the same time.

"Okay, okay."

She took a deep breath, then began silently counting down from ten. He watched her mouth form the word *ten*...

Keo stretched out his fingers before re-gripping the shotgun for the sixth time.

...*nine*...

Gillian was right. This really was a stupid idea.

...*eight*...

She was going to open the door and he was going to step outside and die.

...*seven*...

Because there was no way around it.

...*six*...

If the creatures were outside, they were dead—he and Norris.

...*five*...

He had shotgunned one of those things from point-blank range and blew away the top of its head, and that hadn't even slowed it down.

...*four*...

He had blown off their legs and they still kept coming.

...*three*...

So what chance did they have out there in a hallway full of those creatures?

Not even a snowball's chance in hell.

...*two*...

Dammit, I should have kept on driving yesterday.

"One," Gillian said, and cranked the lever.

BLOOD AND DEATH filled the hallway and assaulted his senses the instant he stepped into the darkened passageway. Keo braced himself for an attack. He waited to feel pain, see bony fingers reaching for him, and be confronted with black eyes piercing his soul from the shadows.

But there was none of that.

No lifeless orbs from the pits of hell in front of him, and when he spun around, there were none behind him, either. The only sounds came from Norris's labored breathing, pounding the air next to him.

Keo became aware of a *slopping* noise and looked down at thick patches of still-wet black blood on the floor and splashed across the walls. Flakes of torn skin and muscle covered the hallway and the smell was horrible, like rotting flesh left out in the sun, even though sunlight didn't have a chance of reaching all the way back here.

He began breathing through his mouth as he moved toward the lobby. Every step meant stepping on and around and through thick patches of blood. Black, thick, and oozing, clinging to the bottom of his shoes.

Slop-slop. Slop-slop...

As he had guessed last night, the creatures had pulled down

the vending machines over the windows and the desks from the front doors, allowing the morning sun to pour into the lobby at will. Wherever direct sunlight touched the room, there were no pools of black blood, only the red *(human)* kind. The familiar acidic smell of the dead creatures lingered in the air.

"That smell," Norris said quietly.

"That's them in sunlight," Keo said. "Their blood evaporates, just like the rest of them."

"This is all pretty messed up, kid."

"You just realized that now?"

Norris grunted back.

They were only able to relax when they stepped into a pool of sunlight and looked out the windows, through the bars, and into the parking lot beyond. It was a hot bright morning, the light against their face the greatest feeling in the world.

"Did we just get really lucky?" Norris said after a moment of silence.

"Really, really lucky," Keo said.

"You always been this lucky?"

"Nope. You?"

"First time for everything, I guess."

"Well, it couldn't have come at a better time."

"Yeah, I'd say." He looked back toward the hallway. "Let's get the girls and get the hell out of here before our luck runs out."

Keo hurried down the hallway, reaching the back room a few seconds later and knocking on the steel door.

Gillian opened it almost immediately. "You're still alive."

"You were supposed to make sure it was me before opening the door," Keo smiled.

"Who the hell else would it be, Keo?" She leaned out and looked up and down the hallway. "Where's Norris?"

"In the lobby."

"Can we…?"

"You want an invitation?"

She smirked before turning serious again. "So, what now? Where do we go and what do we do after we get there? It's always going to be night, Keo. Sooner or later, the sun always goes down."

"Fort Damper, for now," Keo said. "We'll figure out the rest later."

PART TWO

THE WOODSMEN

CHAPTER 14

THE WORLD WAS dead. Or if it wasn't, it was pretty damn close.

"It's the end of the world, Keo," Gillian said solemnly next to him. "We're screwed, aren't we? It's no better out here. Maybe we should have stayed in Bentley."

"We'll be fine," Keo said. "Right now, we just have to concentrate on linking up with what's left of the U.S. Army."

"And then what?"

"We'll cross that bridge when we get to it."

"We're all going to die."

"That's the spirit. Keep that chin up."

She laughed. "Sorry. I guess I was having a little pity party. By invitation only. Attendees: me."

She wasn't entirely wrong. Surviving Bentley had been a miracle, but he hadn't fully realized how dire things were in the rest of the world until they started driving along Interstate 20. Except for the same pileup that Rachel and Norris had braved that first night, the road was mostly clear, and they drove for minutes at a time without seeing another vehicle, much less any signs of survivors.

The silence, along with the emptiness around them, was deafening.

This is it. This is the end.

Hunker down and pass the shotgun shells.

Keo picked up the radio from the Chevy's dashboard. The truck was Jake's, since Keo had left his Lancer buried in the side of the hospital back in Bentley.

"Old timer," Keo said into the radio.

Rachel's Durango SUV followed closely behind them, Norris behind the wheel. Interstate 20 consisted of two lanes of flat road heading west, while two eastbound lanes ran parallel on the other side of a grassy strip. There wasn't much of a view in any direction, and every mile they had passed for the last thirty minutes looked the same as the previous one, with walls of trees along both sides. It had been ten minutes since they had last seen a roadside establishment. Keo didn't like the idea of getting stuck out here at night, even with a shotgun on hand.

"Can you drive any slower?" Norris said through the radio. They had chosen Rachel's car because it was better equipped to carry Lotte and her wheelchair in the back.

"What's your hurry?" Keo said. "Damper isn't going anywhere."

"It's going to have to wait a little longer, because the girls need to take care of business. I wouldn't mind stretching my legs, either."

"Already?"

"I'm fifty-six and retired, kid. I got cramps for cramps."

Keo grinned. "Maybe we can grab you some diapers, too, while we're at it."

"Now you're talking."

"Up there," Gillian said, pointing forward.

"We see something up ahead," Keo said into the radio.

"Roger that," Norris said.

Keo slowed down as they approached a combination gas station and diner. The roadside establishment had appeared unexpectedly out of the wall of green trees that surrounded it. A thick metal sign flopped back and forth in the wind, advertising gas for regular and diesel fuel. Even from a distance, the place gave off an abandoned vibe.

"Looks inviting," Gillian said quietly.

"All we need is a mariachi band playing in the parking lot to welcome us in," Keo said. "You have mariachi bands in Louisiana?"

"I've never seen one. But then again, Bentley is a town of 3,000 people, and I've never seen a six-one Korean guy in real life, either."

Keo smiled. "First time for everything."

"WE'LL HIT CORDEN in less than ten miles," Norris said. "There have to be other survivors there. It's twenty times bigger than Bentley."

"Bigger population, more of those things," Keo said. "They multiply like rats."

"Still, if we could pick up more people on the way, I'd feel better. Strength in numbers and all that." He looked over at Gillian, standing nearby. "You've been to Corden?"

She nodded. "It's a college town. Everything pretty much revolves around Louisiana Tech University."

They were watching Rachel as she was wheeling Lotte back from a bathroom next to the gas station. Keo had searched the single room for them earlier just to be safe, though in the back of his mind he always wondered what he was going to do if there were one of those things inside. Likely he would have ended up wasting a couple of shells on it, only to back out of there in a hurry.

They had found both the diner's and gas station's windows uncovered, which made some kind of sense all the way out here. Keo guessed it was because there just weren't that many people to "turn," so there were no reasons for them to stick around. The creatures weren't stupid. They went where the people were.

Where the food is…

Christine was eating from a bag of chips as she walked over with the other girls. The Doritos bag was one of many they had loaded up from the gas station. The entire store remained the way it was from two nights ago, with only a small pool of dried blood near the front doors. They had stocked up on as much as they could carry, including unopened cases of bottled water and soda. The junk food and chips would come in handy, but the boxes of beef jerky were the real prize. Those could last for up to a year—longer, if properly stored.

Keo hadn't realized how little they had until they began cleaning out the gas station. He was hoping to find a weapon behind the front counter, but there was only a baseball bat. A back room also yielded very little, though he did pick up a couple knives from the shelves. What he wouldn't give for a nice Ka-Bar...

"Let's get this show on the road," Norris said. "We hit Corden, then head south down toward Alexandria and straight to the base after that. We'll pick up any stragglers we find along the way, but let's not lollygag." He blinked up at the sun. "The faster we get there, the better I'll feel."

Rachel helped Lotte into the back seat of the Durango while Norris stowed the wheelchair in the back. The girl could hobble on one leg for short periods of time, but they weren't going to be rid of her wheelchair for a while. Keo and Norris agreed they'd have to make her a crutch soon, in case she needed to be more mobile.

Gillian tapped Keo on the shoulder and handed him a candy bar.

"Ah, you're sweet," he smiled.

"It's just a Snickers bar, Romeo." She opened one herself and took a bite. "How long are these going to last, anyway?"

"Why are you asking me?"

"You look like you'd know. So, do you?"

He shrugged. "Two to four months without refrigeration. Longer, if Fort Damper has something cold to put them in. So eat up. Once they're gone, they're gone."

"There goes my diet," Gillian said, before going quiet and glancing at the flat road behind them. "I keep expecting to see a car going by."

"Me too. The quiet is unsettling."

"Yeah…"

Norris blared the SUV's horn behind them and leaned out the driver side window. "Come on, kids, you can suck face later."

"Suck face," Keo said. "I like the sound of that."

"What are you, fifteen?" Gillian said, walking back to the Chevy. "You coming, lover boy?"

"Yes, ma'am," Keo said, jogging after her.

He climbed back in behind the steering wheel as she settled into the front passenger seat. Gillian picked up a map from the floor and unfolded it in her lap. She took out a marker from the glove compartment and went back to work, jotting down the location of the gas station. She had done the same thing for every notable stop they had made since leaving Bentley.

"We're not coming back here, Gillian," Keo said.

"I know."

"So why do it?"

She didn't answer him until she had finished what she was writing, then refolded the map and slipped it back into the glove compartment. "I just want to make sure we don't forget, that's all."

"Forget what?"

"That these places were once here, that once upon a time they served a purpose. I just want to remember them, even if it's just some scribbling on a map." She shrugged. "It's stupid, I know."

"It's not."

"Yeah?"

He started the truck. "No. Not at all."

"Are you just saying that because you want to get in my pants?"

He smiled. "Not at all."

"Liar."

He cleared his throat. "So, you used to live in Corden?"

"Oh, that's slick—" she started to say, but the words turned into a scream when *a gunshot split the air* and the windshield spiderwebbed.

Keo reached across the seats and grabbed Gillian's head, pushing her down. She struggled against him, caught somewhere between paralyzing fear and surprise, but he was stronger and he managed to get her down just enough that the second and third shots smashed through the windshield and stitched the headrest of her seat instead of her head.

He stuck his free hand toward the dashboard and groped for the radio at the last place he remembered seeing it less than a second ago. Got a hold of something plastic and cold and pulled it down, pressed the lever, and shouted into it, "Drive, drive, drive!"

Keo dropped the radio just as bullets punched into the front hood of the Chevy and he heard the *ping-ping!* of lead slicing through metal. He didn't look up—he didn't have to—letting go of Gillian and grabbing the steering wheel with one hand and pulling the gear into drive with the other, then slammed his foot down on the gas pedal.

The truck lurched forward—*ping-ping!* as two more shots pierced the side and the rear passenger window shattered against a third shot—as Keo struggled to control the steering wheel. He pulled himself up into a sitting position just as he felt a slight bump and knew they were out of the parking lot and back on the highway.

He caught a glimpse of the shooter—no, *shooters*—coming out from behind the gas station as he sped off. Two men, both armed with assault rifles, but it wasn't their weapons that got his attention. It was the fact that they were both wearing black shirts and black pants with the legs shoved inside black army boots, and their faces were covered in green and black paint. They were also wearing some kind of stripped down assault gear, and their waists bulged with pouches he was sure were stuffed with magazines for their weapons.

Ping-ping-ping! as bullets punched into the side of the Chevy even as he drove past them, willing the truck to go faster faster *faster*. The gas pedal was completely pressed against the floor, and he would have shoved it all the way through the vehicle if he could at that moment.

The tires struggled mightily against his control, even with both hands gripping the steering wheel. The two shooters only stopped firing at Keo because they had begun shooting at Norris in the Durango, which was following him onto the highway. He thought he could hear the girls in the SUV screaming, but of course that was impossible with bullets flying around him—

And more shooters were emerging out of the stretch of grass that lined the highway divider. (Jesus, how had he not seen them before?) There were two more of them, similarly dressed, their faces covered. One was firing an AK-47 and the rounds punched into the side of the Chevy behind Keo's seat, one shattering the window.

Keo didn't stop to find out if there were more of them somewhere out there. Four was enough. Four was goddamn too many already.

He kept the gas pedal shoved against the floor, hands on the steering wheel, and the truck pointed west up the road. He glanced quickly at his side mirror and saw the Durango keeping pace, swerving a bit on the road, just a split second before the image—and the glass—exploded in front of his face.

He looked up at the rearview mirror instead. The two shooters at the gas station had moved into the road and were shooting after them. They weren't hitting much of anything at this distance, though Keo imagined they must have been aiming for the Durango behind him and not the Chevy. He hoped the girls had gotten down as low as they could go back there.

He pulled his foot off the gas pedal just enough to let the SUV catch up. He spotted Norris in the rearview mirror, leaning forward against the steering wheel. Norris's own windshield was pockmarked with holes, but the vehicle seemed to be moving fine.

It wasn't until they were far enough down the highway and he couldn't hear any more shooting that Keo allowed himself to relax a bit and pulled his foot slightly off the gas pedal. He looked over at Gillian, picking herself up from the floor of the front passenger seat. She had glass in her hair and there was a small cut along her left cheek. She must not have noticed it as she sat back on her seat, crunching broken glass under her. She didn't seem to have heard (or felt) that, either.

"Gillian," Keo said.

She didn't react to the sound of his voice.

"Gillian," he said again, louder this time.

She finally looked at him. Her face was calm, but that was a façade. He had seen it before from civilians in the aftermath of a gunfight. The real her was in turmoil, every emotion she had ever felt in her lifetime swirling around inside her at this very moment, like ocean waves trying to drown her. He had felt the same thing during his first couple of combat experiences.

"Gillian," he said a third time.

"Yes," she said, and just saying that one word brought her back closer to the surface. She looked down at her hands. They were shaking in her lap. A drop of blood from her cut cheek dripped and landed on the back of one hand, and she finally noticed the wound. "Oh God, I'm bleeding."

"It's okay. It's just a graze. You'll be fine."

She looked at him, and he didn't think she believed him.

"Trust me," he said. "I've seen people shot before. You're not shot. You were just cut by flying glass. Okay?" When she didn't respond, he said again, more forcefully, "Okay?"

She nodded mutely.

"I need the radio, Gillian," Keo said, pointing to the two-way Motorola on the floor at her feet.

She picked it up, looking at it as if she didn't know what she was holding, then finally held it over to him before reaching back up to her cheek to feel the cut. Her fingers came away with some blood, but thankfully not too much.

Keo pressed the transmit lever on the radio. "Norris, you still with me?"

"Yeah," Norris said through the radio. It sounded like he was hyperventilating slightly. It took a moment for Keo to realize that he was, too.

In and out, in and out...

"You and Gillian?" Norris asked through the radio.

Keo checked on Gillian. She was still staring silently down at the smeared blood on her fingers. "We're fine," he said into the radio. "How's everyone in your car?"

"The girls are freaking out," Norris said. "What the hell happened back there? Who were those guys?"

Good question.

Who the hell were those guys? Where did they come from? Where did they get those weapons?

"I don't know," Keo said.

He looked down at his speedometer. He was still going well over sixty miles per hour. That meant Norris was, too. He took his foot off the gas a little bit more.

"Gotta slow down, Norris," he said into the radio. "The last thing we want is to get into a wreck out here."

"Roger that," Norris said.

Soon, Keo was down to fifty miles per hour. He wasn't comfortable enough to go any lower, but he was also wary of going too much faster. There hadn't been a lot of debris or abandoned vehicles for the last few miles, but he had seen plenty of evidence that they existed around Bentley. All he needed was to hit a piece of metal on the road going this speed and they would be tumbling down the highway instead of driving up it.

"What now?" Norris said through the radio.

Keo glanced up at the rearview mirror, expecting to see a

vehicle coming up the road behind Norris. There wasn't any, but then again, they had gotten a pretty good jump on the shooters.

How did they get to the gas station in the first place? They didn't walk there...

He slowed down some more.

The radio squawked, and Norris said, "What's going on? Why are you slowing down?"

"We need to stop for a minute," Keo said.

"What?" Gillian said. She was staring wide-eyed at him. "Why are we stopping? They're back there, Keo! What if they're chasing us?"

"Exactly. We need to find out."

"How?"

Keo stopped the Chevy in the middle of the road and turned off the engine.

"Stay here," he said to Gillian before climbing outside.

He jogged up the road to the Durango, parked a few meters away. Norris flashed Keo a questioning look through the bullet-riddled windshield. Rachel was, too. Keo couldn't see Christine or Lotte in the backseat.

All four of the SUV's door windows were gone and there were holes across Norris's driver side door. For the life of him, Keo couldn't figure out how Norris was still alive after the battering his vehicle had taken. When he glanced back at the Chevy, though, he guessed Norris probably had the same question about him.

Jesus, how are we still alive?

"What's going on?" Norris asked. He swatted at shards of glass still clinging to his window frame.

"Turn off your engine," Keo said.

Norris hesitated, but did it.

Keo walked past them and up the road slightly. He stopped and listened. For a moment, all he could hear and feel was his own heartbeat. The adrenaline was still pumping overtime through his body, making it hard to concentrate—

There!

Car engines. More than one.

Coming up the road toward them.

Keo ran back to the Durango. "Can you hear them?" he shouted at Norris.

Norris shook his head. "Hear what—" He stopped. "Fuck!"

"Drive drive drive!"

He was still running to the Chevy when Norris fired up the Durango and took off, swerving around the parked truck. Keo quickly lunged back into his vehicle and turned on the engine.

Gillian was staring after the fleeing SUV. "Are they leaving us?"

"No," Keo said. He slammed on the gas and chased after Norris. "They're following us."

"Who?"

"The shooters back at the gas station."

He glanced at the rearview mirror, but they still hadn't come into view yet. That was the good news.

"Why are they following us?" Gillian asked, her voice trembling.

To finish the job, he thought, but said instead, "I don't know." He grabbed the radio. "Norris, we need to get off the interstate."

"Are you crazy?" Norris said through the radio. "We don't know this place. We'll get lost without even realizing it."

"Norris, we can't lose them on the highway. If they have faster vehicles, they're going to catch up to us sooner or later. We're not going to win a gunfight with guys carrying assault rifles."

Norris didn't answer right away. After a few seconds, the ex-cop said, "Okay, call it."

"First exit you see, take it."

"Roger that," Norris said, though Keo detected zero traces of enthusiasm in his voice.

Keo didn't like this idea any better than Norris, but it wasn't as if they had a choice. He looked up at the rearview mirror again. There was nothing back there, which meant their pursuers were still too far back. If he concentrated hard enough, he thought he could hear them coming, but that was probably just his imagination.

Up ahead, Keo saw the Durango's remaining rear light come on as Norris slowed the vehicle down. An exit was coming up and the SUV was moving into the right lane to take it.

Keo tapped on the brake and followed, praying to God this was the right move, that they weren't going to get themselves killed by leaving the highway...

CHAPTER 15

"WHO DO YOU think they were?" Gillian's voice was still trembling noticeably thirty minutes after the attempted ambush, but at least her hands had stopped shaking. "Why were they trying to kill us?"

"I don't know," Keo said. "Could be anyone. For any reason. I don't know."

"But why were they shooting at us? Were they soldiers?"

"No, I don't think so. Looked like guys playing soldiers, though. We were lucky."

"Lucky?" She gave him a horrified look. "You call this lucky?"

"The guy who fired the first shot was a lousy marksman. If he'd been better, we wouldn't be having this talk. One of us would be dead. Maybe both."

"Oh." She took a moment to digest that. "I still don't feel very lucky." She looked at the floor and kicked at the pile of glass scattered down there. "God, how are we even still alive?"

"I told you. We were lucky."

"I guess you're right." She frowned. "I still don't feel very lucky, though."

They had turned off Interstate 20 and onto Highway 145 twenty minutes ago before merging onto Highway 146, heading farther south. The Durango had pulled back earlier and let the Chevy take the lead again.

If Keo thought the view from I-20 was trees and green and

little else, the two-lane road along 146 was even less thrilling. The only difference was the lack of a strip between the north and southbound lanes. That, and the endless walls of trees to both sides of them were thinner and older, the branches, leaves, and trunks battered brown and dry from too much sunlight and not enough rain.

Every now and then they saw man-made driveways that led to country houses behind large clusters of trees. Sometimes those houses were more visible from the road, even welcoming (at least on the outside). Other times they were too well hidden to see much of what lay in the back, which he guessed was part of the charm of living out here. The last three homes they had pulled into the driveways of had revealed covered windows up front. They had quickly reversed each time and continued on.

The fact was, they were lost. They didn't know where they were going, and although Gillian still had her map, it didn't show them houses or buildings or any place that could reasonably be considered a viable shelter. The only good news as far as Keo could tell was that the ambushers hadn't followed them off the interstate. He was sure they had lost the pursuit once they left I-20, parked half a mile away, and turned off their engines. The sound of vehicles passing by behind them had been all too obvious.

They're hunting us. Like prey.
Who the hell are these guys?

So they went south off the interstate because they couldn't go anywhere else. According to Gillian's map, the road they were on now wouldn't take them all the way to Fort Damper, though there was a road farther down that would eventually reconnect with highways heading into the city of Corden. That was an option Keo kept at the back of his mind. For now, he was just happy they weren't being shot at or pursued.

"There's not a lot out here," Keo said after a while.

"It's the country," she said, as if that should explain everything.

He guessed it did. They were deep in the boondocks now. The sticks. People didn't come out here unless they were trying to get away. He had seen it in the homes they'd passed. They hadn't been big homes—most were three, four-bedroom bungalows. There was probably a river or a lake nearby. Fishing spots, maybe.

The radio on the dashboard squawked, and he heard Norris's voice. "How much longer, kid?"

Keo picked up the radio. "I don't know. This isn't exactly my backyard."

"Well, it's not mine, either."

Keo glanced at Gillian, who shook her head back at him. "Don't look at me. I've never been out here before. I've always just driven straight to Corden and back on the interstate."

"Let's just keep going until we find some place we can stop and rest," Keo said into the radio.

"We need to find a place soon," Norris said. "I'm running low on gas."

"How low?"

"In another hour, we're gonna be squeezing into that Chevy with you."

THEY DROVE PAST three more houses, each one located so far from one another that Keo was sure the residents probably had no idea the other existed. Each time they pulled into the driveway, they saw covered windows, and each time Gillian let out a sigh of frustration.

"This is hopeless," she said.

"We'll find a place," Keo said.

She flashed him an annoyed look. "How can you be so damn optimistic after everything we've been through?"

"Have you ever been to Mogadishu in the summer?"

"I don't even know where that is."

"It's in Somalia. In the Horn of Africa."

"Am I supposed to know where the Horn of Africa is? Is that, like, in Africa?"

He smiled. "Yes."

"What about it?"

"Well, it's not fun. Especially when you're an American. Everyone in that country has an AK-47."

"What were you doing in Mogadishu?"

"This guy had this thing that the guys I worked for wanted, so they sent me and some people to go get it."

Gillian stared at him in silence for a moment.

"What?" he said.

"What exactly did you use to do for a living before all of this, Keo?"

"I got things for people."

"What kind of things?"

He shrugged. "Stuff. And things. It's always different. Sometimes it's just to take people places. You know—work."

She shook her head. "Forget I asked."

EVENTUALLY, THE GIRLS in Norris's vehicle couldn't stand it anymore. Keo began hunting the side of the road for a place—any place—until he saw an old, rusted sign for an RV park. The road into it was overgrown with grass and there were no indications it had been traveled recently. He pulled into it and drove about 100 meters off the highway until they came to a camping ground next to a river.

The park might have been worth visiting once, but those days were long gone. It was now a junkyard for abandoned vehicles, everything from trucks to bicycles to husks of old mobile homes. The newest piece of junk looked at least a decade old. But while the cars took over one side of the park, there was still the other half left over, with a nice view of the river in the back.

Keo and Norris pulled up next to a couple of picnic benches, both falling apart and beaten by the elements.

Norris climbed out with his shotgun clutched in his hands and scanned the area around them for threats. He looked weary and paranoid at the same time. "No one sits or touches or leans against anything. Understand?"

Gillian had gone over to the SUV, and with Rachel, helped Lotte out of the Durango and back into her wheelchair. They left to do their business, leaving Christine behind. The girl was circling their cars, apparently counting all the holes along the sides, while eating a packet of Ring Dings.

"Jesus, I can't believe we survived all that," Norris said, looking at their vehicles.

"We got real lucky," Keo said.

"You got a good look at those guys?"

"A bit."

"What did you see?"

"Tactical gear and assault rifles. That's all I needed to see."

"Face paint, right? Tell me those guys weren't black."

Keo chuckled. "Yeah, face paint."

"Thank God," Norris said.

They spent the next twenty minutes going over both cars, making sure there were no leaks in the gas tanks or anywhere else that was vital. The vehicles had, miraculously, escaped pretty intact, save for the broken windows and bullet holes. Everything they needed to keep going (with the exception of the Durango's dwindling gas supply) was still in one piece.

"Real lucky," Keo said.

"I'd like to get a piece of those assholes," Norris said. "Send some payback their way."

Norris looked toward the road, as if he could see past the turn and out onto the highway. Fortunately he couldn't, which meant anyone passing by wouldn't be able to see them, either.

Rachel and Gillian were walking back with Lotte, Gillian

pushing the wheelchair. Even from a distance, he thought they looked excited about something.

"How's Rachel?" Keo asked.

"Scared," Norris said. "Shit, I was scared, too. I told you, right? I've never been in a gunfight in my life. Over two decades on the job." He shook his head. "You saw four back there, too?"

"Yeah. Two at the gas station and two more hiding on the highway."

"How'd they sneak up on us?"

"Good question."

Better question: Who the hell were those guys?

"At least we lost them," Norris said. "The question now is, what do we next? The Durango's not going to last for very much longer."

Keo glanced at his watch. The day had crept up on them and it was already noon. Normally that wouldn't be so bad, except it got dark way too fast around this part of the state this time of the year. "We need to start looking for a place to stay the night."

"Yeah, not a lot of options out here."

"Guys?" Gillian called out to them when she was closer. "We found something on the other side of the park."

"What is it?" Keo said.

"It's a cabin," Gillian said. "And there's nothing covering the windows."

THE CABIN MUST have been some kind of manager's office for the park, back when the area was still serving customers. It was just slightly beyond the clearing, hidden behind the pile of cars, and would have stayed invisible if the girls hadn't stumbled across it.

The exterior was old and weather-beaten, and the interior

was covered in cobwebs, signs that no one had been inside for years. Which was exactly what Keo was hoping to find. The absence of any kind of foot traffic meant no creatures, either. The cabin had two bedrooms in the back, and something that was even more valuable—a basement.

While Rachel and Gillian drove the trucks over and Christine stayed outside with Lotte, Keo and Norris looked over the wooden basement door built into the floorboards. It looked as old-fashioned as the rest of the cabin, and it was covered in a thick layer of dust that Keo kicked at.

"Looks good," Keo said.

"How's that?" Norris said.

"A lot of dust means the door hasn't been opened recently. So there's nothing down there that'll want to eat us."

"You hope."

"Only one way to find out."

"Your funeral," Norris said.

Keo flicked on the flashlight duct-taped to the end of his weapon's barrel while Norris got into position and grabbed the brass ring connected to the door.

The ex-cop looked over at Keo. "You ready?"

Keo nodded.

Norris changed his grip on the ring. "Okay," he said. Then, showing surprising strength for a fifty-six-year-old retiree, pulled the door open with a loud grunt.

A cloud of dust and God knew what else erupted when Norris flung the door open. Keo fought through the cough and aimed the Remington into the opening. A thick patch of black emptiness greeted him.

Keo moved the shotgun back and forth and side to side, illuminating some questionable wooden steps leading down. The basement floor was packed dirt, but the walls were block concrete. The flashlight revealed rectangular objects underneath dirt-covered blue tarps. Boxes, maybe. Good supplies, if they were lucky, but that was a stretch given the state of the cabin.

He waited for signs of movement—scurrying, a pair of black eyes—but there was just the stream of loose dirt and dust flitting back and forth across his flashlight beam.

Norris had already unslung his shotgun and turned on the flashlight, shining it down along with Keo's. "What do you see?"

"Nothing," Keo said.

"Doesn't mean there's nothing down there."

"Nope."

"So, what now? Go down there and find out?"

"Not like we have a lot of choices. This might be the best place we'll find all day. Like you said, the Durango's almost out of gas, so that really limits our options."

Norris sighed, then slung his shotgun and reached into his pocket. "Heads you go, tails I—"

Keo had already leaped through the hole and landed on the dirt floor just in front of the stairs before Norris could finish. He straightened up and spun left, then right, then left again just to be sure. His finger was on the shotgun's trigger at all times, ready to pull at the first sign of movement.

This is such a bad idea.

The only sound was his own labored breathing, and the sudden burst of movement and violent teeth coming at him from the shadows that Keo was expecting never came. There was just him scooting left, then right, the *crunch* of his sneakers against the unsteady dirt floor. The fact that the room smelled abandoned meant no one *(no thing)* had been down here in a while. Definitely longer than two days.

"Goddammit, kid, you almost gave me a heart attack, for crying out loud," Norris said, leaning over the hole above him.

Keo gave the basement a final look before lowering the Remington. "There's nothing down here but dirt and old supplies."

"You sure about that?"

"I've been down here for almost a minute and I'm still alive.

Yeah, I'm sure."

"Good enough for me," Norris said, just before he vanished out of sight.

The basement was a decent size, maybe 650 square feet, with concrete walls and shelves that were mostly empty. The ones that weren't held empty gas cans and boxes of plastic cutlery that didn't look usable anymore. At least, Keo wasn't going to be using them anytime soon. He pulled the tarps one by one and was disappointed to find just empty crates.

"What's down there?" Gillian asked, looking through the hole behind him.

"Nothing," Keo said.

She looked around the room, then pinched her nose. "It smells."

"But that door looks pretty solid, and there are no other ways in."

"What about our stuff in the cars?"

"We'll bring in what we need for the night, and maybe something extra in case we have to stay down here a while."

"I'm not looking forward to this, Keo."

"Yeah, well, it beats staying out there when night comes," Keo said.

IT WAS ONE in the afternoon by the time they brought everything they needed (and a little extra, just in case) into the basement. The girls predictably weren't looking forward to sleeping on a dirt floor. They spent the remaining daylight eating and watching the sun go down and didn't climb into the basement until four. The room was just large enough that everyone was able to carve out their own space, with Gillian settling down next to Lotte's wheelchair.

Keo turned on the only portable LED lamp they had been able to salvage from the police station and used the light to climb back up to the door. Every inch of the stairs creaked and groaned with each step he took, and Keo swore he could feel the wood starting to give under his feet. They were both too heavy to climb at the same time, so Keo went up and inspected the door while Norris looked on from below.

The basement door opened outward, so he slipped a tire iron from the Durango through another brass ring on this side of the thick block of wood and tried to lock it in place, but it wasn't long enough. He tossed the tire iron down to the dirt floor and Norris held up his shotgun. The ring was just big enough to fit the Remington, and the weapon had the length to slide across the door, with a good six inches of the barrel braced against the wall.

Keo tried opening the door. It moved slightly, but not enough to reveal any lights from the other side. Even if the creatures found them down here, brute strength alone wouldn't get them inside. He hoped, anyway.

"Looks good," Keo said, climbing back down.

"Well, at least that shotgun will finally come in handy stopping those things," Norris said. "God knows it hasn't done much good before."

Keo walked over and sat down next to Gillian and Lotte. The girls were eating bags of chips and drinking bottled water, their faces bright against the pool of light.

"Is that really going to work?" Gillian asked, nodding up at the basement door.

"It should," Keo said.

Gillian didn't look convinced, but she didn't say anything. Keo thought it was probably for Lotte's benefit.

"This is the first time I'm glad I'm in a wheelchair," Lotte said.

"Why's that?" Keo asked.

"I'm the only one without dirt butt."

He grinned and Gillian actually giggled. He gave her a surprised look.

She smiled back at him. "Thank you."

"What for?"

"Saving my life back at the gas station. Again."

"It's becoming a habit."

"I know," she sighed. "Gloria Steinem's going to revoke my feminist card pretty soon." She pulled a bag of chips from the box they kept the food in. "Chips?"

"Don't mind if I do."

"You save my life, I give you chips. I think we're fair and square, don't you?"

"Absolutely."

Keo took the bag and opened it, sucking in the surprisingly enticing smell of baked potato chips. Maybe he was just starving, because he couldn't remember the last time he voluntarily ate junk food.

For the longest time, there was just the sound of crunching chips. No one really had much to say, though Keo noticed they glanced at the door every now and then.

"Keo," Gillian said after a while.

"Hmm?"

"What would make someone do something like that?"

"Do what?"

"Those men back at the gas station. Why did they try to kill us? I don't understand it." He could see her struggling with the question. "You've been around. I know you've done things. You don't have to say it; I know you don't push papers in offices for a living. Can you tell me why you decided to save us and those people back there tried to murder us?"

Rachel was listening on the other side of the basement. So was Norris, though Keo thought he already knew the answer. You didn't spend two decades of your life working as a cop and not know what man was capable of.

"They want what we have," Keo said. "That's all it is."

"The supplies?"

"Yeah."

"But it's just one gas station. There have to be dozens, hundreds, sitting around for the taking. Why would they care if we just took from one?"

"It's just human nature, Gillian. Some people abide by the tenets of civilization, not because they have to, but because they want to. It's who they are. Others are just looking for an excuse to bring out the monster inside them. The end of the world is a hell of an excuse, don't you think?"

"I guess."

He waited for her to say something else, but she didn't.

Instead, she leaned over and put her head on his shoulder. Keo wasn't sure how to respond at first, but he finally put one arm around her and pulled her tighter against him.

HE STAYED AWAKE long after the others fell asleep, keeping one eye on the door, anticipating some kind of movement to alert him that they had been discovered. Eventually he gave in around three in the morning and didn't open his eyes again until nearly seven, with slivers of sunlight shining into his face from the wooden floorboards above.

He stood up and glanced around him. The others were still asleep, Gillian curled up on the floor next to him. Lotte was drooling out of one side of her mouth and looked dangerously close to falling out of her wheelchair.

Keo walked across the room and kicked Norris's shoe. The ex-cop opened his eyes and groped for the shotgun that wasn't there.

"It's morning," Keo said. "We made it through another night, old timer."

Norris stood up and stretched, his joints popping with every movement.

"Let the girls sleep for a while," Keo said. "They had a stressful last few days."

Norris grunted back and watched Keo walk over to the stairs and start climbing up.

Near the door, Keo stopped and listened for a moment.

"Anything?" Norris asked below him.

Keo shook his head, then pulled Norris's Remington out of the brass ring and tossed it back down to him.

"Still in one piece," Norris said. "Maybe our luck really is changing."

Keo was reaching for the door when it flew open by itself.

He reached for his shotgun, freezing at the sight of a man wearing a camouflage cap and pants and long-sleeve shirt, staring back down at him. But it wasn't the man's hunting clothes or bearded face that got Keo's attention. It was the AR-15 rifle in his steady hands, the barrel pointed straight down and between Keo's eyes.

CHAPTER 16

"HI THERE," THE man with the rifle said. "Tell your friend down there to take his hands off the shotgun, or I'm gonna have to put you down."

"Shit," Norris said behind Keo.

Pale brown eyes flickered past Keo and down to, he presumed, Norris. The man's hands were amazingly steady. Despite the beard, he wasn't really that old. Late thirties, maybe, and he had definitely killed before. Not a killer by any means—Keo had met plenty of those and knew the look—but the man was fully capable of unloading his magazine into Keo from a meter away.

Keo stayed perfectly still and waited for the opening that never came.

He was poised four rungs down from the top, but he was high enough on the stairs that he didn't have to move very much to pop his head through the open door. The Remington was slung over his back and the prospect of actually using it was nil. There were no two ways about it; he was dead in the water.

Or just dead.

A second figure appeared, walking around the door and stopping behind the first man. He was wearing similar hunting clothes, stringy blond hair sticking out from under the sides of his LSU Tigers cap. He was younger, and at first Keo thought they might be father and son, but no; the years weren't that far apart. Maybe ten at the most.

"You were right," the second man said. "There were people in here. How'd you know?"

"This place was abandoned when I came by three months ago," the first man said. "Those cars weren't outside, either."

"Hey, Earl, there're a bunch of supplies in these trucks!" a third voice shouted from somewhere outside the cabin.

The two men eyed Keo carefully. The younger man had unslung his rifle—another AR-15—but hadn't aimed it into the basement. If Keo thought the older man was experienced, the second one looked anything but. He had an almost anxious look about him.

"What are we going to do with them?" the younger man asked.

"I don't know," the first one said, then, "Hey, come on, don't do it." He wasn't speaking to Keo, but to Norris behind him. "This doesn't have to get bloody."

Keo resisted the urge to look back at Norris to see what he was doing down there. He decided to trust that the ex-cop would know what to do in this situation—not that he thought Norris had been in a jam like this before. Instead, Keo concentrated on the figure above him, and to a lesser extent, the one in the back.

If he could get to one of those rifles, they had a chance. A small chance, but it was better than nothing, because that was all he had right now. A big fat nothing.

"Shit, they got kids down there, Earl," the second man said, leaning over the older man to get a better look.

"I see 'em," the first man, Earl, said.

Keo saw something in Earl's eyes and knew the man had instantly made a decision. He braced himself for what was coming, got ready to dive up through the hole for the rifle (was that even *possible?*), when Earl took a step back and pointed the AR-15 away from Keo.

"Truce," Earl said.

Keo stared at him, not quite sure if this was some kind of

trick—a joke at his expense, maybe—or if he was really seeing two men with the drop on him calling for…a truce?

"We don't want to hurt anyone," Earl said. "Least of all kids. I'm Earl and this is Levy. Come on out of there and let's talk," he said, directing that last part to Norris and the others in the basement below Keo.

Keo didn't move. This had to be a trick. Wasn't it?

Earl seemed to have read his face. The older man grinned. "Hey, I'm the one with the AR-15 and you're the one stuck on some stairs, remember? I don't have to do this. Doesn't that count for something?"

He's got a point.

Keo climbed up the rest of the way.

THERE WERE FOUR of them: Earl and Levy, the two in the cabin; and Gavin and Bowe, who were outside with the Chevy and the Durango. Gavin was the third voice Keo had heard earlier. Earl was easily the oldest, while Gavin and Bowe were around Levy's age. They all wore similar camo hunting clothes, but unlike most hunters he knew, they carried pouches stuffed with magazines for their AR-15s, each of the carbines showing the wear and tear of heavy past use.

"You're lucky I decided to circle back here at the last minute," Earl said when they were all outside the cabin. "We usually don't stray too far from the house, but we decided to see what was down here this morning."

"You have a house around here?" Keo said.

"About ten miles upriver."

Earl was friendly enough, and so were the three with him. Their only relation was as co-workers at a warehouse in Corden. The three younger men worked under Earl and it was actually there, working the second shift, that they survived three nights ago.

"You know about them, I'm guessing," Earl said. "That's why you were in the basement."

"The creatures," Keo nodded.

"Uh huh. Bloodsuckers. I guess everyone knows about them now. The ones still alive, anyway."

Norris and the girls were carrying the supplies they had taken into the cabin back out to the vehicles. Earl's people lent a hand and they had everything loaded back up in less than ten minutes.

"Where were you guys headed?" Bowe asked. He had short brown hair and was just slightly taller than Keo at six-two, but he had much broader shoulders. Keo had no trouble envisioning the kid running over people during a high school football game. Bowe also looked about five years removed from his high school graduation.

"Fort Damper," Norris said. "We were headed down there when we ran into some trouble."

"What kind of trouble?" Earl asked.

Norris told them about the men in assault vests and the ambush.

"Shit," Earl said. "Levy swore he heard some shooting when we were searching homes up the road yesterday. Around noon?"

"Sounds about right," Keo said.

Levy smiled triumphantly. "I told you guys, but you wouldn't believe me."

"You always hear shooting," Bowe said. "When do you not hear shooting?"

"It's true," Gavin grinned. He had short red hair and barely came up to Bowe's chin, though he filled out his camo with girth what he lacked in height. "Every single time we're out here."

"Yeah, but I was right this time, wasn't I?" Levy said, and actually reddened a bit.

"And you didn't know who they were?" Earl asked.

Keo shook his head. "They just opened up on us."

"Damn."

"Black assault vests?" Bowe said. "Like what, commandos?"

"Something like that, yeah," Keo said. "You've never run across people like that since all of this happened?"

"Not yet," Earl said. "Hopefully, we never will. We've mostly kept to ourselves down here. Yesterday was the farthest we ever went up toward the interstate. If we need something specific, we just drive to Corden."

"Corden's close?" Gillian asked.

Keo noticed that the men, including Earl, stood a little bit straighter when Gillian walked over to them. He found that oddly amusing and comforting at the same time. He was worried about how the four men would react around Gillian and Rachel. Besides food and shelter, women were likely the third most valuable commodity these days. For some, they might be the number one.

Seeing Earl and the other three's reaction to Gillian, though, put Keo's mind slightly at ease. Not entirely, but he was less concerned than he had been just a few minutes ago.

"Pretty close," Earl said. "Why?"

"We were hoping to find some more survivors there," Gillian said. "Maybe even pick up supplies along the way."

"It's about an hour's drive from here. You don't need to go back to the interstate if you know the right roads to take."

"Wait a minute; you guys said you were headed down to Damper?" Bowe said.

"Yeah," Norris said. "If someone has answers about what's happening out here, it'd be the military. Damper would have had contact with the government in the early going, I'd imagine."

"You don't wanna be going down there," Levy said.

"Why not?" Rachel asked, walking over to them. "Isn't it safe?"

"Fort Damper's gone, ma'am," Bowe said, looking almost

apologetic. "Some fool burned it down to the ground the night all of this happened."

THEY HAD BEEN following Earl's mud-caked black Bronco for the last thirty minutes when it finally turned off Highway 146 and onto a patch of dirt road marked by an old rusted sign that didn't have letters anymore. They drove slowly for a few more minutes, heading deeper into the woods.

The Bronco finally slowed down before turning into an open clearing. Keo followed in the Chevy, Norris bringing the Durango behind him. It was hard to miss the house after he made the turn.

The clearing was a wide-open yard carved out of the surrounding woods. Trees had been felled recently to make extra space, and the ground was brown and flat and easy on the Chevy's tires. The house was red and black brick and mortar, a large one-story building around 2,500 to 3,000 square feet. Antennas jutted out of the roof, and there were two ATVs parked haphazardly in the yard along with three trucks. The two front windows had burglar bars over them, and the front door was protected by a heavy security gate.

It looked like the kind of country home someone who liked hunting would build from the ground up and retire to in his old age. So what were four guys who worked at the same warehouse doing here?

Keo parked next to one of the trucks while Norris maneuvered the Durango behind him. Earl, who was driving the Bronco, pulled up next to them.

Earl climbed out and walked over to them. "This is it. The house."

"You built this place yourself?" Keo asked.

"It was just me for the first five years," Earl nodded. "The boys lent a hand in the last two, so it went much faster after that. I gave them a place to stay in return for the free weekend labor."

"Any objections to throwing our supplies in with yours?"

"Heck no." He walked over to the Chevy and peered in at the boxes of food, cases of bottled water and soda, and everything they had liberated from the gas station. "You guys really stocked up on the junk food, huh?" Then he gave them an amused look. "You know that a lot of your boxes have holes in them?"

"Yeah, we noticed," Keo said. "Got some boxes of jerky in there somewhere."

"One question," Gillian said as she came around the Chevy's hood.

"Shoot, ma'am," Earl said.

"Is that a generator in the background?"

"Good ear."

"Does that mean…?"

"Working plumbing? Yes, indeed."

"Oh, thank God," Gillian said, smiling brightly at him.

Earl laughed. "We'll get you guys settled in, share with you what we have. It'll beat sleeping on a dirt basement floor, I can guarantee you that much."

"I think just about anything will beat sleeping on a dirt floor," Keo said.

"You coming, Earl?" Bowe called from the other side of the Bronco. He and Gavin looked as if they were already preparing to leave again.

"In a sec," Earl said. He turned back to them. "Bowe thought he saw some deer tracks not far from here. We're gonna go see where it leads. Deer population's really thinned out; we hardly saw any the last few days."

Levy walked over. "I can show them the house, Earl. I got a feeling Bowe saw rabbit tracks and thought they were deer."

"Hey, screw you," Bowe said. "They were definitely deer."

"Whatever," Levy said.

Gavin chuckled. "Levy hears gunshots all the time, and Bowe thinks he sees deer tracks all the time."

"Hey, they were definitely deer!" Bowe shouted.

THE DOOR INTO the house was a foot wider than the standard three feet, which made rolling Lotte in easy. There was also a small ramp, though Keo couldn't imagine what Earl needed that for. They didn't have to worry about tracking dirt inside because there was already plenty on the wooden floorboards. Keo could tell it wasn't real wood from the glossy shine, but the construction was solid and it didn't creak under their shoes, which probably meant concrete underneath.

Levy led them inside, then showed the girls where the bathroom was. Gillian and Rachel hurried off with Christine and Lotte, as if the water might run out if they didn't get to it fast enough. Keo and Norris exchanged a brief chuckle.

"Keo," Levy said, walking back to them, "that's a weird name."

"Tom was taken," Keo said.

"Huh?"

Keo smiled. "It's a joke."

"Oh, gotcha," he said, though Keo couldn't tell if he really did "get" it. Levy looked as if he got confused easily.

Now that he was inside the house, Keo noticed the thick slabs of wood fastened over the two front windows. They were held in place by makeshift riggings that could be easily manipulated by pulling on welded link chains to lower the pieces completely over the openings. Both inch-thick blocks of wood had small, rectangular peepholes with a sliding metal covering, and simple latches at the bottom to hold them in place once they were brought down into position. The set-up wasn't anything fancy, but then, it probably didn't have to be to keep the creatures out.

The front door, too, had been worked on. Keo had thought it looked heavy when Levy was opening it earlier, and now he knew why. It was solid oak, but they had attached a second layer of lumber to it, effectively doubling the door's strength. They had also drilled two sets of brackets on either sides of the doorframe, with the two pieces of 8 foot 2x4 that he guessed would be dropped across the door to barricade it leaning against the wall nearby.

"When did you guys reinforce the door and windows?" Keo asked.

"Earl's idea," Levy said. "The four of us put them together the same day we got here, using supplies Earl was going to build a garage with. The burglar bars are strong enough to keep those bloodsuckers out, but we didn't want to take any chances."

"And they work?"

"We're still here, aren't we?"

"Good enough for me," Norris said.

The living room was as big as any house Keo had been in. There was a fireplace in the back with two comfortable looking sofas in front of it, along with an armchair in a corner and a couple of stools next to an island counter in the kitchen. The place clearly lacked a woman's touch, which was something he noticed almost right away.

"Earl bought this place and built the house for his wife," Levy said. "But then they split up and he sort of ignored it for a long time. Then one day he invites us out here for some hunting. That was two years ago, and I guess Gavin, Bowe, and me decided to help him finish the place. Plus, it was a good excuse to come hunting and drinking every weekend. When everything went down, we figured this was probably the safest place. You saw what happened in the cities?"

Keo nodded. "A smaller version of it, yeah."

"We were working at the warehouse when it went down. We got real lucky."

"How's that?" Norris asked.

"It was a small warehouse and we managed to lock it down in time. Man, those things kept trying to get in all night. It was crazy."

Keo looked around the room before stopping at a gun rack on the wall next to the fireplace. There were a couple of hunting rifles and a 12-gauge shotgun, and open boxes of ammo on top of a shelf. "Is this everything you guys have?"

"That?" Levy said, following his gaze. "That's nothing. Wait till you see the armory."

THE HOUSE HAD two back hallways, and Levy led them to the one with the basement. He opened the door and walked down wooden steps, a small squiggly bulb on the wall partially lighting their way. The basement had a solid concrete floor and walls, and a humming noise punctured the silence as a large LED panel powered on in the center of the room.

The basement, like the house above it, was built for space. It was one giant room with small 1x1 foot ventilation grills strategically placed along the top of the walls. Half of it was already filled up with stacks of moving crates, and one entire wall was covered with propane tanks of various sizes and brands—the hundred-pounders in the back and the smaller twenty-pounders up front. There had to be close to fifty in all.

"Where'd you get all the propane tanks?" Norris asked.

"We brought what we could fit into our vehicles from Corden the first morning," Levy said. "We've been looting the rest from businesses between here and the city since."

"What about the houses?" Keo asked.

"We were saving those up for later," Levy said. "They're in there, you know. The bloodsuckers. Hiding in the backs of those houses."

Keo nodded. "We noticed."

Levy headed to the far end, where Keo almost stopped in

his tracks at the sight of the weapons piled on top of a shelf. There were boxes of ammo on the floor, so many that someone had gotten creative and stacked them into one big pyramid.

"Damn, son," Norris said. "The ATF know you have this arsenal down here?"

Levy chuckled. "We grabbed everything we could find, along with the propane, before we hightailed it out of Corden."

Keo picked up one of a dozen or so M4 carbines on the shelf. The M4 was a shorter version of the M16 and was just a shade over a pound lighter. He liked the M4. It was a good fighting weapon.

"Got those from a pawnshop," Levy said. He pulled another weapon from a shelf and Keo smiled at the sight of the Heckler & Koch MP5SD. "Found this little ditty at the same place. The only one, unfortunately."

"Daebak," Keo said.

"Huh?" Levy said.

"Nothing. May I?"

Keo put down the M4 and took the submachine gun. He ran his fingers along the stainless steel suppressor attached at the end of the barrel. The weapon felt light, and he found out why when he pulled out the long but empty magazine. The MP5SD looked in good condition, though he could tell it had been put to use before, and often.

Norris chuckled at Keo. "Jesus, kid, it's just a gun. Don't drool over it."

Keo grinned back at him. He couldn't help himself.

"We always bought our hunting gear from the guy who ran the pawnshop, so we knew he had all these gems in the basement," Levy said. "Figured, what the hell. It wasn't like there was a lot of people left in Corden to take them."

"The four of you are the only survivors?" Norris asked.

"That we know of. But it's not like we spent a lot of time looking. We drove up and down the city for a while that first day, then decided the best course of action was to split for the house. We've been trying to contact other people on the radio since we got here, but so far no luck. How about you guys?"

"Not counting those psychopaths at the gas station, we haven't seen anyone since we left Bentley," Norris said. "Even FEMA's down."

"Yeah, we tried FEMA, too. Nothing. Hell of a thing, huh? Power grid's down, radio's down. There's just nothing out there. But we'll keep looking. I mean, what else we gonna do, right?"

"Anyone claimed this?" Keo said, holding up the MP5SD.

"It's yours," Levy said. "I only play with American." He said to Norris, "You're welcome to the M4s. Complement that shotgun of yours."

"You have any more of those?" Norris asked, pointing at Levy's gun belt.

"As a matter of fact, yeah." He sifted through another box and pulled out two tactical belts with pouches and a gun holster already attached. It was similar to the ones he and the others were wearing. "We brought extras."

"The same pawnshop?" Keo said.

"Yup."

Keo took the belt and picked through one of the crates loaded with handguns. He settled for a Glock G41 .45, then went hunting for magazines.

Norris decided on a G42 .380. "I had one of these back in the day."

"Just like old times, huh?" Keo said.

"Not quite."

Keo found a handful of magazines and loaded the G41, then stuffed the rest into one of the pouches.

"What about you?" Keo asked Levy.

Levy tapped the AR-15 slung over his back. "We got these babies nice and broken in. Plus—" he added like a proud parent "—we converted them from burst to full-auto. So if those assholes you tangled with show up here, they're going to eat some lead and like it, that's for damn sure."

CHAPTER 17

EARL CAME BACK an hour later without any deer. "False alarm," he said.

"Are there supposed to be a lot of deer around here?" Keo asked.

"The woods are usually thick with them." He shook his head. "It probably has something to do with what happened three nights ago. I think those things might be feeding off the deer population."

While the women were getting dressed after their long, hot shower, Keo and Norris helped Earl move his things from his room and over to Gavin's. The house's four bedrooms, each one with wooden floors and the same Spartan design, were split evenly among the two hallways. Earl might have built the house initially for his wife, but apparently she had never gotten around to putting her stamp on the place.

They started by moving Earl first, with Bowe up next. The tall twenty-something would be giving up his room to shack with Levy, whose room was in the same left side hallway. Rachel and Christine would take over Earl's room in the right side hallway, with Gillian and Lotte settling in Bowe's. That would give the women a little more privacy in a house that was suddenly very crowded.

Keo had to admit, Earl and the other three's willingness to give up their space was impressive. He was expecting resistance, even downright hostility, but it was Earl and Bowe who had offered up the rooms to the women without any prompting, though Keo thought it was possible they had discussed it during their fruitless deer hunt.

The stark difference between Earl, Bowe, Gavin, and Levy and the four men with painted faces back at the gas station made Keo's head spin. He had to wonder if he might have shot first and asked questions later if it was him who had stumbled across Earl and the others and not the other way around, especially just a day after the ambush.

Maybe. Maybe…

Although the deer hunt had come up empty, Gavin and Bowe remained in the woods while Earl came back to help Keo and the others settle in. It was more hospitality than Keo had expected from a complete stranger, but he was glad for it. After two nights in Bentley and a third night in the dirt basement, Earl's house was a godsend.

"You really don't mind us being here?" Keo asked Earl as they settled his bags into Gavin's room. Levy's was farther down the left side hallway. "Giving up your room in your own house?"

"Nah. Girls need space. Levy told you I built all this for my ex?"

"He did."

"Turns out, she wanted more than just a house in the woods, I guess."

"Sorry about that."

"Hey, that's life. She got on well, though. Last I heard she had remarried and was pregnant in Baton Rouge somewhere. The best thing the ex ever did was not demand I sell this place and give half of the sale to her. I still love her for that." Then he brightened up, or at least did his best to shake those bad memories away. "Besides, you should see my apartment in the city. It's half as big as this room."

Gavin's room was already filled with duffel bags, dried mud on the floor, and hunting magazines piled in a corner. The bed was a generous seventy-four inch, relatively new-looking blue mattress on a cot that could be folded up and stored when not in use. Gavin's was leaning against the far wall when they entered—unlike Earl, Gavin hadn't bothered putting bed sheets on his—leaving plenty of space for another bed to be placed in the room.

"You used to be in the service?" Earl asked him.

"No," Keo said. "Why?"

"You got that ex-military look."

"My dad was. I was a former army brat."

"That how he met your mom?"

Keo smiled. Earl was definitely a lot sharper than the good ol' boy aw shucks vibe he gave off. "Yeah. He was stationed in Yongsan for a while. She completely married down when she hooked up with him. Were you in the service?"

"Nah. I tried to sign up a couple of times, but I have a bad ticker. Bowe came close to enlisting, but his dad lost the house and he had to go work out of high school. I made it into Boot Camp myself, but only lasted a couple of weeks before they saw my medicals and kicked me out—"

Earl was interrupted by the echoey *pop!* of a gunshot. It sounded far away, somewhere within the woods that surrounded the house.

"Bowe and Gavin?" Keo said.

Earl nodded, but he was too busy listening to speak.

Another gunshot rang out, then a third one. The shots echoed for a bit before fading away.

"Hunh," Earl said.

"What?"

"Gavin and Bowe don't normally miss."

They craned their heads when they heard the *pop-pop-pop* of an AR-15 firing on full-auto.

"Shit," Earl said, running out the door and down the hallway before Keo could even react. The man was faster than he looked.

They were inside the living room and making a beeline for the door when the *pop-pop-pop* came faster and with more intensity, as if Gavin and Bowe were trying to unload their weapons' entire magazine in one pull of the trigger.

Rachel and Gillian came out of the right side hallway at the same time. Both women's hair were still wet, and Gillian's eyes immediately sought out Keo's.

"Were those gunshots?" she asked.

Keo nodded as Levy and Norris raced out from the basement behind them, rifles thumping against their backs. Earl was already at the door. He threw it open and ran out, while Norris and Levy followed.

More gunfire rang out; then there was a long silence, maybe five seconds, before more shots clattered across the woods, a clear indication that Gavin and Bowe had just reloaded and were firing again.

Keo was almost out the door when Gillian said, "Hey." When he looked, she added, "Be careful, huh?"

He smiled at her and she returned it.

He ran out, sliding the MP5SD around to the front of his body before he was out of the front yard. He hadn't had time to look around the area after arriving, and Keo was momentarily surprised by the cool air, thanks to plenty of shade. There was a river to his right on the other side of some trees, and if he strained, he could hear the currents over the chirping birds and—

—the cracking of automatic gunfire chased a couple of birds into the air.

They were really pouring it on now. But at what?

It took him a full two minutes of nonstop sprinting through a sea of trees, leaping over bushes and dodging branches, before he finally reached them. Thankfully, Keo didn't have to worry about getting lost. All he had to do was head straight toward the sound of continuous shooting.

Norris was standing in a line with Levy, Earl, Gavin, and

Bowe, all five men with their backs to Keo. Gavin was pulling another magazine from a pouch that looked more empty than when Keo had first seen it earlier today. Two empty magazines were already lying at his feet. The same for Bowe.

They were staring at an old mobile home that looked as if it had arrived in the woods before the trees even began sprouting. Once upon a time it had had white walls, but the color had faded and sunlight poured through broken windows and bullet holes that stretched from one side of the five-meter-long building to the other.

"I don't think that house's going to bother us again," Keo said as he walked up behind them.

Levy flashed his familiar grin. "Not anymore, it won't."

"Another one of yours, Earl?"

"Nope," Earl said. "It's been here since I bought the property. No one's ever claimed it."

"Owners probably ditched it decades ago, from the looks of it," Bowe said. "It's old enough, that's for damn sure."

"So what were you guys shooting at?" Keo asked.

"I saw something inside," Gavin said. "One of those things."

Levy chuckled. "I hear shooting, Bowe sees tracks that aren't there, and Gavin thinks he sees those bloodsuckers everywhere he turns."

"I'm telling you, I saw it," Gavin said through gritted teeth.

"Sure you did."

"Well, if it was in there, I think you got it," Keo said.

"I wouldn't be so sure about that," Earl said. "I shot one of them that first night. Right in the face. Nothing. I think it just got more pissed off."

"Yeah, I put a hammer in the eye socket of the same one Earl shot," Bowe said. "Damned thing just kept coming."

"Sunlight," Norris said. "They're afraid of sunlight. And with good reason. It's the only thing that can kill them."

The four men exchanged a look.

"He's not lying," Keo said. "I know it sounds hard to believe until you've seen it with your own eyes, but it's true. Direct contact with sunlight turns them to ash, vaporizes them almost instantly."

"The fuck?" Bowe said. "I never saw that."

"Me, neither," Gavin nodded.

"You know this for sure?" Levy asked Keo.

"I know it's hard to believe," Keo said. "One of those you have to see it to believe it things. But it's true." He nodded at the mobile home. "If there is something in there—"

"There was, I swear I saw it," Gavin said.

"—and you got sunlight on it, there won't be anything left of the creature but bones. Bleached white bones."

"Bleached white bones?" Levy said doubtfully.

Keo shrugged. "Abnormally white, yeah."

The four men exchanged another long and uncertain look. Keo wasn't sure if they believed him or thought he and Norris were crazy. Given the last seventy-two hours, it was probably fifty-fifty, whereas they would have tossed him into a hospital with a straight jacket before that. These days, though, a lot of things were possible.

"Sunlight, huh?" Bowe finally said.

"Makes sense," Earl said. Keo could see Earl's mind working, turning over the new information in his head. "We were wondering why they wouldn't attack us in the daytime, even when we ran across them while salvaging. They always stayed away from the doors and never came outside. Shit, it makes sense now."

"And all those covered windows," Gavin said. "Is that why?"

"To keep out the sun," Keo nodded.

Earl looked over at Norris as if for confirmation. "You've seen it, too?"

Norris nodded. "I haven't seen the vanishing act when sunlight hits them, but he's not lying about the rest. I've seen it happen to the blood they leave behind. Trust me when I tell you, these days it pays to believe in things you normally would think were crazy."

Earl nodded. "I can't disagree with that."

"There's an easy way to prove what I'm saying," Keo said, then nodded at the mobile home.

"How many did you say you saw?" Earl asked Gavin.

"One or two...or more," Gavin said. He was suddenly not very certain. "I couldn't tell. It was so dark in there, and I only got a glimpse of something moving inside when I was going through the door. What about you, Bowe?"

"Nah," Bowe said. "Too dark, and you were backing up and shooting already."

"I guess that explains why they didn't follow us out after I started pouring rounds into the place," Gavin said. "It's still day out. The sun."

"We should make sure," Earl said. "See this sunlight thing for ourselves."

"You know about how it works?" Keo asked.

"The biting thing?"

"Yeah."

"We know," Earl nodded, and he exchanged another private look with the other three.

They saw it happen to someone they knew on the first night, too.

"Okay," Earl said, and moved toward the mobile home.

Levy, Gavin, and Bowe hesitated, but then followed reluctantly.

Keo and Norris remained where they were, watching the foursome approach the door, which had also taken a beating during the shooting and now hung from a single top hinge. There were at least a dozen bullet holes in it, and sunlight speared through the openings. Keo couldn't understand how it was still hanging on.

"You get off any shots?" Keo asked Norris.

"A couple. But they were doing a pretty good job of it. I got the feeling they've been itching to shoot something for a while."

"Well, at least they're on our side."

"Amen," the ex-cop said.

Earl had grabbed the doorknob and pulled on it. Keo didn't think he had even put that much effort into it when the perforated door fell loose from its last hinge and tumbled to the ground. Levy, Gavin, and Bowe nervously stepped back, even though the door hadn't come close to hitting them.

They stared into the dark, rectangular opening, as if trying to decide whether to go on ahead with their plan or back out. Despite the broken windows and bright afternoon sun, it was difficult to see much beyond the first couple of feet inside the mobile home. That, more than anything, made them hesitate.

"Well?" Bowe asked.

"Give me a sec," Earl said.

"Be careful," Gavin said, his voice trembling slightly.

"We don't really need to go in," Levy said. "How many magazines did we put into this thing? A half dozen? If that didn't do it, what's the point of getting this close?"

For a moment there, Keo thought Earl had been convinced by Levy's argument. But then he said, "We just have to make sure. It's important. We don't have to go in there; we just have to lure it out."

Earl took a large breath, then took a step toward the door, raising his AR-15 in front of him.

Bullets don't work, Keo wanted to tell him, but Earl already knew that.

"This feels like a bad idea," Norris said quietly.

Keo couldn't disagree with that, even as he watched Earl stick the barrel of his carbine into the open door and lean forward. Bowe, Gavin, and Levy hadn't moved any further and were standing a good four feet behind Earl.

"Be careful," Levy said nervously.

"I'm just going to lure it out," Earl said. "If it's even in there—" He hadn't gotten "there" all the way out when something grabbed the barrel of his AR-15 and pulled, and Earl's body jerked toward the opening.

"Shit!" Keo shouted.

Keo and Norris raced forward just as half of Earl's body disappeared into the mobile home opening. Levy lunged forward and grabbed for Earl's waist, while Gavin got a leg and Bowe groped for an arm. They pulled at about the same time Earl let out a loud, bloodcurdling scream.

"Pull!" Keo shouted. "Pull him out, goddammit!"

Levy, Gavin, and Bowe did, putting every ounce of strength they had into the effort, and Earl's body came tumbling back out of the door. All four men stumbled back, fighting for footing that wasn't there, until their legs and arms and bodies got tangled up with each other's and they fell to the ground in a pile.

Earl was still gripping his carbine when he began his back-pedaling, and it fell out of the opening *along with one of the black-skinned creatures*. The monster let out something that sounded almost human as it was pulled out into the sunlight.

For the second time in his life, Keo witnessed the impossible: the creature's pruned flesh turned ash gray inch by inch, as if the sun was eating it alive. It was one of those things that shouldn't be possible, but the evidence in front of him was irrefutable.

Amazingly, it looked as if the creature was holding onto the barrel of Earl's rifle the entire time it fell out of the door, as if it was trying to hold onto something—*anything*—to ward off what it knew was about to happen.

It didn't work.

The flesh evaporated instantaneously, forming a thick gray cloud that lingered in the air, dissipating in seconds even as bones—white, as if they had been bleached—tumbled free and clattered to the ground. A skull bounced against the dirt and rolled until it came to rest against the sole of Levy's boots. Levy was sitting and trying to get up, and he ended up staring at the empty eye sockets in front of him.

"Holy hell," Norris whispered breathlessly next to Keo.

"I told you," Keo said.

"Yeah, but... Jesus Christ."

Levy scrambled up from the ground, coughing and holding his hand over his nostrils and mouth. "What is that smell?"

"I think I'm going to throw up," Bowe said, stumbling away from the others and grabbing at a tree trunk for support as he bent over and retched. Somehow, he managed not to follow through with it.

"The smell's from them," Keo said. "That's all that's left of them. And the bones. Flesh. Blood. Even organs. They all go, except the smell and the bones."

Gavin was helping Earl up, the older man clutching his right arm. Blood seeped through his fingers, running in rivulets along his forearm and past the elbow. Earl looked more stunned than hurt. Or maybe he was just unable to fully process what was happening.

"It bit you," Keo said.

Earl shook his head. "I don't know. I felt a stab of pain..." Earl stumbled back until he was leaning against a tree by himself for support. Sweat popped out along his temple. "That was so stupid. I shouldn't have done that..."

Levy, Gavin, Bowe, and Norris were looking down at the bones. There was something obscenely pure about the creature's skeletal remains, even the way it looked deformed, twisted at impossible (painful) angles. No one said a word, not even Norris, who had seen more than the others.

Bowe put his boot on the skull and pressed down on it, then jumped slightly when the head buckled. "It's like stepping on a Mexican piñata. I thought skulls would be tougher." He kept pushing down until the skull collapsed in on itself. "It's like paper."

"What do we do about the mobile home?" Levy asked.

"How many did you say you saw in there?" Norris asked

Gavin.

"I'm not sure," Gavin said. If he looked uncertain about the numbers before, Keo didn't think the man could remember his own name at the moment. "Like I said, it could be just the one, but... I don't know."

Keo turned away from them and back to Earl, who was still leaning against the tree. His face was so much paler than a few seconds ago, and sweat poured down his face in sheets. His eyes had widened noticeably, and he was breathing hard, his chest heaving under his shirt.

"You okay, Earl?" Keo asked.

"I gotta stop the bleeding," Earl said.

"Let me help—"

"No, I got it."

Earl pulled a handkerchief out from a back pocket and covered up the wound. Keo hadn't been able to tell the severity of the injury or even what it was. All he had been able to glimpse in the brief second was blood. There was a lot of blood. Keo hadn't seen someone bleed like that since...

Delia.

"Earl," Keo said.

"No, I'll be fine," Earl said, wrapping the handkerchief tightly around the wound—grimacing with the effort—then using his teeth to cinch it up.

"Earl, did it bite you?"

"I don't know," Earl said, and shook his head, sweat flinging off him. "It happened so fast. But it doesn't really hurt that much. Or at all, really." He tried to smile, but it came out pitiful. "You'd think it would hurt more with all the blood."

"Earl, you know what happens when they bite you."

"I told you, I don't know if it bit me." He wiped the back of his good hand across his temple. It came away covered in sweat. "I'll be fine. I'll be fine..."

No, you won't, Keo thought, but he said instead, "Okay, Earl. Okay..."

CHAPTER 18

"ARE YOU SURE?" Gavin asked.

"I've seen it happen in person," Keo said. "It's going to happen to him, too."

"But he's not dead yet."

"Not yet."

"He's gonna be fine," Levy said, though he didn't look at them when he said it. Instead, he was staring out the window, where he had been standing for the last two hours.

"Earl's a tough guy," Bowe said. "The toughest guy I know. It was only a bite, anyway."

I bet that's what the billion other people on the planet said three nights ago, Keo thought, but he said instead, "It's not a normal bite. The bleeding won't stop and the victim gets worse with time. I don't know how it works, or how fast it happens. Maybe it depends on how much they take out of you during the bite. Or put into you. I don't know. I'm not a doctor or a scientist. I'm just telling you what I saw, and what I saw is that eventually you succumb."

Keo stood across the window from Levy, both of them watching Rachel and Christine walking around the front yard while Norris rolled Lotte along in her wheelchair. What should have been a hopeful new day for them had become dour when they brought Earl back to the house. But the kids seemed to be handling it well, Christine in particular. Keo wondered if that was some kind of coping mechanism. Maybe. It wasn't like he knew anything about kids.

Behind him, Gavin sat on the couch with a bottle of water, staring off at nothing while Bowe paced back and forth.

They all looked over when Gillian came out of Gavin's room, where they had put Earl. She was cleaning blood off her fingers with a damp towel, and the look on her face confirmed everything to Keo.

"Is he okay?" Levy asked.

Both Gavin and Bowe waited anxiously for the answer, too.

"I've cleaned and treated the bite," Gillian said, "but the rest of it... I don't think we'll know for sure until tonight." Gillian walked to the kitchen where she poured water into a bowl and washed her hands with soap. Blood quickly muddied up the water, and that encouraged her to rub harder. "He lost a lot of blood," Gillian continued. "I don't even know how you lose that much blood from just a bite wound. And there's something else. The area around the bite looks infected."

"Infected?" Levy said.

"Look, I'm not a doctor. I'm not even a nurse." She sighed, sounding exasperated and tired. "But from what I can tell, he's got a fever, and the body only does that when it's trying to fight an infection. We don't know if this is how the virus works." She looked at Keo. "You said it yourself. It's like an invasion. How they multiplied so fast three nights ago. They bite you, you die...and you turn."

"It's efficient," Keo said. "They don't need a big army. They literally just create one as they go, until there's no one left to resist."

"You don't know that," Gavin said, springing up suddenly from the sofa. "He'll be fine. He's Earl."

"Yeah," Bowe nodded. "Earl's one tough sonofabitch."

Gavin picked up his AR-15. "He'll be fine," he said again before going outside.

Keo watched Gavin through the window as he climbed onto one of the ATVs and rode off. Norris and the girls looked worriedly after him.

"Let him go," Bowe said. "He just needs to cool off. He and Earl were close—*are* close. I meant to say *are close.*" He sat down on the same spot that Gavin had just vacated. "Shit," he said quietly, then looked toward the left side hallway, where Earl was somewhere inside Gavin's room.

"You saw this before," Levy said to Keo. "What happened with your friend?"

"She got bit, like Earl," Keo said. "She was bleeding a lot, too. No matter what we did, she just kept bleeding. I used to think all I needed was a first aid kit and I might have been able to save her, but now... I don't think that's possible." He looked across the room at Gillian. "The wound, it doesn't heal. It just keeps bleeding."

"I changed Earl's bandages twice while I was in there," Gillian said. "Keo's right. It just keeps bleeding and he keeps getting worse."

Levy's face paled. "I gotta go grab some fresh air," he said, grabbing his own rifle and leaving the house.

Bowe stood up and looked at Gillian. "Keep an eye on him, huh?"

"I will," Gillian nodded.

Bowe grabbed his own carbine and fled out of the house after Levy and Gavin. They reminded Keo of children fleeing because dad got sick and they didn't know what else to do. He felt sorry for them. They had survived the end of the world together, likely because of Earl. And now, the man who had saved them was sick and hurt and probably dying, and they couldn't do a damn thing about it.

Gillian walked over and handed Keo a bottle of water. "I'm sorry about your friend."

Keo took a sip. "Thanks." He noticed Gillian was looking at him more carefully than before. "What?"

She shrugged. "It works on you."

"What's that?"

"The gun belt and all those pouches. I guess you've worn them before."

"Here and there."

"How come I don't have one?"

"You want a belt?"

"I'd settle for one of those," she said, pointing at his holstered Glock.

"Can you shoot a gun?"

"I'm a fast learner. You can teach me."

He nodded. "It's a date."

Gillian gazed out the window at the girls and Norris. The ex-cop was alert, his body tense, and he had one hand on the M4 rifle slung over his back while his eyes scanned the woods around them.

Keo looked over at her, standing close to him. She really was a beautiful woman. Her long black hair, spread around her face, gave her a strangely exotic look. Keo had met a lot of beautiful women, one of the perks of being sent around the world by the organization. Delia had been something special, too, but she was almost plain next to Gillian.

"Stop it," she said, still looking out the window.

"What?"

"You're staring."

"I wasn't staring."

"Yes, you were." She gave him a half smile. "It's sweet, but this is probably not the time." She glanced across the house at Gavin's room. "Is he really going to die tonight?"

"Tonight. Before tonight. It only took my friend a few hours."

"It must have something to do with the bite, like you said. How deep it is, or how much of the virus—or whatever it is they transfer into you—that determines how long you last." She ran her hands over her face, looking more tired than he had ever seen her, and turned back to the window. "It's not going to get any easier, is it?"

"No," he said.

"I didn't think so, but you could have at least lied."

"Sorry."

"It's okay," she said. Gillian peered out the window and looked up at the sky. "It'll be night soon."

"It's always going to be night sooner or later," Keo said. "That's the problem."

THE REMAINING AFTERNOON was spent with everyone waiting for the inevitable nightfall. They all knew it was coming, but it was still bright outside. Impossibly bright, in fact. Instead of comforting them, though, all that sunshine only added to the pervading sense of approaching dread.

The girls kept busy by settling into their new rooms. They did it without the same enthusiasm they had shown before Keo and the others had carried Earl back.

Gavin and Bowe continued to stay away from the house by hunting in the woods. Keo could hear their gunshots every now and then. The loud sounds of their ATVs were usually followed by long bouts of silence as they settled somewhere looking for prey. He wondered how they could continue hunting after everything that had happened. Didn't becoming prey themselves give them a new perspective? Apparently not.

Keo and Norris finished bringing in the supplies they had brought with them, piling most of them down in the basement.

Gillian checked in on Earl every thirty minutes or so, and each time she came out of the room she looked less optimistic.

"How is he?" Levy would ask each time.

"He's not getting any better," she would say.

After a while, Levy stopped asking.

"Do you think it's like this everywhere?" Gillian asked Keo when they found themselves at the kitchen together, with Levy having wandered outside to be with his thoughts and the girls still in their rooms.

"What's that?" Keo said.

"People hiding, like us. Inside barricaded cabins in the woods. Or in rooms with steel doors. Places that they can't break into. We can't be the only ones still out here, Keo."

"We're not. You forgot those assholes at the gas station."

"No, I didn't. I just try not to think too much about them."

I don't have that luxury.

Who the hell were those guys?

"Maybe it is like this everywhere," he said. "Survival means abandoning the cities and staying away from places with high concentrations of people. Out here there's less of them, and maybe you have a chance."

"Do you ever wonder, though?"

"About what?"

"What it was like in the cities when all of this started. It was terrifying at the hospital that night, and there were less than a hundred people there. I can't imagine a city with hundreds of thousands of people. Or the ones with millions of souls…"

AROUND 4:30 P.M., with the skies starting to darken, Keo asked Levy to show him the generator and followed the young man out the back of the house and to the supply shack next to the river. Inside, Keo saw a neon green square block flanked by propane tanks and bright-red gasoline cans.

"It runs on propane and gasoline," Levy said. "We've rigged it to run the plumbing and lights, too. Plus outlets to plug in electronic devices, though we haven't really used that yet. It puts out about 6,000 continuous watts and close to eight hours of run time on a single eight-pound tank. Eventually, we're going to have to limit it to a few hours a day to conserve, but for now I think it's worth wasting a few tanks to get the girls comfortable. Earl mentioned that he wanted to install solar panels. Maybe we can do that later when he gets better."

He's not going to get better, kid, Keo thought, but he didn't say it out loud.

Levy pressed a switch and the generator shut down. The shack, which had been vibrating when they entered, went suddenly very still around them. They headed back outside, and while Levy put a padlock over the shack door, Keo walked over to the ridge and looked down at the flowing water, which was surprisingly clear even under the graying sky.

"Norris and I can help around the place," Keo said. "I've been known to swing a mean hammer every now and then."

"He used to be a cop, right?"

"Yeah."

"What about you?"

"Nope. I never could stand taking orders from people in uniforms."

"I thought your dad was in the Army?"

"He was."

"Oh," Levy said, "getting" it that time.

"Earl doesn't have a boat?" Keo asked.

"He's not much of a swimmer. Besides, you can fish from any part of the bank with a rod and reel and catch everything you need."

"What kind of fish do you get around here?"

"Crappies, bass, and some catfish, too. The channel cat can grow pretty big. You fish?"

"Not so much. The funny thing is, I'm a very good swimmer."

"You don't say."

"Nope."

Levy gave him a slightly confused look, but let it go and said, "Come on, let's get back inside. Night's not our friend anymore, remember?"

Keo followed Levy back into the house. It was a short walk, and by the time they reached the back door, Keo had committed the area to memory. The back door, like the front, had its own steel security gate on the outside and similar reinforcements on the inside.

The others were gathered in the living room eating MRE bags from the basement and perishable foods they had brought with them from the gas station. Gavin and Bowe had returned an hour ago without any fresh kills. There was, Bowe told Keo, just nothing out there to hunt anymore.

The front door was closed and locked, the 2x4s settled into their brackets, and the wooden slates had been lowered over the two front windows, along with the windows in the separate bedrooms. Six in all. It was a simple but brilliant setup, and just one more thing to add to his list of Things To Be Grateful To Earl For.

Sorry, Earl. And I mean that.

Every now and then, Keo noticed the girls looking around nervously. They could all feel it, he thought, even if they couldn't see it for themselves through the walls.

Night is coming.

SEEING THE WOODS from a small 2x12 inch slot—a window within the window—was a new experience. The moon had chosen tonight of all nights to hide behind the clouds, which made it almost impossible to make out the trucks from the ATVs in the front yard, much less the dirt trail and the trees.

"It's so dark outside," Gillian whispered over Keo's shoulder, her warm breath against the back of his neck. It wasn't an entirely unwelcome sensation.

She had her arms around her chest, but it wasn't because it was cold. Even though the temperature had dipped outside, it was a nice and comfortable seventy-five degrees inside. They had left just one of the LED lamps on in the living room, but even on its lowest setting it provided surprisingly strong light throughout most of the house and even portions of the two hallways. There were more lamps that were turned off hanging from the ceiling.

"It shouldn't be this quiet," Gillian said.

Keo looked down at his watch: 10:16 P.M.

They were well into the night, and there were no signs of the creatures. Keo wasn't sure if that should have comforted him or worried him. The bloodsucker in the mobile home was proof they were out there in the woods.

But it was too dark outside to see much of anything. That would have been fine, but he couldn't even hear the birds chirping around them anymore. They had gone quiet almost as soon as the sun disappeared. Were the animals in the trees hiding, too? Why? Could the bloodsuckers climb? That was a slightly disturbing thought.

"How are the girls?" he asked.

"They're tired. I don't think they realized how tired they were until they laid down on an honest to goodness bed again."

"What about you?"

"I'm okay."

"You look tired."

"Gee, thanks."

"You're still beautiful."

"It's the end of the world, and you're hitting on me," she said, though she didn't look entirely displeased.

Keo slid the metal peephole closed and they sat down on the floor under the window. Without the generator, the house was impossibly still, and he could hear every single breath Gillian took. He could also smell her, and it was a nice smell. But then again, women always smelled good to him.

He looked across the living room at Norris, cocooned inside a sleeping bag on the floor close to the unused fireplace. Keo wasn't sure if Norris was really asleep or if he was just pretending to be in order to give them some privacy. There was an unused bedroll next to Norris. It belonged to Gavin, who was inside his room with Earl at the moment.

"How long has he been in there?" Keo asked.

"Gavin? Three hours, I think. I've been looking in on them every hour."

"Good. When Earl dies, we need to get his body outside before he turns."

Gillian nodded. "I'll keep checking on him throughout the night." She paused, then, "Gavin still doesn't think it'll happen. He's convinced Earl will make it."

"He's in denial."

"I know." She was looking down at her hands, though he couldn't tell what she was looking for. They were clean, as far as he could see.

"What's wrong?" he asked.

"I didn't know it was so hard to get blood off. It clings to you. I can still smell it."

"You get used to it."

"Do you?"

"Yes."

"Who are you, Keo? Who are you really?"

She was looking at him intently with those green eyes, and he never wanted so badly to kiss someone in his life. She had such soft-looking lips, too, and she was sitting so close he didn't have to make any effort at all to breathe in her intoxicating scent.

Somehow, though, Keo managed to restrain himself and smiled at her instead. "You're going to find out, much to your disappointment, that I'm very ordinary and pretty unspectacular."

"I don't believe that," she said. "But that's okay. If we survive tonight, we can get to know each other better."

"*Daebak.*"

She narrowed her eyes at him. "What did you just say? Did you just cuss me out in Korean?"

He chuckled. "It's something my mom used to say to me

when I was a kid and I did something good, or that she approved of."

"So it's a good thing."

"Yes. Although…"

"What?"

"She said it to me when I did something bad, too, so…"

"You're Korean. How do you not know what a Korean word means?"

"I was born on a military base in San Diego, Gillian. English is my native tongue. Besides, the closest I've ever been to anything remotely Korean is North Korea."

"What were you doing in North Korea?"

"These guys I worked for sent me to get something from these other guys that had this thing they wanted."

"So why didn't you ask someone there what *day*-what? How do you say it again?"

"*Daebak.*"

"Yeah. That. Why didn't you ask someone in North Korea what it meant while you were there?" She looked proud of herself, as if she had just beaten him at his own game.

Keo grinned. "Have you ever been to North Korea, Gillian?"

"Oh God, it's one of those stories," she groaned.

"You don't stop to ask people in North Korea about things and stuff. You run and hope they don't shoot you in the back with an AK-47."

"Smart ass."

"Wanna hear another story?"

"No."

"When I was nine," Keo said anyway, "I went to see a fortune teller. She told me I was destined to meet a cute bank teller and spend the rest of my life with her in an isolated house in the woods. Go figure," he said, gesturing around them.

"Seriously?"

"Which part don't you believe?"

"That I'm cute," she said. "No one's ever called me cute before."

"Stunningly beautiful?" he said.

"Better," she smiled, just before a gunshot exploded across the house and froze both of them in place.

CHAPTER 19

THE GUNSHOT CAME from Gavin's room. Gavin and *Earl's* room.

Norris snapped up from the floor even before the gunshot had finished echoing across the house. He momentarily had to fight with his own bedroll before he could stumble up to his feet and grab his M4 leaning against the wall nearby.

Keo was already running across the room. "Stay here!" he shouted back at Gillian.

She nodded and shouted back at him. "Earl's in there! If he's turned—"

"I know!"

Norris fell in beside him, and they made a beeline for Gavin and Earl's room together. The gunshot had come from inside. There was no doubt about it, and Keo knew right away something had gone horribly wrong even before they heard two more shots—*pop! pop!*—coming in quick succession from inside.

Farther up the left side hallway, a door opened and Levy stumbled outside, the dull black barrel of a Glock glinting in one hand. He had apparently gone to sleep in a T-shirt and the same pants he had been wearing all day. Bowe rushed outside too, his taller frame hovering wobbly behind Levy's.

"What's happening?" Levy said. "Who fired the shots?"

Keo ignored him and reached Gavin's room. Before he could get to the doorknob, the door swung open and Gavin staggered outside. The redhead grabbed the doorframe with one bloody hand, the other holding an automatic pistol tightly in his fist. An LED lamp hanging off the ceiling inside the room was turned on medium setting, illuminating Gavin's wild and frenzied expression, like something out of a horror show.

Gavin looked confused when he saw Keo, and they stared at each other across the open doorway. That is, until blood spurted in a wide arc from Gavin's left shoulder and splashed against the wall.

"Oh, Jesus," Levy said. He stood paralyzed in the hallway, staring at Gavin, as if he couldn't quite process what was happening. "What happened? Are you okay?"

Bowe didn't stand around asking stupid questions. Instead, he rushed past Levy and toward Gavin, who heard him coming and whirled around to confront him. Bowe slid to a stop and stared at his bloodied friend.

"Gavin, Jesus, you're bleeding," Bowe said. "Where's Earl?"

Gavin didn't answer. He didn't seem capable of answering. He turned away from Bowe and lurched out of the room, pushing his way past Keo and Norris. He moved in a crooked line, like a drunk, staggering everywhere. Somehow, he made it to the kitchen, passing a horrified Gillian, who followed him tentatively. Gavin had left bloody fingerprints everywhere as he groped his way across the house.

"Watch it, kid!" Norris shouted.

Keo spun back around, just in time to see Earl lunging at him through the open door.

No, not Earl. The thirty-something, easygoing country boy was gone, replaced by one of those creatures. *A bloodsucker.* Keo only knew it was Earl because it was still wearing Earl's clothes, though they were now absurdly too big for its shrunken frame.

The sight of Earl surprised Keo. When had he died and turned? It couldn't have been that long ago. But to look at him, he would swear Earl had turned days ago. How had he gotten the drop on Gavin? Was the other man sleeping? That made sense. He didn't think even Gavin would continue holding a vigil over a dead body.

Earl used to have brown eyes, but the ones that peered out of the room at Keo now were black and lifeless. Pruned, dark skin glistened against the LED light, but it was not quite tightly pulled against its skeletal frame yet. Keo imagined the thing that used to be Earl only had to walk around another few minutes before it would simply slink out of its now ill-fitting clothes. It still had hair, but not much, and what it had flitted away as it reached for Keo with impossibly sharp and bony fingers.

Norris dove forward and slammed the butt of his M4 into the creature's face.

"Oh, fuck!" Bowe shouted. He had been standing close to the door when Earl appeared.

Keo thought he heard the sound of bone breaking as Norris's rifle found its mark. While that didn't stop the creature, it slowed it down just enough. Clumps of blood *slurped* out of its shattered nose when Earl *(not anymore)* turned its head.

"Earl?" Bowe said. "Oh shit, Earl."

Earl whirled on Bowe, who had kept moving forward.

Too close, you idiot!

Bowe realized his mistake right away and began backpedaling, but he did it too fast and tripped on his own legs and fell. And so did Earl—*over Bowe*, and for an instant the two of them looked like dancers that had gotten their legs tangled and were now falling to the floor in each other's arms.

Then Bowe began screaming because Earl had sunk his teeth into Bowe's neck. The sight of the taller man struggling underneath the smaller *(shrunken)* Earl left an indelible image in Keo's mind. At least, until bright crimson red liquid splashed the floor like geysers.

Levy had smartly (or maybe he just couldn't make himself move) stayed farther back in the hallway. He raised his gun to fire, and Keo waited for the loud explosion in the narrow passageway. Except there weren't any because Levy didn't pull the trigger. Instead, he stared almost in disbelief as one friend

THE WALLS OF LEMURIA   183

bit and chewed another's neck.

Bowe was thrashing violently on the floor, long limbs flailing wildly, trying to dislodge Earl. He grabbed Earl's thin neck and tried to push him off, but Earl wouldn't let go. Either that, or its teeth had sunk so deeply into Bowe's flesh that it couldn't be pried loose even by the Jaws of Life.

Keo unslung the MP5SD and fired.

Despite the attached metal suppressor, the submachine gun wasn't completely silent as Keo concentrated half of the magazine's thirty rounds into Earl's back. Dark liquid *(blood?)* sprayed the air and walls and Earl twitched. Levy had stumbled back down the hallway, throwing his hands over his face to keep back the blood splatters and chunks of flesh and muscle that came loose from Earl's body with every impacting 9mm round.

When Keo finally stopped shooting, Earl looked up and seemed to sneer at him. For a moment, Keo wondered why he thought shooting it would work. Shotguns hadn't done a damn thing, so why did he think submachine gun rounds would prove different?

You're a world class idiot, that's why.

Earl climbed off Bowe, who had stopped moving on the floor. It wasn't because Earl had feasted on him (though that probably had a little something to do with it, too), but Bowe was now bleeding from not just the neck, but also from three bullet holes in his chest. Keo's bullets, he realized, because the creatures had soft bodies and bullets went right through them. What didn't hit Bowe had slammed into the ground around him.

Keo stumbled back, feeling slightly sick to his stomach.

Aw, Jesus. I shot him. I shot Bowe.

Earl had forgotten about Keo, Norris, and Levy, and he *(it?)* grabbed Bowe by one leg and pulled him toward the door. Bowe didn't struggle. He didn't have the strength. His eyes were glassy and blood trickled out of the wounds across his body, though they were nothing compared to the stream *slurping* out of the gash in his neck where Earl had bitten him. How a bite could possibly be worse than bullet wounds defied logic.

The second Bowe's body disappeared into the room, Norris rushed forward and grabbed the doorknob and slammed the door shut.

"Hold on," Keo said.

"I got nowhere else to be," Norris grunted back.

Norris gripped the doorknob with both hands, but he didn't really have to. There were no movements from the other side, no loud crashing against the door, or any attempts by Earl to come back out. Because he—*it*—didn't want to come out. Not yet, anyway. It was busy in the room.

With Bowe...

As if to confirm it, blood appeared out the bottom of the door, spreading into the hallway in a thick *(way too thick)* gush.

"Jesus," Norris said, and moved his feet away. "Do something, will you?"

Keo turned to leave the hallway, kicking spent shell casings from the MP5SD strewn across the floor. It was a timely reminder, and Keo pulled out the half-empty magazine and slapped in a full one.

Half-empty. Because I pumped three of them into Bowe, too.

Aw, Jesus.

He didn't know why it bothered him so much. It wasn't like this was the first time he had shot someone. Not even close. Of course, all those other times he had meant to do it. This time was a little different.

Gillian was at the kitchen with Gavin, holding a rag against his shoulder and trying to stanch the bleeding. It wasn't working, and the proof were two similar rags already in a pile on the counter, both soaked with blood. She met Keo's eyes, and he was impressed by the calmness he saw looking back at him.

What happened to the woman who shook for an hour after the ambush yesterday? She was gone, replaced by this Gillian, who though clearly terrified of what was happening managed to do her part anyway.

"Are you okay?" Keo asked.

She nodded back, probably because she didn't trust herself to answer vocally.

"How's Gavin?" he asked.

"He's...fine," she said hesitantly, but her face told him a different story. "He said he fell asleep and when he woke up..." She didn't finish, because she didn't have to.

If Gavin had heard their exchange, he didn't say anything. He looked like he could barely stand, and if not for Gillian pinning him against the counter with her body, he might have toppled off the stool at any moment.

"Do the best you can," Keo said.

"I will. Go back there and help Norris."

He nodded and hurried back to the left side hallway.

Norris was still leaning against the door, both hands gripped tightly around the doorknob. He had positioned his feet to keep them away from the spreading blood on the floor, but he was quickly running out of space. How many pints of blood did a human body contain? Because it looked like all of it was coming out of Gavin's room at the moment.

"You back already?" the ex-cop said.

Keo looked up the hallway at Levy, standing silently behind Norris. He was there, but he wasn't really there. "Levy, you still with us?"

Levy glanced over at him. "What's he going to do with Bowe?" he asked quietly.

You know damn well what he's doing with Bowe right now, Keo thought, but said, "You have anything in that basement to keep this door locked?"

"Why?"

"We need to keep Earl sealed inside until morning."

And Bowe with him, too.

And Gavin makes three...

"Right. Morning," Levy said. He sounded robotic, on automatic pilot.

"I need you to go get something to lock this door with. Maybe the same kind of latches you guys put on the windows. Do you have any of those left?"

"I think so…"

"We're going to need a screwdriver and screws, too. Grab a drill if you have one. Okay?"

"Okay," Levy repeated, though he hadn't moved.

"Levy," Keo said. When that didn't get any response from Levy, Keo said louder, "Levy." The other man's glazed eyes shifted back to him. "Go. *Now.*"

Levy nodded and hurried off. He was still clutching the Glock in one hand, though Keo wasn't sure if he even knew that.

Norris looked after Levy. "He looked bad to you?"

"He just saw his best friend try to eat his other best friend, and actually succeeded in eating another one," Keo said. "Hard to look good after that."

"Good point." Norris's eyes drifted to the path of blood Gavin had left behind as he ran off. "That kid ain't going to be okay. You know that, right?"

"You just worry about that door and I'll worry about Gavin."

Norris looked back at the door. "I don't think he's going to try to leave the room. Or if he does, I'm pretty sure I can stop him. Unless he can break down the door, he needs to turn this doorknob, and from what I've seen, they're not that strong. So go on."

"I'll be back," Keo said, and returned to the living room.

Gavin was lying on one of the couches now, with Gillian kneeling next to him, wrapping a thick roll of gauze tightly around his shoulder and looping them around his arm. She had already applied so much that Gavin looked like a baseball pitcher with a bag of ice taped to his throwing arm. Rachel was crouched nearby in pajamas and T-shirt, putting scissors away into an open first aid kit. Additional bloody rags were spread out on the floor around them.

Gavin didn't look as if he was even aware the women were working on him. His face was ghostly pale and his eyes were closed. The women had turned on a second LED lamp nearby, and the room glowed unnaturally bright.

"The girls?" Keo said to Rachel.

"They're inside my room," Rachel said. "I told them not to come out unless I came to get them."

"Are they okay?"

"Scared out of their minds from all the screaming and shooting, but I think—God, I can't believe I'm saying this—they might be getting used to it by now. What about Bowe?"

Keo shook his head.

"You were right," Rachel said. "If they bite you, it's over."

Keo walked over and got a closer look at Gavin. He looked asleep, and Rachel had wrapped a thick blanket around him. He was almost peaceful. For now, anyway.

He's going to die. Then he'll turn.

Like Delia.

Like Earl...

"Gillian," Keo said.

"I know," she said softly. She sat back on her haunches, staring at the bandages around Gavin's shoulder as they slowly, ever so slowly, started to redden an inch at a time. "It won't stop bleeding. Just like with Earl."

"We need to put him someplace where he can't hurt anyone."

"Like where? There aren't a lot of choices left, Keo."

"There's the basement," Levy said, coming out of the right side hallway. He had a padlock and a steel hasp in one hand and a battery-operated power drill in the other. His Glock was stuffed into his front waistband, and Levy looked better than when Keo had last seen him a few minutes ago. He seemed to be more in control, as if the initial shock and paralysis had worn off. A little, anyway.

"The basement?" Gillian said. "Will that work?"

"It's a big room and the door is pretty strong. He'd never be able to get out."

"That's not going to work," Keo said.

"Why not? If he's in the basement, he won't be able to hurt anyone."

"Exactly. He'll be *in* the basement. You want to go down there to get him when he turns?"

"We don't know—" he started to say, but quickly stopped himself. Levy looked down at the tools in his hands instead.

"Right," Keo said. "We're going to do this my way this time."

CHAPTER 20

AFTER LEVY WENT back to the basement and got another set of locks, they drilled the steel plate over Gavin's door first, then added the padlock and snapped it into place. Then they stepped back from the door and waited for the creature that used to be Earl to do something, but it never did.

How long does it take to drink Bowe dry?

Keo didn't say it out loud, of course. Levy was standing next to him, and he already looked pale from just being so close to the room.

"You okay, Levy?" Keo asked.

Levy gave him a blank look, as if he didn't quite understand the question. "Bowe's in there."

"Yeah."

"Earl's...eating Bowe?"

Drinking Bowe is more like it, Keo thought, but said, "Try not to think about it. I know it's hard, but it's not going to do you any good imagining what's happening behind this door."

Levy nodded and looked away.

Norris tried opening the door by jiggling the doorknob. It opened just a few inches, but not enough to see inside. Which was good. Keo didn't want to see what Earl was doing in there to Bowe anyway. He already knew.

"They're not strong enough to break the door down," Norris said. "We should be good."

"There are two of them in there now," Keo said.

"Shit, that's right. Bowe, too." He glanced over at Levy, but the younger man didn't seem to have heard him. Levy was focused almost entirely on the thick puddle of blood under the door. Norris said to Keo, "You think it makes any difference?"

"I don't know," Keo said. "I guess we'll find out." He put a hand on Levy's shoulder. "Let's do your door next."

"For Gavin..." Levy said absently.

"I'm sorry, but we don't have a choice. This is the only way."

Levy looked down at his hands again. "I know," he said quietly.

"Let's get the room ready," Norris said.

When they were done putting the lock on Levy's door, Keo went back into the living room while Norris stayed behind with his M4 and stood guard outside Gavin's room. Levy hadn't moved to follow Keo, so he left him back in the hallway with the ex-cop.

Gillian sat in a chair next to the sofa and Gavin's prone form. She had put a second blanket over him, tucking the corners under his shivering body. Rachel had returned to her room to be with the girls.

"Will the doors hold?" Gillian asked.

"I think so."

"Even after Bowe turns, too?"

"They're not very strong, so it should hold."

Hopefully.

Keo sat down on another chair and took in a long breath. He didn't realize how tiring running back and forth between the living room and the hallways could be. Maybe he was just out of shape. Or maybe the night was dragging on for way too long.

"It'll be okay," he said. "We'll get through tonight and tomorrow, and the days after that will be better."

"Do you really believe that?" she asked, looking at him intently.

"Absolutely."

"You're a terrible liar. We're probably all going to die out here. Which would suck, because I always envisioned dying in France when I'm eighty years old with the love of my life holding my hand as I drift off to the big blue yonder."

He smiled. "I'll hold your hand."

She gave him a half-smile. "What about France?"

"I can get you as close as Paris, Texas."

She laughed softly despite herself, but it was only a short burst until the realization of their situation set in again. Still, it made him feel good to hear it from her.

"How many people you think are out there right now?" she asked. "Like us? Huddling around LED lamps."

"I don't know. But we got lucky. A lot of people could have gotten lucky, too."

"For how long, though? We're living on borrowed time." She was looking at Gavin's pale, sweat-slicked face. "A bite, Keo. That's all it takes. A bite, and we become like Earl. Like Gavin…"

Keo closed his eyes and wanted to go to sleep. He was tired. Way more tired than he wanted to admit. It didn't help that he barely slept last night on the dirt floor under the cabin in the RV park.

"We'll be fine," he said quietly. There wasn't much confidence in his voice, and Gillian likely knew it, too.

"How can you say that? After everything that's happened? After everything you've seen? They can't be killed, Keo."

"Sunlight kills them."

"And sunlight doesn't come up for half the day. That's half of our lives we'll be looking over our shoulders." She shook her head. "That's no way to live, Keo. That's no way to survive. Maybe it'd be better if…"

"Don't say it."

"Why not?"

He saw the look in her eyes. The same look he had seen before in people who had given up. Most of the time they were from mortally wounded soldiers and civilians. There had been a girl in the Sudan, with a bullet hole in her chest...

Keo got up and crouched in front of her. He took her hands in his. "What about us?"

She looked back at him. "What about us?"

"You promised to give me a chance. I expect you to keep your word."

This time she managed a whole smile. "It's too bad you didn't come to town before all of this. I would have shown you a really good time."

"Missed it by that much, huh?"

"Just a bit."

He opened his mouth to say something when he stopped.

"What?" she said, seeing his reaction. "No clever responses?"

He put his forefinger to his lips. *Shhh.*

Then he got up and crossed the room to one of the windows, making as little noise as possible.

"What is it?" Gillian said behind him.

He slid back the metal plate over the peephole and looked out.

He saw only pitch-black darkness.

"Keo," Gillian said, walking over to him. "What do you see?"

"Nothing," Keo said.

"But why—"

A pair of darting black eyes appeared in the rectangular slot, their unnatural shape eerily highlighted by the LED light from inside the house. Keo took a step back at the same time Gillian gasped loudly behind him.

He reached for his submachine gun—not to use it, but just to make sure it was there.

It saw them and grabbed the burglar bars and began rattling them against the window frame. Jagged white and yellow and brown teeth snarled, and pruned black skin gleamed under what little moonlight there was outside.

Keo saw a flicker of movement, then two—no, three—*five* more of the creatures emerged out of the darkness. They converged on the window, fighting with one another to grab at the bars and began pulling on them.

The rattling grew louder and louder as more of them got a grip.

One of the shriveled things shoved its hand through two of the vertical struts and smashed the glass pane behind it. It kept pushing its fist through the broken glass until its knuckles landed harmlessly against the wooden plate. Realizing it couldn't get through, the creature pulled its arm back, slicing its flesh and leaving behind dripping black blood on the shards and windowsill.

"Keo, close it," Gillian said behind him.

Keo obeyed, closing the peephole. He hadn't finished sliding the metal plate into place when the same rattling noise and the crash of broken glass echoed from the other window. That was followed by something hitting the door, except the door was impossibly thick with the reinforcements, and the noise only came through as dull *thump-thump-thump* sounds that, somehow, still managed to be unnerving.

Just as Keo and Gillian were focused on the door and windows, there was more pounding from behind them, more rattling and smashing glass, this time from the back door at the end of the right side hallway and from all four bedrooms.

Rachel burst out of her room with the girls. Christine ran out front, Rachel pushing Lotte's wheelchair. They looked terrified, Lotte clutching her wheelchair's armrests, the knuckles already ghostly white.

"The window," Rachel said, out of breath. "They're trying to get in through the window inside our room."

"They won't be able to get through," Keo said.

"Are you sure?"

God, I hope I'm right, Keo thought, but said with as much

conviction as he could muster, "Yes, I'm certain of it."

Norris and Levy came out of the left side hallway with their weapons.

"Jesus Christ, what's happening out here?" Norris said.

"They know we're here," Gillian said. Her eyes snapped from the door to the windows and back again.

"Who?" Levy said, confused.

Them, Keo said.

The noises were getting worse, increasing in intensity and volume. They seemed to be coming from every part of the house now, from the front to the back to the sides. The rattling of burglar bars, the breaking of glass, the *thoom! thoom!* of flesh hitting the doors on both ends of the house.

The ferocity of the attacks from all around drove them to each other. Before they realized it, they were all standing within an invisible five-feet box in front of the fireplace. Then Rachel sat down on the couch with her daughter, while Gillian went to be near the frightened Lotte, putting a comforting hand on the young girl's arm. Lotte managed to grin back her appreciation.

Gavin was oblivious to what was happening. Keo looked down just to make sure he was still breathing, that his wound hadn't taken him yet. The thick roll of gauze around his shoulder had turned almost entirely red since Gillian put it on less than an hour ago.

Won't be long now...

"The lights," Norris said. "It's too bright in here."

Keo rushed over to the LED lamp on the kitchen counter and twisted the knob to its lowest setting, while Levy crouched next to the one in the living room and did the same thing. The room slowly darkened, though there was still just enough light to see with.

He was halfway back to the others when he heard loud banging from in front of him—past the living room and from the left side hallway.

Earl.

Or what used to be Earl. Or maybe it wasn't just Earl. Maybe Bowe had already died and turned, too. Was that why the pounding sounded much louder from Gavin's room? Or was it because it was *inside* the house? Not that it mattered. As hard as he was banging on the door, Earl wasn't getting out of there.

Gillian held out her hand to him and Keo took it. He stood next to her and they listened to the attack in front of them, behind them, and from the sides. Norris was facing the left side hallway while clutching his M4. Levy had sat down on the other sofa and was staring at the floor. Keo thought there was probably a fifty-fifty chance Levy was actually aware that he was still in the living room with them at the moment.

The banging continued.

They didn't stop. They didn't seem capable of stopping. It wasn't as if they were making progress. He could tell they hadn't gotten any further than when they started. The bars over the windows remained in place despite the continued rattling, all the efforts to pull them free. Every pointless smashing of flesh against unyielding wood produced the same dull *thud*.

The reinforcements are holding. Thank you, Earl.

Gillian's hand tightened in his, and Keo looked over and gave her a smile that said, *"We'll be fine."*

She returned a halfhearted smile, one that said she didn't believe him for a single second.

He didn't blame her. It was hard to be optimistic when it sounded like every undead thing in the world was outside the house at this very moment, trying to get in. How many were out there now? He had only seen a dozen with his own eyes, but it was obvious there were more out there.

Silly undead things. You're wasting your time. So why don't you just stop, goddammit.

But they didn't, because they didn't seem capable of ever tiring out. He remembered the night at the police station. How long had they kept banging on the back room's steel door? Hours and hours.

He looked down at his watch. It was past midnight. At this rate, the bloodsuckers would keep at it for at least three, maybe four more hours. That was assuming they stuck to their pattern—

Silence.

Just like that, they stopped.

The last *thud* reverberated against the door before it slowly faded into obscurity. The noises from the windows in front and behind them had also stopped. Earl, too, had ceased his attacks against the locked bedroom door.

They exchanged a look. Even Levy lifted his head up.

"It's a trick," Norris whispered.

"No," Keo said. He hadn't bothered to whisper. The creatures already knew they were inside, so there was no point in being quiet. "I don't think it's a trick. I think they know."

"Know what?"

"That they can't get in."

Norris looked back at the left side hallway. "He's stopped, too. Earl."

"Stay here," Keo said, and moved toward one of the windows.

"Your funeral," Norris said.

Keo reached the window and put his hand on the metal slide, but he didn't pull it back right away. He looked back at them, saw every face—with the exception of Gavin—staring back at him. Rachel and Christine were holding hands and Lotte was clinging to Gillian's.

He turned back to the window and opened the peephole. He expected a surprise, like in the movies when you thought the killer was gone and he pops back up to give the audience a nice little jolt. Keo was prepared for it.

But there was nothing out there.

Even the clearing actually looked brighter than the last time he looked out. He could spot their vehicles again, sitting undisturbed under the soft glow of moonlight. The only movements he could detect were from the trees beyond the yard, moving against a soft wind.

Although he couldn't see them with the naked eye, Keo swore he could *feel* them inside the surrounding woods, watching him back. Of course, it could just be his imagination cranked up to the nth degree.

"What's the verdict, kid?" Norris asked anxiously behind him.

Keo didn't answer right away.

"Kid?"

"They're gone," Keo finally said. "Or, at least, I can't see them outside."

"Maybe they're hiding in the woods."

"Maybe. I can't see them if they are." *But I can feel them. Maybe.* "I think they're just gone."

"That doesn't make any sense," Gillian said. "Why would they just leave?"

"Because it doesn't matter," Keo said. He covered the peephole and looked back at them. "They don't need to take the house tonight. They can try again tomorrow night. And the night after that. All they need is to wait for us to make a mistake. They're always going to be out there because it's always going to be night, day after day after day. If it's not the same ones that are out there now, it'll be a hundred new ones. A thousand."

No one said a word. He could see them absorbing his words. He couldn't tell if they believed him or if they thought he was ranting. He wasn't, but he had never been especially good at rallying the troops.

Time to learn some new skills, pal. It's a brave new world.

"That's our task moving forward," Keo continued. "That's what we're going to have to do from now on if we want to survive. We're going to have to promise each other that we'll never make a mistake, because the first time we do, it will cost us all our lives."

He looked over at the left side hallway, at the blood-covered door of Gavin's room.

"Now, let's talk about how we're going to get rid of what's in there…"

CHAPTER 21

UNDER THE WARM morning sunlight, they found the bare footprints of hundreds of the creatures spread across the clearing, much of it piled on top of one another near the windows and doors. For some reason, the bloodsuckers hadn't bothered with the shack in the back. That was a good sign. The generator was a luxury that probably wasn't going to last forever, but Keo certainly wanted to keep it around for as long as possible. The girls, no doubt, would agree.

Keo walked the grounds with Levy, looking for signs that the creatures had left someone behind, the way they had with the mobile home. Levy was frazzled, his eyes puffy from lack of sleep. They had all drunk instant coffee an hour ago, but that apparently hadn't had much effect on Levy.

"One," Levy said after they had been walking in silence for a while.

"One?" Keo said.

"One of those things. It took out Earl, Gavin, and Bowe. Jesus. *One.*"

Keo noticed Levy was walking faster, and Keo had to increase his pace to keep up.

"How many did you see last night?" Levy asked. "Hundreds?"

"I couldn't see all of them, but that sounds about right."

"Jesus. Hundreds, when just one took out three of us. Earl was tough and he was really smart. He was the only reason we survived that first night. If they can take Earl, what chance do any of us have?"

"What happened to Earl was a mistake. The same for Bowe and Gavin."

"You told us, but we didn't listen."

"I wouldn't have believed me, either, in your shoes."

"If we'd only believed you." He shook his head. "Then Bowe and Gavin would still be here. Maybe even Earl…"

Keo didn't say anything. He wasn't sure if all of that was true, but if Levy needed to believe it, then why not let him?

"What you said last night," Levy continued. "You think that's possible? You think we can keep going as long as we don't make any mistakes?"

"We just have to look out for one another. Keep each other alert and careful, make sure everyone's doing their jobs."

They circled the house a second time, making sure the doors were intact and the burglar bars hadn't loosened during the night. The creatures might have spent hours assaulting the windows, but they hadn't done much to pry the gates from the walls. They had, though, broken all the glass.

"We'll install mesh screens to keep out the bugs in the daytime," Keo said. "No point in putting glass windows back in if they're just going to break them again tomorrow night."

They ended up at the back of the house, where Keo stopped and looked over at the river.

"How deep is the water?" he asked Levy.

"It gets deeper the farther south you go, but around here it's about eight to ten feet. You could swim across if you needed to. Or drown, if you can't swim."

"What's on the other side?"

"The same thing that's on this side. A lot of woods. Why?"

"No reason," Keo said. "I just wanted to get a better lay of the land."

"There are enough woods around here that you could spend months walking around it until you saw everything there is to see."

Keo nodded. "That's the plan."

"What's that?"

"Find a lot of time to waste."

"I don't understand."

"If I have a lot of time on my hands, that means I'm still alive, Levy."

"Oh," Levy said.

GILLIAN WAS STANDING in the right side hallway when they came through the back door.

"They turned," she said. "Gavin and Bowe. They've both turned."

"How long ago?" Keo asked.

"I don't know, but they only started trying to break down their doors about five minutes ago. Norris is there, just in case they manage to get out."

They crossed the living room to the left side hallway, where Norris stood guard outside Gavin's room, watching the door moving in tune to the *thump-thump* coming from the other side. The doorknob jiggled as someone *(something)* pulled at it, but the lock they had put in last night were holding. The same thing was happening to Levy's room down the hall, where they had put Gavin.

Norris looked over. "Gavin started up first, then Earl and Bowe joined in."

"Did they communicate somehow?" Keo asked.

"Not that I heard."

"Maybe whispered?"

"The walls are too thick for whispering," Levy said. He looked from one door to the other and back again. His friends were in there. Keo didn't pretend to know what it was like for him at the moment.

"What now?" Gillian asked. "What do we do with them?"

"They want to come out," Keo said. "So we'll let them come out."

"Are you crazy?"

"Not at all," Keo said, and looked over his shoulder at the open window across the living room. "We'll need to close that up first."

"You really think it'll fall for it?" Norris said doubtfully.

"I don't think they're that smart." He looked back at the door, moving against Bowe's and Earl's fists. "I think once they turn, they're stuck operating on very primitive base instincts. And right now, they want to come out and feed. So let's give them both."

KEO HAD AN idea of how to do it, but it all depended on whether Earl, Gavin, and Bowe would cooperate. They decided to set their sights on the first room, the one with Earl and Bowe inside because it was closer, though Keo had a moment of doubt. He wasn't sure if he wanted to deal with two of them at the same time. What if it all went sideways? They had barely survived Earl, and now they were going to risk it with Earl and Bowe?

To hell with it. Two for the price of one. Now that's daebak.

"Go," Keo said.

Norris slipped the key into the padlock over Gavin's door, but didn't turn it right away. Instead, he looked back at Keo, then over his shoulder at Levy. "We really going to do this?"

"Yeah," Keo said.

"You answered kind of fast there."

"It'll work."

The ex-cop sighed. "Easy for you to say. You're over there and I'm over here."

"Hey, you lost the coin toss."

"Dammit," Norris said, and returned his focus to the door in front of him.

Rachel and the kids were outside the house, but Gillian had insisted on staying behind. She watched from the living room with Levy, standing partially in shadows because they had closed the front door and all the windows back up, which gave the house a dark, cave-like feel. She looked tense, and he guessed she was having second thoughts about being in here at the moment.

"Do it," Keo said.

"Yeah, yeah, hold your horses," Norris grunted back.

Norris took another deep breath, then turned the key in the padlock and tugged it out of the loop and stepped back almost in the same motion.

The door remained closed, Earl and Bowe having given up banging on it a few minutes ago, almost as if they could sense *(Could they?)* what was about to happen outside. Norris backpedaled out of the hallway, not stopping until he was inside the living room with Gillian and Levy, who was clutching his AR-15 in front of him.

Keo remained where he was, partially hidden in the shadows next to the window that faced the left side hallway. He waited, but Gavin's door remained closed. He listened for sounds of movement but could only hear Norris's accelerated breathing across the room, and maybe Levy's and Gillian's, too.

"They're not coming out," Norris said. He was at an angle where he could look into the hallway and see the door.

"Give them time," Keo said.

"How much time?"

"I don't know. It's not like I've done this before."

"Oh, now you tell me."

"If you're so impatient, why don't you go over there and open the door for them? Invite them out."

Norris seemed to actually think about it. "Maybe I should."

"Go on. I'll wait."

"I got a better idea," Norris said. "Let's flip for it again. Heads I go, tails you—"

Click! as the door opened.

Norris took another (involuntary) step back and clutched his M4. Gillian might have gasped out loud, while Levy stood perfectly still, as if he were rooted to the floorboards and couldn't move even if he wanted to.

"One of them's coming out," Norris said.

Keo didn't have to move to see into the hallway from his spot, but it also gave him a very limited angle on the walls themselves. He couldn't tell if Earl's room was open since the door swung inward. So he waited and listened, but mostly he kept tabs on Norris, who had the better view.

"Any day now," Norris said.

They didn't have to wait too much longer before long, blackened fingers slipped out of the open door and grasped one side of the doorframe. The bony fingers dug in, taking a firm hold, before Earl's head appeared in the hallway and tilted, black sockets and tiny slits where eyes used to be searching them out. His black flesh looked at home in the shadows, while sharp bones underneath tight skin moved at unnatural angles.

Then a second creature appeared in the doorway.

Bowe.

The sight of two of them, sticking their heads out of the open door, so far and yet so close that he could *smell* them—like rotting cabbage—made Keo rethink everything. Because this was a stupid plan that depended on too many factors to work. All it would take was one mistake and they would all die. God knew they couldn't shoot the damn things.

Two pairs of black eyes rested on Norris, who stood the closest to them. Gillian and Levy, standing slightly behind Norris, both took an involuntary step further back. Keo didn't think they even knew what they were doing when they did it. It was human nature to back away from overt danger. It was difficult to look at the two shriveled, unnatural things that used to be Earl and Bowe and not see death.

Living, breathing, *moving* death.

Norris seemed undeterred. Or maybe he was just putting up a really good front. Either way, he didn't move from his spot and instead gritted his teeth back at the monsters eyeing him. "Come on out, you ugly sonofabitches. What are you waiting for?"

The creatures bared their teeth at him. Ugly teeth. Cracked, stained teeth. How the hell had they gotten so bad so fast? It was as if acid had chewed on them, turned them into jagged sticks jutting out from gooey, bleeding gums.

"Come on," Norris said. "Come get me, you sonofa—" He didn't get to finish because the creatures bounded out of the room and made a straight line for him.

They were fast. So fast.

Keo didn't realize how fast they really were until he saw two of them moving side by side. He imagined cheetahs stalking prey on the plains.

And Norris was that prey, even as he stumbled back and shouted, "Now, kid, now!"

Norris was backing up so fast that he tripped over his own feet and fell down on his ass.

Just like Bowe did last night...

Keo pulled back on the chains that kept the wooden plate over the window next to him. It wasn't exactly like jerking on a regular window curtain, because the damn thing weighed a ton. The barricade was halfway up, streaks of sunlight pouring in instantly, when the creatures were halfway to Norris. They might have actually made it if they had kept going, but the sudden brightness must have surprised them, and they stopped and their heads snapped in his direction almost in unison.

A splash of morning flashed across the room and hit Earl's legs first because he was closest, and the creature let out a loud squeal as both bent legs turned ash white, the flesh becoming instantaneously brittle against direct contact with sunlight.

The creature that used to be Bowe turned and fled back into the hallway.

Keo kept pulling and the wooden plate kept rising, until a large swath of the living room was flooded with sunlight. Bowe, halfway back to the hallway, seemed to freeze in place and let out a pained noise. It might have even screamed if it had gotten the chance.

But it didn't. Neither one of them did.

Their faces turned white, then gray, then brittle along with their torso and arms and they fell apart as if their entire being had come unglued. Flesh and muscle and organs evaporated in a puff of black-gray clouds, the exposed skeletal remains crumpling to the faux wooden floors in separate piles not far away from one another.

Norris scrambled back up to his feet, brushing at ash that had fallen over his pants. He coughed and so did Keo, the acidic stench of the creatures stinging his nostrils and eyes.

Levy and Gillian walked over, holding rags to their mouths and noses, and stood over the bony remains of the two creatures. They swiped at the lingering cloud and stared down wordlessly at what used to be Earl and Bowe.

"Damn, it worked," Norris said.

"Told you," Keo said.

"Right. You told me. I saw you almost peeing in your pants over there."

Keo grinned back.

Norris crouched next to Earl's bones and took out a hunting knife from a sheath. He jammed the blade into a part of the ribcage and pried something loose, then tossed it to Keo. "Souvenir," Norris said.

"What is it?" Gillian asked, her voice muffled by the rag over her mouth.

"One of the 9mm bullets from last night," Keo said. "It must have gotten lodged in Earl's ribcage when I shot him."

Norris straightened up and put his knife away, looking

down the hallway at Levy's room. "Two down, one to go…"

IT WAS HARDER with Gavin. The fact that he *(it)* didn't come out of the room right away when Norris unlocked it wasn't a surprise. Earl and Bowe hadn't, either. But after an hour of waiting and he still hadn't come out, Keo considered the very real possibility that the creature knew, somehow, what had happened to Earl and Bowe.

Curiouser and curiouser…

Eventually, they were able to lure Gavin out using Norris as bait once again. He stood outside the open door for five minutes, just waiting for Gavin to make his move.

"Come on, you stupid sonofabitch!" Norris shouted into the door. "I can you see in there. Come on out! You know you want this! Prime American beef here, asshole!"

That did it.

Norris practically dived out of the hallway, screaming, "Do it do it do it!" as Gavin lunged out of the open door after him.

Keo yanked the chains for the second time and sunlight flooded the hallway and caught Gavin in the narrow passage. Like with Earl and Bowe an hour earlier, Gavin attempted to flee back into the room, but sunlight splashed across its back and the creature turned to ash. A cloud of remains appeared out of thin air, then the clatter of bones crumpling to the floor.

Norris gave Keo a suspicious look across the room as he picked himself up from the floor. "You waited a little long that time, kid. It almost had me."

"You're imagining things," Keo said, grinning back at him.

THEY BURIED GAVIN'S bones in the woods next to Earl's and Bowe's, using shovels from the shack. Keo and Norris dug the graves and settled the remains into the holes, while Levy stayed back at the house with Gillian and the girls to clean out the two rooms.

Gavin's room was covered in sticky dry blood and bullet holes, but Levy's required less work. In truth, Gillian and Rachel were probably doing most of the work back at the house. Everyone had agreed without actually saying anything that Levy should do as little as possible. The guy had already lost too much. Asking him to clean up after his friends would have been cruel.

When they were finished, Keo and Norris stood over the graves—small bumps in the earth that would, in a year or so, be consumed by the rest of the woods—and sucked in the morning air. He hadn't realized the true meaning of fresh air until he had spent two hours inside a closed house with the dead remains of three bloodsuckers.

"We can do it," Norris said after a while.

"What's that?"

"Stay here." Norris glanced around at their peaceful surroundings. "The house, the generator, the supplies in the basement, and the fish in the river out back. We could stay here indefinitely. Or at least until things get back to normal."

"You still think things will get back to normal, old timer?"

"Everyone needs hope, kid. It's a big planet. I can't believe everyone's gone except for us."

"We know for a fact not everyone's gone. The gas station, remember?"

Norris grunted. "I remember every time I see the Durango. You think they're around here somewhere? Maybe even looking for us still?"

"I don't know," Keo said. "That's the problem. I wish I knew, and I don't."

Who the hell were those guys?

A pair of hummingbirds flickered across the sky above him, drawing Keo's attention. Somehow, knowing the birds were still around gave him some level of comfort. If they could survive the end of the world...

"Let's head back," Keo said. "I'm hungry."

"That junk food isn't going to last long," Norris said. "We might as well eat as much as we can now. Pig out, get fat, die of high blood pressure and diabetes. Wouldn't that be something?"

Keo chuckled. "Yeah. Old-fashioned natural death, huh?"

"That's the dream, kid," Norris grinned back.

As they walked through the woods back toward the house, Keo found himself stealing a glance around them, listening for sounds of movement other than their own. He didn't hear anything, but that didn't mean there wasn't something *(someone)* out there.

Who the hell were those guys?

PART THREE

SUMMERLAND

CHAPTER 22

LIFE WENT ON after Earl, Bowe, and Gavin—at least for Keo and the others. They had gotten to know the three men somewhat, but there wasn't the same familiarity that Levy had. Keo personally liked them enough, especially the older Earl, but it was hard for him to think of Bowe and Gavin as more than just a couple of country kids he met briefly before they left, never to be seen again.

It was different for Levy, of course, but the young man surprised Keo by, if not getting over his loss, then rising above it. He hadn't expected that kind of resilience from the kid, but then, Keo accepted the possibility that he might have misjudged him. A day was hardly enough to get to know someone, especially considering all the emotions that Levy had been forced to endure in just twenty-four hours.

The only remaining survivor of Earl's group showed them the surrounding area in the beginning, pointing out the danger spots they had stumbled across in the first few days while scavenging for supplies. After that, Levy spent most of his time hunting in the woods, coming back with the occasional bird or squirrel, but even those were getting harder to find. It wasn't just the land-based animals that were disappearing, as it turned out.

They raided as many houses around the area they were comfortable with, but for every house they entered, they left alone two. Sunlight was their friend, but sunlight could only go so far into a house even after they knocked down all the doors and windows. Most of the time they steered clear of the bigger homes. The creatures, they found, tended to congregate in large areas. Two-story houses were usually filled with them, especially on the second floor.

The stores were equally dangerous, and they spent most of their time looking through the front lobbies, grabbing all the impulse buys along the cash registers. Clothing was plentiful, and by the end of the first week they had enough of a wardrobe to last for years, negating further need for the girls to raid Rachel's luggage. After that, they concentrated on emergency supplies—non-perishables, canned goods, and batteries. They grabbed anything they thought they could use, either now or later. The basement back at the house filled up quickly as a result.

In the back of his mind, Keo knew the reason he and Norris kept going out wasn't because they needed supplies. They had plenty, and although you could never have too much these days, they weren't the type comfortable with sitting around the house. Even after he retired, Norris was restless, which had resulted in his cross-country road trip. Keo had never thought about what he would do past his thirtieth birthday. The fact that he was still alive, with a year still to go, was a miracle.

Each time they went out, they had to go further from the house, and Keo was always wary of going too far north, which would lead them back to the interstate. So they went south instead, sometimes extending east and west, but staying mostly off the main highway that connected to Corden nearby. The smaller the roads and more isolated the homes, he found, yielded the best opportunities. Like with the cabin back at the RV park, the creatures seemed to ignore far-flung locations, which made some sense.

They feed on humans. Of course there would be more of them where humans are.

Which meant the cities, of which there weren't a lot of out

here. Earl's house, as far as Keo knew, was the only occupied home for miles in every direction.

They also traded up their vehicles, swapping Jake's bullet-riddled Chevy for a year-old Dodge Ram 1500 and Rachel's equally damaged SUV for an off-road four-door Jeep Wrangler. They stumbled across a Nissan Frontier about five kilometers from the house and added it to their collection.

Over the next few weeks, they taught Gillian and Rachel how to handle a weapon and shoot. The women were introduced to the G42, a smaller version of the Glock he and Norris were using. They didn't become Annie Oakley overnight, but they got good enough with the .380 caliber handguns that Keo felt comfortable giving them gun belts.

One week became two, and two became a month.

The creatures returned night after night, but they had stopped trying to break their way in. Not that there was much left for them to break. The windows remained broken from that first night and they had never bothered to fix them. They tried putting mesh screens in place of the broken glass, but the creatures kept destroying them, so they stopped doing that, too. There was no point anyway, with the burglar bars on the outside and the reinforced barricades inside. Closing every window and door an hour before nightfall became everyone's job, and they took it seriously.

Even in the daylight, the bloodsuckers' continued presence around the house was everywhere he looked. At night, all he had to do to was peer out the window if he forgot. They hid in the darkness of the woods, watching him back like stone sentries. And they could afford to wait because the night was theirs. He didn't even know if they could grow old and die. Did age still matter when they could exist without half of their heads?

The girls spent their nights reading books and magazines collected from supply runs, while Keo and the men either played cards or joined the others with board games. Rachel also talked about her family's home on Santa Marie Island, where she and Christine had been heading before their trip was cut short by the end of the world.

"It's beautiful there," Rachel said wistfully. "The most gorgeous place on Earth. Except during hurricane season, I mean, but you can usually ride those out unless it's a really bad one, and those are pretty rare."

"Where is it, exactly?" Keo asked.

"It's within walking distance from the main Galveston Island. You need a ferry to get there from land, unless you have a boat."

"Is it a big place?" Gillian asked. "I've never been outside of Louisiana."

"It's about five miles long, give or take," Rachel said. She looked over at her daughter with some regret. "Christine could be on the beach right now if I hadn't insisted we drive through every state in the union."

"They might be there, too," Keo said.

"Who?"

"The bloodsuckers."

"Oh." She frowned. "I didn't think about that."

"Way to be a buzzkill, kid," Norris snorted.

Keo sighed. "I'm sorry, Rachel."

"No, you're probably right." She gave him a pursed smile. "It would be nice to find out, though. Maybe my family is still there…"

"I could imagine spending the rest of my life on a beach," Gillian said. She smiled at Keo. "What about you?"

"As long as you're there," Keo said.

"Oh, barf," Lotte said.

The girls laughed, and Norris and Levy chuckled.

Keo smiled, but he looked across at Gillian. She had stopped laughing long enough to meet his gaze before returning his smile.

✳

"WE'RE ALL GOING to die," Gillian said the next morning.

She hadn't said a word before then, ever since they left the house. Keo usually walked the woods in the early mornings by himself. He always used different routes, having memorized almost every inch of the immediate area by the first month. The familiarity with their surroundings allowed him to recognize broken tree branches that weren't there the morning before, or a patch of ground that looked softer this morning because of heavy foot traffic from the previous night.

They're around. They're always around. Even when they don't attack the house, they're out here.

Keo still carried the MP5SD and Glock .45, and had added a Ka-Bar knife he had found in the basement. It was a good knife. Sharp as hell and well-balanced. He had one of the two-way radios they used to keep in constant communication when someone left the house clipped to his left hip. Levy and his friends had liberated a half dozen of them from a Radio Shack in Corden before they left town after the first night.

This morning, brittle leaves and twigs snapped loudly under Gillian as she walked beside him. The natural silence was usually one of the reasons why he came out here alone, though he found that he didn't mind all the noises she was making. Not too much, anyway. He decided to concentrate on enjoying her company instead, the way she smelled.

"You heard me, right?" she said. "We're all going to die."

"What brought this on?"

"I was thinking about Levy. The poor guy lost three of his friends last month. Think about that, Keo. They survived the end of the world, only for Earl to do something stupid like stick his hand into a doorway and get bitten. If that wasn't bad enough, Gavin and Bowe followed right along in the same day. *The same day.*" He could tell she had been thinking about it for some time. "We're just living on borrowed time, that's all. One day, like you said, someone will forget to put down one of the barricades and it'll be over."

He wasn't sure what to say, or what he could say. She wasn't wrong. Surviving the end of the world was already like winning the lottery, only to die three days later because of a dumb mistake?

Is that all this is? Borrowed time? We survive until, inevitably, we make a stupid mistake?

"Keo," she said. "Say something."

"Then we just don't make any mistakes."

"To err is to human. Isn't that the saying? Humans make mistakes. We're going to, sooner or later. It's inevitable."

"If everyone does their job, we'll be fine. We just have to remember what's at stake."

"Easier said than done. Even if all the adults do their part, the girls might miss something. They're just kids."

"They're smart kids. They'll do fine. They've been doing fine for a month now."

"It's in our human nature to be complacent. I just don't know who we're fooling. This isn't going to last."

"Maybe."

"When did you get so optimistic?"

He smiled. "The question is, why are you so pessimistic all of a sudden?"

She shrugged. "I don't know. Maybe it was listening to Rachel talk about Santa Marie Island and her family. It just occurred to me that while she was talking about seeing them again, all I could think of was how glad I am that everyone I know is already dead so they didn't have to live through this."

"Everyone?"

She nodded solemnly.

"I'm sorry," he said.

"Thanks."

"We'll be fine, Gillian. I'll make sure of that."

"You're just one person, Keo. You can't be everywhere at

once. Sooner or later, you'll forget something, too. Then what?"

"Gillian."

"What?"

"Shut up."

"Why—"

He kissed her before she could finish and then he waited for her to push him away, but when she didn't, Keo slipped his arms around her waist and pulled her tighter against his body. She moaned against his mouth and he inhaled her scent. She smelled of lavender soap, one of the few luxuries these days.

He immersed himself completely in the feel of her mouth and the surprisingly warm sensation of her skin against his. She was kissing him back, until suddenly she started to push him away. It took every ounce of strength he had to not pull her back to him.

"Keo," she said breathlessly.

"I'm sorry," he said. "I couldn't help myself."

"No, no, it's not that." She was blushing and smiling at him at the same time. "I wanted you to, anyway. It's—I should tell you something."

"Can it wait?"

He moved tentatively to kiss her again, but she put her hands on his chest and kept him back.

"Maybe... I don't know," she said.

"What is it?"

"I haven't had sex in three months."

His reaction to her confession must have been something, because she started laughing and pointing at him.

"Really?" he said.

She nodded between spurts of laughter. "You should see the look on your face right now."

"Three months? How is that possible?"

She stopped laughing long enough to say, "What do you mean?"

"You're beautiful, Gillian. How is it possible you haven't

had sex in three months? What were you doing in the two months before the end of the world?"

"Not wanting to have sex."

"Oh."

"Look, girls *can* not want to have sex, you know. It's sort of our God-given right. That and babies."

"So, it's been a while?"

She had calmed down now. "Well, three months. I guess that's a while, right? I mean, it's not like I'm a virgin or anything. I still know how to do it. It's sex. It's not rocket science."

"That's good to know," he said. Then, "Should I wait?"

"I'm surprised you waited this long to make your move. I'm kind of impressed."

"I have amazing self-control. Either that, or I'm the dumbest man alive."

"But you're not gay, right?"

"I don't think so."

"You're not sure?"

"Not that there's anything wrong with it, but no. I'm pretty sure."

"So why did you wait so long?"

"There was a lot to do. The house. The woods. The creatures in the darkness. You know, surviving and stuff."

"Oh, that old excuse."

He smiled. "That, and I didn't think you were going anywhere. Besides, it's either me, Norris, or Levy. And I was pretty sure you weren't going to end up with Norris."

"Why? I like Norris."

"He's older than dirt."

"Dirt can be sexy. And why not Levy?"

"He's too young and he didn't look like your type."

"Maybe I like them young, and what do you know about my type?"

"You're sarcastic and independent and you'd want someone

with experience. Like me."

"God, you're full of yourself."

"Am I wrong?"

"No," she said, grabbing him and kissing him.

She caught him by surprise, and Keo stumbled back and bumped into a tree. Birds took flight above him, but he wasn't listening to the flapping of wings because Gillian's mouth was crushed against his and it was all he could do to slip his arms around her waist and pull her closer.

After a moment, she broke their contact and smiled. "I always thought my first time with you would be, I don't know, more special."

"What's more special than against a tree in the woods?"

She rolled her eyes. "Charming. But I'm serious."

"So am I." He looked around at the empty woods. "We're alone out here. As long as you keep it down."

"Give me a break. You're the one who's going to be screaming for your mommy."

She untangled herself from him and he let her go—again, with a lot of effort. The sudden start and stop should have made him angry, but all it did was make him want her even more.

She leaned against the tree next to him. "I like you."

"Score."

"But I don't want to have sex with you against a tree. Face it; I'm the one who's going to get the worse of it."

"I'll be gentle."

"I'm sure you will. But still, no."

"It's not what you imagined, I get it."

"Not even close." Then she smiled at him again. "When was the last time we went out for a supply run together?"

"You and me? Never."

"Don't you think it's time? Maybe you can ask Norris if he'd rather stay at the house the next time you go out, and I can come along."

"If he says no, I'll just shoot him in the back of the head."
She laughed. "Let's try asking him first."

THEY DIDN'T MAKE mistakes. Everyone made sure of that. Keo checked everything. And when he forgot, Norris didn't. And when Norris forgot, Gillian didn't. Between the three of them, the barricades always went up an hour before nightfall and stayed up an hour after sunrise.

They also kept listening to the radios, hoping to hear something that would tell them they weren't the only people still out there. But there was nothing on the airwaves. Keo had begun to expand farther out into the woods during his morning walks. Each day, he spent anywhere from an hour to two hours just sitting quietly and listening for sounds that he didn't hear but was sure were out there.

Voices. Footsteps.

Cars.

During the early mornings, when the woods were at their most peaceful, he relived the gas station ambush in his head, replaying the images of the men in black assault vests over and over.

Who the hell were those guys?

They were out there, somewhere, likely probing the interstate for victims. Well-traveled roads, not backwoods ones that would lead them to the house, or like the ones he and Norris took. That made Corden a no-go. A city that size was a prime target for opportunists. If not the men in black, then others.

The creatures continued to probe the house and the woods at night, every night, but they were always gone by morning. There was a certain dependability to it that Keo couldn't help but feel a little comforted by.

There was also a new normal back at the house.

Lotte's leg had healed enough by the end of January that she was able to abandon the wheelchair with the help of a crutch they had found lying on a shelf in a mom-and-pop pharmacy about five kilometers from Corden. Lotte being able to move more freely meant she spent more time outside, either by herself or with Christine and Rachel. That, in turn, allowed Keo to sneak in afternoons with Gillian in her room.

They were careful, but Keo always knew it wasn't going to last forever. They had it too good. The house. The woods. The fish in the river. The stacks of supplies in the basement. It was three months going on four. It was easy living. Even boring.

And it was perfect.

Too perfect.

Keo always knew that eventually something would happen that would remind him the world was still a very dangerous place. Not just at night, but during the day, too.

CHAPTER 23

THE BARBERSHOP HAD been abandoned even before the end of the world. There were three buildings in the small strip center—a diner, the barbershop, and an empty garage that probably used to be an auto body shop at one point. It didn't look like it had much to offer even from the road, but after driving past it the last three times they came in this direction, Keo decided to stop in and search it just to be safe.

His instincts were right. There was absolutely nothing of value in any of the three buildings. But they were running out of places to search without expanding their net even wider, so it made for a minor diversion before they headed back to the house.

Keo was in the barbershop, looking out the dirt-encrusted windows at the two-lane road on the other side of the wide-open parking lot, when his radio squawked and he heard Norris's voice. "You found anything over there yet?"

"Still a big fat nothing," Keo said into the radio. "How about you?"

"We should have kept going like all the other times. There's nothing here but empty cans of motor oil." Norris was in the garage next door. "You got any use for that?"

"Not that I can think of."

"Nothing in the barbershop? Did you look in the closets in the back? How about all the drawers? There's gotta be some shaving supplies lying around. Anything?"

"This place was abandoned long ago, Norris. There wasn't anything here even before the world fell off a cliff."

"Gotta pick up some more razors."

"I'll put it on the list."

"Let's head back. I'm already starving."

"You're always starving."

"And I'd be eating right now if you didn't insist on stopping at this ghost town. Always trust your instincts, kid."

"Gee thanks, Dad," Keo said.

Norris chuckled.

He shared Norris's disappointment in the lack of barber supplies. He would have settled for a pair of styling scissors. The ones they had back at the house weren't exactly designed to cut human hair. They were mostly intended to chop away hair in huge, undesirable chunks.

Keo ran his fingers through his hair. It had been a month since he had his last haircut, and styling scissors or not, it was getting thick up there. He made a mental note to ask Rachel to cut it this afternoon. He had once made the mistake of asking Gillian, but she had proved terrible at it. The one positive from that experience was that Gillian realized her own deficiencies as a barber and refused to cut anyone's hair again.

He clipped the radio back on his hip and was walking to the door when he heard it.

Engines.

Keo darted behind the wall next to the glass curtain window that looked out at the parking lot and unslung his MP5SD. He had to squeeze into the corner to stay out of the reflecting sun and from being seen.

His radio squawked right away, and Norris, slightly hyperventilating, said, "You heard that?"

"Yeah," Keo said into the radio.

He heard the car for another few seconds before he actually saw it. A white Ford F-150 truck. It blasted up the road, going at least fifty miles an hour. It was moving too fast for Keo to have glimpsed anyone inside, though he thought he might have seen a couple of figures in the front cab. Of course, the sun was in his eyes—

Shit, Keo thought, when he heard tires squealing as the Ford's brakes engaged. *This day is going to hell fast.*

He tightened his grip on the submachine gun and raced across the room, passing cracked mirrors and a couple of reclining barber chairs that had been stripped clean of padding. He ducked behind the end of the wall counter. It was wide enough to hide his entire body, and Keo went into a crouch and peered over it just as the Ford reversed back into view.

The F-150 came to a complete stop in the middle of the road. Now that the vehicle was still, Keo could make out two figures in the front through the open passenger side window. He mouthed a cursed when the two men opened their doors and climbed out.

They were both wearing *black assault vests* over black cargo pants and long-sleeved black shirts. That combination would have been impossible a few months ago, but it was already early February and the weather had turned chilly, so the men were perfectly at home suited up like commandos on a mission even in the daytime.

Keo keyed his radio. "Can you see them?"

"No, I'm at the back of the garage," Norris said. "You got eyes on them?"

"Two. And they're wearing black assault vests."

"Wait, are they…?"

"I don't know. Maybe."

"Dammit." Then, "Just two. We can take two."

"Follow my lead."

"Roger that."

Keo clipped the radio back to his hip and watched the black-clad figures walk into the parking lot. They had left the truck idling behind them, the doors thrown lazily open. They had also unslung M4 carbines and were scanning the area as if they expected to find something.

The truck.

Earl's Bronco was sitting in the parking lot. It was also the *only* vehicle in the entire place. If the men were familiar with the strip center, they would have remembered that the parking lot was supposed to be empty from previous drive-bys.

Shit. I should have kept going. Trust your instincts next time, you idiot.

As the two men got closer, Keo saw radios Velcroed to the front of their vests and the pouches around their tactical belts bulged with spare magazines. All of that meant they had come prepared. For what, though? They were both wearing caps, and while he couldn't make out their faces under the brims, he didn't see green and black face paint.

So who were they? What were they doing in this area? Were they actually a part of the four men who had ambushed them at the gas station back in November? The assault vests looked familiar, but there were no writings or anything to indicate these men were part of an organization. Keo spent a few seconds recalling the ambush in his head again. No, the four men he saw back then didn't have any writings on their vests, either.

So what did that prove? Nothing, and maybe everything.

One of the two men was making a beeline for the Bronco with his M4 aimed at the back window while the second one remained slightly behind, pulling security. That told him they had either done this before, or they were reasonably well-trained.

As the men honed in on the Bronco, their path took them across the barbershop's window from left to right. Fortunately, Keo had parked the truck between the barbershop and the diner next door, so by the time the men reached their destination, they had left his line of sight. He couldn't see them anymore, but they couldn't see him, either, when Keo stood up and quickly ran toward the glass wall.

He ignored the door and looked out the window and to his

right. One of them was standing behind the Bronco while the second one, the closest to Keo, was moving toward the front passenger door. Both of the truck's windows were open, so the men didn't really need to get too close to peer inside.

Keo didn't wait for them to discover that the vehicle was empty and turn their attention elsewhere. He switched the MP5SD's fire selector to full-auto and pulled the trigger and shot the black-clad figure closest to him in the back. He landed three bullets while the rest missed their mark and hit the side of the Bronco with three solid *ping-ping-ping!*

He was spinning toward the second man, only to discover that his intended target was already taking aim at him with the M4.

Oh, shit.

If Keo had fired from anywhere else, it would have taken the other black-clad man at least a few seconds to track the sound of his suppressed gunfire. Unfortunately for Keo, the noise of the glass wall shattering and pelting the shredded linoleum tiles like falling rain gave away his position.

He heard a loud *pop!* and braced himself for the first bullet and the pain to follow.

Instead, Keo watched the man behind the Bronco jerk his head sideways and fall to the asphalt floor like a marionette with its strings cut. Blood spurted out of his temple and disappeared under the truck in bright red streams.

Norris appeared in Keo's peripheral vision, moving tentatively toward the two bodies. Keo climbed out through the shattered window and joined him in the parking lot. He moved quickly to the man he had shot and turned him over onto his back.

The man was still alive, and he stared up at Keo, face grimacing with pain. He looked in his thirties, and his eyes darted from Keo to Norris, then back again. He had a full stubble and his slightly fat, pale lips were trembling, as if he was trying to say something.

Keo crouched next to him, avoiding the blood pooling under the man's back. "You have a name?"

The man didn't answer. His eyes snapped to Norris before returning to Keo once again.

"You're going to die," Keo said. "Can't help you with that. But it might be awhile. I don't think I hit any major organs. Have you ever seen someone bleed to death? I have. It's going to be long and painful."

The man swallowed. "Doug," he said, stuttering out his name.

"Doug," Keo said. "I can help you with the pain."

"Do it," Doug said.

"I will, but first, how many more of you are there?"

Doug didn't answer.

"I need an answer," Keo said. "How many more of you are out there?"

"A lot," Doug said.

"How many is a lot?"

"A—" Doug didn't finish. He closed his eyes and died.

Keo sighed and stood up. "Shit."

"I thought you said it was going to be long and painful?" Norris said.

Keo shrugged. "I was just guessing."

Norris chuckled. "Man, you're evil." Then he looked at the Bronco and the holes Keo had put into the side. "And nice shooting there, Tex."

"I didn't want to take a chance I might miss with the glass between us." He looked up the parking lot at the Ford idling in the road. "Besides, I already got you a replacement."

"I can live with that trade." Norris looked over at the man he had shot. "What about them?"

"You heard Doug. There are a lot of them out there somewhere."

"Like some kind of militia, you think? I hear there are a lot of those nuts out here. Wouldn't surprise me if the assholes who took a run at us last year were one of those."

"That's possible." Keo pulled Doug's broken radio free from his vest. "These things aren't for communicating between the two of them, I know that much. They're well-prepared. I'm guessing the others know exactly where these two went this morning."

"It looked like they were headed to Corden. Maybe that's where their base is."

"Maybe, maybe not. But I got money on their friends coming to look for them when they fail to show up or answer the radio."

"So, we dump the bodies," Norris said. "Far from here. If they don't know where these two skells died, they won't know where to start looking for us. And it's a big country. You could get lost out here if you don't know where you're going."

Keo nodded. It was a solid plan. It also helped that the strip center was a good forty-five kilometers from the house.

Still, Keo didn't like what Doug had said when he asked him how many of them were out there.

"A lot," he had said.

How many was a lot?

A dozen? Two dozen?

Too many.

THEY DIDN'T WANT to take any chances that the bodies could be discovered, so they loaded them into the Bronco and Norris drove it while he followed in the Ford. They took the familiar road all the way back to the RV park where they had met Earl and his friends those months ago. Then they dumped the bodies into the river and made sure the water carried them south and out of sight before heading back. The house was up north, so there wasn't a chance the bodies would somehow show up there.

The Bronco had three holes in it that it didn't have an hour ago, but it was still in good condition as they drove it back to the house. They couldn't risk leaving the other Ford behind or ditching it somewhere where it could be found. Even if the chances were remote, the risk wasn't worth it.

Gillian saw them drive up and gave him a curious look when he climbed out of the F-150. Norris drove on and parked the Bronco with the other vehicles on the other side of the yard.

"Do we really need another truck?" Gillian asked him. "I'm pretty sure we have more cars than gas to run them at the moment."

"You can never have too many trucks," Keo said.

"Spoken like a country boy. You sure you're not originally from around here?"

"I'll re-check my family tree when I get the chance."

"So where'd you find this one?"

He told her, and watched her face get paler with every detail.

"Was it the same ones?" she asked when he was done.

"It could be. They weren't walking around with signs around their necks, but it's a hell of a coincidence if they're not from the same group."

"Do you think they were out there looking for us?"

"I don't think so," Keo said. "It's been months since that incident. I think they were doing what Norris and I were. Looking for supplies and expanding their search areas as they wear out the closer targets. Norris thinks they could be based in Corden."

Gillian crossed her arms over her chest and shivered slightly. Keo put his hands on her shoulders and kissed her forehead before giving her his best comforting smile. It wasn't nearly as convincing as he had hoped, and it showed on her face.

"We'll just have to be extra careful from now on," Keo said. "Even more than before."

"Will that be enough?"

"It'll have to be, because we don't have any choice. It's not going to get any safer out there, Gillian. We need to continually adapt if we want to keep surviving. That's the goal, right? Survive?"

She nodded and tried to smile, but it came out poorly. "Yeah, that's the goal."

"Good," he said. "Let's go tell the others."

IT BEGAN HEATING up again around March, and by April he was already walking around in T-shirts like the first few weeks when they arrived at Earl's house. The weather, though, proved unpredictable. Most days it was seventy degrees or higher, but there were times when it dipped to the mid-fifties.

Don't like the weather? Just wait an hour.

He walked his usual rounds, keeping track of where the creatures had been the previous night, using the broken branches, twigs, and impressions on the ground as markers. There was no real pattern to their movements, though that in itself was a pattern.

The winter weather of the previous months hadn't done anything to cut down on the creatures' nightly visitations. They continued to show up night after night, probing the windows and doors, looking for weaknesses. To his surprise, hearing them scurrying around outside the house at nights had ceased to strike terror in him and the others. It was now so commonplace that they were sleeping soundly through the nights.

Keo wasn't entirely sure if that was a good thing, though.

In the mornings, he still spent the same one to two hours walking the woods, listening for sounds of footsteps, for voices, or car engines that didn't belong. Like all the other times, he didn't hear anything this morning, too. That should have made him feel better, but it didn't.

He was turning to head back to the house when he saw it.

Smoke, rising lazily in the distance…

CHAPTER 24

SMOKE MEANT PEOPLE, and he knew exactly where it was coming from. The question was who was there and how many of them there were.

It took him five minutes to reach the origin of the smoke, running full sprint through the woods. Keo ran with one hand on the submachine gun and the other on his radio. "Norris, come in. Norris!"

Norris answered after a few seconds. "You sound like you're running, kid."

"Smoke in the northeast. Can you see it?"

"Wait..." A brief pause, then, "I see it. Where's it coming from?"

"The bungalow."

"I thought it was abandoned."

"It's supposed to be."

"Shit. Where are you now?"

"Almost there," Keo said. "I'm going silent. Get over here when you can."

Keo turned off the radio and put it away, then burst out of the woods and into a clearing. He went into a crouch, sucking in a lungful of air, thankful he had approached the house from the side so he could see its doors and windows, but whoever was inside probably couldn't see him. He hoped, anyway.

The bungalow was a long, squat building about twice the length of their house. The front door and windows were wide open, like the last time he saw them two weeks ago. There were too many shadows for him to see inside from thirty meters away, but there was no mistaking the gray smoke coming out of the chimney. There was definitely someone inside.

He couldn't find a vehicle anywhere, which wasn't too surprising. He would have heard a car coming, even an ATV or dirt bike, for miles in these woods. There were so few noises these days that just about anything that didn't belong—like birds chirping or squirrels scrambling across branches—would be easy to detect. Had they arrived on foot? Possibly. He had searched the entire area in the last few months, and he knew for a fact there wasn't supposed to be anyone inside the bungalow.

Keo stood up and darted across the open ground. He made it to the side of the building in less than four seconds. The nearest window was to his right and he moved toward it. He heard a faint, whispering hiss followed by the random *pop pop* and the smell of dead trees and dry twigs burning in a makeshift campfire from inside. It was a slightly chilly morning, but sixty-something wasn't nearly cold enough for a fire. Of course, they could be cooking something.

He also heard voices. A woman, saying, "...around here?"

A man answered: "Not too far from here. I only saw it from a distance, but it looked pretty livable. We should go check it out. Even if we don't stay, there could be valuable supplies lying around."

A second woman: "You said the house looked livable?"

"Better than this one," the man said.

"In good shape?"

"It had windows and everything, and I think I might have heard a generator in the back."

"That means there are already people there. It's been five months. Generators don't last that long by themselves. Did you see any cars?"

"A few trucks and some ATVs."

"Should we go see for ourselves?" the first woman asked.

"Maybe," the second woman said. "Let's just finish breakfast first, then we can decide what to do later."

Keo moved along the length of the building toward the back. He peered out at the river twenty meters through the woods and found the answer to how the people in the house had arrived here.

There was a white pole sticking out of the water near the bank, wrapped in fading blue canvas. He was looking at the mast of a sailboat, the bulk of it hidden behind the trees and ridgeline. Not a big boat. The river was only so wide that anything longer than a twenty-five-footer was probably pushing it.

A sailboat. So that meant the people in the house had been on it last night and not inside the house. How was that possible? Hadn't the bloodsuckers seen the boat last night? Of course, they could have arrived this morning...

Crack!

He turned around in time to see Norris moving through the clearing when he suddenly slid to a stop at the sound of a gunshot. At first Keo thought Norris had been hit and was falling, but no, the older man had just put the brakes on at the last second and was fighting to keep from slipping. He spun around and ran back toward the tree line.

A voice—one of the women—shouted, "Stay back! Don't come any closer!"

Keo turned the corner and headed for the back door. The bungalow had lost all of its doors years ago. That allowed Keo to look inside at a darkened hallway and make out silhouetted figures at the other end in the living room, crackling fireplace lights flickering off a woman with a shotgun and a man gripping a hunting rifle.

He slipped inside the hallway and moved toward them, glad to have darkness benefiting him for the first time in a long time. He didn't worry about the creatures, not with three humans already inside the house.

THE WALLS OF LEMURIA 235

Since that first shot, it got very quiet again. The figures in front of him seemed to be scrambling around, apparently because Norris's sudden appearance had freaked them out almost as much as their warning shot (at least, he hoped it was a warning shot) had likely put even more grays into Norris's stubble.

The Keo from five months ago would have gone into the house shooting. The MP5SD's attached suppressor would have allowed him to take out one, likely two of them before the third even knew he was inside. On full-auto, the submachine gun was a supremely deadly weapon with or without silent capabilities.

These people didn't sound dangerous, though. Overhearing their conversation had convinced him they were just looking for a place to stay for a while before moving on. It was likely they were more afraid of him and the others at the house. That, more than anything, was why he didn't go in guns blazing. He was tempted, though. After the run-in with the two men in black assault vests, he was leaning heavily toward not taking any chances.

I'm going soft. That's the only explanation.

He tightened his forefinger against the trigger when one of the women, wearing a white T-shirt, stopped moving in front of him. She was clutching a 12-gauge double-barrel shotgun with the barrels pointed up at the ceiling. She looked almost as uncomfortable with the weapon as the man with the hunting rifle, peering out the window looking for Norris across the clearing.

"Is he still out there?" the woman with the shotgun asked.

"The black guy?" the man said.

"How many are out there?"

"I just saw the one black guy."

"I think he's still out there," the other woman said from somewhere to the right of the living room. Keo couldn't see her from his position. "Did you see that gun he had?"

"Some kind of assault rifle," the man said.

"Where'd he get something like that?"

"I don't know. Maybe a gun shop?"

"Gun shops carry stuff like that?"

"Around here, I guess."

"Maybe it was a mistake to come up this far north…"

"We can always go back down."

"Yeah, we should think about that…"

Keo smelled burning fish from the living room. So that was why they had started the fireplace. Fish for breakfast.

The woman with the shotgun had moved directly in front of Keo now. He could make out the New Orleans Saints' fleur-de-lis on the back of her shirt, illuminated by the flickering fireplace light. She was shuffling her feet nervously and he was close enough that Keo could see long black hair that hadn't seen a decent shampoo in a while.

"Hey, you still out there?" the man called out the window at Norris.

There was no reply.

"I don't think he's going to say anything," the second woman said. "You did shoot at him."

"It was a mistake," the man said defensively. "I panicked when I saw him coming out of the woods."

"Did you think he was, you know, *them?*" the first woman said.

"What do you mean?"

"Because he's black."

The man didn't answer right away. Keo couldn't tell if he was turning the question over in his head or if he was slightly offended by the suggestion. He finally said, "Of course not. They can only come out at night. I knew it wasn't them. He just freaked me out running toward us with that rifle."

"Oh," the woman said, sounding slightly embarrassed.

Keo had to smile. Norris running out of the woods with an M4 would scare anyone. He wondered what the ex-cop was doing now. Maybe he was trying to reach Keo through the radio. No chance of that, since he had turned it off earlier as he approached the house. The last thing he wanted was for it to start squawking as he sneaked in to get a good look at the new occupants.

"I think he's gone," the woman whom Keo couldn't see said.

"Can't take the chance," the man said.

"Then what?"

The man shook his head. "We shouldn't have started the fire. I told you that was going to be a mistake."

"Forget about that," the woman said. There was a slight edge in her voice. "Arguing about it won't make any difference now."

"Maybe we should head back to the boat—"

Keo stepped forward and pressed the barrel of his weapon against the back of the first woman's neck. She let out a startled yelp just as Keo grabbed her shotgun with his other hand and wrenched it free from her grip. It hadn't taken much effort at all, as if she were just waiting for someone to come and take it from her. He leaned the weapon against the wall instead of tossing it to the floor. The last thing he wanted was for the 12-gauge to go off involuntarily and kill someone, especially him.

The man at the window spun around, as did the second woman—she was almost as tall as the man, both of them maybe five-eight—who moved forward holding a handgun. A six-shot revolver. Silver-chromed. Fancy. Light brown eyes pierced the semidarkness, and a long blonde ponytail whipped behind her.

They both looked young, maybe in their twenties. Keo couldn't see the face of the woman in front of him, but he guessed she was about the same age. He wondered if she was half the looker as the one pointing the handgun at them.

"What the fuck!" the woman with the gun shouted.

She wasn't really pointing the weapon at him, since Keo had slipped behind the first woman and was now using her as cover.

He was so much taller than her that he had to bend slightly at the knees, which wasn't entirely comfortable, so he hoped this wasn't going to take too long.

"He's got a gun!" the woman in front of Keo shouted.

"Oh, shit," the man said. He kept raising his rifle and lowering it, as if he couldn't quite make up his mind what to do. "Oh, shit," he said again. "What now, Jordan? What now?"

The tall woman, Jordan, held the revolver steady in her hands as she moved forward another step, trying to see Keo behind his shield. "Let her go, you asshole! Let her go right now!"

"No," Keo said.

That seemed to throw them off, and Jordan and the man exchanged a look. The woman in front of Keo was shaking badly.

"What do you mean, 'no'?" Jordan said.

"I mean no," Keo said. "N-o. The opposite of yes."

Jordan's face looked conflicted. Not quite as indecisive as the man's. His response, he guessed, wasn't what she had expected.

Finally, she just shouted again. "Let her the fuck go, asshole!"

Keo almost smiled. He could tell she was trying her best to sound tough, but it wasn't an easy thing to pull off. Her hands didn't waver and the six-shooter remained steady in front of her, which was impressive for a civilian. But did she know that if she started shooting there was a better chance she would hit her friend than him?

"Here's your problem," Keo said. "I have a gun that can fire thirty rounds with one squeeze of the trigger. As luck would have it, so does my friend back there."

The man spun around—and froze at the sight of Norris aiming his M4 through the window at him from less than a meter away.

"Lower your weapons and we won't kill you," Norris said,

the sound of his gruff voice prompting the man to toss the hunting rifle away so quickly that Keo expected an accidental discharge and was thankful there wasn't one.

The woman, Jordan, proved to be made of sturdier stuff than the man. She didn't lower her handgun, and instead glanced back at Norris, then at Keo, and back again. She looked pained from the indecision. She was clearly afraid of being shot (who wasn't?), but she was also afraid of what would happen if she did surrender. He actually felt bad for her.

Jesus, I really have gone soft.

"Relax," Keo said. "I could have killed all three of you before you even knew I was inside the house. You're still alive now because I decided we're not enemies."

"*You* decided?" Jordan said incredulously.

"Yes. I'm the one with the automatic weapon."

That seemed to placate the man. Then again, Keo guessed it wouldn't have taken much, judging by how fast he had tossed his weapon.

"Jordan, please," the man said. "You heard him. We're not enemies."

"Listen to the kid," Norris said, sounding every bit like the ex-cop that he was. "You don't want to make this any worse."

"Jordan," the man said. "Just do what they say. *Please.*"

Jordan didn't look convinced by either one of them, but he could tell she was smart and she knew there was no way out of this. Of course, he had seen very smart people do some pretty stupid things before when they thought they had no choice.

"Listen to your friend," Keo said. "Put down the gun."

Her mouth twisted into a silent scream and she actually looked even more angry. He didn't know that was even possible.

"Dammit!" she shouted, then bent her knees and slowly lowered the revolver.

"Kick it over here," Keo said. "Not that I don't trust you, but you look pissed off enough to try something stupid."

She glared defiantly at him before grudgingly kicking the revolver over.

"Good," Keo said, and let go of the woman in front of him.

She stumbled forward and ran into Jordan's arms. They embraced, Jordan still watching Keo over her friend's shoulder. The man at the window breathed a sigh of relief, and so did Norris behind him.

"Close one," Norris said.

"You okay?" Keo asked.

"Kid missed me by a mile." He grunted. "I think I almost pissed my pants, though."

"Oh, nice."

"What now?" Jordan said.

Keo remembered how Earl had treated him and the others when he found them in the basement of the RV park. Earl hadn't had to do any of those things, but he had anyway because he was a decent human being.

The legend of Earl lives on.

"Well?" Jordan said. "Are you going to shoot us now or later?"

"I like this one," Norris chuckled behind them.

"Oh, shit," the man said. He was looking over at the fireplace, at two large channel catfish spit roasting over the fire. Both fish were turning black.

Keo slung his weapon. "Let's feed you first. Then we can talk about who gets to stand where on the firing squad."

CHAPTER 25

BEING INVITED BACK to the house for breakfast after being held at gunpoint was probably not what the three newcomers had expected. It took them a few seconds to absorb the offer, then another few minutes to talk amongst themselves while Keo and Norris waited outside the bungalow. Eventually, they decided they had nothing to lose. Or Jordan decided. If he thought she was the leader when he only heard their voices, he was proven correct when he saw them together.

Afterward, Jordan and her friends, Mark and Jill, followed Keo and Norris back to the house. Keo had already called ahead on the radio, and by the time they arrived, Gillian and the others had the food laid out and waiting for them. Breakfast was MREs and canned goods that Earl and the others had raided from the same pawnshop where they got most of their weapons. There were large crates of the stuff stacked in one corner of the basement.

Jordan tackled a bag of MRE when she wasn't trying to drink them dry, while Jill and Mark hungrily spooned up fruits dripping with artificial syrup out of cans. All three looked as if they hadn't eaten anything in days, which prompted Keo to wonder what they had been surviving on all this time. They didn't look malnourished exactly, but not entirely healthy, either.

He and the others sat and stood around the newcomers, watching them devour everything put in front of them. It had been such a long time since they'd interacted with anyone from outside the house that the three friends' presence created a noticeable spark of energy. If Jordan and her friends noticed the attention, they didn't react to it. Then again, they were probably too busy eating and drinking.

"How long have you guys been staying here?" Jordan asked.

"We got here a few days after all of this began," Keo said. "We've been here since."

"I don't blame you for not leaving this place. I mean, look at it. Besides supplies, you've got fish in the river and hunting grounds, right?"

"Not so much the hunting grounds."

"No?"

"We think the creatures fed off most of the land-based wildlife. The ones that can't climb, anyway."

"You guys must be really hungry," Gillian said with a smile.

Jordan blushed a bit. "We ran out of supplies about a month ago. We've been traveling up the river since, picking up useful things where we can and staying on land occasionally. But most of the time we stay on the boat. We have some fishing poles onboard that we use to catch fish along the banks."

"How do you sail upriver?" Keo asked.

"If there's enough wind blowing in the right direction, you can sail anywhere," Mark said.

"Mark's the expert," Jordan said. "You have any boat questions, you should ask him. Jill and I are just along for the ride."

"Where did you guys come from?" Gillian asked.

"We were at Lake Pontchartrain in New Orleans when all of this happened," Jordan said. "The only reason we're still alive is because we were on Mark's boat when it started."

"The boat belongs to my dad," Mark said. He tilted his can and sucked down the remaining juices, then wiped his mouth on the back of his hand. "I've been boating with him since I was ten."

"The river comes all the way up here?" Keo asked.

THE WALLS OF LEMURIA 243

"It goes everywhere," Jordan said. "There are dozens of large and small veins. We just followed it north as far as it would take us."

"Why north?"

"South's the Gulf of Mexico."

"Ah."

"We wanted to find out if anyone else was still out here, and going inland seemed the best option."

"Those first few weeks were rough," Mark said. "We kept waiting to hear about what had happened. Waited for the state or the government to come in and tell us what to do. But they never did. And the city…"

"Have you ever seen a city like New Orleans empty in the middle of the day?" Jordan asked.

"Can't say I have," Keo said.

"It's spooky. Like walking through a cemetery." She paused for a moment. "They almost caught us the first night…"

"They got Rick and Henry," Jill said. Her voice was squeaky, as if she was afraid to talk too loudly. Keo guess that was a habit from being "out there."

"Yeah," Jordan said, and went back to her MRE bag of beef stew without elaborating.

Keo exchanged a brief glance with Norris and Gillian. No one had to tell them what had happened to Rick and Henry. Everyone knew. They still remembered the first night vividly, almost half a year later. It was hard to forget when you discovered everything you thought you knew about the universe was wrong.

Jordan stood up from the living room couch where she had been sitting with the others and walked over to one of the windows. She rasped her knuckles on the thick block of wood on top of it. "This is how you keep them out?"

Keo nodded. "That and the bars."

"I've seen them break down doors, but this stops them? The burglar bars and this block of wood?"

"We've been here since November of last year. So yeah, they work pretty well."

"It's a hell of a place you guys got here. I can see why you didn't keep moving."

"Definitely more leg room than in Mark's boat," Jill said.

"Speaking of the boat," Rachel said. She had kept quiet all this time that the sound of her voice surprised Keo a bit. "Have you ever heard of Santa Marie Island?"

Mark looked up from rooting around his empty can of fruit. "Santa Marie Island? Near Galveston?"

"Yes!"

"My dad took me sailing around the Gulf of Mexico when I was fifteen. We stopped by Galveston for a while. One of the islands we passed along the way was Santa Marie. It looked like a nice stretch. Plenty of marinas to dock."

"You can get there from New Orleans?" Keo asked.

"If it's in the Gulf of Mexico, you can get to it by boat," Mark said. "My dad and I have even crossed the Panama Canal once or twice and sailed the Pacific Ocean."

"So you can sail to Santa Marie Island from here?" Rachel asked.

"It'd take weeks and we'd need a lot of supplies and good wind, but yeah, I don't see why not. And if we could find fuel, we would get there faster using the outboard motor, but we try to limit it to emergencies."

"Why the river?" Keo asked.

"What about it?" Jordan said.

"You guys said you've stayed on the river since New Orleans. Since all of this began, except for the occasional supply runs on land, or like back at the bungalow to cook the fish. So why the river?"

Jordan, Mark, and Jill exchanged a brief look.

"You don't know?" Jordan said to Keo.

"Know what?"

"It's the water."

"What about it?"

"They won't cross it," Jordan said. "Even back at Lake Pontchartrain. We could see them on the shore, watching us at night, but they never tried to attack the boat. It doesn't matter how close we get to land; as long as we're on the water, they stay away. I think they're afraid of it."

"'It'?"

"The water."

"Why?"

"I haven't a clue. They just are."

"Sonofabitch," Norris said. Then to Keo, "Did Levy say anything about Earl keeping a boat around here?"

"He said Earl didn't," Keo said.

"Speaking of which, where is Levy?" Gillian asked.

Keo looked around them. He swore he had seen Levy standing around and listening to the conversation just a few minutes ago. Where the hell did he sneak off to, and how did no one notice until now?

KEO WALKED WITH Jordan back to the bungalow. She was wiping oily fingers from some potato chips she had eaten back at the house on already-dirty jeans, while well-worn sneakers caked in dirt and mud *crunched* the morning ground.

"Mark and Jill trust you," Keo said.

"I guess," she said, though she didn't look comfortable admitting it.

"Was it always like that?"

"No. Rick was supposed to be it. We depended on him the first few days while trying to figure out what the hell was going on. But after he...what happened to him, happened, someone had to step up. I guess that was me."

"You're doing a pretty good job."

"Maybe..."

"You've kept them alive all these months. That's no small accomplishment."

"Yay me," Jordan said. She glanced up at the trees, at the birds in flight, and the animals perched on tree branches without a care in the world. "You said they're feeding off the animals too?"

"I think that's a fair bet. There hasn't been a single deer in these woods, and Levy says there are supposed to be a lot of them."

"Levy's the one that snuck off when no one was paying attention?"

"Yeah."

"Strange kid."

"Kid?" he smiled.

She grinned sheepishly back at him. "I guess we're about the same age." Then she looked around her again. "Do you think they do to the animals what they do to us? I mean, turn them?"

"I don't think so. At least, I haven't seen one yet. Then again, sometimes it's hard to tell what those things used to be once they've turned."

"Yeah, I guess you're right. Once...one night I saw one of them come very close to us along the banks. It didn't attack, because like I said, they never do, but this one was watching us very curiously. You know what I mean?"

"Not really."

"Like it *knew* us. Or recognized us." She went quiet for a moment, and there was just the sound of their footsteps. Then, "Afterward, I thought that it could have been Rick. Or Henry." She shook her head. "But it couldn't be. Like you said, once they turn, it's hard to tell them apart, or if they're even male or female."

Keo couldn't help but think about Delia. Or the thing that used to be Delia. If it was still alive, it was probably still out there right now, somewhere...

"Hey," Jordan said.

"What?"

"What kind of name is Keo, anyway?"

"Paul was taken," he said.

THE BOAT WAS a twenty-two footer, just over six and a half meters long, with an almost two-and-a-half meter beam. The white paint had seen plenty of activity, including overlapping and month-old dirt-caked shoe prints along the deck stretching from bow to stern. Mud clung to the sides, and the cabin was visible through long windows on the sides and front. It was in reasonably good shape.

"It looks like a tight squeeze," Keo said.

He stood on the bank looking down at the boat, anchored in place against the soft river current, just within climbing distance from land.

"The five of us spent a whole day in and around it before everything went to shit," Jordan said, standing next to him. "It was a pretty tight squeeze, even with Mark and Henry spending most of the time on deck."

"What about the motor?"

"We still have some fuel left for it. Not much, but some. We grabbed as much as we could from the marina back at Pontchartrain, but we don't use it unless we absolutely have to. Mark is really good at sailing with just the wind."

"Have the creatures ever tried to board the boat in any way?"

She shook her head. "I told you, they have a thing about the water. They'll go right up to it—along the banks, like where we are now—but they never step foot *into* the water. There were times when we came so dangerously close to land that I was sure they might try to leap onboard. I mean, it wouldn't have been much of a risk because they would have made it easily."

"But they didn't."

"Never. Not once. I used to spend days and weeks trying to understand it. Now, I just accept it as a gift from the gods and move on."

"So we now know they have two Achilles' heels: sunlight and bodies of water."

"What about that?" she asked, nodding at the MP5SD slung over his back.

"I'd like to tell you the thirty rounds make a difference, but they don't. I emptied half the magazine into one of them at point-blank range. It just gave me an annoyed look and went on about its business."

"But it's so awesome looking."

He chuckled.

"You got another one?" she asked.

"You like guns?"

"I hate guns. But I hate dying more."

"I don't think there's another one in the basement, but we can probably get you something equally awesome looking."

"Cool." Then, "You never told me how you guys found this place."

He told her about leaving Bentley, then meeting Earl, Gavin, Bowe, and Levy.

"Doesn't sound like you guys have had it too bad," she said.

"You've met others before us?"

"A few. A couple of them took some pop shots at us. I don't know why. They just opened fire. We became leery of other survivors real fast after that."

"But you still kept moving north on the river."

She shrugged. "I guess we were hoping we might find some non-assholes still hanging around. Hope springs eternal, I guess. It's disappointing, you know?"

"What's that?"

"Most of the planet's dead, and we still can't completely trust the few human beings that are still around. That's why it took me so long to put down my weapon back there."

He nodded. "I understand."

Then she narrowed her eyes at him. "So what's the deal?"

"Deal?"

"I know you didn't ask me here just to show you the boat. That's Mark's department. Jill and I just try to stay out of his way when we're on the water. So what's on your mind, Keo?"

Smart girl.

"What are the chances you, Mark, and Jill are staying with us?" he asked.

"Are you kidding? Did you see the two of them back there? You're going to need a crowbar to pry us away."

He laughed.

"So what's the catch?" she asked.

"You said the boat can fit five comfortably?"

"Comfortably," she nodded. "But you can squeeze more in there if you need to."

"How many more?"

"How many you got?"

He nodded. "A couple of days after all this began, we were heading for Fort Damper to find some answers. On the way over, we were ambushed by men with assault rifles at a gas station along the interstate. Like you said, it's still hard to trust people these days. That's why I think we should talk about an exit strategy, in case we ever need one."

"And you want to use the boat for that?"

"I think it's perfect, don't you?"

"Maybe. What's in this for us?"

"I'll let you stay at the house."

"You mean you weren't going to before?"

"Not if you said no to my offer."

She smirked. "Some Good Samaritan you turned out to be."

"Nothing in life's for free, Jordan. Especially these days. So, you wanna hear the details?"

She nodded. "I'm listening…"

CHAPTER 26

THE CREATURES CAME out in force that night. Keo wondered if it was because they knew *(somehow)* that there were more people in the house than in previous nights. He didn't need to look through the peepholes to know that there were a lot more of them out there than there had been the last few months. He could hear them moving around, sometimes rattling the metal bars.

Still probing. Still looking for a weakness, for a mistake…

Keo and Norris gave the room that they had been sharing so Jordan and Jill could have it, while Mark slept in the living room with them. To Keo's surprise, none of the three friends were sleeping together, though it was obvious Mark had some affections for both girls. They didn't share his feelings, apparently, even after five months of being crammed in the same boat.

Jordan told him as much when he asked about it one day.

"No," she had said.

"No?" he had repeated.

She rolled her eyes. "He's a guy. Of course he wanted to. But he's our friend. We've known him since high school. It's one of the reasons we all ended up at Tulane University. Rick and I were a couple, and Jill had Henry. Mark was always sort of the odd man out." She had shrugged then. "I mean, I don't know, maybe Mark and I might have gotten together eventually. Or he and Jill. It just hasn't happened yet, that's all."

Keo was impressed with Mark's self-control. Both Jordan and Jill were attractive women, and to live in the same twenty-two foot space with them day and night for five months with nothing happening was a hell of a feat. Keo wasn't sure if he could have lasted more than a few months. Just one month of waiting for Gillian had been torture.

With Keo and Norris back in the living room, that left Levy as the only man in the house with his own room. For his part, Levy didn't seem to have any problems with three new people joining them. Keo had expected at least some token hostility toward the idea, but Levy was surprisingly fine with it.

Mark's boat was moved over from the bungalow and tied out back at the pier behind the house. Keo and Jordan made arrangements to squirrel away supplies in the boat in case of emergencies. They didn't worry about someone stealing it. Anyone who got close enough to do that would probably try to take the house instead. Besides, a boat was not like a car; you needed to know more than just how to steer it in order to "drive" one.

Keo and Norris taught Jordan, Mark, and Jill how to shoot with weapons from the basement, though mostly it was just Jordan and Mark. Jill didn't have her heart in the lessons and after a while, they stopped insisting she keep it up. Jordan showed tremendous promise, even more so than Mark. For some reason, Keo wasn't surprised by that. Jordan, he thought, was the kind of woman who could do just about anything, given the time and necessity.

The world had come to an end going on six months when Jordan was comfortable enough with her Glock to ask to go out on supply runs with him. Her presence allowed Keo to leave Norris back at the house, which made both him and the ex-cop feel better. After the run-in with the two men in assault vests, Keo was always worried about leaving the house undefended. As comfortable as Gillian and Rachel had become with their weapons, there was a stark difference between shooting at trees in the woods and shooting a living, breathing target.

Keo and Jordan were coming back from one of their supply runs when the radio Keo always kept on the dashboard of the Bronco squawked, and he heard Gillian's voice: "Keo. Are you back yet?"

He picked up the radio. "We're coming up the trail now. What's up?"

"It's Levy," Gillian said. "Rachel found out where he's been spending all his time."

Levy.

"That doesn't sound good," Jordan said from the front passenger seat.

"Nope," Keo said.

Levy had been spending more and more time alone and away from them these days. It was easier to lose track of him with three more new bodies around, but on the days when Keo noticed that Levy wasn't there, it always struck him as odd that the guy simply disappeared without telling anyone. There were even times when Levy beat Keo out of the house in the mornings, which meant he had to have been up pretty early. Levy always came back hours later, though, and he always seemed in a good mood. That, more than anything, convinced Keo that the kid was okay.

Now, though, he wasn't so sure, especially when he heard the anxiety in Gillian's voice.

"Is it bad?" he said into the radio.

"It's pretty bad," Gillian said. "Hurry back."

CURIOSITY HAD GOTTEN the better of Rachel, but coincidence offered her the opportunity.

"She was in the back, washing the girls' clothes in the river this morning," Gillian said. "Levy came out and didn't see her. I guess she was just curious about where he goes all day, so she decided to follow him."

"And he didn't notice?" Keo asked.

He was in the front yard with Norris and Gillian. Jordan was there, along with Mark, but Jill was inside the house somewhere with the girls. She had become very close to Lotte and Christine in the last few weeks.

"I guess not," Gillian said.

"She can be pretty light on her feet," Norris said.

"She came back about an hour ago," Gillian added.

"Where is she now?" Keo asked.

"She was telling us about what she saw when she started throwing up. She's in the house changing her clothes—"

Rachel came out before Gillian could finish. "I'm okay," she said. "I just had to get myself together, that's all. Sorry, Gillian."

Gillian rubbed the other woman's shoulders. "Don't be. Are you sure you're okay?"

Rachel nodded, but she didn't look close to being okay. Keo had never seen her so pale.

"You don't have to come," Keo said to Rachel. "I think I know the house you're talking about. Norris and I could probably go there by ourselves."

She tried to smile. "I'm fine, Keo. Let's just go."

"All right. Lead the way, then."

She started off with Norris.

Keo turned to follow when Gillian reached for his arm. "Be careful. And remember what he's been through, okay?"

He nodded. "I'll be on the other side of the radio if you need me." He looked at Jordan. "Keep an eye out."

"Don't worry about us," Jordan said.

Keo jogged after the others, catching up to Norris and Rachel halfway to the tree line. "How far?" he asked Rachel.

"I think about half a mile," she said. "I almost gave up following him a couple of times because he just kept walking. I guess this is why it takes him so long to come back every day."

"And he didn't see you?"

"No. I think he was too busy with…whatever he was think-ing about." Rachel looked down at her hands, which were shaking a bit. She stuffed them into her pockets. "It wasn't wrong, was it? That I followed him? I was just curious where he went every day, and it was the first time I saw him leave the house."

"Don't beat yourself up over it," Norris said. "I would have followed him too, if I could wake up early enough to see him leave the house."

Rachel clearly knew where she was going, and looking around them, Keo could spot shoe prints along the slightly damp ground. Some were fresh, but many had been tread over the weeks and months. This was definitely where Levy had gone every morning.

After about thirty minutes of walking in almost near silence, Rachel slowed down. Keo recognized the area, and as they stepped out of the woods and into a clearing, he saw the familiar carcass of a burnt out two-story house and the unattached two-car garage next to it. The garage was the only thing still standing, and the last time Keo had stumbled across the property during one of his scouting passes, there had been a rectangular hole where a door used to be. That hole was now covered up with a partially burnt door still bearing the scars from the fire that had gutted the house next to it. The padlock over it was new, though.

As they got closer, Keo saw jagged gutters along the surface of the door, and it took him a moment to realize they were actually created by clawing fingers. Someone (*somethings*) had been trying to get into the garage very recently.

Rachel stopped between the woods and the garage, and Keo and Norris stopped with her. She gave him a hesitant look. "He's in there."

"Is he alone?" Norris asked.

She shook her head. "No."

"Okay, kid, you did your job, now stay here," Norris said.

She nodded gratefully and took a step back. Keo expected her to turn and run back to the woods at any second, but she didn't. She wanted to, though. He could see that much in her eyes.

He and Norris exchanged a look, then they walked the rest of the way to the garage. Norris had subconsciously (or maybe purposefully?) slid his M4 from behind him to the front. Keo made a conscious effort to leave his MP5SD where it was, behind his back. He didn't want Levy to see the two of them on approach with weapons at the ready.

"Be careful. And remember what he's been through, okay?"

They were five meters from the door when it opened and Levy stepped outside.

He didn't look surprised to see them, and Keo guessed he had either spotted them coming or heard them talking to Rachel. Sounds carried these days.

Levy was smiling at them, but the important thing was that he wasn't reaching for his sidearm. "What are you guys doing here?"

"What's in the garage, Levy?" Norris asked.

"The garage?"

"Yeah, the garage. What's inside?"

Levy looked past them and at Rachel. Keo couldn't tell if that was anger, indifference, or amusement playing across his face.

"Levy," Keo said, drawing his attention back to them. "Show us what's in the garage."

He looked indecisive, and for a moment Keo thought he might reach for the Glock in his hip holster. Levy always left with his AR-15, but it was nowhere to be seen at the moment.

"Levy," Keo said again. "Show us the garage."

"You want to see the garage?" he asked.

"Yeah," Norris said.

"Okay, then. Come see what's in the garage."

He turned around and led the way. Keo and Norris followed. Rachel, not surprisingly, hadn't gotten any closer. She looked rooted to the ground behind them.

Levy opened the garage door and disappeared inside, leaving the door open invitingly for them. They went inside, but they hadn't gone more than a few feet before Keo smelled it.

It wasn't a smell you ever forgot. Like rotten cabbage inside a trash Dumpster left out in the sun for too long. As physically nausea-inducing as anything he had ever had the displeasure of sniffing. He remembered it from the motel that night, then from the police station in Bentley during the attack. It was unmistakable, and it assaulted his senses like sharp knives. Even breathing through his mouth did little to deter it now that it had invaded his system.

"Jesus, Levy," Norris said. "What the fuck?"

It took a few seconds before Keo's eyes could adjust to the semidarkness inside the two-car garage. One half of the room was filled with piles of burnt furniture, most of them still covered with the heavy plastic tarps Keo had discovered when he first looked through the building months ago. It was the unoccupied half of the structure that drew his attention.

Keo knew what he would see there before his eyes became accustomed to the dim lighting. The stench had given it away. He just wasn't sure how he would react, and it took everything he had not to throw up.

It was perched in the corner, which allowed it to stay as far away from the sunlight pouring in through holes in the roof and along the walls. A metal spike had been driven into the floor and was connected to a thick rawhide rope that disappeared into the darkened corner. Inside the small section of blackness, Keo heard movement. The dirty, mud-caked rope, in response, slithered against the ground.

"I found them in here," Levy said. "There were two of them. What I think happened was, they must have overslept and got stuck inside after sunrise. Did you know they could oversleep? I was surprised, too."

THE WALLS OF LEMURIA   257

Overslept?

Keo wasn't sure if Levy sounded desperate to believe his own explanation, or if he had actually gone off the deep end. Oversleeping was a human trait, and what was inside that corner was *not* human.

Or at least, not anymore.

"At first, I thought about shooting them," Levy continued, "but I realized that wouldn't have done anything. And they couldn't hurt me. Not in the daytime, anyway. All I had to do was stay in the light. That was before I found a way to capture them. It wasn't easy, but with a little ingenuity and patience, it all worked out."

Keo took out his flashlight and clicked it on. He splashed the bright LED beam into the corner, illuminating the creature hiding within.

He didn't know what he expected to see exactly, but the shriveled, emaciated thing that looked back out at him wasn't the least bit frightened by the light. It bared its devastated teeth, oozing black liquid dripping from rotting gums. A single black eye glistened, as if wet. Where the other eye should be, there was just a malformed hole. The end of the rope was wrapped tightly around its throat, so constricting that black blood coated the part where the rawhide bit into its flesh. Its entire left arm was missing.

"You said there was two," Keo said.

"I had to kill the other one three weeks ago," Levy said. "Just to be sure."

"Be sure of what?" Norris said.

"That they don't regenerate after death. Or re-death, I guess," Levy said, and grinned oddly at them. He didn't seem to notice the smell.

How long has he been in here with this thing, doing God knows what, that he doesn't even smell it anymore?

"I've been thinking about it, you know," Levy continued. "Since what happened to Earl, Gavin, and Bowe. What do we really know about them? Not much. It's all just guesses. So I did some tests."

"What kind of tests?" Keo asked, though he wasn't entirely sure he wanted to know the answer.

"I started with the first one. Cut its limbs off one by one."

Levy walked over to the wall and unhooked a machete hanging from one of many hooks that hadn't been there when Keo checked the garage previously. The baseball bat was also new, as were the ax, the hand saw, the pruning saw, the sickle, the hedge shears, and what looked like some kind of makeshift spear on a wooden pole. It was like looking at a medieval armory. The only thing missing were shields, but Keo guessed Levy didn't need that when his victims were tied up.

Levy returned with the machete. The blade was sharp and glinted against the stray beams of sunlight. He swung it around, the *whup-whup* eliciting a shuffling movement from the creature in the corner of the room.

It knows what that noise means...

"I even decapitated it," Levy said. "Not that it did any good. Do you know they can still live even after you chop off their heads?"

Keo thought he heard Norris swallowing loudly behind him.

"It's crazy," Levy continued. "I swear, the blood was moving by itself. *By itself.*"

"How?" Keo said.

"I don't know. I took Science and Biology in school like everyone else, but this is beyond me." He grinned that strange grin again. "But it's interesting, isn't it? I mean, these things...they're like a new race. Where did they come from? *How* did they come to be? Maybe I'll write a book."

"And?" Keo said. "What did you find out after...all of this?"

A part of him was intrigued, the other half horrified by what he was hearing. And yet, and yet, wasn't Levy right? What *did* they know about the creatures? Most of it was trial and error.

What else could they know about the enemy?

What was that line by Sun Tzu from *The Art of War*?

Something about knowing your enemy and blah blah blah.

Close enough.

"It's kind of disappointing," Levy said. He walked back to the wall and put the machete away. "They don't grow back their limbs. When they're exposed to sunlight, it's gone. There are just the bones left." Levy looked down at the floor. Keo wondered if that was where the dead *(again)* creature's severed limbs had been twenty-one days ago. "I just had to make sure, though."

"Be careful," Gillian had said. *"And remember what he's been through, okay?"*

He wondered if Gillian ever thought *this* was what Levy was up to. It sure as hell had caught him off guard. The kid didn't look like he had the makings of a Josef Mengele. Keo didn't think Levy could have been the Nazi doctor's unwitting assistant.

And yet here he was, talking about torturing these undead things like it was the most natural thing in the world.

Kid's come a long way from that first night.

"How long has this been going on?" Keo asked.

"I found them six weeks ago." He looked into the corner at the remaining bloodsucker. If the creature didn't react at all to Keo, he thought he sensed a bit of fear coming off it now, directed at Levy. "I've been taking my time with this one. I don't want to just kill it. That's not going to get us anything."

"'Us'?" Norris said. "I didn't know there was an 'us' in any of this, kid."

Levy gave Norris an almost hurt look. "We're all in this together, Norris. Aren't we? The more we learn about these things, the better we can protect ourselves and keep what happened to Earl, Bowe, and Gavin from ever happening again. Isn't that what we want?" He turned to Keo. "Isn't that what we all want, guys?"

Keo exchanged a brief look with Norris. He couldn't quite tell what was going on in the ex-cop's head at the moment. Norris looked almost pained by the whole thing.

"Now what?" Keo said to Levy. "What are you going to do with it?"

"What I've been doing," Levy said. He glanced over at his wall of weapons. "I haven't used everything on it yet, and I have a lot of ideas I want to try." Then he looked back at them and narrowed his eyes with suspicion. "You're not going to stop me, are you?"

"This isn't right," Norris said.

"What do you mean?"

"You can't do this…"

"I'm trying to find a way to save us."

"By torturing it?"

"That's not what I'm doing," Levy said. He sounded exasperated, as if he couldn't believe he was being forced to explain something that should have been readily obvious to them. "It's already dead," he said. "You can't torture something that's already dead."

"HE'S ALREADY KILLED one of them?" Gillian asked.

"The way he said it, it was an accident," Keo said. "When he cut off its head, the rest of the body stumbled into the sunlight and…well, you know what happened then."

"They vaporize."

"Yes."

"And he told you he wanted to see if they would regenerate?"

"That's what he said."

"What about the head?"

"He said he kept it around for a while…"

Gillian was speechless for a moment, and remained sitting

on her bed looking across the room at him. Keo wasn't entirely sure what Gillian was thinking. Maybe she was wondering if he were crazy, too.

Just like Levy.

"I told you it wasn't pretty," Keo said.

"Maybe I should go talk to him," Gillian said softly.

"And say what? 'How's the experiment on the undead things going today, Levy?'"

She gave him an annoyed look. "So what do you think we should do about him?"

"I think we should leave him alone."

"How can you say that? He's *torturing* those things out there, Keo."

"Thing. There's just one left."

"You know what I mean."

"Look, we hardly knew the guy before he lost everything. For all we know, losing Earl, Bowe, and Gavin all in the same day was too much for him to handle, and this is his way of making sense of it. Maybe he just needed a mission, and this is it. I'm frankly shocked the guy lasted this long. I expected him to do something this insane months ago."

"Do you think he's dangerous?"

"To who?"

"Us. The girls. In general, I mean."

"I don't know," Keo said honestly.

"We have to do something. He goes to it every day, and he stays with it for hours. I don't want to think about what he does to it."

"It can't die."

"I know that, Keo. But he does *things* to it. It's not right."

"It's already dead."

"Keo, stop justifying it."

He sighed. "I'm not."

"Aren't you?"

"I…" He stopped himself.

Was he justifying Levy's actions? Maybe. He knew one thing: The old Keo would have had no trouble with what Levy was doing now. That Keo would want to know everything about the enemy. Even if nothing was learned, and even if all of it was Levy's crazy way of coping with his friends' deaths, the ultimate goal wasn't a bad one.

Maybe I haven't gone all that soft, after all.

"What should we do, Keo?" Gillian said, watching him closely.

"We should leave him alone," Keo said. "He's not hurting anyone."

"What about it?"

"What about it?"

"He's hurting it."

"It's already dead, Gillian. He can't hurt it anymore than that."

"But you don't *know* that. Maybe they still feel pain and fear. We don't know for sure that they don't."

He recalled the creature shifting inside the dark corner of the garage when Levy whipped the machete in the air...

"I don't know," Keo said. "Anything's possible with these things. Levy's right about one thing: What do we know about them? Practically nothing. Where they came from, *how* they came to be."

"Be serious, Keo. Levy's just a country kid pulling wings off flies. He's not going to discover anything groundbreaking about their origins." She stood up and walked over to the window and looked out the burglar bars at the woods outside. "This is nuts," she said after a while.

"Which part?"

"All of it." She sighed. "This is sick. You have to know that." She looked over at him, and he could see the pleading in her eyes. "Please tell me you know that, Keo."

He nodded. "I do."

She looked relieved, before turning back to the window.

Did he really know that what Levy was doing was sick, though? Keo guessed his values were a little out of whack compared to someone as upright as Gillian. Or Norris, Rachel, and everyone else in the house, for that matter. He hadn't exactly had to make a lot of moral decisions in his life. It had always been a matter of doing what the organization tasked him with. This was uncharted territory. He was being asked to make decisions about people's lives, and the strangest part was, no one was even paying him to do it.

Tread carefully, pal. Really carefully.

"Norris and I will keep an eye on him," Keo said. "We'll make sure he doesn't do anything that'll hurt us."

"What happens if he goes...over the line?"

The line? Where's that, exactly? Who knows where the line begins and ends these days.

"We'll deal with it when that happens," Keo said. "I'll deal with it."

CHAPTER 27

LEVY WAS A problem, even if Keo couldn't convince himself what the kid was doing back in that garage was entirely wrong. Doing something about it, though, was where things got murky. Keo wasn't convinced he should stop Levy. What did it really matter to the house what Levy did with his free time? As long as the *thing* in the garage was half a mile away from them. That was probably all that mattered. Wasn't it?

"That kid's trouble," Norris said.

"Trouble or troubled?" Keo said.

They were outside the house, looking in the direction where they knew Levy had gone again this morning.

"Both," Norris said, sipping the instant coffee from the same white and yellow LSU Tigers mug he had rescued from a convenience store.

"What did you used to do with troubled kids back when you were walking the beat, old timer?"

"Put them in a hospital."

"With your nightstick?"

"Yeah, that too."

Keo chuckled. "Not a lot of hospitals around anymore. What are we going to do? Arrest him for kidnapping? Read him his Miranda rights? Sic the United Nations on him for war crimes again non-humanity?"

Norris grunted. "I'm telling you, kid. I've seen this before."

"This?"

"Not *this*, this. But the same ballpark. People ignoring all the obvious signs that someone's headed for trouble. It only encourages them."

Maybe Norris was right. Gillian seemed to think so. But she didn't have any answers either, and from the sounds of it, neither did Norris. What exactly were they going to do with Levy if they did decide he was too dangerous? If his "experiments" came home to roost? He recalled those scratches on the garage door. Were the other creatures trying to get in to save their own?

There you go again, assigning them human behavior. They're not human anymore. Get that through your head.

"You know I'm right about this," Norris said.

"Knowing and doing something about it are two different beasts."

"You gotta make the decision."

Keo stared at him. "Me?"

"Yeah, you."

"Why am I the one who has to make a decision?"

"You're the de facto leader, aren't you?"

"When the hell did that happen?"

Norris shrugged and sipped his mug. "I guess it was that night back in November when you told us how it was going to go down. You basically set yourself up as our fearless leader."

"Not on purpose."

"Maybe not, but there it is."

"And you approve?"

"I'm already too old for this shit. I'm basically Murtaugh to your Riggs."

"Rigs what?"

"Riggs. R-i-g-g-s. You know, *Lethal Weapon*?"

"What is that?"

"It's a buddy cop movie from the '80s." Norris grunted. "You've never seen it."

"I don't watch a lot of movies," Keo said. "When I do, I try to watch one made after I was born."

"You're missing out."

"What was it about?"

"These two diametrically opposed guys who also happen to be cops. One's insane and single, the other's by the book and married with children. They're thrown into a situation where they basically have to trust one another with their lives. Hard to do since they're so different and all, which is where the movie's conflict comes in. You've really never seen it?"

"Nope. So, Murtaugh and Riggs?"

"Yeah. One was an over-the-hill black guy. Like me. The other was a loose cannon white guy with a death wish. Like you."

"I'm not white," Keo grinned.

"You're half white, so that makes me half right."

"Question."

"Shoot."

"Did Murtaugh and Riggs live at the end of the movie?"

"Oh, hell yeah. They even did three sequels in the next ten years after the first one."

"Ten more years?" Keo said. "I'd take that. Hell, I'd take five more years."

"That's the spirit, kid; think high."

"You don't understand, old timer. The things I've done, even before all of this…" He shook his head. "The fact that I've survived this long is a miracle."

"Like I said, loose cannon with a death wish." He slurped his coffee. It was probably already cold by now. "On the plus side, we know where he goes now."

"Are we still talking about Levy?"

"No, the Pope." He wrinkled his nose like he had an itch. "It's a mistake. What's happening back there at the garage isn't helping us, but it could hurt us. Karma's a bitch, kid. If we let him keep doing what he's doing, how does that make us better than the Nazis during World War II?"

"You sound like you've been thinking about this for a while."

"It's a problem. Can't just stick your head in the sand and pretend what he's doing isn't wrong."

Keo nodded. "Maybe you're right..."

"It's been known to happen."

Keo noticed that Norris's beard had become less salt and pepper and almost entirely gray these days. "You getting any sleep?"

"As much as the rest of you, I guess. Gotten a few more extra hours since Jordan and the others showed up." He shrugged. "I don't think I've had a full night's sleep since all of this began."

"Yeah. Me, neither."

"What kind of night's sleep you think Levy gets every day?"

"I don't know. He seems pretty damn cheery in the mornings, though."

Norris snorted. "Maybe we should ask him what his secret is."

"I would," Keo said, "but I'm a little afraid he might tell me."

THINGS WITH LEVY came to a head two weeks later and caught everyone off guard, especially Keo. He would have been fine spending the rest of his life not having to deal with the "Levy Problem," as it had become known around the house when Levy wasn't around. Reality, unfortunately, had its own ideas.

With no supply runs scheduled for the day, Keo was walking the woods when his radio squawked and he heard Gillian's voice, panicked, but clearly doing her best to stay calm.

"Keo. Please come in."

"I'm here," Keo said. "Are you okay?"

"I'm fine, but Lotte's missing."

"What do you mean, 'missing'?" Norris asked through the radio.

"I mean she's not here, and no one's seen her since this morning," Gillian said.

Keo began jogging through the woods back toward the house, while Norris said through the radio, "Didn't I see her this morning during breakfast?"

"No," Gillian said, "she wasn't there. I didn't realize that until an hour ago. She usually has coffee with me and Rachel."

"And Rachel hasn't seen her either?" Keo asked into the radio.

"No," Gillian said. "No one has. And I asked everyone, including Christine. No one has seen her, guys." Then, more panicked, "Hurry, Keo."

"I'm coming," Keo said.

He put the radio away and ran faster.

GILLIAN AND RACHEL, along with Jordan and the others, were waiting outside the house when Keo arrived. Norris was already there, having been closer when Gillian called.

The ex-cop looked over and shook his head. "She's not here. We looked everywhere."

"She wasn't here when we woke up this morning," Jordan said. "She was with us all last night, talking about school. She wanted to be a nurse and was asking me about college courses." She looked pained. "I'm sorry, Keo. I thought she'd just gone back into her and Gillian's room when I didn't see her this morning."

"What about her crutch?"

"It's gone, too," Gillian said. "I found her radio inside our room."

"And no one saw her leave?"

He looked from face to face and they all shook their heads.

"What about Levy?" Keo asked.

"Levy?" Gillian said.

"He didn't answer the radio."

She frowned. "Why would Levy know where Lotte is?"

"I don't know," Keo said. "But he should have answered the radio. You don't ignore something like that." He unclipped his radio and pressed the transmit lever. "Levy, are you there? Come in."

He waited, and so did the others. Norris shifted his feet anxiously, as did Gillian.

"Levy," Keo said into the radio again. "Come in if you can hear me."

Then, just when Keo didn't think he would ever answer, Levy said through the radio, "What's up?"

"What time did you leave the house this morning?" Keo asked.

"Early. Why?"

"Did you see Lotte?"

There was a slight pause, then, "No," Levy said. "Is something wrong? She okay?"

"We don't know. We can't find her anywhere. You sure you didn't see her leave the house this morning?"

"I'm sure, yeah. Sorry."

"Okay, let me know if you see her."

"I will," Levy said.

Keo put the radio away and looked back at the others.

Norris was staring at him. "He's lying," he said. There was no trace of doubt in his voice.

"You don't know that," Gillian said.

"I do know," Norris said. "I've been listening to people lying to me half my life, Gillian. He's lying."

"It doesn't make any sense. Why would he take Lotte?"

"Only one way to find out," Keo said.

✳

"HE'S LOST IT," Norris said. "You know that, right?"

"We don't know anything for sure," Keo said. "You're jumping to conclusions."

"I'm pretty good at jumping, kid. But I also know when something isn't right. And that kid isn't right."

"You can jump all you want, just don't pull the trigger until we know for sure."

They walked through the woods in silence for a moment, the only sound the *crunch* of soft ground and twigs under their shoes. The others were staying behind at the house, even though most of them wanted to come, including Gillian. He had managed to talk them out of it, though. Keo didn't want Levy to see everyone converging on him at once.

"I'm right," Norris insisted after a while.

"We'll see," Keo said. Then, "What would Riggs do in this situation?"

Norris chuckled. "I don't know. Probably run in blind with guns blazing."

"He do that a lot?"

"Yeah, he was a lethal weapon, see. Thus the title of the movie."

"Maybe we can look for the Blu-ray when we hit that Wall-bys near Corden later next week."

"Why stop at one Blu-ray? Grab the whole boxed set. All four parts. They're all pretty good."

"Did they die at the end of part four?"

"Nope. Last I heard, they were still hoping to make a part five."

"Wouldn't they be pretty old by now?"

"Have you looked around you, kid? Old age is the least of their problems these days."

Norris didn't say much after that. Keo guessed he was trying to think about what was waiting for them up ahead. Keo was doing the same thing. He spent the long walk back to the burnt-out two-story house trying to come up with a scenario where Norris was both wrong and right.

What the hell was he going to do if Norris *was* right? Keo didn't have a clue. If he thought the idea of taking charge was foreign and uncomfortable, having to decide what to do with a stray member of the flock was borderline nauseating.

"What do you think he's doing with her in there?" Norris said.

"We don't know she's there."

"She's there," he said, with that same absolute certainty.

He's probably right, Keo thought, but said instead, "Maybe."

Norris was holding his M4 tightly in front of him, and every now and then he adjusted the Glock holstered at his hip. The ex-cop looked a little nervous as they approached the familiar clearing. They had both slowed down without a word, as if they were trying to prolong the walk to the garage, to where Levy was at the moment. But eventually they had to finally reach the edge of the woods, where they stopped and looked out.

The fire-gutted house was still on the left side, with the partially burnt garage next to it. Keo noticed right away that there was something different with the garage door, which was partially open. He saw what may or may not have been movement from inside through the small opening, but it was impossible to tell for certain from his angle.

"If we find what we think we're going to find in there, let's keep calm so things don't escalate," Keo said.

"If he has Lotte in there..." Norris said, but didn't finish his thought.

"All of this could be one big misunderstanding. She could be there because she wants to. *If* she's there at all. For all we know, she went exploring in the woods and got lost and couldn't find her way back."

"She's moving on crutches," Norris said. "Hard to get too far into the woods with one good leg, kid."

"It's just something to consider."

Norris shook his head. "I'm telling you, I can tell when

someone's lying to me."

"Even through the radio?"

"Even through the damn radio. Even through the damn phone." The older man gritted his teeth. "She's in there."

Keo sighed. "I'll go first. You follow—"

Crack!

The gunshot split the air and Keo twisted his entire body as the bullet chopped into his side.

He thought, *Aw, hell, this is gonna be bad,* even as his legs buckled under him and he sank to the ground, just as a loud explosion of continuous gunfire shattered the woods around him.

CHAPTER 28

"SHIT SHIT SHIT!" Norris shouted as he dived for cover behind a tree. As he slipped behind the large trunk, the bark on the other side came undone against a torrent of bullets.

Keo didn't have time to see if Norris had survived his little leap. He was too busy trying to get his bearings as the ground around him seemed to turn to mush and dirt kicked so high into the air that all the brown and black temporarily blurred his field of vision. He was on his knees and twisting until his survival instincts kicked in and he managed to engage his legs to lunge out of the open and behind his own tree for cover.

The *pak-pak-pak* of rounds hitting the trunk on the other side, over and over again, sounded like someone playing a tune. More bullets dug lengthy trenches in the earth to the left and right of him.

"You all right, kid?" Norris shouted over the roar of gunfire.

Keo didn't answer right away. He looked down his left side and saw blood. Not a lot, and it probably looked worse than it really was. After the initial impact, Keo didn't really feel like he had been shot—or at least, it didn't hurt nearly as much as the last few times. This almost felt like a bee sting. A really, really painful bee sting.

He pulled his T-shirt up and saw blood pooling around a sharp line, almost like a scalpel's incision, along his side. A bullet graze.

Daebak.

He was lucky. Goddamn lucky.

"I'm good, I'm good," Keo said.

"You sure?" Norris said.

"Pretty sure, yeah."

"You must have nine lives, kid."

Six lives now, but maybe I'm being overly generous.

Keo got up and turned around. The gunshots had lessened; their ambushers had realized they had lost the advantage and were conserving ammo. Either that, or they were reloading. What mattered was that dirt wasn't flying at his eyes and the giant trees in front of him and Norris had stopped falling to pieces.

"Was that Levy?" Norris said.

"I don't think so," Keo said. "That was more than one gun. At least three."

"Three? Where the hell did three guns come from?"

"Let's ask them when we introduce ourselves."

"Sounds like a plan—" Norris said, but didn't finish because the garage door in front of them banged open and Levy came out with his AR-15 at the ready.

Levy spotted them right away, and he must have also seen the state of the trees they were hiding behind, or maybe Keo's blood-soaked shirt did it, because he spun around to face the shooters somewhere on the other side of the clearing. He was moving toward the edge of the building when someone snapped off a shot and Keo saw the muzzle flash, along with a chunk of the unattached garage tearing off in front of Levy's face.

That sent Levy scurrying away from the corner as the gunfire picked up again, this time directed at Levy. Pieces of the garage began snapping loose under the assault, but luckily for him, Levy was still well hidden. He threw himself to the ground in front of the door and folded his arms over his head, waiting out the fusillade.

Keo took the opportunity to lean out from behind the tree and picked up the muzzle flashes aimed at Levy. He was right; there were three shooters, all on the other side of the estate. They were well-spaced, about five meters apart, and they were firing assault rifles—one AK-47 mixed in with a couple of carbines. Probably M4 or AR-15. He knew one thing for sure: they all had full-auto firing capability. The trees in front of him and Norris could attest to that. The first shot, the one that had drilled through his shirt, was fired from fifty meters away. It wasn't a bad shot, just slightly off target. Thank God.

He glanced across the narrow space at Norris, who, like Keo, hadn't returned fire yet. The ex-cop was biding his time, looking for his opportunity. He seemed calm, almost serene, while watching Levy trying to brave the rain of gunfire.

Their radios squawked and they heard Gillian's voice, loud and anxious. "Keo, Norris, what's happening over there? Are you guys all right?"

Keo unclipped his radio. "We're fine. But I need you and everyone to lock down the doors and windows at the house."

"Is it Levy?" Gillian asked. "Is he okay?"

"It's not Levy. There are other people in the woods. Get everyone inside and don't open for anyone but Norris and me, okay?"

"Okay," Gillian said. Then, "Be careful."

"We'll see you soon." He glanced across at Norris again. "Hey."

The older man looked over. "What?"

"I'm going to try to outflank them."

Norris's eyes shifted down to Keo's bloody shirt. "Can you even run with that?"

"It's just a scratch."

"Your funeral."

Keo held up his radio. "When I squawk it three times, open fire."

"That your plan? It sucks."

"It's gonna happen whether you want it to or not. But I need you to be good with it."

Norris grunted. "Hey, you wanna get yourself killed, be my guest. I'm not the one with the pretty girl waiting back at the house."

Keo grinned, then jogged back further into the woods, moving in a straight line so he couldn't be shot at. Hopefully they hadn't seen him moving, but even if they did, he might look as if he were just retreating.

That wasn't what he was doing, of course, but they didn't need to know that.

THERE WERE THREE shooters, one for each of the three muzzle flashes he had seen earlier. Spacing themselves out to see all of the clearing, and the garage in the middle of it, was a smart move on their part. It gave them coverage and made their numbers seem larger.

But there was a fault in their tactics. They couldn't see Keo now as he retreated, then maneuvered sideways and started moving forward again. Obviously they hadn't expected him and Norris to pop out of the other side of the clearing. Bad luck for them, good for him.

Keo crouched now, grimacing a bit at the sudden stab of pain. He looked down at his blood-soaked shirt. It had stopped bleeding a few minutes ago after the cotton fabric became sticky, and the inside of the T-shirt stuck to the wound. He would have liked the time to clean and dress it, but he guessed this worked too in a pinch.

He looked across the woods at the closest ambusher about thirty meters away, the man's left side visible to Keo. A man in his thirties, give or take, wearing green and brown camo hunting gear that covered him from the dirt-stained boots all the way up to his tightly fitted cap. He wore a sidearm in a hip holster and had pouches bulging with spare magazines. The man was leaning behind a tree, peering through a red dot sight mounted on top of an M4. His finger kept tugging on the trigger, coming dangerously close to pulling it, but somehow always not going far enough to finish the pull. A man who clearly put value on each shot. Keo wondered if this was the one that had almost ended his life if he had shot just a few inches higher.

Keo couldn't see enough of the man's partners from his vantage point to know for sure if they were male or female. He saw enough to know that all three had found nice cover, which explained why they hadn't bothered to switch up after the initial burst of shooting. At the moment, they seemed to be biding their time. Maybe they had friends coming, or maybe they just weren't in a hurry.

He glanced down at his watch: 1:16 P.M.

Plenty of time.

Keo unclipped his radio and squeezed the transmit lever three times, then quickly clipped it back to his hip.

Norris began firing from somewhere on the other side of the clearing. Branches snapped and a tree or two lost chunks of bark, but as expected, Norris didn't come close to hitting any of the three ambushers. It did spook them enough to drive the man in front of Keo to move further behind the tree, just before he and his two pals started returning fire at Norris's position.

Keo stood up halfway behind the bush he had been watching from and shot the ambusher in the thigh. The man looked more surprised than hurt, and he lowered his rifle and started looking around, eyes darting under the brim of his cap. When the man turned, he presented his chest to Keo, who shot him dead center. The man leaned back against the tree, as if he were sitting down to rest. Before he could slide all the way to the ground, though, Keo shot him a third time just to be sure.

Then he was up and running forward, keeping low as much as possible while still swallowing up the distance between him and the dead man at a fast clip.

By now Norris had stopped shooting, probably to reload, though the other two ambushers were still firing back at him. He wasn't surprised both men were clueless as to what had happened to their friend. The suppressor attached to the MP5SD rendered Keo's three shots with the decibel level of a slight cough. Barely audible against the loud *pop-pop-pop* of assault rifles filling the woods at full blast.

He reached the tree and gave the dead man a quick look to make sure he hadn't somehow clung on to life. Or maybe he was wearing a bulletproof vest. The man looked younger up close—maybe early thirties—and he had surprisingly bright blue eyes.

Keo leaned around the tree and picked out the next man.

Like the first, this one was also clad in camo from head to toe. Except instead of a cap, he had black hair with streaks of gray. The older man was crouched behind his hiding spot and was busy reloading an AK-47. The assault rifle, like the man's wardrobe, sported a camouflage paint scheme.

The ambusher must have sensed Keo, because he looked up after loading his rifle and instantly squeezed the trigger without a moment's hesitation. Keo ducked behind the tree as bullets chopped into it at a relentless pace from the other side.

"James, are you okay?" the older man shouted while still firing. Then, "Sonofabitch! You're going to pay for that!"

Keo pressed his back against the tree trunk and waited out the gunfire. The man would have to reload sooner or later. Probably.

Then there was a new round of shots, this time coming from Keo's left. He looked over into the clearing and saw Levy running up, pouring rounds from his AR-15 into the woods, in the direction of the second ambusher. He looked wild, but there was a strange grin on his face, as if he were having the time of his life.

Keo sneaked a peek around the other side of the tree trunk

and saw the second man staggering away from his spot, blood pouring out of his hip and right leg. Bullets were zipping relentlessly around him, until one of them found their mark and the man stumbled and dropped, disappearing behind a thick bush.

Then Levy ran up and shot the man two more times in the back.

Aw, Jesus, kid.

Levy looked over, and Keo saw a wild man staring back at him. Levy's face was flushed red and he seemed to be breathing way too hard, using more effort than was necessary. Despite all of that, he was still grinning, bloodlust dancing across his eyes.

Keo looked past Levy, expecting to see the third ambusher either taking off or attacking in a last-ditch effort to salvage the day.

But there was no fleeing form or a last charge.

His radio squawked, then Norris's voice: "All clear. I got the third one. All clear."

"Roger that," Keo said into the radio.

He came out from behind the tree and walked over to Levy, who remained standing over the camouflaged form lying still on the ground. The blades of grass around the man were covered in blood, as was the damp earth under him.

"I've never killed anyone before," Levy said. Despite his heaving chest and large eyes, his voice was amazingly unhurried, even calm. "He's dead, right?"

"Looks dead to me," Keo said.

"Feels weird, taking a life."

"It should, Levy."

"Yeah, I guess." He looked at Keo. "Am I supposed to feel bad about it?"

"Do you?"

"I'm not sure." He seemed to think about it for a moment, then shook his head. "I guess I don't feel too bad. What's it like?"

"What's that?"

"The second time killing a guy?"

Keo didn't answer him. He didn't know how. Then again, he had never sat down (or stood around) talking about his feelings after killing a man, either.

"You all right, kid?" Keo asked.

Levy nodded. "Yeah. I've never felt better in my life." He looked down at his victim. "Who do you think he was?"

"I don't know. You've never seen him before?"

"Never saw him in my life."

"You didn't know they were here until they started shooting?"

"Nope. They must have been really quiet. It's a good thing you and Norris showed up. They probably would have snuck up on me." Suddenly, the grin left his face and was replaced by suspicion. "What are you guys doing here, anyway? Are you checking up on me?"

"We were looking for Lotte."

"I told you, I haven't seen her." He looked slightly annoyed. "You don't believe me?"

"We're checking everywhere."

"Well, she's not here. Why would I lie about that?"

I don't know, why would you lie about that? Keo thought, but said, "We're just looking everywhere."

"And you just happened to walk in this direction?" Levy said, slightly amused.

"Yeah, that's pretty much it."

"Where have you guys looked so far? Maybe I can help. I like the kid, too."

Keo didn't get a chance to answer before their radios squawked again and Norris said, "Third one's talking, and he's got a pretty interesting story."

"What's he saying?" Keo said into the radio.

"They came here looking for a missing friend, and they thought he was in the garage."

Keo looked at Levy.

"He's lying," Levy said.

"Yeah?"

"Yeah," Levy nodded with absolute conviction.

"Good to know," Keo said, and punched Levy in the gut.

When Levy doubled over in surprise, Keo hit him in the face. Levy dropped, landing on his stomach on the ground next to the man he had killed.

Levy groaned and tried to get back up.

"Don't," Keo said.

Maybe Levy didn't hear him, or maybe he was just stubborn, but he reached for his sidearm. Keo hit him across the face with the stock of his submachine gun, and Levy flopped back to the ground again.

This time, he didn't try to get back up.

CHAPTER 29

"JESUS CHRIST," NORRIS said, doing his best not to choke on the stench.

Keo was already breathing through his mouth, and it was barely helping. Even though he had shut down his sense of smell, his eyes still stung from the tainted air. It was all he could do to stare at the darkened corner and not throw up.

There was blood all over the half of the garage that wasn't covered with leftovers from the burnt house next door. Fresh blood. It pooled in the sunlight, originating from the corner where Keo had last seen Levy's creature.

It was still in there, but it wasn't alone anymore.

He took out his flashlight and flicked it on.

They glanced up from what they were doing and glared at him, as if he was an annoyance interrupting their work. There were two of them now, and one of them was clearly smaller, though size was always tricky with the creatures. One of them was missing an arm and had a hole where its eye socket should be.

He knew without a doubt that the other one was Lotte. Or it used to be Lotte.

He only knew that because it was still wearing Lotte's shirt and pants, both soaked in blood that glistened against his flashlight. She hadn't turned all that long ago. The pebble turquoise bracelet that she always wore barely clung to her shrunken wrist, on the precipice of falling free at any second.

Her chest was sunken, her body impossibly frail. Her right leg, which still hadn't healed entirely, was bent at an odd angle, though she moved on it as if there were no pain.

Do they even still feel pain?

A rawhide rope was wrapped tightly around Lotte's throat and attached to the same spike driven into the ground that leashed the other creature. It wasn't just Lotte and the creature in the corner, though.

There was a third. A man. Not really a man. A *kid*.

He was wearing dirt-caked camo pants and a shirt, like the three men who had tried to ambush Keo and Norris earlier, though the boy's clothing looked too big for his slight form. Blood was spurting out of his neck and wrists where he had been bitten, teeth marks still visible around the gaping wounds. Lotte and the creature were perched over the boy, the sound of wanton suckling filling the garage.

Norris shuffled his feet restlessly behind him. "This is going to kill the girls. Rachel, Gillian... Jesus."

Lotte. The fourteen-year-old had been easy to like. He remembered all the times when she "accidentally" fell asleep in the living room whenever he forgot to leave her and Gillian's room in time. How she looked after Christine when Rachel was busy, or humored Norris when he started telling another one of his dull stories from his time as a cop.

She was a good kid. A really good kid...

"She looks fresh," Norris said. "How long does it take for them to turn?"

"I don't know," Keo said. "I guess it depends on when they die."

He shook his head. He didn't want to have this conversation. He didn't *need* to have this conversation about Lotte.

"He's going to turn," Norris said. "The kid in the camo. Just like Lotte. Jesus, this is going to kill the girls."

The thick and crisp *slurp slurp* of Lotte and the creature working on the dead body was like a sledgehammer in the quiet of the garage.

"We can't let them leave," Keo said.

"Which ones?"

"All of them."

Keo clicked the flashlight off, pocketed it, and took a step back. Norris did the same thing and they turned without a word and left. Keo slammed the door shut behind them.

Outside, Levy was lying unconscious on the ground on his side. He had a strangely contented look on his bruised face, even with his hands tied behind his back with a pair of zip ties they had found on one of the dead ambushers. Keo stared at Levy, wondering what the hell they were going to do with him.

The last surviving ambusher, whom Norris had caught while the man was fleeing across the clearing, sat on his butt a few feet from Levy, his own hands bound behind his back along with his feet to keep him from running off. He was almost as young as the boy inside the garage with Lotte and the creature, but maybe a few years older. Eighteen, at least. He had told Norris his name was Joe.

Right now, Joe glared at Keo and Norris, as if he were prepared to tear them apart with his bare hands if given the opportunity. "Is Bobby in there? Is he alive? He's dead, isn't he?"

"There was someone else in there," Keo said.

"Bobby. It was Bobby, wasn't it?"

Yeah, probably, Keo thought, but said, "I don't know what Bobby looks like."

"It's Bobby," Joe said, as if just making that declaration sapped all the energy and anger from him. He looked down at the ground between his legs instead. "There was a lot of blood where we last saw him. He was bleeding pretty bad all the way over here."

"You followed the blood here?"

"Yeah. He must have stabbed Bobby," Joe said. He flashed Levy's unconscious form a disgusted glance. "Sneaked up on him, probably. Bobby couldn't hear too good out of his right ear."

"Sorry, kid," Norris said.

Joe looked up at Norris, the fire suddenly reignited. "You killed him. You killed Bobby."

"Not us."

"You're with him," Joe said, nodding at Levy. "You're just as responsible as he is."

"No..."

"Admit it!"

Norris opened his mouth to argue, but stopped himself. He was probably thinking the same thing Keo was. Maybe the kid was right; maybe they were just as responsible for Bobby's death *(and Lotte's)* as Levy was. They had left him alone after discovering the creature in the garage. They had allowed Levy to do what he did this afternoon.

To Lotte. To Bobby...

"You're right," Keo said. "We should have put a stop to him sooner."

That seemed to deflate Joe, and he looked down at the ground again. "Why'd you have to kill my uncles, too?"

"You shot at us first," Norris said. "You shot to kill, too, so don't start thinking the three of you have clean hands in this."

Joe's eyes went to Keo's blood-soaked shirt. It looked worse than it really was, since he couldn't really feel the pain anymore. Not that he had forgotten about it, but he had been in worse situations.

"What now?" Joe said, looking from Keo's face to Norris's, and back again. "What happens to me?"

"We haven't decided yet," Keo said.

"You got family left?" Norris asked.

Joe shook his head. "I ain't got no one. You killed them all," he said, and looked down without another word.

✳

"I TOLD YOU I never shot anyone while I was a cop?" Norris said.

"You mentioned it," Keo said.

"I'd never even discharged my weapon in the line of duty." He grunted. "It's funny how life works. I spend most of my fifty-six years carrying a gun, patrolling some of the shittiest neighborhoods in Orlando, and I never had to shoot anyone. It takes the end of the world to change all that. Crazy."

They stood just far enough from Joe and Levy that the two men couldn't hear them. Levy had woken up and now sat on the ground next to Joe, doing his very best to avoid eye contact. Joe looked as if he wanted to strangle Levy, and no doubt his zip-tied hands were the only thing keeping him from doing just that. Levy, for his part, seemed to know he had messed up. He had only looked at Keo and Norris once after gaining consciousness and hadn't done it a second time.

"I get the feeling you're better at this than I am," Norris said.

"'This'?" Keo said. "What are we talking about here?"

"All this killing stuff." He added quickly, "That's not an accusation or some kind of backhanded compliment, kid. That's just a statement of fact. Tell me I'm wrong."

Keo didn't. Because Norris wasn't.

"See the world. Kill some people. Make some money."

He glanced up at the sun. The brightness stung his eyes, but it was a good sting, and it took away some of the lingering pain in his side. He was going to have to tend to it sooner or later. A scratch or not, it was still an open wound, and he had seen infections in the field develop from something as minor as a scratch, never mind a bullet graze.

"We can't take him back with us," Norris said.

"I don't see how," Keo said. "Not after what he did."

"So, what's left? What are our options?"

"I think we both know the answer to that."

"Do we?"

"He can't be trusted." Keo looked at Levy, who was doing everything possible not to stare back. "Not around us. Not around the house or the girls."

"Maybe it's just one of those temporary insanity things. Should we ask him why he did it?"

"Does it matter? The point is, he did it."

Norris didn't answer right away. After a while, he said, "The kid needs psychiatric help."

"No chance of that now."

"I guess not." He paused, then, "I can do it."

"No, I'll do it," Keo said. "I promised Gillian."

He began walking away before Norris could say anything else.

Joe and Levy heard him coming and looked over. He wasn't quite sure what was in Joe's eyes, but Levy's were clear as day—they were wide with terror, as if he could already read Keo's mind and knew what was coming.

"Keo, don't," Levy said. "Whatever you're thinking of doing, don't do it. I didn't meant to hurt anyone. The kid—Bobby—he surprised me, that's all. I didn't have a choice."

"What about Lotte?" Keo asked.

"She followed me. I'm sick of people following me, not trusting me. I just...*snapped*, that's all." He was struggling with the right words, or what he thought were the right words. "She started badgering me about what I was doing to the bloodsucker. I tried to explain it to her, the way I explained it to you, but she couldn't understand. I couldn't make her understand."

Maybe that's because she's a more decent human being than me...

"She's just a kid," Levy said. "She didn't have a right to talk to me like that. Not after what I did for her. For all of you. That house is mine now that Earl's gone. I let you guys stay there. And that dumb kid trying to tell me what I could and couldn't do to that bloodsucker just pissed me off."

Keo glanced at Joe, who was watching on in silence. The kid's face was unreadable. Keo guessed he had come to the same conclusion as Levy and was content now to sit back and watch and not interfere.

"You know I'm right, Keo," Levy was saying. "I saw it in your eyes. You know what I'm doing here is right. We need to do this. We need to know the enemy. It's the only way we'll survive."

Keo didn't answer.

"Keo, what are you going to do?" Levy asked. His voice had trembled slightly for a split-second there. "There's still so much I want to do. We can do this together. You're the only one at the house who understands. You know this is the right thing to do, don't you?"

"Why did you give Bobby to Lotte and the other one?" Keo asked.

"Huh?" Levy said.

"Why did you feed Bobby to them? Inside the garage?"

"Because they were hungry," Levy said, as if the answer was obvious. "I need them to keep up their strength. The other one, it was getting weak, dying on me. The blood should keep it fresh for months. Don't you want to know how that works? How one person can sustain them for *months* at a time?"

He did want to know. *"Know thy enemy."* Wasn't that the saying? How could you hope to defeat the enemy if you didn't know what made them tick? What hurt them, and what killed them? Levy was doing them all a big favor, whether the others realized it or not.

"Keo," Levy said, trying desperately to read his face. "You know I'm right. You and me. We know what we have to do. You have to trust me—"

Keo drew his Glock and shot Levy in the forehead.

Joe flinched at the loud *boom!*, then stared at Levy's body as it slumped to the ground next to him and lay still. A small trickle of blood dripped from the hole in Levy's forehead, but most of the damage had gone out the back of his skull and splattered a healthy gob of blood and brains on the ground.

Keo holstered the gun.

"What about me?" Joe asked.

Keo looked at him for a moment. "We killed your uncles."

Joe nodded. "I know. It was a big misunderstanding."

The fire that Keo had seen in Joe's eyes before was gone, replaced by something more subdued, even resignation. The kid was way more mature than his age.

"You didn't have a choice," Joe continued. "I know that now. I accept that."

Keo stared at him, trying to read him. Joe's face was placid.

"Is your place around here?" Keo asked.

"It's a cabin about thirty miles north of here. I guessed we found a place in the woods like you guys did, to hide from those things."

"What were you doing this far south?"

"Hunting," Joe said. "There aren't a lot of wildlife left these days, so we've been going out farther and farther to try to find some. Then Bobby went missing…"

"You'll be alone now," Keo interrupted him. He said it harshly, without emotion, because he wanted to see Joe's reaction.

"Yeah, I know," Joe said quietly, and looked down at the ground.

Keo pulled out the Ka-Bar. "You make me regret this and I'll gut you like a fucking pig the next time I see you."

"You won't regret this," Joe said. "I just want to go home. This entire day has been one big nightmare."

"What will you do next?"

"There are some people in a house about two miles from us. We've traded with them before." Joe shrugged. "Maybe I can stay with them. They're nice people."

Keo nodded. "Don't make me regret this, kid."

"You won't," Joe said. "I swear it."

CHAPTER 30

THEY BURIED LEVY and the two hunters in the woods near the clearing, digging just deep enough to put down the bodies. They had found shovels inside the garage, where Lotte and the creature were still suckling at the dead Bobby. Keo kept expecting Bobby to rise at any second, but he never did.

While they were shoving dirt over Levy's surprisingly youthful-looking face—he seemed to have de-aged in death, though of course that was impossible—Keo spent a few seconds wondering if Levy and the other two buried next to him were going to come back when night fell.

We know nothing about them. Levy's right about that. We are just guessing about everything. Who knows what we've been wrong about?

They thought about burning down the garage and the creatures inside with it, but the risk of setting a fire that they couldn't control was too great. Instead, Keo and Norris spent ten minutes knocking down enough of the back walls to expose the creatures to sunlight. He heard them hissing, then smelled the familiar acidic scent. Leashed to the spike on the ground, the only path available to the creatures was to flee the formerly darkened corner. But there was nowhere to go and they died *(again)*, leaving piles of bones and Bobby's cold, bloodied remains abandoned on the ground.

Keo and Norris thought about burying Bobby, too, but decided one more of the creatures running around wasn't going to make any difference tonight or the next thousand nights.

Besides, if he did turn while the sun was still up, he would just die *(again)*.

They left the clearing, Keo expecting to see Joe back at any second gunning for them, trying to exact revenge for the relatives he had lost earlier at their hands. The Keo from six months ago would have just shot the kid after dealing with Levy. He remembered thinking the same thing when he had found Jordan and her friends in the bungalow.

I really have gone soft. God help us.

"You think he'll come back?" Norris asked. "Joe?"

"I hope not," Keo said. "I'd hate to wipe out the kid's entire bloodline. Too little of that left these days."

"For what it's worth, I think you did the right thing. I don't think I could pull the trigger on the kid, either. What was he, eighteen?"

"Looked about eighteen. You have any kids before all of this?"

"I was married twice, but never managed to squirt out a brat. I guess that's a good thing, considering what happened to the world. Otherwise I would have spent all my time trying to get back to Orlando. I'm way too old for that shit."

"Just like Murtaugh."

Norris chuckled. "Yeah. Just like Murtaugh. We're both way too old for this shit, though Murtaugh had a family in the movies. That was one of his weaknesses, actually. The bad guys kept using his wife and kids against him."

"Sounds like a chump."

"Up yours," Norris said.

They picked up their weapons and carried the shovels with them back through the woods. It was a long walk, made longer by what had happened back at the burnt house. Keo tried not to think too much about it, but of course it was impossible.

"What does Riggs look like?" Keo asked after a while. "If I'm supposed to be Riggs to your Murtaugh, I mean."

"Well, he was crazy, like you. Had a questionable past, like you."

"So I'm basically him, is that what you're saying?"

"He had a mullet, too."

"Ugh," Keo said. "I'd rather be Murtaugh, then."

HE EXPECTED A fight with Gillian, but instead she listened quietly and didn't interrupt once. While he talked, she helped him out of his shirt, then disinfected and treated the wound. When she was done, she grabbed a fresh T-shirt from one of the drawers in the back. It was either Earl's or Gavin's. It fit him just fine, and Keo didn't spend another second thinking about whom it used to belong to.

When he finished the story—he didn't tell her where he and Norris had buried Levy in the woods—Gillian put her arms around him and pressed her head against his chest. "I know it wasn't an easy thing for you to do."

"It wasn't," Keo said.

"I know. You did what you had to. What you thought was right."

"What do you think?"

"It doesn't matter."

"It does. To me."

"Keo..."

"Tell me."

She pulled back and gave him a pursed smile. "I wasn't there. I didn't see what you saw. With Lotte, with that kid Bobby..." She shook her head. "I'm not going to second-guess you, Keo. After all, the day I met you, you drove a truck through a hospital wall."

He smiled at the memory.

"You're crazy," she continued, "but you're also a good man."

"Am I?"

"You don't agree."

"I've never considered myself a particularly good man, no."

She watched him carefully for a moment, trying to read him, to understand him. She had such deep green eyes and she had let her hair grow out even longer in the last few months. He often joked that pretty soon she would look like Rapunzel, except with jet-black hair.

"You are," she said after a moment. "Whatever you did before all of this was before all of this. That's in the past. Right now, I trust you. Okay?"

He nodded and kissed her. "Okay."

"You look tired. Lie down and I'll go grab some soup from the basement."

He lay down on the bed and listened to the door open and close softly after her.

Keo stared up at the ceiling, thinking about Levy. About Lotte, who slept on the other side of the room. Losing the two of them on the same day reminded him why this leadership thing was for dummies.

He'd never wanted it. Never needed it. If it were up to him, he'd give it all up tomorrow and go back to being the guy who did the work and clocked out afterward. He knew guys who took the job too seriously, who had nightmares about the things they had done for the organization. Keo had never been one of them because he had never really cared.

Well, he never used to, anyway.

He intended to stay awake until Gillian came back with the soup, but he must have lost more blood than he thought, because he was tired from head to toe. He closed his eyes for a bit, but was somehow snoring a few minutes later.

HE OPENED HIS eyes to sunlight inside the room, which instantly set his mind at ease, and Gillian looking down at him.

Soft hands stroked his hair, and his head was in her lap. He didn't think waking up to the sight of her could ever feel so right, so at home. He had forgotten how beautiful she was, how perfect everything was about her, even that twinkle of mischief in her eyes.

"Stop staring," she smiled. "Although, I admit, it's flattering—especially with that stupid grin on your face."

"Where's my soup? Didn't you promise me soup?"

"It's over there," she said, nodding to a foldout table. "But it's already cold. And yucky. I'll warm it back up for you later and you can have it before dinner. It'll be like we're married, or something equally distasteful like that."

"Would it be so bad being married to me?"

"Not as long as you don't grow a beer belly and start fooling around with every floozy around town."

"That's a lot to ask from a man."

"Well, marriage is a big deal. It requires commitment."

"True enough. What time is it?"

"An hour before nightfall." She added quickly, "Don't worry. Everyone knows what to do. You're not the only capable guy around here, you know."

"But I'm definitely the handsomest, right?"

She shrugged. "Eh. Mark's pretty cute."

"What about Norris?"

"Too old."

"You don't like them old?"

"I don't like them *that* old."

He smiled. "I'm going to tell him you said that."

"Don't you dare." She continued stroking his hair before finally saying, "We'll be okay, won't we?"

"We'll be fine."

"You said that pretty fast."

"Because I don't have any doubts about the answer," he said, hoping it was more convincing than he felt.

The truth was, he wasn't sure about anything anymore.

Joe, Levy, Lotte…

Did he make the right decisions today? Was letting Joe go the right thing to do? Killing Levy? Lotte's death?

"I almost believed you," Gillian said.

"You should, because it's true."

"No, it's not. I'm not an idiot, Keo."

He nodded. "I know."

"You'll do your best. And so will Norris and me and everyone else here. Jordan and Mark and Jill. But every night, they'll still be outside our doors, waiting for us to make a mistake. Like you said, all it'll take is one small mistake."

Like not dealing with Levy in time…

She looked off across the room, and he knew she was staring at Lotte's empty bed. He reminded himself to get rid of it tomorrow. It didn't need to be there anymore. It was a reminder of what they had lost and, more importantly, the bad decisions that had led to it. *His* bad decisions.

Live and learn, live and learn…

"She was a good kid," Keo said.

"She was," Gillian nodded. "Did he tell you how…?"

"No," Keo lied. "But he admitted he was responsible for what happened to her."

"God, she must have been so afraid at the end." Gillian closed her eyes and leaned back against the wall. "Six months, Keo. That's how long we've been out here. It feels like an eternity, doesn't it?"

"It does."

"We don't even know what's happened to the rest of the world. What's going on out there? What about the cities? The other states? We don't know anything."

"It's not our problem."

"Isn't it?"

"No. I'm just some guy who worked for some people with questionable ethics, and you're just some girl who once worked for a bank. Norris is just an ex-cop from Orlando. Rachel,

Christine, Jordan and the others...we're just people doing the best we can to survive. What happens out there isn't our problem."

"Maybe you're right. Maybe I'm overthinking it."

"Hey," he said.

"Hmm?" she said, looking back at him.

"We'll be okay. I promise."

She nodded and smiled, but he could tell that she didn't believe him.

THE DAYS WENT on, minus Levy and Lotte. They left Levy's room empty for two days, and on the third Keo decided it was time to get it over with. The sooner he got everyone putting the past where it belonged, the faster they could all pick up the pieces. Gillian wanted to wait at least a week, but Keo was adamant. If they wanted him to lead them, then he would, and that meant making all the decisions.

He helped Norris clean Levy's room out and moved the ex-cop in, along with Mark. He also moved into Gillian's room, which meant everyone at the house finally had their own space and no one had to sleep in the living room anymore. No one was particularly enthusiastic about their newfound privileges, but he figured they would all get over it eventually, so they might as well start now.

Every now and then, Keo wondered what had happened to Joe. Had he gone back to that cabin where he stayed with his uncles and cousin, and continued on? Was it possible to make it out there by yourself? Or did he join those neighbors he had mentioned? Did they take him in? Spurn him? Maybe he should go check on the kid one of these days.

Keo put it on his to-do list, near the very back.

EVENTUALLY, KEO DECIDED it had been a while since they had gone on a supply run. Not that the house was in desperate need of any one thing, but he didn't like the idea of never venturing beyond their small corner of the world again. The idea of living like hermits was not very enticing.

There was also the presence of Joe and his family, which had convinced him they weren't nearly as alone out here as he had once thought. It wasn't just Joe, though; it was also those two men in black assault vests that he and Norris had killed a few weeks back. The presence of those two still gnawed at him.

"How many more of you are out there?"

"A lot."

So where were all those others? Did they ever come close to finding their fallen comrades? He was pretty sure the bodies had never been recovered. Jordan said the river went all the way to New Orleans. That was a hell of a long way from where they were now.

No, the others tracking the bodies back to the house for a vendetta wasn't what worried him. What did, though, was the knowledge that they were *out* there.

Somewhere. Doing what?

"You worry too much," Norris would say when Keo brought it up. "It's a big state. The chances of them running across us by accident are miniscule."

"Like Joe and his family?" he had countered.

That had made Norris think twice. "Good point," he had said.

It was a good point. So good, in fact, that it stuck with him and made him want to go out there again.

CHAPTER 31

NORRIS HAD HIS M4 in a sling, the rifle thumping against his chest as the Bronco rumbled along the dirt trail. Keo drove, as usual. He liked driving. It kept his mind from wandering. He was already doing too much of that lately.

"Mark says he wants to come along one of these days," Norris said.

"Really. Mark?" Keo said.

"Yep. Mark. I think he feels bad, especially since Jordan's been going out on runs with you. It's a manly thing, I guess."

Keo had a hard time envisioning Mark out there with him. The guy was good on a boat, but he hadn't shown the same kind of proficiency with a firearm that Jordan had. In fact, none of the others had come close to her, including Gillian and Rachel. He wasn't too surprised, though. Jordan was a natural athlete who had been going to Tulane University on a softball scholarship when the end of the world cut short her college career.

"They're fitting right in," Keo said. "Especially Jordan."

"You would like her, wouldn't you," Norris said. It wasn't a question. "She's the female you, after all."

Keo laughed. "Is that supposed to be a compliment to me or an insult to her?"

"Take it however you want."

"I'll go with the compliment, then."

"I would, too. That's a pretty girl."

"You like them young, old timer?"

"I like them liking me back. I don't think it's going to happen with her, though. She's not even interested in Mark, and he's at least slightly more handsome than me."

"And younger."

Norris grunted. "Don't remind me."

Keo saw the trail opening up ahead and the long stretch of empty highway on the other side. It had been three weeks since their last supply run, and Keo didn't remember the road being this long.

"How far are we going out this time?" Norris asked.

"I'm thinking north, halfway back to the interstate—" Keo said, when the loud *crack* of a gunshot smashed into the air.

He jammed on the brake instinctively, and Norris, not wearing his seatbelt, nearly sailed into the dashboard. Keo was lucky; he had the steering wheel gripped tightly in both hands and barely lurched forward.

Norris opened his mouth to say something, but before he could get anything out, the *pop-pop-pop* of automatic gunfire erupted *from the house* behind them.

Keo jerked the gearshift and slammed on the gas and the truck shot backward. He used his side mirror to see with, but he was going so fast that the Bronco was swerving from left to right, right to left, each time threatening to plow into the woods on either side of him. Every time he almost came close to rear-ending a tree, he managed to wrench the steering wheel back just in time.

"Jesus, that was close!" Norris shouted. "How are you so good at this?"

Keo thought about all the hours of tactical driving training, the security details through gun-ridden neighborhoods hauling people whose lives were worth more than a thousand of him put together over a few thousand lifetimes.

But he didn't answer Norris because he was too busy keeping the steering wheel under control, absorbing every bump in the road, concentrating on every emerging tree and blade of grass swiping at the sides of the vehicle.

Gillian. Get to Gillian!

Norris was looking out the rear windshield, one hand gripping his M4, the other on the handlebar above the door to keep from flying out of his seat again. He didn't say a word even as the *pop-pop-pop* and loud *boom!* of gunfire echoed back and forth behind them, getting closer with every second that passed.

Keo drove with absolute focus, eyes on the side mirror, the truck moving so swiftly under him that he wasn't really aware of how fast he was going. Forty miles per hour, maybe fifty, possibly even higher than that. He didn't care because he *still wasn't going fast enough.*

"Watch out!" Norris shouted.

Keo saw the same thing Norris did at the exact same moment: A man in black clothing *(and black assault vest!)* appeared out of the woods like a ghost, stepping into the road behind them. The man raised a rifle, and the very distinct clatter of an AK-47 on full-auto filled the air.

Norris pulled his head down and screamed an incoherent curse as the back windshield exploded. Keo did the same thing—going down just low enough to avoid getting shot in the back of the head, but still high enough to see the side mirror and continue guiding his path back, back—

Wham! He crashed into the shooter, and the man disappeared under the truck.

Keo kept his foot hard on the gas, heard the *thwumph! whumph!* as the back then the front tire ran over a large object. He straightened up and looked forward just long enough to glimpse a black form lying in the middle of the road.

They found us. Jesus Christ, how did they find us?

He glanced back at the side mirror just as he almost slammed into a towering tree. He jerked on the steering wheel at the last instant and managed to dodge a close one. Norris let out another loud curse, but his words were lost in the squealing tires and constant gunfire behind them back at the house, getting louder and louder as they got closer.

The *pop-pop-pop* of automatic gunfire continued to ring out in a nonstop barrage, only occasionally broken up by the loud *boom!* of shotguns. There were too many sounds now—the roar of the truck under him, the crunch of tires against the dirt, and the shooting—for him to clearly make out what was happening.

Then he saw the clearing coming up less than twenty meters away.

"Get ready!" he shouted.

"Do it!" Norris shouted back.

As soon as Keo hit the opening, he pulled at the steering wheel, spinning it like a top. The Bronco obeyed reluctantly, turning in a wide arc, the tires fighting ferociously to maintain its balance against the ground. The view outside the front windshield switched from the trail over to the familiar sight of the house.

The bullet-riddled house.

Keo slammed on the brakes, shoved the gear into park, reached for the door handle with his other hand, jerked it, and dived outside in almost the same continuous motion—all of it made possible by pure adrenaline coursing through every inch of him. He prayed Norris was doing the same on the other side, and when he heard the passenger door opening, he got his answer.

Bullets shredded the Bronco's front windshield, the loud clatter of gunfire like a never-ending supply of firecrackers. Keo was already leaping out of the Bronco and running backward, sliding on the ground as he careened toward then around to the back bumper, which was now facing the trail. Norris appeared next to him, having circled back from the other side. The ex-cop gasped for breath, the expression on his face halfway between terror and exhilaration.

Two loud popping sounds overcame their senses just long enough to tell Keo that the front tires had just been shot out.

That noise was quickly drowned out by the *ping-ping-ping!* of bullets piercing the sides and front hood of the vehicle. As far as Keo could tell, based almost purely on a few seconds of what he could see as soon as he burst out of the trail and into the clearing, the shooters were gathered on the other side of the yard.

"You bleeding?" Keo asked.

"Nah," Norris said. His chest heaved erratically, and he was blinking sweat out of his eyes. "You?"

"Not this time."

"Your luck's changing."

"Tell those guys that."

Keo glanced over at the house, and the first thing he saw were the thick blocks of wood on the other side of the windows. They were pockmarked from the barrage, but that was the good news, because the barricades were down, which meant someone had made it into the house.

After he made sure they weren't being outflanked, Keo leaned around the Bronco and looked toward the front of the house. He saw a body just a few meters from the door. He knew it was a woman right away by the curves and shape of her still form, but it took him a few extra seconds to see the side profile of her face.

Jill.

She had been shot in the forehead, wet blood still pooling under her. There was an odd expression on her face, almost a look of shock. Her eyes were wide open and staring up at the bright sun.

The front door of the house was closed, and like the barricades over the windows, it too was pockmarked with tiny craters. Keo was wondering how many rounds the reinforced door could take when bullets shattered the truck's remaining windows and falling glass fell around him. Norris grunted out another curse, and Keo brushed the small shards out of his hair and off his shoulders.

Running for the front door was out of the question. He wouldn't make it halfway before they picked him off. At the moment, the Bronco was his best option. For now, anyway.

He slipped out from behind the car and moved along the side, staying low. The shooters were gathered in *front* of the house, which meant they were to his right, with the front of the house to his left. The sound of gunfire was so close that he was sure they were either hiding where the other vehicles were parked across the yard or close by. He couldn't tell how many there were by the shooting, or where they were firing from exactly. The fact that they hadn't shot him dead yet was an indicator they didn't have a solid bead on him.

There was a sudden burst of gunfire—*Norris's M4*—from behind him. Keo fell to his knees and looked back and saw the barrel of Norris's rifle pointing toward the house.

There was a body on the ground next to the side of the house that hadn't been there earlier. The man lay motionless on his stomach, his face buried in the grass on its side. He had on black clothes—black pants and a black assault vest over an equally dark shirt. His face was covered in green and black paint.

Who the hell are these guys?

Norris leaned over and gave Keo the thumbs up.

Keo grinned back, then continued on his way. He was halfway to the front of the Bronco when he caught movement from the corner of his eye and looked over, seeing a pair of eyes peering out from the peephole in the window directly to his left. He recognized the color green and smiled.

His radio squawked almost at the same time that the shooting mercifully ceased. Either the assaulters were reloading or they had realized they didn't have the angle to take him and Norris out. He didn't really care, because it allowed him to hear Gillian's voice coming through fine *(and alive, thank God)*.

"Keo, what are you doing?" she said, almost screaming through the radio. He hoped the bad guys hadn't heard that.

"I'm trying to save you, sweetheart," he said.

She laughed. "You're insane. But what else is new?"

"You okay?"

"In one piece, but Jordan's been shot. And Jill…"

"I see her," Keo said, looking across the yard at Jill's prone form. "What happened?"

"I don't know. They came out of nowhere and shot Jordan and Jill. The rest of us were in the house. We locked the doors and put the barricades down."

"Good, that's good."

"What do we do now, Keo?"

"I don't know. Give me a sec—"

Another round of bullets slammed into the other side of the Bronco, the *ping-ping-ping!* cutting Keo off. He stayed where he was and kept his eyes forward in case they tried to rush him head-on. There was no point shooting back. He couldn't even see anyone, and standing up to get a look would probably get his head shot off.

So he crouched where he was and let them go at it for a while, until finally the shooting stopped again and the last gunshot faded into the woods around them.

Gillian was watching him the entire time through the peephole. Bullets pecked the wall around the window, some embedding pointlessly against the thick wooden plate.

He held up his hand to get her attention. "Can you see them?" he said into the radio.

"There's too many of them," Gillian said. "I can see five. I think there were six before."

"Where exactly are they?"

"They're almost right in front of you. Two are hiding behind the trucks and one's crouched behind the ATV, and I think there are more in the woods. Be careful, Keo; they might try to get behind you."

"Norris is keeping an eye out. Where did they come from? Did you see?"

"I don't know. I think from the woods."

So they walked here. Which meant what, exactly?

He had no idea and he didn't particularly care, either, at the moment.

"What do we do, Keo?" Gillian asked. He could hear the urgency in her voice, along with the fear, even though she did her best to hide it.

"Stay put," he said.

Keo glanced back at Norris behind the back bumper. The ex-cop had heard the conversation through his own radio, and Keo liked to think Norris was thinking the same thing he was.

Five men with assault rifles. Probably more.

Those were some bad odds right there. And the assaulters had come fully loaded, based on the large volume of fire they had unleashed so far. They had gone silent now, probably because they couldn't get a clear shot. That, or they were already trying to outflank them.

I think there are more in the woods," Gillian had said.

She had only seen five, but there could easily be more.

Who the hell are *these people?*

He took a chance and stood up quickly, peering through the broken driver side window. He figured he had a second, maybe two, before they saw him. In that brief second or two, he glimpsed three figures—all wearing similar black assault rigs—biding their time behind vehicles parked across the yard. One was behind the Nissan Frontier, another at the large hood of the Ford F-150. Two more black-clad figures appeared in the corner of his eye, moving through the woods at the far end of the yard. They were heading toward the trail.

"Be careful, Keo; they might try to get behind you."

The assaulter behind the Ford saw Keo, and for a split-second they stared at each other across the wide space.

Keo wished he was surprised to see the familiar face looking back at him, but a part of him wasn't. Not that it made it any easier to stomach, but maybe he always knew, deep down, that he had made the wrong decision that day.

*Sonofa*bitch.

It was Joe. He was back and wearing the same rig as the others. Even through the face paint, Keo knew instantly who it was. He recognized the fire (hatred) in the kid's eyes.

Joe took aim and opened fire with his assault rifle, and Keo ducked back behind the Bronco as bullets punched into the other side.

"In the woods!" Keo shouted back at Norris. "They're trying to outflank us!"

"I see them!" Norris said, and his M4 unleashed a half dozen rounds.

There was a moment of peace as Norris's last shots faded.

"Norris!" Keo shouted.

"They're moving farther back into the woods," Norris said. "I don't think I hit any of them, but it definitely got them running. What did you see?"

Joe. I saw fucking Joe.

"We're in trouble," Keo said. "I don't think they're going to leave until we're dead."

"You're full of good news today, kid."

"Sorry."

"Well, they're gonna get around us eventually. I just chased them off, but that just means they'll run farther back into the woods to stay out of my line of fire. We probably got five minutes tops before they're completely around us. You got something in mind, you better get to it soon before we're dead."

Keo sighed. He had made a mistake, and it was now coming back to bite them. Letting the kid go had seemed like a good idea at a time. A concession to the "new" man he had become.

You screwed up. Now everyone's going to pay the price for it.

Fucking Joe. He had given Keo a nice song and dance. It was believable, too. The kid would have won an Oscar with that performance.

And Keo had swallowed it. Hook, line, and sinker.

Fuck you, Joe.

"Well?" Norris said behind him. "Four minutes and counting, kid."

"You're not going to like it," Keo said.

"Does it involve us not dying?"

"Fifty-fifty chance of that."

"Well, shit. What about the girls?"

"I think we can save them."

"Then do it," Norris said without hesitation.

Keo took a moment to think about what he would say before pressing the radio's transmit lever. "Gillian..."

She answered quickly. "What took you so long?"

"Is there anyone at the back of the house?"

"I'll ask Mark; he's back there." He waited a few seconds, then she was quickly back. "Mark says someone *was* back there, but he's gone now. He doesn't know where he went."

Keo glanced over at the man Norris had shot, still on his stomach on the ground next to the house.

"And Mark's fine?" he asked.

"Yes. Why?"

"What about Jordan?"

Keo saw another pair of eyes—soft brown this time—appear at the peephole next to Gillian's green eyes.

"I'm here," Jordan said through the radio.

"You hit?" he asked.

"Yeah, in the left arm, but it doesn't look fatal."

"Can you shoot?"

"Yes. I can't say how well, but I can shoot."

He paused.

"Keo," Jordan said. "How are we gonna do this?"

He remembered the talk he had with her back when she had first shown up. There was a reason he had chosen her instead of Mark. Because she was the obvious leader of the three friends. Jordan had kept them alive all these months.

"Jordan, I need you to get everyone out of there," he said

into the radio.

"I don't understand. We're safe here in the house, aren't we?"

"For now. Once they finish us off, they're going to come for you."

"We have all the doors and windows covered," she started to say, but he cut her off.

"Jordan, look at them. *Really* look at them. These are the guys I told you about. The ones at the gas station. They didn't come here to shoot up the house. They came here to take *down* the house. Once they have the place surrounded, they'll bring everything they have and take it. Do you understand? That place can withstand bloodsuckers, but it's not going to last long against a bunch of well-armed paramilitary assholes."

She didn't answer right away.

Come on, Jordan. You know I'm right. You're too smart not to see it.

Finally, she said, "What's your plan?"

"This is it. That emergency option we discussed. Get everyone into the boat and tell Mark to get the hell downriver as fast as he can and keep going. We stashed those emergency provisions for a reason. It's time to put them to use."

Gillian took over the radio. "Keo, are you crazy? We're not leaving you and Norris behind!"

"Five is too many," Keo said.

Five? More like six. Maybe seven. And those are just the ones here. How many do they have out there?

"How many more of you are out there?" he had asked the guy.

"A lot," the guy had said.

"Keo, what are you saying?" Gillian said.

"You need to go with Jordan and Mark. Take Rachel and Christine and get the hell out of there. Make your way to the boat through the back door. Use the outboard motor and get downriver as fast as you can and keep going."

There was a pause, and he imagined Gillian struggling with everything inside the house. He couldn't see her eyes anymore, and the browns of Jordan's had disappeared, too.

"Jordan," Keo said.

"Yes," Jordan answered. She sounded calm, which was good.

"You understand?" Keo said.

"Yes," Jordan said without hesitation.

"We'll provide you with covering fire just in case they try to send someone else back there."

"All right. When?"

"Grab as many supplies as you can, but only what you can carry and still run. Food and water only. Some ammo, if you have room. You'll have to rely on the emergency provisions for the rest."

"Then what? Where are we going?"

"Downriver."

"But *where*, Keo?"

He didn't even have to think about it. The name came tumbling out of his mouth naturally, as if it had always been on the tip of his tongue. "Santa Marie Island. Norris and I will find a boat and meet you there as soon as we can. Okay?"

"You'll follow us down there."

"Yes."

"Okay," she said, though she didn't sound as if she believed a single word he had just said.

Smart girl.

"Keo," Gillian said. "You promise me. You'll follow us to Santa Marie Island."

"Yes," Keo said. "I promise." Then, before she could say anything else, "Reserve a spot on the beach for me. I also wouldn't mind if you were wearing a bikini when I get there."

She laughed. "I'll wait for you. Just hurry."

"I will," he said. Then, "Jordan."

"Yeah," Jordan said.

"You have five minutes to get ready. Starting *now*."

CHAPTER 32

"*SEE THE WORLD. Kill some people. Make some money.*"

It had been a simple life plan, and it had been going splendidly for the last ten years. Then, the world decided to stop making sense and everything went out the window. He found himself leading a bunch of people he didn't know, kinda/maybe falling in major like with a girl, and now hoping against hope to keep them alive at the cost of…what? His own life?

Daebak. You've certainly come a long way.

What a sucker.

Keo lowered the radio and glanced at the back bumper.

Norris was staring back at him with a slightly crooked grin. "We're going to follow them downriver to Santa Marie Island, huh? I almost believed you there for a second."

Keo grinned back at him. "Keep an eye on our six, old timer. I'll make sure no one tries to sneak back behind the house from this side while they're getting ready."

"They'd have to think you were crazy to make the girls abandon the house and run to the river for them to send someone else back there."

"Yeah, well, it's better they're not trapped in the house when we get killed."

"That house is pretty strong. It can withstand a lot."

"You know how I got Gillian out of the hospital in Bentley?"

"No."

"I ran a truck through a wall. That wall was just as strong as the house's."

"You really are insane," Norris said. "I should have—"

Norris was interrupted by a long string of gunfire from the back bumper—all of it from Norris's own M4. Keo waited patiently for Norris to stop shooting, the *clink-clink-clink* of bullet casings pelting the ground around the ex-cop's feet.

Then the sound of reloading, and Norris, sounding more agitated than a few seconds ago: "They're almost behind us, kid. You better tell them it's now or never."

Keo looked forward to make sure no one was making a run for the other side of the house. He didn't think they would. Why would they? There was no point because they had the house surrounded, and no one would be crazy enough to make a run for the boat in the back. Why trade the safety of a house with walls for something that floats on the water?

Maybe they're all right. Maybe I am a little bit crazy.

He pressed the radio's transmit lever. "Are you ready?"

Jordan was out of breath when she answered. "Almost ready."

"It has to be now."

"What's happening?"

"We're running out of time. They've almost outflanked us."

"Okay, okay…"

"Go, Jordan, get them out of there. *Now*."

"Okay, okay," she said again. "In twenty, okay? In twenty."

"Twenty," Keo repeated.

He put the radio away and got into position behind the driver side door, then began counting down. The windows of the Bronco were all shot out, and he couldn't move more than a few inches without *crunching* glass on the ground. That made for a lot of noise and he cringed each time, thinking the assaulters had heard his every step. The only good news was that the tires were all blown, and that was preventing someone from shooting his feet out from under him. So there was that.

Ten seconds had passed, which left...

Ten...

He glanced over at the house one last time. The peepholes were closed.

Eight...

Keo sucked in a breath. "Ready, old timer?"

Six...

"No, but what the hell," Norris said from somewhere behind him.

Four...

"It'll be fun," Keo said.

Two...

Norris chuckled. "Fucking Riggs. That's what you are. Minus the mullet."

One!

He popped up from behind the shattered driver side window and sought out the Ford F-150 where he had last seen Joe. A head bobbed on the other side of the vehicle and Keo opened fire, the cycling mechanical whine of the MP5SD almost immediately lost in the *ping-ping-ping!* of 9mm rounds puncturing the truck across the yard. The head dropped out of sight, though Keo didn't delude himself into thinking he had hit anything.

Behind him, Norris was firing on full-auto with the M4, and Keo was very glad they had loaded up on ammo before heading off on the supply run. The belt around his waist held four magazines for the submachine gun and two more for the Glock. Norris had about the same amount, though he had already used up one while Keo hadn't fired a single shot until now.

While he kept Joe pinned down behind the Ford, he glimpsed two figures moving on the other side of the Nissan nearby. Keo switched his fire to that vehicle, piercing tires and shattering windows. He didn't stop shooting until he had drained the magazine, then he ducked back down and began reloading.

They returned fire, 5.56 and 7.62 rounds drilling into the Bronco, sharp and metallic and so close he was almost certain he was going to be filled with holes in the next few seconds. Keo wondered what the truck looked like to someone from a distance. All four tires were gone and the vehicle was essentially sitting on its undercarriage like an abandoned piece of junk. Which, he guessed, probably wasn't too far from the truth.

Norris had also stopped firing and was reloading while the assaulters returned the favor.

Keo waited to hear the sound he knew *(hoped)* was coming, knowing that even over the pummeling gunfire wouldn't be difficult to detect—

There!

The loud roar of an outboard motor firing up, at first with some difficulty—loud coughing spurts—before it caught and increased in volume.

"Watch the sides!" Keo shouted. "Don't let them make a run for the back of the house!"

As soon as he said it, a black-clad figure raced across the yard toward the side of the house in front of him. He switched the MP5SD to semi-auto and fired twice, hitting the running man in the thigh with his second shot. The man stumbled and rolled forward on his shoulders but somehow still managed to keep his grip on his AK-47. As he was coming to rest on the ground, Keo shot him two more times, hitting him in the chest with both rounds. The man went down for good this time.

Keo's radio squawked, and he heard Jordan's voice. "Keo—"

"Shut up and go!" he shouted back into the radio.

There was no reply. Instead, Keo heard the outboard motor revving as someone hit the throttle. He couldn't hear the river parting under the boat from this distance, but he imagined it heading downriver at this very second, and Keo couldn't help but smile to himself.

"See the world. Kill some people. Make some money. Get killed for a

bunch of people you didn't know until six months ago."

Fucking daebak.

Norris screamed, and Keo turned around to find the ex-cop on the ground, shooting at two black-clad assaulters hiding in the woods behind them. Norris's bullets tore into the trees and branches as the men sought cover.

Keo rushed over and poured half of his magazine into the woods after the two men. He might have hit one, but they were too far away—over fifty meters—and he couldn't tell for certain either way.

"You good?" Keo shouted.

"Fuck no!" Norris shouted back, simultaneously reloading his carbine while flat on his back. Blood spurted out of his left leg, near the thigh area.

"I'll pull, you shoot!" Keo said, and grabbed Norris by the shoulders and began dragging him across the yard toward the side of the house. Thank God he had at least parked the Bronco close enough that it wasn't too big of a distance—

Spoke too soon, he thought, when an AK-47 sent bullets *zip-zip-zipping* around his head. Keo did all he could to ignore the rounds and kept dragging. Not an easy feat, because the bullets seemed to be getting closer with every step he took. He was moving as fast as he could, but even he knew it wasn't fast enough. He was out in the open, exposed, dragging a bleeding man with him.

Any minute now, and one of them's going to get lucky.

Get ready for the pain. Get ready…

Norris was firing into the trees before turning at the waist and unloading at the vehicles in the yard. That silenced the enemy assault rifle for a moment, but then it was back again just as Keo reached the side of the house. Brick exploded, showering both him and Norris in thick red and gray clouds.

He kept pulling Norris along the side of the house, trying to reach the back and safety. He couldn't stop. Not for a second. Couldn't reach for his MP5SD and return fire, because that would mean stopping completely. And he couldn't do that, because not constantly moving *back back back* would result in doom for both of them.

And Norris was heavy. Jesus. Had Norris put on some pounds since they arrived at the house? It felt as if he were dragging a boulder—

Crack!

Keo grunted as the bullet chopped through his left shoulder. Pain speared his body like flames, enveloping every inch of him.

He kept moving, dragging Norris with him, doing his best to ignore the pain, because there was no choice, because stopping meant death, so he had to keep *going and going and going*—

A second *crack!* tore a big chunk from the brick wall a few inches from his face, throwing debris into his eyes.

He coughed and kept moving and dragging.

Finally, after an eternity, he reached the back of the house and pulled Norris behind it just as the two black-clad assaulters peeked out from behind the Bronco *(Jesus, when had they made it across the open ground from the woods?)* and fired at them, half of their rounds hitting the corner of the house and the rest going into the trees in the back. There were two more thick clouds, like some kind of man-made fog, in front of them by the time Keo dropped Norris to the ground and unslung his submachine gun.

Keo heard the loud rush of footsteps and spun around just as a figure took the corner on the other side of the house. The man froze when he saw Keo looking across at him.

Joe.

The kid's AK-47 was just halfway up when he rounded the house. His eyes widened and he was in the middle of taking another ragged breath. Sweat poured down Joe's forehead, gliding smoothly over the waterproof paint on his face.

"Wait—" Joe said, half a second before Keo shot him in the

chest, and as the eighteen-year-old fell, Keo shot him a second time, hitting him in the neck. Blood spurted as Joe went down. He didn't get back up.

Norris was reloading when Keo looked back. The ex-cop was staring at Joe's still form on the other side of the house. "Fucking kid," he said. Then, "You're bleeding."

"Yeah," Keo said. "So are you."

"So what does that tell you?"

"We're fucked."

"That about covers it," Norris grunted.

He was bleeding and it hurt, too, but he ignored the pain. The feel of wetness trickling down his shoulder and running along the length of his left arm was strangely cold.

He noticed right away that the pier was empty and there were no signs of the boat. He couldn't hear the roar of the outboard motor anymore, either, which meant they were far, far downriver by now.

Next stop, Santa Marie Island.

"What now?" Norris said. His eyes were glued on the corner in front of him, M4 poised and ready to shoot.

Good question.

Keo looked around them. He hadn't really thought this far ahead. Getting the hell away from the Bronco had been the priority, and now that they were behind the house, what was left? He had no delusions that the assaulters would leave now, not after the casualties they had taken. They were probably coming at this very moment. Either from one side or both. Likely both. That's how he would do it.

The same reason he told Jordan to abandon the house was the same reason they couldn't use it to make their stand. Too easy to surround, too easy to destroy once they were locked inside with no way out.

No, the house wasn't going to do it.

So what was left?

Then he heard his answer. It had been there all this time.

The river.

"Can you swim?" he asked Norris.

Norris sighed. "You call that a plan?"

"Cover us!"

Keo slipped his hands under Norris's shoulders and began dragging him backward again, this time toward the river. It seemed a lot further today than it usually did, but maybe that was because he was moving with a 200-something pound burden this time.

Norris fired another burst at the corner in front of them just as a man with camo on his face sneaked a peek around it. Clouds of loosed brick floated in the air, thick and red and gray. A second later, a figure burst through the makeshift smokescreen, and Norris shot him in the leg. The man went down screaming when a pair of hands grabbed his legs from behind and dragged him back through the fog.

Keo thought that was ironic. A lot of people were being dragged around bleeding today.

"Stay back if you know what's good for you, whippersnappers!" Norris shouted.

Keo wanted to laugh when he felt the ground under him slanting and knew he was close to the river. He looked back to be sure and saw that he was almost at the ridge overlooking the bank below. The pier was to his left and the flowing river was directly behind him. The sound of rushing water had increased. It wasn't a strong current today, but maybe it would be just good enough.

Hopefully.

"Ready?" he shouted.

"Fuck no!" Norris shouted back.

"In you go!"

Keo swung Norris around as if he were a sack of meat. Norris might have been screaming obscenities at him as he flew through the air and splashed into the river face-first.

Norris disappeared under the water, only to pop back to the

surface, gasping for breath, a couple of seconds later. He had, miraculously, still held onto his carbine.

"You're going to pay for that!" Norris shouted at him just before he was carried downriver.

Keo didn't have time to make sure Norris didn't sink back under the surface, because bullets began screaming around him. One of them hit him in the back of the right leg, and he fell off the ridge and just barely managed to stick out his hands as he landed on the muddy banks. He half-crawled and half-ran toward the river and leaped toward it with every ounce of strength he had left, which wasn't very much.

He sank under the surface like a lead weight, the stinging cold making every inch of his skin howl with a combination of unbearable pain and surprise. He struggled to right himself underwater even as the world rippled in slow motion as bullets penetrated from above. He could barely hear the *thudding* clatter of gunfire from the bank as they poured round after round at him, but for some reason the bullets were coming down further and further behind him.

Keo decided to give in and embrace the current. He stopped trying to fight his way up to the surface where, in all likelihood, he was going to get his head shot off the second he popped it back up. He was thankful for the cold river water because it helped to dull the pain from his shoulder and leg as he floated downriver.

His eyes were open and he saw that he was leaving tendrils of blood in his wake. A lot of blood.

Jesus, he was literally bleeding to death in the river.

There was a bright side to all of this, though. He was probably going to drown before those two bullet wounds finally got the better of him, so there was that.

CHAPTER 33

NORRIS FISHED HIM out of the river, though Keo didn't know how or when exactly, since his entire body had gone numb from the cold and he had trouble clinging to any specific thought, much less pay attention to his environment. The bleeding and pounding pain from his toes to his head didn't help, either.

He woke up sporadically throughout the day, first on a muddy bank with Norris pumping on his chest. When he opened his eyes a second time, he was traveling through the woods, hoisted over one of Norris's broad shoulders. The ex-cop might have been grumbling the whole way, but Keo couldn't really be sure since he could barely keep his eyes open.

He was also only dimly aware of the sun setting in the distance.

That's not good, he remembered thinking. *That's not good at all.*

The third time he opened his eyes, he saw only darkness. Alarm bells went off and he willed himself to sit up, but he couldn't move a single part of his body.

Slowly, the darkness gave way to light—or well, sort of light. He could make out dirty scarred gray walls, and the ground under him was hard and cold. A concrete floor. He was in some kind of room. A dark room, but it wasn't necessarily dark outside...yet.

"Still alive?" a voice said.

Keo managed to turn his head toward the sound of the

voice. Norris, sitting against a wall, watching him with a grin. He looked dry, which meant they had been here a while. Norris still had his M4 across his lap and Keo's MP5SD slung over one shoulder. His left leg was wrapped with what looked like strips of fabric.

"Thirsty?" Norris asked.

Keo nodded.

"Well, too bad; we don't have any water," Norris said and chuckled. "Of course, I think we've both had enough of water to last us a lifetime. You're still alive, though. That's good, right?"

Keo managed to sit up. He was close enough to a wall that he only needed to scoot back a few inches. Which was good, because any farther and he wouldn't have made it. His right leg had a tourniquet wrapped around it. It looked like a piece of a shirt. Another tourniquet was tied tightly around his left shoulder, which probably explained why he could barely move it, even though he could feel the pain from it just fine. *Too* fine, in fact.

"Where are we?" he asked. His throat was parched, which he found surprising. He was sure he had swallowed most of the river earlier in the day.

"Remember that house we searched about a month ago? The one with the swing set out back?"

"Yeah…"

"We're in the basement. Got lucky. It only took me carrying you for an hour to find it again. Luckily, I haven't gone senile yet. Well, not entirely." He grinned, white teeth visible in the semidarkness. "It's a good thing you're taller than you weigh, kid, or I would have dumped your ass back at the river bank."

Keo glanced down at his watch. It was still ticking after being drowned in water for…how long?

5:16 P.M.

"Any pursuit?" he asked.

Norris shook his head. "We floated down the river pretty

far. I almost didn't catch you when you flew by, you know. It's a good thing I'm pretty fast even with this bum leg."

"Thanks," Keo said. "You saved my life."

"Hey, you saved my ass first. Just returning the favor."

Keo laid his head against the wall. The basement smelled of abandonment, but it looked secure, with a door to his left at the top of a flight of stairs. He remembered checking the house with Norris before and finding the place empty, with the basement door held tightly shut with a padlock, which meant none of the creatures were waiting inside when they opened it.

It was a good thing Norris remembered how to get back to it.

"Go to sleep, kid," Norris said from across the room. "Door's locked. They can't get in. We'll look for food and water tomorrow. Until then, let's try to just survive the next twenty-four hours. It's been a really shitty day."

Keo couldn't disagree with that. He closed his eyes and allowed himself to slink back down to the floor. He was tired. He didn't think he could actually sit back up if he tried. Or at least, not on the first try.

Maybe on the sixth…

He was asleep again in seconds.

A WEEK AFTER the firefight at the house, they were still following the river down south toward New Orleans, keeping in mind that Mark and Jordan had sailed the others upriver to them from the same fork.

Traveling on foot was a pain in the ass, especially with their wounds. They hobbled more than they actually walked, and they made pathetic time. It seemed as if they had been walking for months without seeing any signs of civilization, a reminder again that while they were hiding out back at the house, there was still a very big world beyond the woods.

They broke away from the river only to find shelter and food, which further cut into their progress. Even then, they didn't move very far from the river because Keo didn't trust that they could find it again if they ever lost sight of it. Neither one of them had a map or knew where the hell they were going. Every tree they came across looked like the last hundred (or thousand) they had already passed in the last seven days.

Eventually, the sun would always begin its descent, which meant they had to find safe haven for the night. At first they carved out an hour at the end of every day just for that, but when that proved too risky and they almost got caught outside on Day 3, they decided two hours was the better number.

By their first week in the woods, they were looking for shelter at around noon. That really cut into their time, too.

Norris never said anything about whether the girls and Mark had made it to Santa Marie Island or not. He seemed just as content as Keo to keep moving, pushed on by a shared goal. The fact that they hadn't encountered wreckages along the river in the first few days was a good sign. Of course, Gillian and the others would be moving faster on a boat powered by a combination of outboard motor, sails, and going downriver with the current. They might have already reached New Orleans by now and slipped into the Gulf of Mexico on their way to Galveston, Texas.

He hoped, anyway.

Keo was trying to convince himself that Gillian and the others were safe and sound, either on their way to Santa Marie Island or already there and sitting on the beach waiting for them, when the *crack!* of a rifle shredded the branch an inch in front of his face.

"Run!" he shouted.

Not that he had to. Norris was already ahead of him, moving surprisingly fast for a man in his fifties with a wounded leg.

Keo unslung his MP5SD as he ran, keeping as low as possible while still maintaining his speed as rifle fire shattered the woods behind him. Bullets *zinged* past his head and one came dangerously close to putting another hole in his body, this time much higher up than his leg but below the one already in his shoulder.

He kept running, telling himself not to look back.

The gunfire was hellacious, which meant more than one shooter.

Run. Don't look back. Keep running!

But he couldn't help himself, and Keo threw a quick look over his shoulder.

He glimpsed black clothes, assault vests, and painted faces emerging out of the woods all around them. At least three that he could see, possibly more.

Who the fuck are these guys?

Norris looked back at him.

"Don't stop!" Keo shouted at him.

Norris didn't stop, and neither did Keo, even though his leg and shoulder and every inch of his body was killing him.

Around him, the woods continued to explode as if they were being bombarded with heavy artillery shells. Keo had never seen anything that could be mistaken for a full-blown battlefield, but he imagined it had to look and feel and sound just like this.

Who the fuck are these guys?

THEY RAN FOR hours, stopping to rest whenever they could, then ran some more.

Keo wasn't sure what direction they were going; he was only aware that soon he couldn't hear the river anymore, which meant they had unwittingly run *away* from it. He told himself they could locate the river again later. It was a long stretch of water, reaching all the way to the Gulf of Mexico. It was difficult to lose track of something that long. Sooner or later, even just stumbling around, they'd eventually run across it again.

He hoped, anyway.

By nightfall, they had found salvation on a wooden platform about twenty meters off the ground. It was a hunting perch, high enough that they could see most of the woods even lying down on their bellies so they wouldn't be seen from below. In the months since someone had used the basic construction to stalk wildlife, the branches had grown back, providing enough cover that they had almost missed it when they walked across it during the day.

Keo hated the idea of being outside at night, but there wasn't much of a choice with no signs of a possible building to take shelter in. Thankfully, it was a cloudy night, and what little moonlight there was wasn't enough to illuminate them on the scaffolding. He could barely see Norris lying a few inches from him, so he assumed they were safe from prying eyes on the ground.

The coming nightfall had also sent their black-clad pursuers into hiding. He wondered if they had gotten caught by the darkness and kept waiting to hear desperate gunfire, and was disappointed when he didn't hear a single thing throughout the night and early morning.

There were also no signs of the creatures below or around them, which wasn't too much of a surprise. There was no humanity around here, and if he had learned anything, it was that the bloodsuckers always seemed to know where people were hiding, and they flocked there like moths to a flame.

He drifted off to sleep thinking about Gillian and the sandy beaches of Santa Marie Island...

HE WOKE UP in the morning to Norris elbowing him in the gut.

"Wakey wakey, Sleeping Beauty."

He opened his eyes and rolled over onto his back, staring up at what parts of the sun he could see through the thick canopy above him. He took in the brightness and let last night's dream slowly drift away.

They didn't say anything for a while, and Norris was content to stare down at the ground below, his carbine in front of him.

Finally, Keo said, "You know what this means, right?"

"What's that?" Norris said.

"They're not going to give up."

"I kinda figured that."

"They followed us for a week, for God's sake. That's some goddamn determination right there. Makes me wonder if Joe lied about those three back at the garage being his only living relatives."

"Oh, I'm pretty sure the little bastard lied about a lot of things. All he did was run back for his pals."

"Doesn't matter now. What matters is they're going to keep hunting us."

"Yeah," Norris said quietly. He had clearly come to the same conclusion during the night. "So what are we going to do about that?"

"We can't lead them to the others. Not if they're still downriver waiting for us."

"You think they might be?"

"Gillian's stubborn enough."

"So we try to lose them first. Don't give them a chance to stumble across the kids. I don't like the idea of doing all of this, risking my life and jumping into a river, only to lead them right back to the others."

"That's what I figured. It's a big state. If they want a fight, we'll give them one. Besides, Santa Marie Island isn't going anywhere."

"Sounds about right."

"You good with this?"

"Shit, I've already overstayed my welcome," Norris said. "Why the hell not?"

Keo grinned. *"Daebak."*

Norris grunted. "Yeah, *day*-whatever."

Snap!

Keo rolled onto his stomach and peered out over the edge of the hunting stand as a black-clad figure stepped out from behind two thick bushes in front of them, clutching an M16 rifle. The man's face was painted black and green, and he was carrying a tactical pack and wearing heavy boots that *crunched* and *snapped* everything under him as he moved.

"You see him?" Norris whispered.

"Yeah," Keo whispered back, while peering through the sight mounted on top of his MP5SD.

He lowered the red dot over the man's forehead, clear as day under the swarming sunlight. Keo flicked the fire selector to semi-automatic and slipped his forefinger into the trigger guard.

"We really gonna do this?" Norris whispered. "We're probably going to die, you know."

"Yeah, I know," Keo said.

He pulled the trigger.

"One down…"

7127

36169785R00200

Made in the USA
Lexington, KY
09 October 2014